# Introduction

*From birth he never stood a chance; once his umbilical cord was cut, the slippery slope of fate began. Toxic role models dragged him through a feral upbringing, leaving him to make choices that no rational mind ever would.*

*He believed that his altered ego would give him the strength to cope; yet it just took him to darker places where his immaturity was in turmoil. AKA Casey was just a mask to hide his frightened inner child.*

**Mike Bowden**

# Casey

Casey now had to navigate the breakfast with his shaky hands. He was embarrassed to eat in front of other people so he was glad Sarah was engaged with other customers as he dropped some egg yolk onto the table; seeing the egg was under cooked, he flicked some raw egg white with his knife, splattering the contents like semen across his plate. He chuckled thinking about the blonde in his bed the night before. It seemed a military operation to manoeuvre his knife and fork through the platter in front of him. Resorting to him making sandwiches, which were easier to manage. His unsteady hand spilt the contents of the overfull cup onto the table and to his annoyance, splattered the liquid onto his favourite Ben Sherman shirt. *"Oh bollocks!"* he scowled himself.

His second cup of tea was delivered as Sarah collected his empty plate. Casey was starting to feel a little steadier and his shaking hands became calmer. His late breakfast was his only meal of the day; alcohol would be his only other substance to see him through. Most of the time he either lived on his nerves or pumped to the brim with adrenaline, there seemed very little in between. Constantly living his life on the edge, alcohol became more and more of a dependable friend, sometimes his only friend. It was almost like sitting at the bar raising his glass with the devil, yet the evilness lay deep inside him.

Casey waited by the phone for his boss to call with the details of his appointments for the day. In essence it was a list of people he would need to extract money from and issue violent warnings on those unwilling to pay. He got a buzz from dominating other people and enjoyed earning commission in the process. His employment was a place where he could release all the pain and suffering he had endured in his adolescent years, a place to vent his uncontrolled anger; he wasn't a skilled fighter, yet his aggression compensated for it. The demons inside him never got tamed. His festering anger was left unchecked, like a boiling cauldron ready to scald unsuspecting victims of his rage.

Life had not been kind to him. Growing up had thrown him more challenges than most people could have coped with. He was left bitter, feeling rejected by the society that should have protected him. He often wished that he could have turned the clock back to rewrite his journey; he had never felt loved, therefore couldn't even comprehend the concept. Casey knew something was missing, he had a chasm that needed to be filled, but he didn't know what would satisfy his craving.

On answering his Motorola phone, better known as, '*The Brick,*' Casey was greeted by the stern Italian accent of his boss, barking his instructions. Marco was a cruel man that saw himself as a modern day gangster, demanding people to be submissive to his will. He had given Casey the bulky mobile phone a couple of months before as a means of instant contact and anonymity, yet the device was fickle to an appropriate signal resulting in most conversations being, *'Hello can you hear me?'* or *'I'm losing you'* These frustrations compounded the aggressive mood of the call until Marco screamed, "*Fuck the fucking fucker phone, I'll get you a pager!*"

Although Marco got a thrill from administering beatings to anyone that crossed his path, he realised he had to use his head rather than his fists, so as not to get his own hands dirty. The police were always on his case and were looking for any opportunity to bring him and his empire down. Marco had to play things cute, which is why he employed people like Casey. He was very well connected to many unsavoury characters that would do anything to win his favours. Although Casey wasn't frightened of him, he treated him with healthy respect, mindful of his violent associates.

Casey quickly wrote down the list of visits and the amounts for collection in his notebook then ended the call. There was nothing sociable about their conversation, just business, which suited him fine. Marco could be very unpredictable so it was best to interpret his mood when he could look into his eyes. At the end of the day, the list would be discarded with the strike of a match, leaving no record of the mayhem that he had left in his wake.

He studied his new shopping list that his boss had just relayed to him and psyched himself up for the day ahead. There were a few regulars, who were very compliant causing him no trouble, also a couple that would try a sob story to get out of their payment. Those were the ones Casey would violently remind of their debt and take whatever he wanted over and above the instalment to justify his extra effort that was his perverse enjoyment of the situation.

On the list was a businessman who owed a huge debt. Casey knew this visit would be more of a challenge and he'd need to keep his wits about him as he may encounter other staff in the building. This storage unit had some ambush points if the proprietor wished to utilise his workers to defend him. Casey enjoyed extracting money with force from men who had looked down on him in the past; the last time they had

11

locked horns over a payment, Casey had left him sprawled on the floor covered with blood. This appointment could either be easy or difficult, he was unsure what to expect.

Another name on the list that gave him concern was that of Tina. He hated forcing money from women and never raised a hand to them, just intimidating them with his bellowing voice and menacing stare. Tina was a drug addict who rarely paid her instalments. Occasionally she would manage to find a few pounds but never enough to satisfy the debt. Casey would warn her not to let him down next time, but allowed his soft side to make up the shortfall from other money he'd extorted. He wanted nothing else from her as she reminded him of the pitiful sight of his mother when he was a child. Not to appear weak, he would kick over some furniture and mess up her room but never inflict pain on this cowering female.

With his stomach filled and his nerves a little calmer, he picked up his Foster Grant sunglasses and he headed off to the local bar to consume a couple of pints to set him up for his first call. As much as Casey thought the shades were a cool look to his image, in fact they were more of a necessity to block the glare from his vision. Bright sunlight stung his eyes and made his damaged eye water; blinking was futile, so the sunglasses eased the discomfort.

He was never motivated to start his day and often questioned why in the hell he should lead this way of life, but once he was in the midst of his daily quest he was okay. The Crown Inn was a haunt of several heavy drinkers who could be easily drawn into an argument. This was where Casey could taunt the beast within and prepare himself for the day ahead.

Casey sometimes felt that he'd been dragged into a hostile world and stripped of his innocence; almost left feral from an early age to bring himself up in a world with no adult guidance. From his earliest memories life had been no different, with his parents leaving him to his own devices to survive, as a child shouldn't have done. His parental role models were very negative and his only motivation was to not end up like them, but he had no knowledge how to live a better life. There were no peers to show him the way and no true friends close enough to guide him. The only emotion that was branded into his DNA was loneliness.

He now had a new persona, a new image and performed each day, as a villainous actor would do on the stage. There was no way his old look would have created the intimidation needed to execute his craft and earn his wages. He liked his newfound confidence and was comfortable with his nickname to suit his tougher image, an AKA derived from the initials of his real name KC; this is what he wanted to be known as.

Part 2

Kelvin Carter was raised in a toxic household where he received many beatings from his father. There was always a cold eerie silence at home, only broken by the reassuring tick of the grandfather clock in the lounge. That was the only thing that wasn't frightening to hear, the constant mark of time that would move from the last moment of fear, to the unknown fate yet to come.

He was an only child to his parents Terry and Brenda, feeling a burden to their meagre lifestyle. They lived in a two-bedroom terrace house, which was run down compared to the neighbouring houses. People surviving on the poverty line occupied the street, but even that said the Carter household stood out as the scruffy blight in the neighbourhood, often being the attention of complaint.

After a brief relationship with Terry, Brenda found herself pregnant and desperate. She had been living rough after running away from home and had very few options for her future. Her fate seemed sealed, kipping on one sofa after another or the sanctuary of an unlocked church in the darkness of night. She was scared of the shadows and the eerie noises of the night. Sleep never came easy until exhaustion took its grip on her teenage body.

When Terry agreed to stand by her with their future child, she felt a sharp pang of the inevitable submissive fate, which she knew would take away any freedom that she could hope for. She had no direction in life before the conception of her unborn child and now her life was being mapped out before her without her consent, without her control. She was only a child herself, just passing her eighteenth birthday when she missed her period. Could her future be worse than her past? Only time would tell.

Terry was devastated to hear that Brenda was pregnant. He was a '*Jack-the-Lad*' character with slicked back wavy hair and his groomed moustache, sowing his wild oats when the unthinkable happened. All his friends were out having a good time with the local girls, yet he was the one that literally got caught with his trousers down. His father was a mean man and was the commanding force in their household. On hearing that his son had stupidly messed up his life, he insisted that Terry do the right thing and marry Brenda.

Terence John Carter and Brenda Siobhan Murphy were married by special licence just a few weeks before the baby was born. There was no pomp or ceremony to the service, low key was an understatement. Terry in his best suit and Brenda in her maternity frock were blessed in marriage at the Shrewsbury registry office with Terry's parents as witnesses. Afterwards they celebrated with a couple of beers at The Boathouse pub and then returned to live in Terry's cramped bedroom at his parent's house as husband and wife.

There was a lot of underlying tension within the Carter household with his mean father controlling the routine that he'd become accustomed to. Housework had to be done to military precision and meals to arrive hot and on time; after all, he was an ex-serviceman in the Infantry, a merciless Sergeant Major. Brenda was expected to help out with the chores and managed to cope as well as she could in the latter stages of her pregnancy. She tried to build up a bond with Terry's downtrodden mother, winning the odd favour or two, but spent most of her time exposed to solitude in the bedroom she shared with Terry.

Terry Carter was a store man, working in the warehouse of a food wholesaler. He was employed to pick orders and load them in a delivery sequence on a distribution lorry, ready for the next day. He had been working there since he had left school and after five years of service received his first salary raise. His boss knew that he'd recently married and was due to become a father, so wanted to help him out. Terry was a good worker, although he made every excuse under the sun to go to the office so he could flirt with Jessie the secretary. Even with a ring on his finger and a baby due, he wasn't ready to settle down. He was raging inside how his life would change so dramatically because he couldn't keep it in his trousers that one fateful night. He knew that his life would change forever and that his frustrations would fester out of control.

Just after two o'clock on the morning of 2nd December 1960, Brenda gave birth to Kelvin with the help of Terry's mum Joan. There was no time to summon medical help; the baby was in a rush to join the havoc of the Carter household. If he'd known beforehand I doubt he would have been in such a hurry. Brenda held her newborn son close to her chest wrapped in a clean blanket until the midwife arrived. She felt for the first time in her life what pure unconditional love was towards another human being. Although she'd loved her parents, she hadn't felt this intensity before; this sensation was new and comforting. She hoped that one day she would feel some sort of feelings

17

towards Terry rather than being thrust together through circumstance, at that moment she just felt contempt towards the sperm donor of her child.

The next few weeks was an arena for so much frustration and many arguments between Terry and his father Alfred. The women kept a low profile and tried to maintain some normality, whilst Alfred complained about the mess in the house, the dirty nappies and the constant crying of the baby. His booming voice did nothing to instil calmness and created far more tension than their small house could cope with. One argument too many caused a flash point where Terry, Brenda and baby Kelvin were told to leave. Alfred had put his foot down and Joan could do nothing other than to comply with his wishes.

A work colleague of Terry's confided that he intended to do a moonlight flit after his next pay packet, leaving his small two-bedroom house vacant. Jack had built up a large gambling debt and couldn't afford to pay his rent, let alone pay the people he owed money to. *"Terry we're scarpering Friday night. Leave it until Monday then ask Old Frenchie if he has any empty properties,"* he said with a wink.

The landlord was pissed off being left out of pocket and intended to track down the, 'Thieving bastard who owed him money.' Knowing Terry was desperate and a workmate of Jack, he hiked up the rent and demanded a large deposit. Reluctantly Terry pawned his watch and a couple of keepsakes to raise the money. The junior Carter family moved in within a couple of days. They had very few possessions, most fitting into a couple of suitcases. Alfred sat stubbornly in his chair saying nothing as they left his house, Joan slipped Terry a few pounds that she'd saved

little interest in his offspring, just seeing him as a financial burden, just as his leach of a wife was to him.

"*Here you go son,*" Terry said throwing a copy of The Beano comic at Kelvin. It was one of those rare days when he wasn't too drunk. '*That must mean that daddy loves me,*' the youngster thought scooping up the crumpled comic to read. Clearly it wasn't new, maybe discarded by some other child, but Kelvin didn't care, his daddy had given him something nice.

Kelvin's hopes of his father love were shattered the following day, when he found the torn pages smeared with faeces and shoved unceremoniously down the toilet. Tears couldn't express the disappointment he felt, the betrayal of the love that he yearned.

Brenda spent her meagre housekeeping on food and cleaning products, which left nothing for luxuries such as clothes. "*That's very kind of you,*" she humbly said, eagerly accepting neighbour's cast-offs. Much of her time was spent scouring jumble sales and charity shops for bargains that she could utilise in various ways. Threadbare jumpers would be a source of wool to unravel and knit again into something wearable for either herself or Kelvin. Occasionally when she was desperate, she would steal food from the local corner shop, until the day she was caught red handed and banned from the establishment. She was lucky the owner took some degree of pity on her and didn't call the police.

The embarrassment and shame raked through her body as she sobbed on the pavement. Mrs Francis from number forty-seven found her huddled on the ground holding the toddler Kelvin in her arms and helped her home. The young boy couldn't understand why his mummy was always sad, he'd never seen her smile but felt comforted by her tight grip as she cocooned him inside the wrap of her cardigan. He was starting to ask questions that she either didn't want to, or couldn't answer. It was best he kept his innocence as long as possible.

Brenda became insulated in the confines of their shabby house, the only lock and key that contained her was in her head. Her confidence was shattered into tiny pieces; she was a broken woman in so many ways. Her clothes were in tatters, her hair was unkempt and she was painfully thin.

Everything she had went to provide for Kelvin; Brenda had whatever was left, even eating the scraps on his plate to sustain her existence. If drunken Terry fell asleep without eating his meal, she would gorge on this feast too without remorse. Although she had a roof over her head, at times she felt almost feral in her existence. This was so far removed from the innocent upbringing that she had received from her kind and loving parents. She was ill prepared to deal with the intense shame she felt and the burning stares of the outside world, so it was easier to live as a numb recluse for as long as possible.

* * *

Random moments in time where everything seemed to stand still, allowed Brenda to escape from the torment she endured. Standing at the kitchen sink peeling potatoes allowing her mind to wander. The chore was associated to memories of her childhood, recalling happy thoughts of her stood in the potato fields in Ireland on sunny days. Wearing her favourite floral dresses and her hair tied back in a ponytail, she would laugh and play with her brother and younger sister. She felt safe and protected as if cocooned in a sugar coated shell.

As she developed into a young woman her understated beauty drew the attention of many a young lad who would cautiously flirt with her on every occasion. Her slender physique still had a childlike innocence as she stole her first kiss from Patrick on her sixteenth birthday. She remembered the sun so bright on those carefree days, those naïve days where life was simple, until a cloudy day in June, when her uncle enticed her into his shed and locked the door shut behind them.

As he turned to face her in the confines of the timber chamber, Brenda could see his flaccid penis hanging from his open flies. She was frightened and confused. He had always been a little too affectionate for her liking, touching her and stroking her in public, but this made her panic with pure fear. "*What are you doing?*" she croaked, trying to clear her throat. He said nothing. As his hands started to paw at her young body, she squirmed to evade his touch. She tried to resist his efforts to pull up her pretty floral dress. "*Stop! Please uncle stop!*" she cried, clinging onto the hem of her dress. Brenda hadn't seen the evilness in his eyes before. He leaned over and whispered into her ear, "*I'm going to make you a real woman.*" He forced himself on her, ripping the virginity from her innocent body.

The timber chamber resumed normality when he left a few minutes later. Brenda could see a cobweb in the corner with a spider busying itself to repair a hole with newly woven thread. A muddy spade and hoe hung on hooks on the wall.

She had never noticed the practically of the shed before, after all she had only been inside once before with her brother for a dare. It was just a shed, not the setting for disgusting vile depravity. *"No, it wasn't possible?"* she questioned herself.

She was still in a state of shock, a state of denial as she stepped outside into the wide-open space. The clouds now hung heavy in the sky and a few spots of rain dripped onto her face. No one was around to hear her sobs. Her tears mingled with the raindrops to trickle down her face, hiding her shame. *"The last few minutes must have been a bad daydream,"* she told herself. After all her uncle was the local mayor. A man like him wouldn't do such a thing to a young girl like her, but the evidence was plain to see from her soiled dress and her discarded knickers. No one would believe her; they would say she was asking for it. Panic swept through her body unable to tell anyone.

*'Why did you go into his shed?'*
*'Did you encourage him?'*
*'What did he do to you?'*
*'Why didn't you run away?'*
*'Why didn't you tell your parents?'*
*'Are you making up stories?'*

These questions swirled around in her head. These were the questions the Garda would ask if she reported it. Brenda doubted anyone would listen to her claims against an upstanding member of the community. Her home was eerily quiet as she grabbed a few things and decided to run away, as far away as possible, maybe as far away as England where no one would know her. She couldn't face explaining to anyone what had just happened, she just felt numb.

The postmistress gave her a quizzical look as Brenda withdrew the last ten Irish Punts from her savings account. *"That's a lot of money, what are you going to spend it on?"* She mumbled something about treating herself to some new clothes and left quickly before the postmistress could ask any more questions.

Brenda had never left Ireland before, so the bumpy ferry crossing was a terrifying experience for someone so young and vulnerable. She found a bench in the quietest part of the lounge and curled in a ball, fighting sleep to keep the memories out. Once at sea there was no going back. There was no going back anyway, no choice but to flee on the night crossing from Dublin to Liverpool, leaving behind the broken sanctuary of her small home town.

Liverpool at dawn terrified her even more. The hustle and bustle of a busy city had taken her from one hellhole to another. She only had five punts left and to her shock couldn't spend her money over the counter to buy any breakfast. *"Only sterling in here if you want scran."* Tearful Brenda fled the cafe racked with embarrassment, as she didn't understand the accent or what had been said.

Wandering the streets aimlessly made her feet sore until she had to rest on the steps of the town hall. She had noticed several posters dotted around advertising a new group called The Beetles appearing at The Cavern Club. Two young girls pawed over a poster, trying to draw Brenda into their excited conversation, but soon realised how upset she was. Brenda briefly relayed the events of the last twenty-four hours, trying to leave out the vile details. One of the girls pressed a shilling into her hand and said, *"Get yourself some brekkie."*

The kind gesture forced a tear to drip into the palm of her hand as she studied the silver coin. Her hunger pangs had dissolved, just as her hope of escaping the living nightmare that she was wrapped in. In the distance Brenda could hear the rumble of a train, which drew her like a magnet. Could another place be better than this? She hoped so.

She managed to dodge the station guard amidst the crowds of people and stow away on the first train that arrived. She was so petrified to be discovered, that she hid in the toilet curled up on the lavatory seat; her heart pounding every time someone tried to use the locked facilities. In the distance she could hear the stern voice of the conductor shouting, *"Tickets please!"* In panic she unbolted the door and dashed through the carriages away from the impending confrontation.

The train slowed and an announcement was made from the platform, *'You have now arrived in Crewe.'* Brenda had no idea where that was but it gave her an opportunity to escape before being apprehended for having no ticket. Stepping across the platform she jumped on an awaiting train; finding the goods cart, she hid behind some mailbags and fell asleep.

Silence strangely woke her. The rhythmic rumble of the tracks had comforted her, but this eerie stillness caused her more fear than she had expected. Creeping out from her hiding place she could see an empty dark platform. There were two guards chatting at the far end under a glowing light, unaware that she was lurking in the shadows. Brenda slipped off her shoes to quieten her steps and escaped through the entrance to the cobbled street outside.

*"Oh shit,"* she cursed under her breath as she stepped on a piece of broken glass. Blood smeared one of her shoes a she put them back on. There was a surreal nothingness around her, the hush only disturbed by the meowing of a cat. She was frightened and alone, flinching as every unexplained noise made her jump. Brenda started trudging up the hill before her, wincing with the pain of her cut foot. She had to find some protection from the nighttime, somewhere safe until daylight. After a few minutes she came across a building with an unlocked door, The Abbey Church of Saint Peter and Saint Paul, Shrewsbury.

* * *

As Kelvin grew his demands increased. He was oblivious to the problems his mother was facing and the challenges she had to overcome to just survive. When he started to play with other children on the street, he could compare his lifestyle to theirs. Even at an early age, he felt different to other children, confused and full of questions. It wasn't until he played with them that he learned how to laugh; that made him feel sad to go home to the sombre shell that was his house. He'd only ever heard his dad shout and his mum cry, so laughter was a strange and uncomfortable concept he had to get used to.

Brenda sunk to an all-time low when Kelvin reached school age. Her drunken husband still denied her of money, her cupboards were empty and her son was asking questions that she couldn't answer. *'Why can't I have?'* was Kelvin's latest phrase, followed by *'The other children do.'* Looking in her purse she found the last two shillings that had to see her through the week. Her abusive husband would expect feeding after his drinking spree, even if he didn't eat it and her son wanted to feel the same as his peers. Her mind was in turmoil as she slid to the floor sobbing.

Handing over a few tarnished coins to a local shopkeeper in payment of a loaf of bread, she cheekily asked, *"Could I have some credit to see me through the week?"* With a sarcastic laugh he replied *"No chance! Try Fred, he'll charge you through the nose but you can pay weekly."*

Fred was a local grocer that delivered food door to door from the back of his tatty Bedford van. Brenda had often seen him plying his trade along her street but never summoned up the courage to speak to him. Times were tough and she had to ask if he could show pity on her. Waving him to stop as he drove by Brenda shyly asked, *"Excuse me sir, could I be one of your customers?"*

Fred was a pot-bellied man in his late fifties, with greying hair and a weathered face. Deep furrows on his forehead rippled from his puffy eyes, whereas his stubble goatee framed his tobacco stained teeth. With a twinkle in his eye he replied, *"Ah an Irish rose."* Brenda dropped her gaze not to make eye contact. Fred paused for a moment to scan her petit body through her thin cotton dress, his lecherous eyes mentally undressing her before him. *"Yes I'm sure we could get along very well."*

As he opened the back of his van she felt like a child stepping into Santa's grotto; Brenda's eyes lit up, she smiled for the first time in so long. Her arms were like an octopus as she shovelled food into carrier bags, Fred barely having time to jot down what she was having. Two bags full she scurried off with an insincere thank you. Fred shouted after her, *"Don't forget to pay at the end of the week!"*

Brenda nodded through the crack as she closed her front door.

The bags of food barely covered the empty shelves but Brenda felt happy that she could eventually provide. Simple things could lighten her sombre mood. The last time she could remember opening a cupboard door and seeing such a plentiful stock was as a child in her mother's kitchen. She never went hungry at home, there was always food to make a meal and home baked cakes to snack on. She loved to spend her Sunday mornings baking cakes with her mother and rolling pastry to make pies. Brenda's happy childhood was a far cry from the mere existence that she now was subjected to.

As the week went on the food depleted and her anxiety grew, fearful of Fred tapping the door for his money. Every sudden noise made her jump out her skin, not knowing what to expect. Brenda had made a stupid mistake getting involved with such a scam on her own doorstep; she had nowhere to hide. She knew that the small amount of housekeeping money that Terry gave her wouldn't cover the debt. She had taken the credit knowing she couldn't pay and now had to face the consequences; maybe she could sweet talk him for another week or avoid him for as long as possible.

Friday came and so did the tap on the door. Brenda looked out of the window and saw Fred's tatty Bedford van parked outside. Her heart sank as she realised that he had seen her through the window so she couldn't avoid him. Nervously she opened the door to the feared grocery man. He said with a beaming smile, *"How's my Irish rose? Have you got my money?"* She could see before her the face of a gargoyle from the local churchyard, spitting those words from an awkward leering smile; draped in a dirty brown overall he wrung out his sausage like fingers in anticipation.

Brenda could hardly splutter out her words *"My husband doesn't get paid until tonight, so can I pay you next week?"* Fred's smile slipped from his face and challenged, *"Umm, you wouldn't be holding out on me would you?"* Brenda dropped her gaze and shook her head. *"Okay"* Fred agreed to her surprise, *"I'll call in next week, but no more food until I get paid."* He threw her another beaming smile as he left, waving over his shoulder as he swaggered down the path. Brenda's heart was visibly pounding in her chest. She tried to put the matter out of her head for a short while, having managed to dodge the bullet this time. Next Friday she had to be more prepared to avoid the confrontation.

Tuesday came with a tap on the door, taking Brenda unawares as she opened it to Fred. She hadn't seen his van and guessed he'd parked it around the corner so as not to alert her. *"Good morning my Irish rose, have you got my money?"* he questioned with his false smile stretching from ear to ear.

*"Oh umm, no I haven't, I said last week that my husband doesn't get paid until Friday"* Brenda nervously stretching the truth. Still holding on to his cheeky grin, he quipped *"We both know if that were true, you'd have last week's money now. I'm not leaving until you either pay me in cash or pay me in kind."* Brenda looked at this grey hair man in disgust, he reminded her of her uncle and she started to shake. She dropped her head to avoid his gaze and started to whimper, *"No please give me more time."*

The house was empty, Kelvin was at school and Terry was at work. *"No more stalling!"* he insisted, as he pushed her inside and closed the door behind him. Brenda stood petrified staring at this seething monster before her, frozen to the spot just as a rabbit fixated by the headlights of a speeding car. She only had a blurred memory of him pawing at her clothes and ripping her knickers as he pushed her back onto the table to take his payment in flesh. She couldn't bear to look into those abusive eyes tearing away any dignity that she had left; she couldn't bear to remember the day she had been stripped of her innocence for the first time. Brenda let her mind drift whilst staring at the clock, the second hand slowly ticked around the face marking time for this horror to end.

Brenda had been subjected to sex over the years, mostly against her will, until it became just a numb act of going through the motions. Every time, she had frightening flashbacks to when her uncle took her virginity in that cramped shed. That vile place had stripped away her innocence and cheated her of a loving gesture with someone special. This time was no different to the countless times her husband had forced himself upon her in a drunken stupor. Her self-respect had been wrenched from her soul many years before; the only way she could cope was to take her mind back to the potato fields on a sunny day.

She often wanted to pick up the phone to call her mum or perhaps write her a letter to say she was okay, but knew in her heart that she was a broken woman, doubting she ever would be fine again. Her father and his abusive, disgusting, vile brother were identical twins. They were very close and she was afraid of never being believed if the truth came out. She feared that if ever she looked at her father again, she would visualise him weighing heavy on her instead of his perverted brother, frightened that she would see the rapist in his eyes; that single detail was one thing that she couldn't cope with. Brenda never wanted to darken the image of her father in such a putrid way, so she had no choice but to keep the abusive secret to herself. She didn't have the courage or resolve to confront her fears, so they continued to eat away inside her.

Fred blew her a kiss as he dressed himself then left without saying a word. Brenda curled into the foetal position on the table and allowed a tear to roll down her cheek. The thoughts of her sunny childhood had turned into a darkened shed; she felt an uneasy numbness as her mind retraced the awful details of the last few minutes. Her attention was brought back to earth by a loud banging on her door. As she stood up a trickle of semen dampened her thigh. Straightening her clothes, she opened the door to an arrogant Fred. He was holding a bag of groceries, which he placed on the step. *"I'll be back again next week to see my Irish rose, see you later alligator,"* he chirped as he blew her another kiss, then turned to swagger away.

Brenda knew this was something that she couldn't control; she was now a victim of another abuser that would take what he wanted from her. She picked up the groceries and hugged the bag to her chest before sobbing uncontrollably, maybe trying to justify her actions to feed her son or maybe accepting her worthless existence. She felt like a piece of meat that the depraved could feast upon whenever they wanted. Brenda had no strength to fight off the vultures pecking on her frail carcase.

She ran a scolding bath of hot water, then violently scoured herself with a wire-wool pad and caustic soda until her ripped flesh turn the water red with oozing blood. Kelvin calling from downstairs broke her trance as he came home from school. The water was stone cold, time had dissolved but her vivid memory had not. *"I'm having a bath, I'll be down in a minute!"*

Terry had recently become impotent due to his excessive drinking, so took his frustration out on her with his fists, leaving her bloodied and bruised whenever he chose. His drunken nights left her no escape from the painful pounding that she was exposed to. She was frightened to scream in case it woke Kelvin. Brenda had found ways to detach herself from the countless times that Terry had previously raped her when he was consumed by alcohol, but the punches, those painful punches wanted to explode from her vocal chords. She wanted to scream and never stop.

Part 3

With his mop of long curly hair and dishevelled clothes, Kelvin stood before the school gates to face another challenging day. He was unlike the other children at the school who donned school uniforms and satchels; he stood out from the crowd as the poor relation that never quite fitted in. With his baggy home-knitted jumper and scruffy trousers that crept up his legs higher than they should, made him a target for mockery. Holding a carrier bag containing jam sandwiches for lunch and a few pencils he'd acquired from previous lessons, he headed off to his classroom.

His school years hadn't been kind, suffering taunts from the school bullies and the ridicule of his teachers. He knew that he was never going to achieve good grades, let alone pass his exams in a few years; it seemed like his teachers had written him off, showing no encouragement or enthusiasm to even help him gain the most basic of education. At the age of thirteen years old he was a shy insular boy that metaphorically hid in the corner to avoid confrontation; he'd learned how to do that at home to avoid mental torture and physical punishment, the same applied at school.

*"Kelvin Carter you are late again,"* roared his teacher to the amusement of the other children in his class. He scurried to the back of the class to find his empty seat, a place he could become anonymous for a short time. His mind wandered to the evening before where he could hear the sobbing of his mother as his brutal father beat her; they never tried to muffle the din or consider how the mayhem

may affect this small vulnerable boy, but it did affect him and would leave lasting scars deep within.

His mother had found a small radio discarded on the street and had given it to Kelvin as a birthday present. It had become escapism, drowning out the noise of the fighting beneath his bedroom floor. Hidden under his covers he could listen to music crackling from this transistor; it didn't worry him that the aerial was broken; he improvised by forcing a compass into the fractured metal to improve the signal.

The chatter in the classroom gave him an opportunity to eavesdrop on conversations of normality, although he couldn't concentrate on the content of what was being said or comprehend the laughter that grew from their excitement. He could only think of how people laughed at him rather than including him in their humour. He desperately wanted to fit in, to be accepted by his peers, but every time he tried to engage with them he was rejected.

*"Can you move over a bit, I've got no room?"* said an annoyed Tess who shared his desk. They had sat together since the beginning of term and had developed a way of tolerating each other. Kelvin liked her because she wasn't mean to him, but knew she lived in a totally different world to him, a world of acceptance. Tess was a kind girl that gravitated towards the waifs and strays of society, often getting criticised by her parents for bringing home sick animals that she would find on her travels. She had a kind heart, but was aware to keep Kelvin at arm's length to avoid the wrath of her classmates for befriending the oddball.

Tess was a petite girl with long blond hair tied back in a ponytail. Kelvin thought of her as the most beautiful girl in the world, which not only came from her beaming smile and freckled cheeks, but also from her warm personality. She herself felt insecure and lacked confidence, which is why she chose to opt for a backseat in the classroom. Her desire not to stand out came from shyness rather than any toxic way of life; she came from a warm loving home and naively couldn't imagine the horrors Kelvin faced on a daily basis.

The school day was over and the class dispersed. Kelvin held back from the scuffled exit of his fellow pupils and was the last to leave. Heading down the corridor forced him to run the inevitable gauntlet of verbal taunts from the schools bullies, lined either side of his exit route. They formed an ever-decreasing funnel that he had to navigate, until it reached a narrow point only wide enough for one. This is where the bully of the day would step into his path and stop him in his tracks. They seemed to rotate on a daily basis so it was difficult for him to identify a singular person as the alpha male.

The experience created a deep distrust for everyone rather than a specific person. Today Johnny was the one who spilled the books he was carrying onto the floor and continued to call him 'Clumsy' and 'Stupid' as the group laughed at him. Tomorrow it may be someone else assuming the role. Kelvin visibly cowered as the verbal assault reigned over him and they knocked him to the floor as he bent to retrieve his books. The group quickly scattered as a teacher approached them, leaving Kelvin sat alone on the floor. *"Get up boy!"* the teacher bellowed and yanked him to his feet, then hurriedly left. The corridor was now empty and eerily silent.

As Kelvin crossed the playground heading for an uncertain reception at home, the group had reformed and continued their jeers from afar. He bowed his head in submission and scurried home without lifting his gaze from the path beneath his feet. The nearer he came to their tatty house, the place he shamefully called home, the more anxious he became. Leaving one nightmare at school, to be faced with another at home didn't make him feel safe or secure. The uncertainty of the night to come filled him with dread.

Opening the front door, he could see his pitiful mother stood at the sink peeling potatoes. She seemed to be miles away and didn't acknowledge his arrival home. Kelvin uttered nothing, just kicked off his shoes and headed upstairs to his bedroom, the tiniest sanctuary you could imagine. He had a single bed covered with a Batman duvet, a chest of drawers to house his clothes and a couple of pop-music posters on the wall that he'd torn from magazines found discarded on the street. The only pleasure that his mother Brenda could provide for him were sheets of white paper and a few worn pencils that she got from the mobile grocer that often delivered on a Friday when he was out. Kelvin had only seen him driving passed as he went to school, a weathered man with grey hair.

Drawing became Kelvin's passion and a way to release all his darkest thoughts. Often he couldn't make sense of the macabre masterpieces that unfolded before his eyes, the images that burnt deep within his soul. The best sketches where taped to the wall alongside his prized poster of leather clad Suzi Quatro, but if ever he should wake from a nightmare and saw their staring faces bearing down on him, his love for Suzi gave him comfort. Pictures were his way of communicating with an outside world that was only real

38

to him. Once he drew an image of his brutal father towering over a frail figure and his tears splashing onto the paper forced him to stop before his inner self allowed the horrors to unfold. He knew what happened after dark when he lay in his bed but he was too young to deal with the severity of the situation. For now, he felt safer in a bubble of ignorance not having to see it with his own eyes.

Brenda called him from the bottom of the stairs to say that his dinner was ready and hungry Kelvin marched down the stairs. Sitting at the dining table his mother brought him his plate of food, almost dropping it out of her frail hands. A few boiled potatoes and a slice of ham was his feast for the night, it was bland and tasteless but satisfied his empty stomach. She never ate with him, just leaving him alone at the table whilst she returned to the kitchen and shut the door. He could hear the sound of saucepans being washed and the crash of a broken plate as it hit the floor. She cried out loud and then the sound of more breaking crockery, sobbing was all he could hear through the closed door.

He left the table, not wanting to open the kitchen door to return his empty plate. In the corner of the room was a small television, which he could watch when his father was out, so he switched on the device and waited a moment, for the image to come to life. Only the evening news was available to watch at the moment, then afterwards his favourite soap opera series. Brenda entered the room and without saying a word sat next to him, wrapping her arm around him. Kelvin could see from the blotches on her face that she had been crying. As she sniffed, Brenda dabbed her nose with a tissue. Nothing was mentioned, they just sat there in silence watching the surreal world of images on the glass screen in front of them. The ticking of the clock kept a rhythmic count of time as the programme on the television unfolded, but they were just background noises from the thoughts spinning in their heads.

The click of the front door opening created sudden panic forcing them to bolt off the sofa like two young lovers caught in a compromising position. Quickly turning off the television, Kelvin scampered to his bedroom, whilst Brenda hurried to the kitchen just as Terry drunkenly stumbled into the room. Neither of them wanted to know his mood or how he would react. Today he fell onto the sofa unable to control his simple functions. After several attempts to remove his shoes, he rolled onto the furniture with dirty feet and fell asleep. Brenda had been watching his antics through the crack of the door and felt relieved for a moment in time. She left it a few minutes then crept passed him, heading for her bedroom hoping he would remain there until morning. His deep snoring gave her some comfort.

Kelvin had camped out cross-legged on his bed, underneath the tent-like cover of his blanket. His crackling radio blurted out, *'When I get me moped out on the road, I'm gonna ride, ride, ride!'* This lightened his mood recalling Jasper Carrot on Top of the Pops. He popped his head out from under the covers and was greeted with a strange calmness. All he could hear was the loud snoring of his father in the lounge below. Relieved to be spared from the usual commotion, he return to listen to his favourite show on Radio Caroline.

Terry had already left for work when Brenda and Kelvin came downstairs in the morning. Muddy footprints left their mark on the sofa and vomit on the floor was a stark reminder of where he had spent the night. It was a usual occurrence for her to clean up after him, but for once she was glad that he hadn't urinated in his sleep whilst lying next to her; those nights would force her to change her wet nightie and sleep on the floor.

Brenda seemed to be in an anxious mood as Kelvin ate his breakfast. The mould was cut off the dried bread before she made his jam sandwiches for lunch, wrapping them in paper. It was Friday and the groceries were due to be delivered so maybe they could have a treat for tea; perhaps his mother would bake one of her famous cakes or make a treacle tart. Kelvin loved anything sweet and hoped his mother could convince the grocer to leave some chocolate for him; recently he'd noticed a bottle of gin hidden under the kitchen sink every Friday, so he must be a generous man.

Almost through another week, Kelvin headed off to school. He hated being there and the only thing that made that time bearable was sitting next to Tess, the one person that didn't call him stupid when he didn't understand the lesson or tell him he was clumsy when he dropped things. She would even let him copy her answers and cheat on exams so he wasn't so much of a target. He liked her for that and had a secret crush on her.

His mood was fine until he approached the schools gates, until he saw some of his intimidators standing guard. As he got nearer he could hear their taunts, he cowered inside and dropped his gaze so he couldn't look into their eyes. He wanted to ignore them, to block them out as if they no longer existed. He felt a sharp nudge, knocking him off balance forcing him to fall to the ground. Pain shot through his knee as it hit the tarmac. *"Clumsy Kelvin, he'll trip over his own feet"* Johnny howled, as the group chuckled.

41

Johnny stepped onto his sandwich, twisting his foot, grinding Kelvin's lunch into the pavement. The bell rang and the group dispersed leaving Kelvin to hurry to class after them. His lunch was ruined and the knees of his trousers dirty, he was sure the ridicule would continue inside.

Tess noticed that his lunch bag had a footprint on it and guessed he'd been bullied on the way into school. Under the desk she slipped a chocolate bar to him from her lunch box, he smiled with gratitude, he loved her for that. The classroom bullies kept looking back over their shoulders laughing between them at their earlier antics. Tess was getting annoyed and told them to grow up which turned some negative attention onto her, making Kelvin feel uncomfortable. She had been so kind to him that he didn't want her drawn into the onslaught he faced on a daily basis. *"Please let it go Tess,"* he begged. The teacher started the lesson and the situation calmed.

Kelvin kept a low profile for the rest of the day, ducking and diving any situation that he felt would escalate the tension. He didn't want Tess to suffer by sticking up for him. He spent most of the lunchtime hidden in the toilets and after school managed to squeeze through the gauntlet amidst a group of other pupils. With a sigh of relief he was through the school gates and heading home. His mum was in a better mood when he got home and she gave him a big hug as he stepped through the door. He could smell gin on her breath but didn't care, he wanted to enjoy one of the rare embraces he got from her, making him feel warm inside. There was food in the cupboard and the smell of baking from the oven. He noticed a glass of orange juice on the side, which his mother kept sipping from; each time it made her giggle. When she wasn't looking he sniffed the glass and smelled alcohol, he guessed the grocer was generous today.

He'd not seen his mum as mellow as this in ages and guessed the gin had eased her mood. She was slurred in her speech, but she was chatty. He felt for the first time in a while that he had a mum, a real mum that wanted to look after him. The radio was playing when they heard the front door open, Kelvin froze on the spot but Brenda continued to sway her hips to the music as she took a cake from the oven. Terry looked stunned as he entered the lounge. He stared at the frightened Kelvin who was transfixed like a rabbit in the headlights of a car. His gaze swung towards the kitchen and could have almost melted Brenda to the spot with his laser like vision. *"What in the hell is going on here?"* he bellowed at the top of his voice. Totally out of character Brenda replied, *"Feck off you gob shite!"* and continued to prise the cake from its container.

Kelvin had never seen his mother behave like this, standing up for herself was new to him. He had also never seen a flash point develop as quickly or violently as it did in that moment. Terry barged his way through to the kitchen and slapped Brenda so hard around the face that she fell to the floor, taking with her the warm sponge that she had baked and also the remaining ingredients that were left on the work surface. Her face was dusted in self-raising flour, which started to soak up the blood running from her mouth. Terry began kicking her in the ribs. *"You bitch, don't you ever answer me back!"* he roared as another blow landed on target. Kelvin bravely ran into the affray to pound his tiny hands onto his father's back. *"Leave her alone, leave her alone"* he cried, only to be greeted with a back handed slap for his trouble.

Attention was turned on the defiant Kelvin. *"You're a pathetic little runt"* Terry spat, *"When you are man enough to take me on, you can take your best shot"* then punched Kelvin in the face. Terry's ring gouged through the skin on the child's forehead and split his eyelid open like an overripe peach. His head was ringing as he fell backwards, crashing his limp skull onto the edge of the coffee table. Blood seeped from his gaping wounds as he passed out to a spinning room. The young hero or possibly fool came back to consciousness to the sound of the ticking clock, the constant noise that magnified the eerie silence.

As he sat up he could see the broken radio smashed in the corner of the room and his mum sat on the kitchen floor. She was propped up against the wall with her knees under her chin, arms wrapped around her legs. Brenda had gone beyond crying to a place of surreal silence, where she could scream with the mute button on and no one would hear her. The trickle of blood from her mouth and the shining black eye were the only obvious injuries but many more lay hidden beneath her clothing. The kitchen looked like there had been a food fight with flour and broken eggs on the floor, her newly baked caked stamped into the lino.

There was no sign of Terry. Brenda looked over and spluttered, *"He's gone out, back down the pub"*. Kelvin eased himself up and headed for the kitchen to survey the chaos. As he tried to help his mother to her feet she screamed in pain from her suspected broken ribs. Once upright she cradled herself to relieve the agony she was in. Brenda recoiled from the sight of her injured son, instantly overcome with panic at the splatters of blood that had run down his face, her own painful plight forgotten.

She damped a towel and gently blotted away the red smears from his skin. His eye socket was a mess; the amount of damage was hard to distinguish with the amount of puffy purple skin. A piece of flesh had been torn from the back of his head, matting his curly hair with congealed blood. Brenda tore a clean tea towel into squares to create wadding for the wounds then secured them in place by tying an old pair of tights around his head.

They helped each other up the staircase, stopping first at Brenda's bedroom. Kelvin helped her remove the torn and stained dress that she was wearing. The sight of the large purple bruises spreading from under her left breast, around to her back made him feel sick. Kelvin helped his poor mum into bed and covered her with a blanket, leaving her to sob like a tortured animal. He closed the door on his own bedroom to recall the enormity of the scene that had unfolded before his very eyes, the ferocious demon that his father had unleashed upon an unsuspecting world. The image of the devastation frightened him, but what frightened him even more was the adrenaline that was rushing through his own body; the excitement that he felt in that bitter sweet moment between pain and pleasure that he couldn't explain. He fell asleep nursing his own wounds, yet the pain made him feel alive for the very first time.

Still feeling sore and frightened from the night before, Kelvin and his mother cleaned the kitchen and straightened the house, staying on alert for the front door to open, expecting an angry Terry to appear, but he didn't. Two days and two nights Terry stayed away, only to appear on

Sunday evening drunk and verbally abusive. Brenda left him to fall asleep on the sofa and went to bed. This evening was no different to any other evening. There was no mention of the violence on the Friday night. Not a word was said, but Kelvin could vividly recall every frame that unfolded on the screen of his mind, just like a movie in slow motion. He became a voyeur as he studied each picture with curiosity rather than fear. What he couldn't explain was the unexpected excitement spinning around in the pit of his stomach.

Kelvin didn't return to school until his lesions had healed. Brenda was shocked at the extent of her son's injuries, feeling extreme guilt for not protecting him. She felt worse for not getting medical help for him, yet she was too frightened, too worried to explain the incident. As the swelling in his eye subsided, she was horrified to see that his upper eyelid was split open from eyelash to eyebrow. The skin was already healing into a jagged inverted V shape, as the cut had not knitted together. *"Mum my eye is sore,"* as he blinked against the light. Brenda applied clean wadding but couldn't find any words to reassure him. *'The fecking bastard'* kept ringing through her head every time she recalled that fateful night. She hoped Kelvin's curly fringe would disguise the scar; she hoped Terry would die a painful death.

Part 4

Another long summer break over and Kelvin was dreading his return to school, albeit his last year in education and last year of school torment. He had spent most of the sweltering summer of seventy-six, loitering in the local supermarket car park, offering to load grocery bags and to return customer's shopping trollies in the hope of a tip. Some days he was successful enough to buy his favourite chocolate and occasionally treat his mum in the process. He was honing his skills as a small time hustler, an entrepreneur in the making, searching out opportunities to exploit. A few coins in his pocket made him feel like a king on the inside, yet his clothes looked more like a pauper.

He had managed to buy a second-hand radio with his supermarket trolley venture, to replace the one broken in the skirmish; this one had a bigger speaker and longer aerial. He was pleased with his investment, now being able to listen to the top-twenty on a Sunday evening without a crackly reception. Two pencils sufficed for imaginary drumsticks while he sang out loud, *'The boys are back in town ........ Spread the word around!'*

His mother had managed to find him a white shirt from the charity shop that he could wear to school, blending in a little more than normal. It wasn't exactly white, but Kelvin felt pleased with it. He was mindful that any stains he made on the first days would be highlighted throughout the week, as this was also his only shirt, so he had to be careful to save embarrassment. Standing at the school gates a little earlier than usual, he took a deep breath and headed inside before the bullies arrived.

He found his usual seat at the back of the class and assumed his normal pose of hunching shoulders and stooping his head, trying to avoid eye contact with the pupils as they arrive. *"Oh hello, you look smart,"* said Tess as she slid into the seat next to him. Kelvin visibly blushed, but didn't say a word in reply. A couple of lads from the bullying group had left this term, leaving Johnny to head up the few remaining in the group. He threw Kelvin a smirk then stuck his fingers up in defiance. It seemed like things would pick up from where they left off, the abuse would continue without respite. *"Okay class listen up!"* The teacher called order and the lesson began.

Kelvin's mind was never focused on his education, daydreaming of his freedom at the end of this school year and doodling sketches in his workbook to consume his time. His teachers never paid attention to his lack of concentration or his unwillingness to be involved, they had written him off as a waste of time quite a while ago. He was just a number to them filling a seat, as long as he didn't disrupt the class, he was left to his own devices. The days were long and blended into each other.

Absentmindedly, Kelvin scratched Tess's name into the top of his wooden desk and came under the wrath of his teacher for damaging school property. *"Stand up boy!"* shouted Mr Stanhope the geography teacher. Kelvin was instantly subjected to the roars of laughter from other pupils in his class. He was so embarrassed and caught a glimpse in the corner of his eye of a red faced Tess cringing with humiliation. *"Err, sorry sir."* He had no intention of hurting her in such a way and wished the ground would open up beneath his feet, allowing it to swallow him whole. He wasn't given such an easy option, but was made to stay behind after class with a sheet of sandpaper to scour the desktop to remove the offence.

A heckling group had formed in the corridor as Kelvin left the classroom. As he approached, he could see an upset Tess circled by the group with Johnny taunting her about the antics in the class. *"Looks like Kelvin l-o-v-e-s you, the saddo!"* Johnny screamed with laughter. Others in the group joined in the verbal abuse as Tess cradled her books to her chest and sobbed. Rage erupted inside him; without a thought Kelvin barged through the group and pushed Johnny away, *"Leave her alone,"* he shouted creating silence in the group. Pain shot through Kelvin's nose as Johnny landed his fist square on target, making him lose focus before he hit the floor. A couple of kicks were administered by the group to show solidarity, then they disappeared like ghosts in the night as a teacher approached. *"Oh it's you,"* blurted Mr Jenkins the science teacher, as he marched off without stopping. Tess crouched down offering Kelvin a tissue to blot his bloody nose. *"Are you okay?"* she asked out of genuine concern. *"Yeah I'm okay, sorry that I got you involved,"* he replied as he stood to his feet. Bowing his head in embarrassment, he scurried off along the corridor without another word, leaving Tess to find her own way.

Brenda never noticed the blood stain on Kelvin's shirt when he got home. He stormed passed her heading to the bathroom to check out the extent of his humiliation. His face was still throbbing and his eyes watered as he locked himself in the bathroom. The only evidence that he could see was a glowing red nose. In any other circumstance you could laugh off his likeness to Rudolph the red nosed reindeer, but now wasn't a time Kelvin wanted to laugh. He sponged off the offending dried blood from his shirt, and then skulked off to his bedroom to feel sorry for himself. He was proud that he'd stood up to the bullies to defend the honour of his precious Tess, but felt a fool in front of her that he had so feebly left his mark on the situation. He was angry deep inside that he hadn't been prepared for such an altercation. Next time he would have to find an edge.

He hung up his shirt and slipped on an old tee shirt before returning downstairs for his dinner. Brenda was in her usual trance at the kitchen sink as she prepared the meal. It was sausage and mash tonight which Kelvin loved; adding her special touch to the feast by frying onions, then smothering the entire plate with rich gravy. Kelvin turned on the television and waited for his meal. The smell wafting through made him feel hungry and distracted him from the throbbing of his nose. Brenda called him to sit down as she placed his meal on the table. She hadn't noticed the trail of gravy she had spilled along the floor until she slipped on the contents as she returned to the kitchen. She cursed herself but never attempted to clean it up, just slamming the door in frustration. The atmosphere felt tense. Kelvin quickly scoffed the platter and retired to his bedroom to recall the events that had unfolded earlier that day.

Lying on his bed he quickly sketched the altercation with Johnny, distorting the facts so he became the brave victor. The bullies were scattered on the floor whilst he triumphantly puffed out his chest, winning the praise and admiration from his Princess Tess. He wanted to be her knight in shining armour instead of the court jester. The image unfolding before his eyes as the pencil scratched over the paper gave him a sense of hope, a feeling that maybe one day he would be top dog so other people would no longer laugh at him. His mind raced at the possibilities, allowing him to daydream as his clenched fists twitched in sequence to his thoughts. He drifted off to sleep with a warm confidence growing in his stomach.

He was jolted back to consciousness by a load scream from his mother. It was pitch black in his room and only a glint of light from under his door gave him any perception or direction. A thud followed by another scream made his heart race as he headed for the door, grabbing the handle and swinging it open. He could see his drunken father towering over Brenda, as she lay on her bed covered with blood, waiting to receive the next blow that would reign down on her. Terry's hand was raised above his head as he shouted abuse at this pitiful woman, whom he disrespectfully called his wife. Kelvin saw red and couldn't allow this punishment to continue. Without thinking, he picked up a table lamp next to their bed and smashed it over his father's head, forcing him to crumple to the floor. Grabbing his hysterical mother, he dragged her downstairs to the safety of the lounge.

There was an unnatural silence that neither of them could comprehend. Kelvin sat her on the sofa and fetched a towel from the kitchen to mop her bloodied face. His body was shaking through pure fear at what he'd done and what may happen next. It had been a brutal attack on a defenceless woman that made no sense. He was angry that his mother didn't stand up for herself, but knew she had no chance against such a fierce adversary, therefore pity was all he could offer as a form of comfort.

They both recoiled in fear as the door swung open. Before them Terry stood swaying with blood running down his neck. He looked strangely confused, struggling to focus on the pair sat on the sofa before him. Kelvin could see the rage starting to build and the redness developing in his father's eyes, becoming genuinely scared for their safety. Without a second thought, Kelvin sprung from the sofa and charged screaming at him knocking him off balance. As Terry regained his composure, Kelvin punched him square in the face and howled, *"You bastard, don't you ever touch her again!"*

There was a moment where time stood still and nothing was uttered. Terry was clearly shocked that his son had become man enough to take his best shot. Kelvin stood his ground with his raised fists ready to defend the next onslaught, but it never came. Terry stared at him, then cast Brenda a disbelieving glance, then left. As the front door closed, Kelvin and Brenda looked at each other and burst into tears.

The slam of a neighbour's front door shocked them back into reality. It was early in the morning and they could see the sun lighting up a new dawn through the kitchen window. Brenda's face was still covered in dried blood from the night before and the graze on Kelvin's knuckles was the only evidence that he had done the unimaginable thing of hitting the man he was ashamed to call his father. Although nothing was spoken, it was clear to see, the fear they both held for the reprisals due to them when Terry sobered up. They felt like they were living on a knife-edge, listening out for the click of the front door and became spooked by sudden noises outside.

Kelvin decided to take the rest of the week off from school and set about clearing up the mess from the night before. Picking up the remnants of the broken lamp, he recoiled nicking his finger on a sharp fragment. "*Oh bollocks,*" he cursed under his breath. A spot of blood from his hand dripped onto the floor, blending in with the dried blood from the night before. He froze for a moment and wondered whose blood it was, his father's or his mother's, then proceeded to paint images in his mind to unravel his quandary. Picking up the lamp to attack his father was a blur but watching the slow motion collapse of this towering man could be recalled in the smallest detail.

Sweeping up the final shards, Kelvin managed to place them in the dustbin just before the dustcart arrived. The bins were always emptied on a Thursday, so he was happy that any evidence of wrongdoing was taken as far away as possible; he doubted that his drunken father would report it to the police but wanted to be sure. Returning to his mother's bedroom he stripped the blood soaked sheets and placed them in the bath. With a little soap, he let the water dissolve the offending stains.

Brenda was sat on the back door step transfixed by the glowing sun now raised above her garden shed. The colour was vivid against the clear blue sky peppered with the occasional distant cloud. Everything felt surprisingly normal considering the mayhem of the previous night. Her mind had managed to escape to a safe field in Ireland, playing with her friends in a cornfield. She didn't want to come back to face reality, she didn't want the daydream to end; it felt safe and calm until the glaring face of her vile uncle filled her vision with a letchful grin. Shivers run down her spine as she visualised herself backing away. *'No!'* screamed from her silent mouth.

She jumped as Kelvin handed her a cup of tea, then showed him gratitude with a nervous smile. Brenda knew that life would never be the same again and feared for the worst, knowing how violent Terry could be; she feared for her life and that of her son. Pulling the belt of her tatty dressing gown tightly around her waist, she sipped her tea whilst her mind spun into overdrive.

After washing and getting dressed, Brenda placed a carving knife under her pillow and put a glass bottle next to her bed. *"No fecking more. You bastard, no fecking more!"* On the sofa she strategically placed her knitting bag with needles easily accessible and sharp scissors in the inside pocket. Sliding out her biggest needle, she thrust it forward like a dagger into thin air, *"Take that you fucker!"* She made a decision in that moment of time that she would never be anyone's punch bag again, so she had to be prepared to fight back. She was so scared but had nothing to lose; every scrap of dignity had been stripped away from her until her life was worse than a meagre existence. Her son was all she had left to live for and he would never be his punch bag.

Between them they continued to clean up the place in an eerie silence, focusing on any sounds they heard, fearing the click of the front door opening, but for that day it didn't happen. They managed to get through the day without incident and felt a little bit of normality in their abnormal world. Kelvin decided to have an early night and left his mother to barricade the front door with a heavy dresser in an attempt to feel a little safer. She also went to her bedroom, sitting upright in her unmade bed listening for every sound. Tightly holding the handle of her secreted knife she never slept a wink, watching the blackness turn into another sunny dawn.

Brenda, woke Kelvin early Friday morning, *"Get yourself off to school."* He protested, as he hadn't intended to return this week after the upset with his father. *"You're getting under my feet, just go to school"* she complained, as his bedroom door loudly slammed. Kelvin was in no mood to face the bullies at school, let alone conform to any dress code, so he slipped on a creased tee shirt and his favourite blue jeans. Heading into the kitchen he found his mother sipping a cup of tea as she sat on the back door step surveying the flaming ball in the sky.

*"What's for breakfast?"* he asked. Brenda pointed to the bread bin on the side. Lifting the lid revealed a depleted loaf covered with green mould, which Kelvin looked at with disdain. He preferred to go hungry. *"Now get out!"* Brenda bellowed, as she ushered him out of the front door, before he could argue. The door slammed behind him as he started walking down the street. The rumble of the grocer's van caught his attention and they locked eye contact as he sped past.

As Kelvin approached the school gates he still had the violent events of the week locked in his mind; he was feeling anxious and nervous, flinching at every sound that startled him over the loud din of the surging pupils. On guard were the usual gang of persecutors that would browbeat anyone vulnerable, under the supervision of self-elected alpha male Johnny. They jostled each other in play fighting to draw attention to them, intimidating those unfortunate enough to be in close proximity. *"Hey you curly haired tosser, didn't your mother dress you today?"* shouted Johnny to the laughter of the group. *"Maybe she was shagging the grocer to pay for her food!"* It felt like Kelvin had been hit with a sledgehammer taking all the breath from his body, stopping him in his tracks. *"They say she's just a whore!"* screamed Johnny to provoke a reaction.

A raging fire ignited in Kelvin's stomach as he charged at Johnny screaming a warrior cry from the top of his lungs. The group froze on the spot as Kelvin rugby tackled Johnny forcing them both to tumble over a low wall. As they wrestled on the wet grass Kelvin managed to get the advantage, sitting on Johnny's chest, then proceeded to mercilessly pound his fists into the face of the cruel oppressor that had made his school life a living hell. Every wrongdoing that this ruffian had subjected Kelvin to was now vividly pictured in his mind as each blow struck. Exhausted and panting he climbed off Johnny and ran from the school with no intention to return, the score with the bully settled, he needed to escape.

His mind was spinning as he jogged down the street, finding a gap in a fence he crossed over some waste ground until he reached the canal, a familiar place where he had hidden in the past. He sat on a bench and nursed the stitch in his side that caused him to wince in pain. All he could hear in his head was Johnny's taunts *"She's just a whore, she's just a whore!"* He turned and threw up behind him leaving a splatter of liquid on the ground from his empty stomach. Wiping his mouth with the back of his hand was the only action he could remember over the barrage of chants in his head, he had no recollection of his walk home.

Outside his house was parked the tatty Bedford van with its front wheel on the kerb. There was no care how it had been left and seems to have been abandoned in a hurry. Kelvin noticed the bald tread on the tyre and recalled the balding head of the grocer, bringing into his mind the weathered face he'd only seen from afar. His thoughts were still spinning out of control as he clicked the front door open and walked in. Two bags of groceries were propped against the wall in the hallway with a large bottle of gin peering from the top. He absentmindedly stumbled over one of the bags, noisily spilling the contents as he opened the lounge door.

He found his mother naked from the waist down laying on the sofa, with the grocer towering over her pulling up his trousers. They both had a shocked look upon their faces as Kelvin barged in. *"You dirty bastard, leave my mum alone!"* he screamed at the defiant Fred, who stood now smirking as he buttoned up his flies. Kelvin launched himself at him, only to be greeted with a backhand swipe, which sent him careering off towards a hard floor. Brenda quickly grabbed him to stop any further attempts to inflict harm on the grocer. Fred looked at the pair of them and spat, *"This is too much hassle, you aren't a great shag anyway,"* then slammed the door as he left. Kelvin wriggled free from his mother's tight grip and went to his room. He stared at the ceiling of his tiny room without shifting his gaze. He was right, that bastard Johnny was right, "*She must be a whore.*" Darkness fell leaving him transfixed all through the night.

Brenda dressed herself and gathered up the scattered food in the hallway. She was too embarrassed to look at Kelvin and didn't have the words to justify her actions. He was too young to understand; she also was too young to understand how she could betray herself, just like Judas Iscariot, for thirty pieces of silver.

Eggs had been broken and the bag of potatoes had split open, as Fred had kicked the contents on his way out. She salvaged what she could realising that her free supply of food had now expired, not knowing what her penniless fate would bring her. The bottle of gin gave her cold comfort as she sat on the kitchen step staring at her garden shed, noticing how the panels were cracked and broken, just like her life. The entire bottle consumed, she completed her ritual of barricading the front door earlier than normal before climbing the stairs to her bedroom.

Sitting upright in her bed, holding the handle of the knife secreted under her pillow, she still feared the return of the bastard Terry. It had now been a few days that he'd been away and she was sure that he would soon be back to rein his terror once more. Every tick of the clock was like water torture bouncing droplets on her forehead, until she wrapped a pillow around her ears to muffle the din. She curled into a ball and sobbed, waiting for the tears to wash away her pain, but they didn't. The rattling of the milkman delivering his bottles and the cooing of the pigeons on her roof brought her attention back to the morning hangover that was now occupying her head. She had no idea what hellish day was in store for her to endure.

Part 5

Tuesday morning felt like just any other day, with Kelvin rolling out of bed to the sounds of a horn blasting on a car outside his house. He looked through his curtains to see a neighbour jumping into a taxi, shouting instructions at the driver before it sped off down the road. He slipped on his jogging pants and a baggy tee shirt, then headed downstairs. His mother sat on the kitchen step staring at the garden shed, sipping a cup of tea, as if transfixed on a movie playing on the wooden slats. She groaned an acknowledgement to Kelvin as he entered the room, but that was the extent of their conversation.

He slipped a dried slice of bread under the grill and waited for the aroma of freshly cooked toast to hit his nostrils. Once covered in butter, he quickly devoured it and headed for the front door. *"I'm going out,"* he yelled to Brenda but no reply. In the hallway he could see the torn flooring where the heavy dresser had been dragged so many times; under his breath he mumbled to himself **'Happy fucking Birthday'** as his sixteenth year went unacknowledged. Outside he had to dodge the puddles formed over night from a downpour, but the holes in his shoes still allowed his feet to get wet.

It had been two weeks since he decided never to return to school, also the same time since his scuffle with Fred the grocer. Their food supply was running low and they were literally living hand to mouth. Kelvin noticed the Bedford van parked at the top of the road outside number forty-two, a single mother with two kids, guess he'd now got a new

59

place to satisfy his needs. Kelvin picked up a jagged rock and left a deep scratch along the side of the vehicle as he passed.

*"Dirty bastard!"* spat from his lips as he tossed the rock onto the grass verge. He headed for the supermarket car park, hoping to retrieve some financial gratitude from busy shoppers. That became his routine, lifting heavy bags of groceries into customer's cars so they would be more likely to tip him. The meagre earnings allowed him to buy basic food supplies.

It didn't take long that day, before the manager confronted him in the car park. *"What are you doing boy?"* Kelvin was unsure whether to run or to try and talk his way out of it. *"I'm taking the trolley back for my auntie,"* Kelvin spluttered unconvincingly.

*"I've been watching you boy and you seem to have quite a little scheme going on, shouldn't you be at school?"* challenged Mr Yates the store manager. *"I'm sixteen sir and have left school, I need to earn money for my mum,"* he replied quite reluctantly. Sweet-talking the customers had been how he'd persuaded them to hand over tips; maybe he could use the same skills to wriggle out of this situation.

*"Um, you can't keep hassling my customers, but I'll tell you what, I could do with a school leaver to help out around here if you want to work for me?"* Yates asked without thinking. He could see how desperate Kelvin was and felt sorry for him. Kelvin jumped at the chance and was told to report for duty the next day looking smart.

Brenda managed to raise a slight grin at the news. Kelvin handed her some potatoes that he'd bought with the few coins that he'd acquired, feeling like he was now the man of the house. It had been several weeks since Terry had left, but they still felt the nervous tension in the air of his impending return. They both jumped at sudden noises and Brenda still continued to barricade the front door after dark adding an eerie atmosphere to the nightly routine. She continued to sit awake all night, gripping tightly on to the handle of her secreted knife, demons consumed her thoughts; not being able to remember the last time that she had felt safe enough to sleep and yearned a drink of gin to soften her pain. Maybe her shaking hands were through fear or anxiety, but possibly due to the lack of alcohol that had been supporting her system for so long.

Drawing the blade from beneath the pillow she studied the shining metal with a newfound curiosity, imagining how she would use it if a violent assault happened. She slowly swung the blade in front of her as if she was the fourth musketeer, lunging at a vision of a brutal attack whilst grunting with every motion. The knife came slowly to rest on her naked thigh, it felt cold yet reassuring, like a dependable friend. Turning the sharp edge onto her warm skin, she pulled the blade very slowly towards her, gouging into flesh, allowing a trickle of blood to slide off her leg onto the bed. It felt like all the tension in her body was leaving her with the stream of red lava. An involuntary sigh accompanied her long exhale of breath; a relaxing calmness enveloped her being.

In that moment there was no pain just relief, until guilt filled her mind, *'Shite, what have I done?'* Her thigh started to throb in pain. The blood smeared as she rubbed the wound in disbelief. Limping to the bathroom, she closed the door and burst into tears. She bound her leg with a towel and ran the blade under the tap to wash away the evidence of her misdemeanour. The cut wasn't very deep and soon started to dry, allowing her to apply a long plaster strip before washing the blood soaked towel. Returning to her bedroom, she placed the knife under the pillow and reflected on the throbbing in her leg. For the first time in so long she managed to doze, until two cats fighting in the garden awakened her. It was three o'clock as she checked the time. She'd gained four hours respite from the horrors in her mind, yet they came back with a vengeance to occupy her thoughts until dawn.

Kelvin felt a nervous excitement as he woke the next morning. It was his first day of legitimate work at the supermarket. Mr Yates was going to be his first boss and he was told to dress smartly. His faded white shirt and school trousers was all he had to offer from his insufficient wardrobe, but he remembered Tess saying '*he looked smart,*' so that is what he wore. After eating a slice of toasted bread, he headed off with a smile, not noticing his mother's pain as she limped towards the kettle to refresh her cup of tea.

The sky always looked sunny when he wasn't at school and this day was no exception, as he walked the short distance to the supermarket. Mr Yates greeted him in the entrance, then ushered him into his office. Sitting behind his desk, Kelvin's new boss seemed quite intimidating, as he passed him an application form to fill out. *"I'll need to phone your school and speak to the headmaster, which one is it?"* Kelvin felt knots tighten in his stomach as he reluctantly supplied the information, expecting his day to be shattered by rejection. He completed the form as best he could whilst Mr Yates was deep in conversation with the headmaster. *"Umm okay, thank you for your time,"* were the last words Kelvin heard as the telephone conversation ended. *"It sounds like you won't be missed at school, who did you upset?"* Before Kelvin could reply to Mr Yates's question, he continued, *"Not to worry Kelvin I'll give you a chance"*.

He was at Mr Yates beck and call, running errands and completing chores. Kelvin didn't mind, he was pleased to feel useful and no longer a target of the school bullies or being ignored by the education system that was duty bound to protect him. He kept a low profile and shyly spoke to other people so as not to draw attention to himself. He didn't have a lot to say to them or have any witty replies to their playful teasing; Kelvin just flushed with embarrassment and continued with the tasks at hand. First day over and his happy mood was brought down to earth when he'd realised that he wouldn't get any pay until the end of the week. His daily trolley heist had come to an end, his cash in hand income gone. Stepping through the front door of his home, Brenda greeted him, *"Did you have a good day son?"* she asked. *"Yes mum but I don't get paid until Friday,"* he sadly replied. *"It's okay,"* she reassured him as she patted him on the shoulder as she headed for the kitchen. Jam sandwiches were their feast for dinner that evening, but neither complained. It didn't seem important what filled their stomachs as long as they didn't feel hungry.

Brenda struggled to shift the heavy dresser to barricade the front door; her leg began to throb with the exertion, making the task more difficult than normal. After climbing the staircase and propping herself up in bed, she studied the blood soaked plaster on her leg. Tugging at the corner, the dressing came swiftly off to reveal a red gash diagonally across the front of her thigh. The wound was clean and tingled as the air hit it. She ran the tip of her finger along the tender injury in disbelief, wondering why she had done it, but more frighteningly why she had never done it before.

She slid down the bed and adopted a foetal position so her hand could clench the knife under her pillow. *"Would the air tingle on Terry's wound if she cut his throat?"* she wondered. *"Would things have been different in the dark shed if she had plunged a knife into her uncle's gut?"* New demons blended with old demons to keep her mind working on overdrive throughout the night. She spent the darkness staring at shadows and never slept.

Kelvin enjoyed his job and was excited to receive his first wage packet at the end of the week. Opening the brown envelope revealed a couple of five pound notes and a few coins. He'd never held paper money before and felt like a millionaire as he slid his earnings into his pocket. After his shift had finished he ran along the aisles in excitement, collecting groceries to fill his basket, proudly handing a note to the cashier to pay for the goods. The few coins of change were enough for him to buy a bar of chocolate, which he hungrily ate on his way home. Presenting his mother the bag of groceries gave him a sense of achievement; it made him feel like head of the household. He then handed her the second note, which he'd earned. *"Thank you son,"* she said and headed to the kitchen to store away the supplies. Kelvin kept the loose coins from his wage packet, which would be his own spending money, it felt like life was on the up. Meat pie and mash was their feast to celebrate his new job.

The next few weeks seemed to bring a little order to their lives with Kelvin earning money at the supermarket to pay for groceries and their bills, which were deeply in arrears. The meagre instalments kept the debt collectors away and gave them a little breathing space. A loud knock on the front door took Brenda by surprise. She opened it just enough for her nose and one eye to peer through, *"Is Terry there?"* barked a man dressed in a suit and tie. Brenda's heart raced in fear just at the sound of his name. *"N-no,"* she stuttered.

*"Well, he hasn't been to work for the last two weeks, next time you see him, tell him he's fired,"* spat the man as he turned and left. Brenda closed the door and slid to the floor as panic racked her body. She was clearly suffering depression and sleep deprivation, unable at times to communicate well. This was one of those moments when things couldn't compute in her mind, nothing made sense.

She was still slumped in the hallway when Kelvin returned from work, struggling to get any logic from her. She mumbled that Terry had been fired for not going to work, which made no sense to Kelvin, as they hadn't seen his father for quite some time. *"Good riddance to him, I never want to see him again,"* he replied. Helping Brenda to her feet he guided her to the sofa, then went to the kitchen to make a cup of tea. They sat in silence, each with their hot brews consumed by their own thoughts; this event had provoked memories that they wanted to forget.

The next day at work Kelvin managed to slide a bottle of gin into his coat pocket from the storeroom without being detected. He could remember that bitter sweet day several months ago when his mother was happily baking, swaying her hips to the music, smelling of gin. He wanted her to be happy again but was only sixteen years old, too young to buy alcohol, so this seemed the only way he could try to cheer her up. Buttoning up his coat, he marched home with the contraband securely held in place. As he presented it to Brenda her eyes became fixated on the bottle as she snatched it from his hand. Without a word she slammed the kitchen door behind her hunting for a glass. Kelvin went to his room disappointed that she hadn't thanked him but soon heard his mother singing as she prepared their evening meal.

Brenda began asking Kelvin to pilfer her a little '*pick-me-up*' in the form of gin, to help her get through the day. He was worried about getting caught but liked to see her happy and to hear her sing Irish folk songs. It soon became a daily routine for him at work, to cut a freshly baked loaf in half, scoop out the contents and secrete a bottle of gin inside, then pay for the loaf. He was becoming too cocky, too confident for his own good.

The day before his seventeenth birthday, Kelvin noticed a small article in the local paper that caught his attention. The headline read *'Homeless man found dead.'* It went on to say, *"Terry Carter of no fixed abode was pronounced dead on the scene after a fight between him and another vagrant. The police are holding a man for questioning.'* When Kelvin shared the news with his mother, they both held each other and sobbed, shedding tears of relief that the torturous Terry would plague them no more. Brenda celebrated with the contents of the bottle Kelvin had stolen that day, offering the boy a glass of happiness, which he quickly consumed.

Kelvin was late for work the next day, waking with a sore head. He was an hour behind schedule and was expecting a dressing down when he arrived at work midmorning. It was his birthday so he was hoping to get some leniency from his boss. Yates blocked his access to the storeroom as Kelvin went to hang up his coat, *"You can't go in there, we're having a stock take, looks like we have a thief working here."* He was ushered to the staff room where he was greeted with a security guard conducting a bag search with his colleagues. A bottle of whiskey was found in Carol Peter's handbag and she was quickly escorted to the manager's office. A few minutes later Yates entered the staff room and boomed, *"We've had a lot of whisky and gin go missing, Mrs Peter's has been sacked, let that be a lesson to all of you, now back to work!"* Kelvin was shaking at his near miss, but grateful that he hadn't been caught red-handed. The news that his supplies of free gin had to stop wasn't received well by Brenda, launching her into a string of verbal abuse at the bewildered young man. The next few days were tense between them, until she ventured out of the house to buy her own supply with the housekeeping money he had given her.

It became a regular occurrence that when Kelvin got paid, Brenda got drunk. She knew that alcohol was driving her to behave in strange and uncontrollable ways, believing that drink would take off the edge to her pain. When the bottle was empty, Brenda would torture her flesh with the blade still kept under her pillow, carving lines into her thigh next to the rows of scar tissue already there. She knew through repeated practice how deep the cuts needed to be, to get the affect she desired. As the emotional pain increased so did the amount of pain she had to inflict upon herself. Every aspect of her mind, body and soul were broken beyond repair. Now she was just a functioning shell looking for her next mouthful of booze.

Saturday morning was Brenda's opportunity to go to the shop to grab a bottle to satisfy the monster deep within her. Kelvin had handed her a five-pound note, along with a bag of groceries to see them through the week. He knew he was feeding her addiction but felt he had no choice. Even a heavy downpour didn't dissuade her from making the pilgrimage to the store to gain her prized gin. Whilst waiting in the queue to pay, a poorly dressed man tried to engage her in conversation, encouraging her to join him in The Rose and Crown, a local pub for a quick drink. *"Oh go on lass, it's only a drink"* he slurred. Holding her purchase tightly to her chest she followed him into the adjoining public house. She was told to sit at a table with two of his friends whilst he went to buy the drinks. His friends were already drunk, heckling her and making sexual innuendos to the amusement of their friend at the bar. Brenda quickly drank the glass given to her on his return then attempted to leave. *"Just a kiss for my trouble"* he smirked blocking her exit. She reluctantly obliged then hurriedly left.

One bottle a week was never enough to satisfy her cravings, and the self-harming that she caused to herself had become an ugly reminder of how desperate she had become. She purposely broke every mirror in the house so she couldn't see her pathetic self-image staring back at her. She hated herself and hated the life that she was living. She mourned the carefree days of her youth and grieved for the life that she could have had, if only she had been stronger.

Midweek was hard for her to cope with her cravings and she found herself loitering outside The Rose and Crown on

Wednesday lunchtime, with only a pound in her pocket. Connor, the man who had enticed her in for a drink previously, noticed her standing outside as he approached. *"Hi lass, are you back here for some more?"* smirking under his breath. She nodded and followed him to the bar. After a couple of drinks he suggested, *"How about a blow-job and I'll buy you a bottle of gin?"*

Brenda was shocked at the suggestion and his boldness to ask. *'No ... No ... No!'* screamed through her mind as she rhythmically shook her head. She wanted to refuse, to take control, yet her body craved the release that alcohol supplied; that pull was stronger than her dignity. Dropping her gaze she nodded and followed him into a cubicle in the gent's toilet to humiliate herself, sucking on the end of his rigid cock. The moment he exploded into her mouth, she vomited the contents onto the floor. Connor laughed as he fastened his trousers, *"The gin will wash it away."*

Now she had crossed a line that she never thought she would, succumbing to a hidden abuser deep within herself that only offered cravings and hangovers. With no money to *'pay the piper'* so she had to trade with her worthless soul. Brenda had slid into an abyss of desperation, a place of no return or respite, where the dark evilness of alcohol drove her to behave in ways beyond any rational thought. Shame and guilt were only reserved for others, not for an alcoholic whore.

Kelvin quickly noticed his mother's midweek drunken episodes and couldn't understand where she was getting the alcohol; maybe she was stealing it from another supermarket and could end up arrested by the police. Wednesday seemed to be a regular day for her to have excessive amounts of drink, but strangely these midweek sessions didn't make her happy, they didn't make her sing. He decided to skip work and follow her; he had to stop her stealing gin just as he had for her. She may not be as lucky as he was and could end up in court.

He dressed for work and left at his usual time the following Wednesday morning, making it clear to Brenda that he was going out. *"See you later mum!"* Kelvin walked up the street then climbed through a gap in the fence, which led to a small area of wasteland. Using a discarded wooden box as a seat, he camped out waiting for his mother to pass. He sat there for quite a while worrying what crimes she had committed to feed her habit, until he saw Brenda scurrying along the road about eleven o'clock. Peering his head through the gap to see her disappear around the corner of their street. Squeezing through the gap in the fence, he jogged to make up some distance, but also mindful to hold back far enough for her not to notice her tail. Kelvin felt like a private detective as he followed her to the High Street.

A tall man with dishevelled clothes and unkempt hair engaged Brenda in conversation outside The Rose and Crown pub, before they both went inside. Kelvin jogged over and peered through the window to see his mother sat at a table with three men all busily engaged in conversation. Brenda sat silent and downed a large glass of spirits in one mouthful. One of the other men, who was slightly short with balding hair stood up and headed for *'The Gents,'* immediately followed by his mother. The open toilet windows faced the street outside where he was stood. Soon there were muffled groans and a man's voice boomed, *"Take that bitch!"* Kelvin's stomach knotted. He turned and

70

threw up on the pavement, unable to comprehend what was happening. He sprinted home, oblivious to a car that nearly knocked him over as he bolted across the road.

Barging open the front door of his house, he proceeded to ransack the lounge kicking over chairs, upturning tables and breaking the few pictures they had acquired. The rage was burning inside him, he felt out of control. He punched the wall in frustration, forcing his hand to recoil in pain, which angered him even more. Kelvin had to get out of the cage that encased his fury, wrenching on the handle of the front door to find an escape. Returning to sit on the upturned box on the waste ground he hoped his anger would subside. Inside his skull, it felt like a pinball machine being operated by a skilled professional, firing the metal ball at speed to maximise their score. The high pitched pings and flashing lights consumed his thoughts, briefly distracting him from the staggering figure of his mother as she passed the gap in the fence; but he did notice her, causing his rage to build once more.

Climbing back through the gap in the fence caused him to snag his shirt, leaving a small tear; Kelvin swore and kicked the fence in disgust. The front door of his house was wide open when he arrived, allowing him to see Brenda stumble to the floor as she tried to lift a discarded dining chair. She threw him a dazed looked as he entered the room and tried to smile, although she could see the anger in his face. Towering over he spat his words, *"You slut, I saw you, I saw you at the pub with those men. I heard you, I bloody heard you!"* then raised a hand above his head as if to reign down a punishing blow. **"No, stop!"** Brenda bellowed, **"You're turning into your father!"** then burst into tears. The thought of her son becoming the image of the

71

monstrous Terry destroyed her more than any other abuse could. Kelvin lowered his head in shame, leaving her sobbing on the floor, as he stormed out the front door.

Kelvin returned after dark to find the house as he'd left it earlier. As he straightened the scattered furniture, he could hear the tearful moans of his mother in her bedroom. Tapping on her closed door he called, *"Sorry mum,"* and went to his room feeling guilty that he'd reacted so badly. He couldn't condone her actions and hated how alcohol had consumed her so badly, but realised she needed help. He had been part of her destruction and he needed to help her but didn't know how. He could hear her muffled sobbing through the thin bedroom wall as he dozed in and out of sleep. Brenda wasn't up that morning when Kelvin was getting ready for work. It was unusual for her not to be sat on the kitchen step with a cup of tea in her hand, but he guessed she was still upset from the day before. He made a slice of toast before he headed to work; his mind was still racing from the events of the previous day.

Returning that Thursday evening around five o'clock, Kelvin opened the door to a silent house. *"Hello mum,"* he called, but there was no reply, no sign of his mother. He went up to his room to change and noticed her bedroom door was still closed. *"Are you okay?"* he asked, tapping on the door as he opened it. Brenda was laying on her bed lifeless with an empty bottle of gin next to her and a pool of blood soaking the sheets from a gaping wound in her groin. The bloodstained knife was still in her hand as her opened eyes burnt holes into nothingness. Kelvin slid to the floor in disbelief, too shocked to make a sound, too shocked to shed a tear. He could only vaguely remember crawling out of that room and stumbling down the stairs to raise the alarm with their neighbour. An ambulance arrived at the same time as the Police. A female officer ushered Kelvin into the lounge, where they sat down on the sofa together to talk. He couldn't comprehend what was being spoken, as his mother was taken on a stretcher out of the house and could only focus his attention on the guilt gushing through his body. If he hadn't raised his hand to her, if he hadn't acted like his father, maybe she would still be alive.

*　*　*

Brenda was broken in every sense of the word. She had been subjected to brutal slavery at the hands of an abusive Terry. Having no money or any place to go, she felt trapped in a loveless marriage. Any thoughts of running away were squashed under the fear of what he would do if he ever caught up with her. Constant dread sucked the life from every fibre of her body, until nothing was left, then fear attacked her mind in the same way. Brenda could barely function mentally or emotionally, leaving her body in a state of disrepair. No amount of tender loving care could ever drag her back from the abyss; feeling loved was a distant memory. She couldn't visualise the happy teenager that she used to be, ever being part of her life, and she now cowered in the corner like a neglected animal.

Feeling the escapism that gin offered was a turning point in her life, a different direction to hell, accompanied by a different form of abuse. Alcohol took over her behaviour very subtly but also very forcefully until she had to submit to its evil ways. Addiction was never her intent, but she had to find respite from her tormented life. She wanted to die so many times, to escape from the nightmare that possessed every corner of her mind; alcohol took the edge off, allowing her thoughts to float from her mind, allowing the pain to subside before she passed out. In those moments she still felt fear, but there was no pain. Her panic to comprehend any sensations became engulfed by numbness. Brenda looked forward to alcohol turning off the light switch of her existence, allowing her to fall into the never-ending darkness.

She never felt as close to Kelvin as a mother should, leaving him to grow up as a feral street kid. Brenda was too consumed by her own problems to provide any more than basic care; she was a victim of abuse, a victim of neglect and became a victim to herself. There were moments that she wanted to tell him that she loved him but the words got stuck in her throat as she tried to speak. Her way to protect Kelvin was to keep him from entering her world, let him run from the house of horrors and never stop running. Brenda didn't have the strength or resources to battle with what fate had thrown at her, so tried to be a sponge, soaking up the suffering before it reached her son.

Sobriety laughed in her face as she craved her next drink. Her churning stomach and trembling hands would force her to shake the last drop from an empty bottle in an attempt to satisfy her needs. The single drop of nectar that landed on her tongue left her feeling cheated by the effort. She could see at the bottom of the bottle the face of her rapist, the face of her husband, the faces of the men in the pub and the face of the devil all laughing at her. Brenda smashed the bottle against the wall, sliding to the floor wailing.

Her trip to meet the men in the pub felt like a last resort to quench her thirst for alcohol. She had no money and knew their filthy hands crawling over her body would make her feel sick to the core, but the demons inside her showed no mercy, their hands were crawling over her soul. Brenda had no idea that she was being followed and could only concentrate on suppressing her cravings, in that window of time that is all she could think about. Sitting in the pub with the vile group of men, while they discussed who should go first, brought vomit into her throat; quickly washing it away with a large glass of spirit. A bottle of gin was placed on the table before her as the incentive to degrade herself, to humiliate the decency of a normal person.

Staggering home with the bottle of liquid payment clenched tightly to her chest, she stumbled over a kerbstone, grazing her knee as she fell to the pavement. There was no pain or no reaction as she stood to her feet and continued her journey, only briefly checking the safety of her bottle. After several attempts to place her key in the lock, she managed to open her front door and fall into the hallway. Crawling on her hands and knees to the lounge, still tightly clenching the bottle of gin, she saw the furniture scattered and over turned. There were no thoughts in her mind what may have happened, she was consumed by a drunken stupor where she didn't care. Brenda stumbled as she tried to stand up a dining chair, and then heard a noise behind her. She turned and smiled at the raging Kelvin who was towering over her.

Her son was livid and spat, *"You slut, I saw you, I saw you at the pub with those men. I heard you, I bloody heard you!"* In an instant, her thoughts became very clear as she saw him raise his hand in anger and shouted, ***"No, stop! You're turning into your father!"*** which seemed to freeze Kelvin to the spot. Brenda felt heartbroken to think that her own son could hold the evilness inside him that his father possessed. Kelvin didn't hear her say, *"Sorry son"* as he stormed out the door, leaving Brenda to cry more than she had ever cried before. She blamed herself for not protecting him from such an awful world, she felt guilty that she had let him down so badly.

Brenda was still crying as she closed the bedroom door behind her. Sitting on the bed with a bottle of gin in one hand and her trusted knife in the other, she whimpered like a beaten animal recalling in detail every one of her sordid indiscretions, trying to justify to herself every single one, but she couldn't. As it became dark she heard Kelvin tap on her door but couldn't hear his words over the sounds of her sobbing. She didn't want to see him, to see those judgmental eyes burning into her soul; she just wanted to die, to release herself from the pain that would never go away.

Quickly drinking the bottle of gin gave her the courage to do what she never thought she could and that was to bring her life to an end, to ease the pain that was inside this battered shell of a body. She could see no other option, no other way out. As the alcohol started to work a comforting spell, she gouged the knife heavily across her groin, hoping for an artery rather than muscle. After a couple of slashes with the blade, a warm glow engulfed her whole body as blood pumped freely from the open wound. She was ready to go, she had had enough.

Part 6

The female police officer quickly scanned the lounge and suggested, *"Kelvin, let's go down to the police station and get you a cup of tea."* Kelvin, still in a state of shock nodded and followed her to the car. He hadn't been in a police car before, nor many others as a matter of fact, so he felt a little travelsick over the bumpy roads. The gurgling in his stomach and the bouncing sensation of the ride, forced bile to burn his throat; he tried not to retch, holding his hand over his mouth.

Sitting opposite him in an interview room she said, *"I'll need to take a statement, then find you somewhere to stay, you can't go back there."* Nothing registered in his mind, he felt consumed by confusion, barely managing to say yes and no in the right context. His thoughts drifted until he gripped the table in front of him imagining that he was on a roller coaster of a ghost ride, spiralling into the abyss. The police officer ushered him into a more comfortable room where he fell asleep on a sofa, twitching at the horrors beneath his closed eyelid. Seventeen and a half years of his toxic life was played out on the cinema screen of his mind, forcing him to make sense of the senseless.

Reality struck him like a sledgehammer as the bright lights hit the back of his eyes as he woke. It seemed like that one sleep had changed him in some way that he couldn't quite describe; as if he morphed himself into a new character from the cocoon of his slumber. Kelvin was angry and frustrated, kicking out at the furniture in the room.

Hammering his fists on the walls as his screams brought the police officer running to see the commotion in full flight. She grabbed him, holding him tightly to her, reassuring him that everything was going to be okay, but how could she possibly know what the future held for him.

When things became a little calmer, Kelvin was introduced to Barbara and George who explained that he was going to live with them. Their home was within walking distance of the supermarket where he worked and they would inform Mr Yates of what had happened. He could take some time off until he felt better. As the three of them left, Kelvin uttered nothing, with the exception of leaving WPC Linda Little a stare that sent chills down her spine. She had seen that look of evilness before with the criminally insane, but never with someone so young, someone that appeared so vulnerable.

Barbara and George Tyler were experienced foster carers and agreed to take Kelvin into their home to help him through this crisis. Both in their late fifties they had seen many young people who had lived through difficult times, but none as severe as Kelvin. Challenging situations were normal to them, yet this adolescent felt different, he seemed hardened to life, he'd been exposed to far more than his young eyes should have seen and that made them feel a little uncomfortable.

The Tyler home was a comfortable semi on a tree-lined street. Kelvin knew the location but had never ventured into such a posh area and he felt out of his depth. As they showed him around their home, he felt guilty that his dirty clothes and muddy shoes were fouling such a perfect home. He took off his shoes to climb the staircase, only to reveal a toe poking through a hole in his sock. His bedroom on the first floor consisted of a single bed and a wardrobe filled with clothes of varying sizes that he was told he could use. The bathroom next door had clean towels and a shower, a luxury he'd only experienced on school sports days; at home he could only wash in the sink, the scum filled bath was hardly used as they couldn't afford the hot water to fill it.

Although the Tyler house was warm and clean, Kelvin felt uncomfortable and didn't know how to behave. Barbara suggested that he shower and change his clothes, and then she would prepare supper. Standing under that hot shower, Kelvin allowed the putrid stench of his mind to swill down the drain with the dirty water. The soapsuds seem to knot his curly hair even more, forcing him to claw his fingers through the tangled mop on his head. He stayed in his room that night, accepting food from a tray left outside his door, contemplating what the future would bring.

Brenda's passage from this earth was marked with a pauper's funeral attended by Kelvin, Barbara and George. The hollow church echoed the words of the priest performing the service, the meaningless words for a troubled soul. There was nothing of note to say for his mother, no words of her achievements or legacy left, his own memories of her far detached from other people's reality. A wave of guilt swept over him as her coffin was lowered into the ground, his guilt for not stepping in to save her from his punishing father; his guilt for killing her with his actions. He felt like he was the one holding the knife as her blood spilled onto the bed sheets. He walked away from the grave, his mother's tormented soul weighing heavy on his shoulders; consumed by his thoughts and overwhelmed by his feelings.

* * *

At the end of the street a group of youths were sat on a wall, laughing between them, as Kelvin approached, one said to him sharply, *"What are you looking at?"* Without a second thought Kelvin launched himself at him, wildly waving his fists until the youth was floored. His friends came to his defence and a brawl broke out, leaving Kelvin bloody and bruised as they punished him with kicks and punches, but he didn't care, he felt no pain. Arriving back at his temporary abode, he shouted at Barbara and George as they tried to fuss over him. He was angry and wanted to be alone in his room. He climbed onto his bed fully clothed and stared at the ceiling whilst the blood from his nosebleed dried to a crust on his top lip. In the heated moment of his altercation he managed to suppress the demon voices in his head, to focus on releasing the anger inside; receiving the punishing blows seemed to fuel his fury even more, building his desire to explode the tension out of his body through his fists.

Mr Yates allowed Kelvin to have compassion leave from work and was surprised to see him attend for duty the day after his mother's funeral. Although he had noticed the black eye developing on Kelvin's face, he didn't think it was appropriate to ask him about it, instead he allowed him to go about his normal work. The day slid into the normal routines of retail life, where Kelvin could immerse himself into functioning without thinking, he kept his head down and toiled on autopilot not speaking to anyone. His colleagues had been gossiping about his events, yet they also felt sorry for him, struggling to say the right words of comfort, so they said nothing.

Leaving work he headed in the wrong direction, towards his mother's house. When he realised his error, he chastised himself; swearing profusely into thin air and taking his frustration out by kicking a street sign. Onlookers seemed puzzled by his actions, and then quickly scampered away before he caught their gazes. He was confused, angry and frustrated by the transformation of his life. He was accustomed to the toxic and abusive lifestyle that he'd been subjected to from birth and didn't know how to handle the introduction to a calmer way of life. He felt very naked and exposed to this uneventful world of nothingness; he yearned the rush of adrenaline that came with fear. Kicking the street sign to release his frustration brought him back to a world that was familiar to him.

The kindness shown to him in the Tyler household was often too sickly for Kelvin to bear, resulting in him creating arguments with them so he could storm out of the house. *"I fucking hate you and your fucking house!"* He wanted to goad them into shouting back to fuel his fury, but they never did. Slamming the door behind him he headed down the darkened street screaming swear words inside his head and kicking every inanimate object that he happened to find. His frustrated march took him unconsciously back to the site of his previous altercation with the group of youths. To his surprise, the six lads were sat huddled together as before, glancing up, as he got nearer.

Kelvin shouted, *"What are you looking at?"* which made them all swiftly stand up, positioning themselves in menacing stances ready to engage. Kelvin launched himself at the person nearest to him, flooring him with one punch; quickly turning to kick another in the groin and followed up with a thump to the third. The other three youths in the group froze in horror to see their friends dispatched in such an easy manner. Kelvin roared like a lion at them and they quickly ran away, leaving the three injured staring up at him from the pavement. He swiftly kicked, whom he thought was the ringleader, in the ribs and roared at them, *"Fuck you ... Fuck you ... Fuck all of you!"* then ran off before they could retaliate.

Kelvin felt much calmer now that he had released all the built up tension of the day. The anger that rose from deep inside him came without warning. He was struggling to cope with his new life. He couldn't express how he felt or manage the stress he now endured, dealing with a life that others may call normal. It wasn't normal to him; his irrational thoughts took his mind down pathways that only made sense in an abstract world of demons and dragons. When he got back to the Tyler house he apologised for his actions and went to bed to recall the fight as a slow motion cinema reel playing in his head. He felt excited and exhilarated as the human dominos fell with ease as he stared into darkened space. Sleep came easily for him that night, he felt satisfied.

Waking the next morning, Kelvin could feel his bruised knuckles throbbing, bringing his attention straight back to the fight from the night before. Guilt rushed through his body like a lava flow as he heard his mother's words **"You're turning into your father!"** burning deep within him. The horrific scene of his blood soaked mother lying lifeless on her bed engulfed him with shame; if he hadn't acted the way that he did, maybe she would still be alive.

He pulled his bedcovers over his head and curled in a ball like a chastised child. He was too afraid to leave the sanctuary of his bedroom. He was fearful of who else he may hurt as he unleashed his anger on the world, frightened that he may turn his frustrations on himself.

Barbara Tyler shouted through his bedroom door, *"You'll be late for work, are you getting up?"* He had no intention of going to work and let out a muffled reply from beneath his covers, *"No I'm sick, I'm staying here."* He was in no mood to speak to anyone, let alone engage in the pleasantries expected of him with the supermarket customers and staff. Kelvin felt imprisoned by the cotton shroud of his bed sheets, which forced him to unwillingly revel a bittersweet feeling between power and shame. His mind spun out of control, unable to cope with the barrage of thoughts that blocked out any rational thinking. He placed his pillow over his face to dampen the screams that exploded from his mouth, until he drifted to sleep with exhaustion.

Waking after lunchtime to an empty house, he crept to the bathroom to relieve himself, only to recoil at his reflection in the mirror. His eyes were bloodshot, casting him a menacing stare born from deep within his evil core. Drawing his face closer to the mirror, his eyes became fixated on the eyes looking back at him, the look of a demon who wanted to control him. The glass began to steam from his breath, as he studied the side of himself that he so badly wanted to suppress, a part of his character that yearned to be fed. Kelvin screamed, *"No!"* as he head-butted his reflection, shattering the image as the glass cracked on impact.

A kaleidoscope of confused images looked back at him, each identical in their broken triangular frames; his mop of dishevelled hair seemed to make a mockery of his intense feelings, trivialising the hatred that he had for himself. Finding a pair of scissors in the broken cabinet, Kelvin began to hack the locks from his head allowing them to fall into the sink. He wanted to rebel against society, just as the Punk Rockers were doing at the time. He loved their music, their anarchic attitude and their statement. Fashioning a Mohican line of curly hair across his head, he continued to trim the sides.

When his scalp resembled a badly mowed lawn, he applied shaving foam, proceeding to shave his head until it glistened under the ceiling light. He winced as the razor hacked into a deep scar on the back of his head, making it bleed. He had forgotten the injury that was previously buried under his thick hair. Scooping up the debris, he flushed the offending hair down the toilet.

Kelvin teased the dishevelled hedgerow of a hair with soap to create limp spikes on his head. He hadn't manicured his creation very well, having uneven lines and irregular spikes. He didn't care he thought it looked fashionable. Retrieving a safety pin from the bathroom cabinet, he swiftly forced it through the reluctant skin of his nostril, piercing his nose.

A newfound curiosity greeted him as he examined his reflection in the broken glass, a dozen intimidating faces looking back at him as he whispered to himself,
*"Hello K.C."*

Part 7

A spot of blood on his pillow was the first thing that Kelvin noticed as he climbed out of bed the next morning. He smoothed his hand over the naked skin of his scalp, finding where the razor had gouged his skin the day before. The air caused his head to tingle as it adjusted to the fresh sensations of his new appearance. His curly mop now a thing of the past, the submissive side of his character locked securely in an imaginary box; he decided to face the world on his terms. The thought of adopting a new persona filled him with feelings, which were polar opposites. He was excited at the prospect of becoming Casey, as if released like a butterfly from a cocoon, but also apprehensive about not being accepted, looking out of place like an ugly moth on a beautiful flower. He convinced himself that he didn't *'Give a shit'* and was ready to fight for his place in the world, to fight harder than he'd ever done before.

Barbara stuttered, *"Oh, Kelvin,"* as he entered the kitchen for breakfast. He didn't give her eye contact; he didn't respond to the tension that he could feel projecting from her judgemental tone. Sitting at the table he buried his head into a bowl of cereal that had been prepared for him, eagerly eating the contents. *"Are, are you okay?"* Barbara asked feeling quite puzzled by the unexpected change to his appearance. *"Yeah, I'm alright,"* Kelvin replied, *"I've got to go, I'm running late for work,"* as he stood up from the table, closing the door behind him as he left.

Today felt a good day for him as he stepped onto the street outside. The sun was shining in his eyes, making him squint, but he smiled as he adopted a new swagger to his walk. His chest puffed out and his shoulders rocked rhythmically with each step, for that moment in time life felt surprisingly good. His heart started to pound in his chest as he approached the supermarket; he had gone absent the day before, claiming he was sick.

*"What in the hell have you done to yourself?"* Yates roared at him, *"Get to my office."* Kelvin bowed his head and followed Mr Yates along the short corridor, already defaulting to his defence mode, feeling at a disadvantage. *"Well?"* questioned the boss as he lowered himself into the chair behind his desk. *"Well boy?"* he prompted a reply.

*"Um, I'm sorry I didn't come to work yesterday. I wasn't really sick, I had head lice and had to shave my head, I was just too embarrassed to come in,"* Kelvin submissively replied hoping to get sympathy, yet his new fashion statement was a contradiction to his excuse.

**'Bull-Shit!'** screamed through his head, but with everything that his young employee had recently gone through, Yates felt horrid for being so hard on him. He was also shocked to see how badly the youngster's eye had been scarred; it had not been obvious with his previous fringe. He guessed from conversations with him that he'd had a tough upbringing, but never expected such visible reminders. Yates didn't want to lose face as he had standards to maintain; he felt Punk Rockers were sticking two fingers up at society and there was no place for that sort of thing in his employment. *"Comb down your hair and take out that bloody safety pin"* he told him abruptly. No more was said.

Kelvin allowed a smirk to spread across his face as he headed towards the staff room. In his head he thought, *"Yeah, I got one over on him, sucker!"* then chuckled to himself. His cheeks flushed a little as his supervisor Cynthia remarked on his appearance. *"Oh look at you, you look trendy!"* she chuckled as she rubbed his head. Kelvin busied himself during the day, raising his head and puffing out his chest every time he noticed someone giving him a second glance. He managed to stand his ground with the onslaught of banter throughout the day from his fellow workers; feeling satisfied that he got through the day unscathed. On leaving work Yates pressed a pair of sunglasses in his hand and said, *"These may make you feel more comfortable."* Kelvin was genuinely grateful for the gesture.

Kelvin's walk home took him past a bus shelter where a group of youths loitered. There were two punk rocker lads slouched on the bench openly sharing a bottle of vodka and chuckling at their brazen display. Two punk girls were engaged in horseplay dancing in front of the lads. Kelvin noticed their short tartan skirts, almost pristine in comparison to their torn fishnet tights and red tarnished Doc Marten boots, finished off with yellow laces. He almost missed a third girl curled up in a ball on the floor with a clear plastic bag pressed to her face. Through the transparency he could see the outline of a tube of glue; she appeared high on solvent abuse.

*"What'cha got there?"* asked Kelvin as he pointed to the obvious bottle of vodka. The lads giggled as they handed over the bottle. He took a large gulp of the clear liquid, trying not to choke as the alcohol burned his throat. A second swig took the edge off the fire, allowing Kelvin to say, *"Who are you?"* A wry smile spread across one of the

87

youth's face as he quipped, *"Jamie, and you bro?"* Kelvin paused for a moment, studying the cautious expressions of the others and said, *"Casey, just call me Casey"*.

Barbara and George's stares over dinner made Kelvin feel a little uncomfortable. Small talk about their daily events was the only conversation between them. The tense atmosphere of unanswered questions left Barbara and George frustrated, they were too frightened to confront this tormented youth about his need to destroy his appearance in such a severe way. They had never noticed how severe the scar was over his eye as his fringe had always hidden it. The deep valley of missing flesh from the back of his head made them wonder if a *'Bash on the head'* had mentally affected him in some way. Clearly he was a disturbed young man with many issues.

They were too frightened to question him about the alcohol on his breath or the strange gaze in his eyes. It appeared to them that Kelvin was trying to cage some sort of demon deep within him, to contain a monster that he had no control of. They feared for his safety if this evilness exploded onto an unsuspecting world, they worried how he would cope with such a responsibility. George noticed how the movements of Kelvin's lips and the expressions on his face, weren't in sync with the thoughts in his troubled mind; he resembled an absentminded ventriloquist.

The speckles of blood were still on his pillow when he got to his bedroom. They transfixed him as they spread in his mind, until they knitted together into one picture. The vision of the blood soaked sheets where his mother bathed, in the last moments of her life, was all he could think of; the knife in her hand and her empty stare haunted him. **'*It was my*** *fault, I killed her'* were the only thoughts spinning around in his head, as he uncontrollably sobbed himself to sleep. He was mixed up, his mind was screwed and his emotions were in tatters. The mask that he showed the world only hid the insecure child that lay deep within. Guilt consumed his body, as if he'd fallen into a raging volcano.

His routine was likened to a professional artist applying strokes, painting a mask over the fragile interior that the world wasn't allowed to see. Rather than using a brush, the razor stripped away the stubble on his head to change his persona. The touch of his smooth scalp reassured him that Kelvin was locked away in a padded cell, gagged and bound unable to utter the horrors he could see. Casey was tougher and could cope, or so he believed, he had to believe there was nothing else. Yet, under the cover of darkness, in the silence of his bed, the shackles were removed and Kelvin could scream freely. He was frightened to sleep.

Unable to comprehend the turmoil of his troubled mind, anger exploded from his body without warning, sometimes verbal, sometimes physical, but always leaving a sour impression on the recipient. His toxic upbringing was centred on abuse, never giving him positive life skills to even cope with the kindness others tried to show him. The Tyler's became an easy target for him to vent his frustrations, causing many arguments, often resulting with him staying out on the streets all night. Sitting alone on a park bench throughout the hours of darkness, were no different to the hours he spent staring at the shadows on his bedroom wall. His thoughts clouded his mind and his judgement, like stirred silt in a muddy pond. He couldn't identify who or what he was really angry with. He was just

89

angry at everything, angry at the world, angry at the sperm from the sick bastard that started the sick joke of his life.

The group of youths that he disrespectfully called *'The Punk Tossers'* became his only contact outside of work. Those words that he used never got reflected back onto himself, as maybe they should, because he was slowly entering their world. They became the passage into a seedy urban madness, which created another distorted dimension in his already confused mind. Sharing bottles of vodka bolstered their courage, intimidating people passing by. Kelvin felt vulnerable to their influence, whereas Casey wanted to be in control. The transition between his two personas became the amusement of the group, taunting his reactions, so his anger could be released on an unsuspecting public. They were more streetwise than him, using him as a weapon to extort cash from the defenceless to buy even more alcohol.

Tensions were running high in the Tyler household, with Barbara and George feeling out of their depths with the mood swings of Kelvin. He would be either subdued and quiet or fiercely hostile, making them uncomfortable within their own home. Although, they had several years of experience dealing with younger people put into their care, Kelvin was the most challenging that they had faced. George tried to empathise with this adolescence's plight, but was concerned for their safety, when Kelvin was in a drunken rage. Choosing his moment, George broached the subject, *"You'll be eighteen years old next month, and maybe it's time for you to start looking for a place of your own?"* Kelvin shrugged his shoulders and muttered, *"Yeah, sure,"* then went upstairs to immediately pack. Within hours he was slumped on a park bench, clutching his bag of meagre possessions, crying like a small child.

Kelvin slipped into work early the next day to change in the staff toilets; stowing his holdall out of sight in the storeroom. His eyes were heavy, he hadn't slept and was feeling hungry. Purchasing a packet of biscuits from the supermarket to suppress his cravings, he scoured a discarded paper for accommodation. Most rental properties insisted on references, which he could ask Mr Yates to provide, but since he also had to be over eighteen years old to be considered, the local hostel seem the only short-term solution. He had just been paid at work, so Kelvin headed over to the location straight after his shift. The cheapest option was to share a bunkroom, where he quickly commandeered the top bunk. The days, weeks and months that followed saw a stream of strangers passing through the bunk beneath his slumbers. It was all he could afford with his limited budget, but for now it was his independence.

He had the freedom to roam as he chose, adopting the persona of Casey at every opportunity; if he weren't back to the hostel before lockup, then a park bench would suffice. Kelvin was kept solely for the supermarket. He knew that his regular source of income was important, so he consciously kerbed his attitude within the confines of the workplace. Casey felt comfortable, this persona felt strong and in control, sticking two fingers up to the world. The streetwise skills that the gang had taught him, allowed Casey to extort from the weak for his own needs. A few extra pounds and a bottle of vodka were the ill-gotten gains from his nightly encounters. Alcohol allowed him to fall asleep in his uncomfortable berth, cuddling the dregs of an empty bottle.

The gang were now redundant they were surplus to requirements. He wanted his independence, he hated his independence; the turmoil made him angry, his deep-rooted guilt made him angry, often for no reason he was angry. Confusion consumed him, forcing him to barely function. By night, the alcohol dominated his behaviour; by morning the hangovers tore his head in two. The constant headaches woke the demons in his mind, only being suppressed by the next slurp of vodka. Days turned into weeks, weeks turned into months and months turned into years; he was consumed by the false numbness of alcohol to calm the guilt raging inside him, but that was all he saw from the toxic role models that tutored his upbringing.

His identity confused him, as much as he loved the music and rebelliousness of Punk Rock, he wanted his appearance to be more mature and meaner than the anarchists of the time. The brief trend was sliding out of popularity as quickly as it had appeared. Standing before the mirror he wanted to make a personal statement against the new wave of music and fashion that was sweeping through. Scissors snipped away at his short-lived Mohican friend; '*Punk Rock is dead, long live Punk.*' Now with a totally smooth head and accessorized with dark sunglasses, the next stage of his life could begin. As much as he would never admit to the world his secret liking for some of the songs of '*Hot Chocolate*' he thought Errol Brown's look quite cool.

Standing before the mirror Casey checked his appearance before heading out for the evening. He wanted to look as mature as possible to get past the doormen without being questioned about his age. He'd bought a chocolate brown shirt, covered with small flower motif designs and beige trousers. As he slipped on his mirrored sunglasses he leaned closer to the mirror; popping a lollypop into the corner of

92

his mouth, he said to his reflection, *"Who loves ya baby,"* chuckling to himself at the memory of the TV show Kojak.

The Roxy was a nightclub that Casey started to visit on a regular basis. Now he was twenty years old; his appearance could easily overcome the twenty-one year old age limit. He had become a familiar face to get past the burly bouncers that stood in the doorway. It used to be a cinema situated at the end of the High Street, but now converted into the trendiest place in town, attracting the good, the bad and the ugly of society. It was a darkened place of flashing lights and loud music, where Casey could blend into the crowd, giving him excitement from his mundane lifestyle. He had heard rumours of the hard fisted boss that owned the place and the muscle-bound security guys scattered around the venue reinforced a no-nonsense atmosphere of the place; adrenaline pumped through his body even more when he became a voyeur to the fights that broke out regularly.

*"Tess! Is that you?"* screamed Casey over the din of the loud music. He'd caught sight of a petit blonde girl stood at the bar; she looked so familiar, could it be possible that their paths had crossed? She squinted trying to focus her sight through the flashing lights that blurred her vision; all she could see was a strobe light flickering on the reflection of a bald man, but the voice was one that she'd always recognise. *"Oh my God, is that you Kelvin? You look so different!"* she cried, trying to make her tiny voice heard over the thumping bass of the music.

She threw her arms around his neck in a drunken embrace, evidently pleased to see him. Tess was out with a group of girls, celebrating a rowdy birthday of one of her friends. Clearly the drink was making her head spin and her speech slur, but she clung onto to Casey rocking to the beat of the thumping music. One of her friends tugged on her arm and said, *"Tess the taxi is here, we've got to go."* Grabbing a flyer from the bar top, she rummaged in her handbag for a pen. All she could find was her lipstick, which she quickly used to write her phone number and handed it to Casey. *"Give me a call, it'll be great to see you!"* Tess bellowed as she got pulled into a crowd of girls, heading for the exit.

Casey stood there staring at the flyer in disbelief. He felt happier than he'd been in such a long time, recalling the memories of them both sat next to each other in school, just a few years before. It seemed surreal to him that they should meet at that moment, in that place, on that day. He carefully folded the flyer so as not to smudge the number and secured it in his back pocket. A beaming smile flashed across his face as he ordered a drink from the bar to celebrate his good fortune. His happy mood muffled the din of the music, consuming his thoughts, taking him far away from the twilight zone of madness that surrounded him.

A couple more drinks reminded his bladder that he had to find a toilet to relieve himself. Thoughtlessly navigating himself through the dancing crowd, still overwhelmed by the warm glow of his encounter, he carelessly stood on the toes of a barefooted girl dancing around her handbag. Her squeals of pain were quickly followed by, *"You prick, watch where you're treading!"* He quickly apologised and continued to bustle his way through the crowd, heading for the corridor housing the toilet block. Any other time he would have been on a heightened awareness approaching a pinch point where trouble could lay. Today he was elated and absentminded as he knocked into a man holding a full pint of beer, spilling it down his clothes. *"Sorry mate,"*

Casey joked with a smile on his face. The spillage wasn't taken as a joke, nor was his feeble apology.

Casey narrowly avoided the venomous fist that was hurtling towards his face, followed by a string of abuse. This flashpoint took his mood from calm to fighting mode in a blink of an eye, returning a counterpunch that floored his assailant. Casey kicked away broken glass that was lying on the floor, in fear that it could be used as a weapon, and then stamped on the stomach of the man crumpled in front of him, causing him to groan in agony. Three other men piled into the affray, throwing punches at Casey. He managed to avoid most of them, but a couple landed on target, momentarily stunning him before he launched his own retaliation. Two of his violent attackers received bloody punishment as they floundered and fell. The other launched himself at Casey with a bottle, only to receive a kick in the groin for his trouble. For a split second, there seemed to be a strange silence, before he felt two burly bouncers pin him to the wall.

These two formidable forces held him aloft, his toes barely touching the floor, bringing his gaze level with their own. He could smell their beer soaked breath as their faces closed in on him. He could see the unpredictable evil in the blackness of their eyes. Adrenaline kept Casey's fear at bay but he was unsure what his fate would be, what punishment was in store for him; there was no point trying to struggle, they left him no room for escape.

Between the faces of his captors, Casey could see a figure slowly appearing from the shadows. It was a large man, well over six feet tall, with a distinctive black quiff donning his forehead. His shirt was unbuttoned halfway down his chest, the buttons taut over his rounded stomach. A crucifix hung around his neck on a thick chain and he wore heavy rings on each of his sausage-like fingers, reminding Casey of gold knuckledusters. He needed no introduction; Casey knew without doubt that he was the club owner, Marco Rossi, a fearsome man with a reputation for violence. The nightclub was a front for his money laundering operation. He was also well known as a loan shark that you only crossed at your peril, someone you would regret borrowing money from, someone you would forever owe.

As he approached, Casey could see a deep scar across his left cheek and a gold tooth exposed as he started to grin. Squeezing his face between those of the captors, Marco eerily whispered, *"I could do with someone like you, do you want to work for me?"* There was no time for Casey to consider his offer, because his offer was one that couldn't be refused.

Part 8

Tess managed to make it to the end of the school year unscathed. She missed Kelvin and wondered what had happened to him after his sudden departure. He was the talk of the school when his mother committed suicide, from then on he seemed to have disappeared. Her grades were okay; she never studied that hard knowing that she would have a job in her father's factory anyway.

Bert Clifton adored his only daughter Tess, and cocooned her from what he believed to be a dangerous world. He was a portly man, whose stomach bulged over his oversized trouser, only held up by his trusty bracers. His balding head was circled by a wisp of straggly grey hair, which extended down each side of his face as sideburns. Bert's small-rimmed glasses perched on the end of his bulbous nose, gave him an aura of a warmly gentle man. Trimmed with his bushy eyebrows, he could have easily been caricatured as a *'Spitting Image'* character or a member of *'The Muppets.'* Although Tess could twist him around her little finger, his loyal workers hugely respected him.

Tess's mother, who was called Doris, was rarely seen without her trusty apron. She was a proud housewife who kept a clean and tidy place. The smell of baking filled their home; her homemade pies were Bert's weakness and the workers revelled in her fruitcakes during their lunch breaks. Their house was in the factory grounds, near to the entrance gate, therefore doubled up as a reception for business visitors. Delivery drivers got to know Doris well and would always arrange their routes to take in a cup of tea and a slice of homemade cake as they went by. She was the hub of the house, and the hub of the factory; nothing got past her. Although Bert ran the factory, she was the driving force that ran Bert; between them they made a great team.

Their factory was originally set up twenty years earlier, as a table cloth manufacturer, but with the popularity of Formica wipe clean tables, their sales started to plummet. Over time they had to diversify into readymade curtains and taking on commissions from clothing manufacturers. The factory sewing machines sang a sweet tune, reassuring Bert that the bank balance was healthy. Also the supply of Doris's freshly baked cakes, reassured the workers that their jobs were safe.

Tess stretched her arms towards the ceiling as she roused herself from her cosy bed. The smell of warm toast wafted up the staircase making her feel hungry. Quickly dressing and tying her hair into a ponytail, she followed the aroma and the chatter of her parents coming from the kitchen. *"Good morning sleepyhead,"* chirped a cheerful Bert. Reaching over to steal the last piece of buttered toast from his plate, Tess quipped, *"Love you dad, ha!"* They both giggled as Doris poured hot tea into their cups and served up more toast. She loved their horseplay over breakfast and was pleased to see her daughter in such a good mood. Their kitchen was the heart of the house where everyone gravitated to; family, friends and workers alike, would confide in this inner sanctuary to the kind matriarch they lovingly referred to as Dot.

Bert glanced at his watch it was eight thirty. *"Come on Tess, it's time to start your first day at work,"* he proudly stated as he slipped on his tweed jacket. Tess clamped a fresh piece of toast in her mouth as she tried to pull on her shoes, almost tumbling over in the process. A muffled profanity slipped from her lips as the toast fell butter-side down onto the floor. Carpet fluff was encrusted in the limp bread that she retrieved from the floor, much to her disgust. Discarding the spoiled slice into the rubbish bin, she trotted after her father across the factory courtyard to the office where she would be working.

She had been to the office many times before to see her father, but this time she felt different as she sat at one of the three desks in the main office. Bert's office was off to one side with a half glazed door to segregate him from the hustle and bustle of the daily routine. Sitting behind his leather-bound desk, his persona changed from playful father to respected businessman. Tess was watching her father engrossed in a telephone conversation as her co-workers arrived at nine o'clock.

Cathy Joules was the office manager who would allocate the workload and supervise the smooth running of the administrative tasks. In her late thirties with two small children, she had to juggle the school drop-off and getting to work on time with military precision; sometimes she would arrive in a fluster when things didn't go to plan. Cathy had joined the firm straight from school and had given Bert almost two decades of loyal service, so he was happy to turn a blind eye to accommodate her work/life balance.

Colin Trott had joined the company a few months earlier after dropping out of his first year at college. Tess would describe him as a bit geeky, with his ginger hair, spotty face and glasses. His tall gangly posture made him look awkward and clumsy, much to the amusement of his colleagues. He shyly blushed at the teasing that he received, but he was a conscientious worker and warmly welcomed into the arms of his extended work family. Tess had met him several times before and noticed that he appeared to find excuses to bump into her, then mumbled his words with embarrassment. She guessed that he had a crush on her, but he wasn't her type.

That night the family celebrated Tess's first day at work with her favourite feast slow cooked stew and dumplings. Doris left the savoury delight bubbling on the cooker all afternoon, only adding the suet mix when Bert and Tess came through the door. Their mouths watered at the aroma as they sat at the kitchen table in anticipation. They had to console themselves with a fresh cup of tea as they waited for the fluffy dumplings to rise, but this was an opportunity for Tess to tell her mother about the exciting day she'd had. Bert managed to devour second helpings, whereas Tess could only manage an extra dumpling. All three of them sat around the table stuffed to the brim and feeling very content.

Over the next couple of years Tess transformed from a caterpillar into a cocoon, then blossomed into a confident butterfly. She no longer looked like a schoolgirl, now she was a pretty young woman. The wages she earned allowed her to replenish her wardrobe and update her hairstyle. Bert wasn't so keen on the shorter skirts that she wore. He knew that she was growing up but in his eyes she would always be his little girl. Cathy supplied her with more work, leading to more responsibility; she relished the opportunities and felt proud that her father trusted her to make decisions, even if they were small by comparison.

Tess was now part of the well-oiled office machine with Cathy and Colin. They worked well together and became good friends, although Colin secretly read more into their friendship than Tess did. He almost became like her lapdog fetching and carrying at her whim, much to the amusement of Cathy. There was always a lot of jovial banter in the office, but sometimes Bert would open his office door and say, *"Shhh, I'm on the phone."* The din would quieten to cheerful sniggers as the humour continued. Tess did like Colin as a friend often chatting to him during their lunch breaks, but never thought of him as anything more.

For her twentieth birthday, Bert gave Tess a promotion to Assistant Office Manager, giving him an excuse to increase her pay. He was pleased with her work and cherished the fact that she was part of the family business. Reminiscing, Bert wondered how different things would have been with a son; Bert Clifton and Son over the door, but it was not meant to be. Doris had health problems after the birth, which resulted in her having a hysterectomy, Tess was their only child and he was still grateful for that.

Tess retained her innocent charm and youthful cheek, although she could respond to flirtatious banter with comic genius, keeping the conversation appropriate. She was a friendly young woman that everyone warmed to, an attribute that she could subtly exploit to her advantage, especially with her father. She was comfortable to be herself in the safe environment of her home and work space, but rarely ventured out socially. Although she had a few close friends, she didn't have self-confidence outside her domain, so relied on group events where she could hide in the crowd.

Colin grew into a reliable and sensible young man, but always seemed to remain in the shadows, never pushing himself forward. He seemed content with his life, coming from a stable background similar to Tess, yet his parents hadn't been so fortunate. His father was a shopkeeper and his mother a cleaner; they were good people and salt of the earth. Colin was close to his parents, but found it difficult to deal with his father's occasional dark mood swings. Although his father was a gentle man, these episodes seemed to come from nowhere. One moment he was laughing, the next ranting and storming out of the house. He would always come back to apologise for his behaviour, not knowing what had sparked his rage.

Being the people pleaser that he was, Colin often brought a variety of chocolates to work as a treat for his colleagues; never cakes, that privilege was left for the queen of the kitchen, Doris. The stream of workers passing through the office collecting their instructions for the day would often tease him. Hence, the chocolates depleted very quickly, as one by one they cheekily said, *"Thanks Colin, and all because the lady loves Milk Tray!"* munching on any chocolate, treats whatever they were. Colin didn't mind the banter and felt accepted as one of them.

The receiver rumbled into the cradle of the telephone as Tess ended her call. She had just finished a flirtatious conversation with Charlie from one of their suppliers. He often called her on the pretence of confirming an order, and over time they had struck up a telephone friendship. Charlie seemed more interested in how she looked and what was going on in her personal life than securing business. Tess didn't mind, she looked forward to his calls. She had painted a mental picture of his appearance and lifestyle from the detailed description he gave. Tess thought he was perfect.

Colin cast Tess a disapproving look as a bunch of flowers were delivered to her desk. The attached card simply said, *'Will you be my Valentine?'* There were no clues to identify this anonymous admirer. Tess blushed as she looked up to see Cathy smirking at her; Colin didn't seem pleased. *"Lucky you, who are the flowers from?"* quizzed Cathy, Tess just shrugged her shoulder and replied, *"I've no idea."*

A few minutes later the phone rang, it was Charlie, *"Hi Tess, did you like the flowers?"*

*"Oh Charlie they are lovely, thank you so much,"* blurted the stunned Tess; her heart pounded with excitement and a huge smile beamed across her face as he asked, *"Would you like to go out for a meal with me?"*

Without a second thought she agreed, asking, *"Where shall we meet later?"* There was a moment's silence before Charlie answered, *"Errrr! I've got plans later, could we meet Friday in the Rose Tavern about eight o'clock?"* Tess was a little disappointed, but still excited at the thought of a blind date with Charlie, so replied, *"Yes that sounds great, see you then."*

Cathy and Tess squealed with delight as the call ended, Colin looked upset and left the office in a huff. The two of them started to write a list of what they believed to be essential for the big night, which meant painting nails, a trip to the hairdresser and a shopping spree. Tess was excited as the plans were made for her big date and promptly made an appointment with a hair stylist. That evening she was eager

103

to share her news with her parents so they could give her encouraging support. *"Do you mean Charlie from Fabric Supplies? Oh!"* Bert questioned. *"Yes dad, isn't that great?"* Tess happily replied as she sat at the kitchen table, missing the look of concern on her father's face.

Twisting her father around her little finger, Tess managed to get the next day off work and went shopping for a new dress and shoes. After trying on several garments and eventually returning to the first shop where the purchase was made; a fitted cream dress with a brown pattern, with matching brown shoes, Tess felt very pleased with her decision. Next, she was off to the hairdresser for a pampering. That evening she proudly showed her parents what had been purchased, Doris gave her enthusiastic praise, Bert smiled and chuckled, *"That's lovely."* He could see his daughter was growing into a woman.

Tess returned to work that Friday morning to the squeals of approval from Cathy, she loved the new hairstyle that Tess gently puffed into place. Even Colin was complimentary saying, *"You look nice."* Tess responded with a beaming smile. Cathy and Tess excitedly chatted about the big date that night, whilst Colin kept his head down, beavering with his tasks.

Bert appeared through his office door and said, *"Tess can I talk to you in my office?"* She guessed that she was going to get a telling off from her father for being so disruptive, but nothing could dampen her spirit. Bert closed the door behind them so they could have some privacy.

Bert perched on the edge of his desk as Tess sat down in a chair. *"I've been speaking to my friend F-frank: at Fabric*

*Supplies,"* Bert, stuttering over his words. *"The reason Charlie didn't offer to take you out on Valentine's Day, was because he was having a meal with his wife."* Tess felt like she had received a sucker-punch, taking all the breath from her body. She only managed to gasp her next breath as Bert crouched down and put his arm around her, saying, *"I'm so sorry Tess."* She sobbed on her father's shoulder for what seemed an eternity.

Cathy could see how upset Tess was as she came back into the main office. *"What on earth is the matter Tess?"* Dabbing a tear from her eye, she replied, *"It's Charlie, the bastard is married!"* Cathy rushed over to her to console her, reiterating, *"Charlie is a bastard! You're better off without cheating scum like that."* Tess sat at her desk as Cathy left the room to make them all a cup of tea.

Colin was annoyed that she had been upset, but was secretly pleased that the big date wasn't going ahead. He crept over to her and mumbled, *"I'm sorry to see you upset, but would you like to go out with me tonight instead?"* He'd wished he had made a Valentine gesture before Charlie had. Tess looked up at him, taken by surprise at his offer. *"Um, that's kind Colin but I don't think so."* Colin's look of rejection was clear on his face as he returned to his desk to continue working.

The phone rang on Saturday morning, *"Hello Tess how did your date go last night?"* chirped Sally, one of Tess's close friends. *"Dad found out that the bastard was married, so I didn't go."* There was a moment of stunned silence. *"Oh Tess I'm so sorry. What a lying bastard!"* Sally scorned. *"You can put that new dress to good use; next Saturday it is Tracy's 21ˢᵗ birthday and we're all going to The Roxy.*

105

*You've got to come."* Feeling a little more cheerful, she agreed.

Tess was feeling anxious returning to work on the Monday morning, dreading the awkwardness of the telephone calls from Fabric Supplies. Her heart jumped each time the phone rang. Around eleven o'clock, she received a call from Frank at Fabric supplies. He was Charlie's manager and said that he would be taking over the account from now on; he would be her direct contact for any future dealings. Tess felt relieved as she ended the call, but noticed her concerned father staring at her through his glass door. When their eyes met, Bert turned away and returned to his desk. She guessed that he had spoken to Frank and was anticipating his call, and she felt safe under her father's protection.

\* \* \*

*'Beep!'* sounded the taxi's horn outside her house. Tess hugged her mum goodbye as Doris slipped her some money, *"Have a lovely time Tess."* Through the opened front door she could see an excited Tracy waving frantically from the front seat, wearing a sash to celebrate her birthday. Sally had opened the back door of the taxi and beckoned her to get in. Tess quickly checked her handbag for her essentials, keys, money and makeup, then teetered to the taxi on her high heels. The taxi driver winced as the three of them squealed in delight, as he drove off to their venue.

Tracy was a tall slender redhead that would stand out from the crowd, she always attracted a lot of admirers wherever she went. Tess was happy to stay in the shadows, leaving Tracy to revel in her birthday attention. As her long legs swivelled from the open front door of the taxi, she seemed to rise like a phoenix from the ashes, until Tracy towered above the group of friends waiting for her outside The Roxy. *"Happy Birthday!"* they all screamed, *"Let's get drunk."* Two of her waiting friends linked arms with Tracy, crumpling her birthday sash, much to their amusement. Sally and Tess joined the back of the group negotiating their way through the burly doormen at the entrance. Finally inside, the raucous beat of the music and the flashing lights marked the beginning of their celebrations.

Sally grabbed Tess by the arm and tried to shout over the loud music, *"Let's get a drink."* Sally squeezed through revellers at the bar, waiting to draw the attention of the barman who was already serving the person next to her. Tess stayed back from the bar so she didn't have to endure the sea of sweaty bodies jostling for refreshments. She looked around the venue with interest, as she hadn't been there before. She was still underage but the group had brazenly strutted past the doormen. A couple were stood in a dark corner kissing, a group of four lads were involved in horseplay near to the toilets and she also noticed two unsavoury characters, trying to discretely exchange money for a small package of drugs.

As she continued to scan the room, she could pick out the muscle-bound security staff positioned at strategic points, making her feel a little intimidated, but reassured. The writhing mass of people on the dance floor lightened her mood, seeing her friends moving harmoniously to the music made her smile. Sally returned with two drinks, tapping one of the glasses on Tess's arm, distracting her from her transfixed gaze. *"What do you think?"* Sally asked, but before Tess could reply she noticed with curiosity a man sat on a stool at the end of the bar. She guessed he was in his

107

forties with a big belly and jet-black hair. From his appearance she instantly thought of the film Godfather and nervously smiled to herself. It was her favourite film but he seemed so out of place in this setting. Although she couldn't see him clearly, she noticed how the flashing lights illuminated the mass of gold rings on his fingers and the heavy cross hanging around his neck; a shiver went down her spine for no apparent reason.

*"Yes it's a lively place, great music,"* Tess roared over the loud music, trying to be heard. They both started to dance on the spot, trying not to spill their drinks, Sally was the first to falter, licking the spilt contents from the back of her hand. The birthday party regrouped by the bar and downed a few drinks in quick succession. Tracy grabbed Tess's hand and dragged her onto the dance floor, swiftly followed by the others. The atmosphere was electric, they all bounced around singing '*Everyone's a winner baby that's the truth* ...' with enthusiasm. As the night wore on, more drunken revellers showed their dance prowess with varying degrees of success. Tess was beginning to feel hot and uncomfortable as she was jostled in the mayhem. She squeezed her way through the crowd, heading for the bar to retrieve a napkin; to her annoyance some idiot had spilt their drink on her new dress and she want to blot it out as best as she could.

*"Tess is that you!"* screamed a familiar voice. All she could see was the silhouette of a bald man walking towards her. As the light hit his face, she let out a squeal, *"Oh my God, is that you Kelvin? You look so different!"* Tess threw her arms around him in a drunken embrace, really pleased to see that her school pal was okay. The hug evolved into a brief dance to the music, until Sally interrupted it, *"Tess the*

108

*taxi is here, we've got to go*." Tess didn't want to lose touch with Kelvin again, so she grabbed a flyer from the bar to write her phone number down. The only thing she could find was a lipstick, which made do. *"Give me a call, it'll be great to see you!"* she bellowed as Sally pulled her away.

As the birthday party headed for the exit, Tracy stumbled to the floor in a fit of laughter. Tess was the first to her rescue and helped her to her feet. Flicking her bright red locks from her face just like Miss Piggy and straightening her sash, Tracy slurred, *"I love you Tess, hic, and you are a good friend."* Tess managed to steady the birthday girl and arm in arm staggered to the exit, closely followed by the rest of the drunken entourage. Outside they quickly said their goodbyes, then split into two awaiting taxis for a bumpy ride home. The driver seemed to hit every pothole in the road, sloshing the liquid contents of Tess's stomach, making her feel sick. Luckily she was the first to be dropped off.

Fitting the key into the lock proved to be a challenge, but finally managed to hit the target, allowing her to creep into her darkened home. A sidelight had been left on in the hallway so she could see her way. The creaky top step alerted Doris that she was home, *"Are you ok Tess?"*

*'Damn'* she thought, and then replied, *"Yes mum, goodnight."* Tess quietly closed her bedroom door behind her, slipped off her dress and fell on to the bed, still wearing her underwear. The room started to spin as she recalled the evening, the music, the alcohol and Kelvin, oh Kelvin. It was great to see that he was ok and *'Wow!'* how hot he was looking now. That was her last thought; she began to snore sliding deeply into a dream world.

Part 9

He tried to focus through his blurred vision at the three men towering over him. Another punishing blow rained down on his battered face, forcing him to turn his head and spit out the bloody contents of his mouth on the floor. He caught a glimpse of a terrified Sofia being restrained by a fourth menacing thug, pleading for the onslaught to stop. Marco turned his head to face the attackers once more; the cold steel of a pistol was forced into his mouth. The young waiter gagged as the weapon hit the back of his throat, muffling any sounds that he could make.

Looking down the barrel of the gun and along the extended arm that seemed to be erupting from his mouth, he could see a very angry mobster known as The Scorpion. As the trigger was pulled, Marco emptied his bladder, filling his lap with a stream of warm urine. It felt like time had frozen; the click of the gun boomed over the surreal silence that engulfed the room. The world no longer existed in the elongated moment of his last breath; his mind was consumed by the simple click that rippled through his soul.

As the gun was slowly withdrawn from his mouth, a stunned Marco realised that the gun wasn't loaded; it didn't contain the fateful bullet that would bring his early demise. *"You little fuck,"* ranted The Scorpion, *"You thought you could steal from me?"* The handle of the pistol landed a painful blow to Marco's jaw, distorting his vision once again. *"I owe your father a favour or you would be dead right now,"* roared The Scorpion, covering Marco in venomous spit as he ranted. *"I'm coming back tomorrow*

111

*and will put a bullet in the pistol if you are still here,"*
barked the mobster.

Sofia was released and rushed sobbing to comfort Marco,
who was bound to a chair unable to defend himself. The
wire that they had used to tie his hands behind his back had
already cut into his skin, causing blood to trickle down to
his fingertips. The Scorpion etched an intimidating stare on
the back of Marco's eyelids, and then placed a single bullet
on the coffee table. It stood upright like a menacing sniper
waiting for the order to fire. The men left in silence, nothing
more was said, nothing else needed to be, the message was
clear.

Marco fell to the floor as Sofia untied him, unable to
comprehend the severity of what had just happened. He
could remember answering the door, then being greeted
with a blow from a piece of wood that knocked him out; he
regained consciousness as a bucket of cold water was
poured over his head. He pointlessly struggled to free
himself, only to receive a pounding blow for his trouble. He
now sat on the floor in his blood soaked clothes, reaching
for a bottle of whiskey to numb his physical punishment.
Sofia prepared a warm salt bath for him and helped Marco
slide into the watery cocoon. He winced as his injuries came
in contact with the salt, but the discomfort strangely felt
soothing and allowed his mind to clear. They couldn't stay,
they had to run for their lives and never look back.

There was no room for luxuries or sentiment as they stuffed
two suitcases with essential clothes. Marco prised up a
floorboard from beneath their bed to retrieve his hidden
stash of money. He placed a pile of notes on the coffee table
next to the erect bullet as some form of peace offering for

his misdemeanour. He knew The Scorpion was a man of his word and would be back the next day, he hoped the gesture might distract any thoughts of reprisals against his family. The remainder of his ill-gotten gains were squeezed into the suitcases, wrapped in dirty clothing that he hoped wouldn't be searched by the authorities as they left the country.

They couldn't stay in Italy any longer, they could easily be traced; next time he wouldn't be so fortunate. Leaving their home under the cover of darkness, they caught a taxi to Naples airport. Switching to a connecting train, they started to weave their way through Europe, regularly changing trains to cover their tracks. After several stressful days of watching over their shoulders, they arrived at Calais. The English Channel was a stormy crossing, but they arrived safely at the port of Dover. He knelt down to kiss the ground.

They needed to lose themselves in the crowd and keep a low profile for a while. Marco had a cousin who lived in Shropshire, which seemed as good of a destination as anywhere. After a brief telephone call and a further six-hour train journey, they reached Shrewsbury station to be greeted by his cousin Nancy. They had not seen each other since her marriage to an Englishman called John eight years before, but embraced warmly as they met. Staying under the roof of Nancy Wilson would be harder for The Scorpion to trace them, rather than the obvious Rossi family name; Marco felt a little more relieved, allowing them to sleep for the first time in days.

* * *

The young Sofia quickly succumbed to the smooth talking Italian waiter that served her coffee in a Naples café. His charm and flattery enticed her back on a daily basis, trapping her in his spider's web. *"Hello pretty lady my name is Marco, are you here for coffee again or just to see me?"* The arrogance slipped easily off his tongue. Sofia was brought up in a strict Catholic family and her father objected to her associating with boys; the lunch breaks from work allowed her to slip away for a few minutes to naively entwine herself in the charms of the handsome waiter. Blushing she replied, *"Err, an espresso please,"* and promptly sat herself at a table near the window. She had positioned herself so her gaze could be transfixed on his every movement. She was nineteen years old and never been kissed, leaving her vulnerable to his will; she thought she was in love.

Marco was ambitious and determined to make something of his life. The café gave him a great opportunity to meet and befriend the criminal influences that could find him fame and fortune. Seizing any chance to do a favour for the local villains started to earn him trust with them; although he was streetwise, his overconfidence would land him in trouble with the law. Sofia sobbed as he was arrested at work and couldn't concentrate on anything until his safe return the following day. *"They have nothing on me,"* he smirked when she questioned him about the incident. She felt reassured that he must be a good guy, although the rose tinted glasses of love blinded her from rational thinking. Marco soon talked her into meeting him after work and took her to his flat to consummate their relationship. Both, interpreted that moment in different ways, Sofia thought it was a statement of his love, whereas Marco saw her as just another conquest.

Her father found out about the affair and was livid. He knew of the reputation of boys like that and forbid Sofia to see him again. She refused in a heated exchange, enraging him even more. *"Pack your bags and leave. I disown you, never come back!"* he roared.

Her tears bounced off the lid of her suitcase as she gathered her belongings. As she looked around her bedroom for one last time, her gaze was drawn to the cross hanging over her bed; she knelt down and prayed for forgiveness. No one was there to see Sofia close the front door behind her, that moment of gut-churning rejection she felt went unnoticed, ousted like a tramp into the night.

Sofia reached Marco's flat just after dusk. She could see his light on from the street below and a silhouette of him moving behind the half-drawn curtains. Taking a deep breath she tapped on the front door. Nothing. She tapped a little harder before hearing footsteps as he walked down the internal stairs towards his front door. The metallic clunk of the lock made Sofia flinch as Marco opened the door; he looked surprised to see her standing there with a case in her hand. *"My father has thrown me out. Can I please stay with you?"* Marco stood speechless. *"Please Marco I'm desperate."*

Marco beckoned her inside. His gesture showed his reluctance to agree. He selfishly saw it as an imposition that would cramp his style, but consoled himself with thoughts of sex on tap whenever he wanted it. *'I guess she owes me now,'* mulled through his mind. Without concern for her feelings he made small talk as he ushered her to his bedroom. Thinking, *'I'll start as I mean to go on,'* he unbuttoned her dress and pushed her backwards onto the bed. Marco was feeling horny as an orgasm brewing inside; his cock growing hard, being restricted by his tight trousers. All that was on his mind was to be inside her, to stamp his manhood authority. There was no finesse, he just needed to be satisfied. Unzipping his trousers freed his rigid penis. Pulling her knickers to one side allowed him to bury himself inside her. The sex was short lived, exploding without warning, but he had been pleasured.

Marco's love affair with himself took centre stage, taking whatever he needed to bolster his inflated ego. Whether that was promiscuous encounters with easy women or extorting money from vulnerable people, he had honed his skills like a thief in the night. He was building his own pedestal to stand on; ignoring despise of people he had wronged, who were prepared to topple him at every opportunity. Naively, he thought he was untouchable; his arrogance caused him to make mistakes, yet he was no more than the pond life of his street. He was the tiniest cog in a giant machine, an insignificant part that was as unimportant as the appendix to the body, yet the youngster creates a fantasy in his head as a would-be tough guy. He never realised that he was no better than a pimple on a badger's arse that could be scratched off any time it became irritating.

The café was a hive of activity. Lunchtime and evening meals were the busiest times, that kept Marco occupied; entertaining the customers with his charm, much to their delight. He was a likeable rogue that people tipped well, but unbeknown to them, Marco had already inflated their bill to pocket the difference. Morning and afternoon sessions had less customer flow allowing him to observe the secret meetings and seedy exchanges of the underground criminals. Envelopes stuffed with cash and precarious parcels wrapped in brown paper would be passed underneath the tables. It became a well-known haunt for black-market dealings and occasional violent disputes. Marco thrived on the electric tension in the room.

Marco noticed a regular occurrence at three o'clock on a Friday afternoon, when a smartly dressed man would enter the café with a green canvas bag. He always sat at table number fourteen, situated in the darkest corner furthest from the door. After quickly drinking the espresso that he had ordered, he would leave empty handed. The green canvas bag remained under the table. Exactly three minutes later another dapper man would enter the café with an identical bag and sit in the same spot. Once again, he would quickly drink his coffee, switching the bags under the table, before exiting with the first abandoned green canvas bag. Exactly three minutes later the first man returned to claim his unattended baggage.

The routine appeared quite comical as they tried to remain inconspicuous, but often would absentmindedly knock a chair or spill the drink held in their shaky hands. To the other customers, these mishaps went unnoticed, but caught the attention of Marco who watched with curiosity. He had to discover the contents of the green bags that became his kryptonite, drawing him in like a moth to the flame.

Marco eagerly watched the clock on the following Friday. One o'clock, two o'clock, and now it's ten minutes to three; he purposely left used crockery on adjacent tables as a prop so he could loiter more freely. As the church clock chimed three bells in the market square, the first gentleman arrived to take up his regular seat. He could be described as a smartly dressed businessman with perfectly creased trousers that mirrored his pristine matching suit jacket. His designer tie complemented his crisp white shirt and his shoes polished to mirrored finish. The cheap green canvas bag looked out of place, something you could easily buy, and nothing like the quality of his tailored clothes.

*"The usual sir?* Marco quipped with a cocky smile, only to be greeted with a piercing glare from the seated man. *"An espresso waiter!"* the man snapped. Marco had realised that he had been too forward and highlighted the man who was trying to go unnoticed. He cursed himself under his breath and returned with the hot beverage without making eye contact with the man. The waiter busied himself clearing the adjacent tables. As usual, the man gulped his drink, threw some coins on the table and left empty handed. Marco looked over his shoulder to see the man disappear through the door. He knelt by the table in anticipation and gently pulled the heavy bag from under the table.

The green canvas bag had two brown plastic handles and brown decorative piping along the seams. The bag was cheaply made and appears to have been heavily used. The shiny gold metal zip that extended along the top transfixed his stare, enticing him like a mermaid luring sailors to the jagged rocks. His mind jolted back into consciousness, forcing his heart to race, time was against him. It sounded like marbles being sprinkled on a tin tray, as Marco tugged on the zip, breaking the eerie silence. Pulling the handles apart revealed the menacing sight of a dozen or more handguns. The images of the people being brutally killed by these intimidating weapons made him feel fearful and excited at the same time. He quickly secured the zip and slid it back under that table, just before the next man came in.

This man had a more stylish dress sense, an air of eccentricity about him that oozed confidence. A yellow waistcoat covered his bulbous stomach, extending through his unbuttoned chequered brown suit jacket. Marco's attention was drawn to his manicured moustache, which curled at the ends, then noticed the scar running down his cheek. *"I'll have a white coffee,"* he muttered as he secured the second green canvas bag under the table. Marco placed some dirty glasses on his tray from an adjacent table and scurried off to prepare the drink. Returning with a white coffee as instructed, he realised that it was the first time that he'd studied these men in such detail. Marco noticed a heavy ring on the man's right hand and scars on his knuckles; he placed the cup in front of him and quickly busied himself so he wouldn't get drawn into conversation.

A few minutes later, coins bounced onto the table as the man finished his coffee and left with the exchanged green canvas bag. Marco dashed to the table knowing that time was limited; he had to know what the trade was. Ripping the zip quickly open to revel a stack of money, bound with paper sleeves, Marco's eyes bulged like an excited frog. Not having time to count the loot, he estimated at least twenty bundles, if not many more. Securing the zip, Marco lifted the bag to assess its weight, and then slid it back under the table. He was behind the counter when the first man returned. He made sure that he never gave him eye contact, although he did see him leave with the green canvas bag from the reflection of the counter mirror.

The next seven days consumed him; Marco thought that this was his big break to become rich. Consequences seemed insignificant in comparison to the prize. He found a similar green canvas bag for sale in the local market place, his

119

excitement built as he purchased his decoy. At home he gathered books from his shelves and filled the bag, checking the weight to make it feel like the bag of loot for exchange. Sofia never questioned him about his strange antics, nor the rough degrading sex they had that night, he seemed like a man possessed. His violent orgasm filled her with fear, she had never seen him like that before. He rolled onto his back staring at the ceiling, dripping with sweat, not a word was said. Sofia looked at him in disbelief, then turned her back on him and curled into a ball.

Since she had moved in, he hadn't treated her in the same loving way as before. On previous occasions that she'd been to his flat, he had been charming and attentive. He had wooed her and showered her with compliments. Now she was under his roof she was just his skivvy, cooking and cleaning and satisfying his sexual demands. This wasn't the fairy tale she had hoped for or the reason she fought with her father. Maybe he had been right all along but her pride would never let her admit her mistake.

His heart pounded on Friday morning as he hid his own green canvas bag behind the counter, then tried to forget it as he went about his work. Marco was very clumsy that day, breaking crockery and spilling drinks, his mind was preoccupied; he kept one eye on the clock counting down the minutes. The café was empty as usual on that Friday afternoon. As the church bells chimed three times, the businessman with the green canvas bag entered. Sitting at his adopted table and consuming his usual espresso, he placed the exchange under the table. Casting Marco a piercing stare as he walked out of the door unnerved him, but the plan was hatched and he had to keep his cool.

120

Exactly three minutes later, the eccentric gentleman arrived carrying the identical green canvas bag for exchange. He called to the loitering waiter to bring him a coffee as he assumed the same spot as his predecessor minutes before. Marco's shaking hand spilt some coffee on the table in front of his customer. He quickly retrieved a napkin so he could dab up the offence, apologised and made a sharp exit. That day he wanted to keep a low profile, so far he hadn't succeeded. Returning to the counter he grabbed the handles of the decoy bag with his sweaty hand and waited for movement at that table. His heart pounded loudly in his ears, as if listening through a stethoscope. The gritty feeling in his throat forced a dry cough to escape breaking the silence, drawing a brief glance from Mr Eccentric. Moments later his coffee was finished and he left with the exchanged bag.

Marco rushed over to the table with decoy in hand, almost slipping over in the process. He knelt next to the table and opened the bag to reveal what he had expected, several bundles of notes. Placing two bundles on top of his bag of books, he exchanged the bags and slid his decoy into position. Time seemed to stand still, although the second hand was racing around the clock face. Grabbing the bag of loot, he scuttled back to the counter, not reaching his sanctuary before seeing the other accomplice heading towards the door. Marco dropped the bag and kicked it under a table on his way back to the counter, whilst trying to casually collect a crumb filled plate and the remains of a strawberry milkshake, froth still clinging to the inside of the glass.

The business-like gangster was on a mission to retrieve his canvas covered bounty, departing as soon as he could. He didn't even give the waiter a second glance. Marco was sure he could see his own heart pounding through his white shirt, which was soaked in nervous sweat. When footsteps faded and an eerie silence engulfed the café, Marco retrieved the bag of loot and locked it in a cupboard under the counter. The chiming of the church bell counted down the eternal hours before he could take the heist home under the cover of darkness. He tried to focus on the steady stream of customers that arrived late afternoon, but his mind wasn't on the job, making several mistakes with customer's bills, most not in his favour. He consoled his frustration with the promise of his payoff later.

Marco sighed at the reassuring clonk of the bolt as he locked the front door of the cafe. He had experienced the most fearful, stressful but exciting day of his life; his mind was on overdrive and his body felt electrically charged. His shaking hands dropped the key to the locked cupboard; his third attempt to insert the key into the barrel was successful, revealing his treasure trove. He imagined music and lights as he was entertained by a string of dancing chorus girls, spilling out of this confined space. The razzamatazz stopped as the green canvas bag hit the floor to an abrupt stillness. The frayed brown handles and an oil stain, which spread like an inkblot from the bottom corner, took his mind in a different direction. Seemingly framed by the dark void of the empty cupboard, he could visualise a round table in a smoky room surrounded by gangsters laughing. They were playing poker and swigging shots of whiskey; an upturned ace of spades, a wad of cash and a loaded revolver drove shivers of fear down his spine. Marco transferred the twenty-eight bundles of money into another bag that he had stored earlier, and then secreted the offending green bag in the waste bin in the back yard.

122

His walk home took twice as long as normal, as he kept taking back-doubles and side alleyways to throw off any chance of being followed. Every noise spooked him, forcing him to seek refuge in the shadows. Sofia could clearly see his distress as he stepped through the door of their home, *"What is wrong Marco?"* Perspiration was streaming down his face, his knuckles white as he gripped the bag tightly to his chest. *"Nothing, just business!"* he snapped as he closed the bedroom door behind him. He prised up a floorboard underneath their bed to expose the hiding place for his ill-gotten gains, then preceded to unite the twenty eight bundles from today with the other bundles of cash, stored from other petty scams. He was relieved to replace the floorboard. Sofia had prepared the evening meal and knew not to interrogate him regarding his business exploits, so made small talk as they ate.

The monster between the sheets that night tore at her nightie, ripping at the fabric in his urge to feel naked flesh. He didn't acknowledge her pleas to stop or her struggles to ward him off. Marco wrestled her to turn her onto her stomach and used his strong hand to bury her head into the pillow, muffling her cries. He had had raging lava spewing inside him, a mixture between excitement and pure fear that had to be released from his body, whatever the cost. Without warning he rammed his hard cock into her anus making her scream with fear as the intense pain raked through her body. He defiled her that night, making her scared for her safety and unable to resist his sexual advances; she felt like a whore as he rolled off her. Within minutes the panting Marco was asleep leaving Sofia to whimper like a tortured animal. She was in total shock at the violence of his attack and too innocent to comprehend what had just happened, but knew not to challenge him.

Something had possessed him and she didn't know how to deal with it.

Over breakfast the next morning a strange normality ensued between them, *"Can I have some more coffee Sofia?"* Not a word was mentioned from the night before. Marco knew he had to act cool and maintain his daily routine so as not to arouse suspicion. He donned a smile and charmed the customers in the café as he usually would, trying to put the stash under his bed to the back of his mind.

The next few days seemed like Groundhog Day, the repetitive cycle of regular customers ordering the same things, except for one glaring difference. Friday afternoon at three o'clock no gangsters appeared and no exchange was made. This unsettled Marco more than if they had reappeared as normal, he had psyched himself up for that, but not this. There seemed to be evil spirits drawing a cloak over table fourteen in the corner. Every few minutes he had to check, to reassure himself that no one was there.

After closing the café at the end of the day, he rushed home as quickly as he could, scanning the shadows and listening for footsteps. He sharply refused the meal Sofia had prepared, spilling the contents on the table as he pushed the plate away. Glass after glass, he found solace in the bottle of brandy they had kept for special occasions this was a macabre special. A knock on the door startled him. The television was booming out music so it was obvious they were at home. He nervously opened the door to see four suited men and the flash of a pickaxe handle just before it struck him unconscious.

Marco was jolted back into the conscious world with a dowsing of water. His hands had been bound behind him; he was sitting on a dining chair in the middle of the room. He could feel wetness on his hands and a searing pain in his wrists; his head throbbed from the impact of the strike. He recognised the menacing figure of a well-known mobster called The Scorpion standing before him; two of his henchmen stood behind him. *"You made a mistake you stupid fuck, I know it was you!"* roared The Scorpion inches from Marco's face. *"I found your name in one of the school books you put in the bag!"* A pounding blow landed on Marco's cheek spinning his mind and blurring his vision once again.

\* \* \*

Sofia and Marco struggled to come to terms with a new life at Nancy's home. They didn't speak English so found it difficult to communicate outside the household. Nancy connected Marco with the local underworld to exchange his currency into sterling, a few useful contacts for him for the future. Sofia was scared and hibernated in her bedroom. Over the next few weeks, Nancy invested any spare time that she had teaching Marco and Sofia to speak English. Marco was a quick learner allowing him to go out and befriend connections in the underworld, with his Mafia style speech. *"Hey, how'ya doing?"* accompanied by his nodding head. Sofia was less able to learn and spent most of her time in her bedroom, reading books and practicing her speech in the mirror.

Their marriage was never official they never had a ceremony. It was easier to let the world believe they were husband and wife from their previous life. They had only known each other for barely a year and lived under the same roof for a few months. There was no mention of getting wed or creating a long-term commitment; circumstances had taken control of their fate and Sofia was just as frightened as Marco to stay in Italy. *'The Mob'* never forgave, nor did the many levels of crooks below; she was uncertain who the money belonged to, so had to flee as an accessory. If things had been different she would have never stayed with Marco, but her destiny was out of her control. She was being swept along with a tsunami of terror.

Nancy received information from her family in Italy that The Scorpion and several of his key henchmen had been mowed down in a spray of gunfire in a gangland attack. The Mafia had been alerted to his underhand deals and his reluctance to cut them in. He was killed in an eruption of gunfire, which terminated twenty men in the process, to demonstrate their dominance and as a message to other likeminded people.

There was a sense of relief from Marco and Sofia that the link had been broken, but also the knowledge they would be safer to stay in Shrewsbury. They would have to make a new home and hope they would never be traced by *'The Mob'*; they hoped that they were insignificant. In essence Marco was the shrimp that fed on the vulnerable plankton of society; whereas The Scorpion was an opportunist fish unaware of the perils of the sharks above. He was an irritating small fry and Marco was just speck floating in a watery abyss. Naples was dominated in the darkness by much larger predators; Marco and Sofia hoped they had stayed off the radar and gone unnoticed.

Marco took the chance to create a new persona, an Italian man with a string of exaggerated stories and imaginary connections. He wanted to become a big fish in a small pond. To do so, he had to become angry and aggressive, almost fearless in his resolve. No one could verify his claims so he had to act like a mobster to become a mobster. As much as he hated to admit it, he needed Sofia by his side, not just for appearances sake, but also as someone to confide in. He thought she would be loyal and stand by him, *'Why shouldn't she, he had given her everything?'* spun around in his arrogant mind. In essence he had bought her with a material lifestyle.

Two decades further on and Marco had successfully carved a niche for himself, which had made him rich in the process. He was a wheeler-dealer rather than a fighter, but that said, he still had to show his prowess to gain respect. He had lost a couple of teeth and gained a deep scar on his left cheek in the altercations that tested him with his adversaries, but these just made him look more intimidating. Although in the early days he'd had scraps with the police, the older and wiser Marco didn't need to confront people anymore; he had the money to pay people to do it for him. He had made his fortune lending money to people living on the poverty line, and then extorting weekly payments with huge interest rates, ensuring the debt would never be paid. As things grew, he lent larger amounts to businessmen who needed instant cash to complete deals or pay debtors; this was where the big money came from to finance his nightclub, a place to launder even more money.

His wealth had financed a large house on the outskirts of the town, furnished with Italian marble and Mediterranean furniture. This luxury abode was a statement of his unsavoury success and a sign of dominance to the victims of his antics, but this was also a prison for Sofia. She had become a recluse, barely leaving the house or conversing with anyone else. Marco expected her to keep the house pristine and also herself, so he could showcase his lifestyle to any visitors that he chose to invite. She had to be at his beck and call to satisfy his whims, either as a glamorous hostess or the target of his lust, but never as a wife. She felt trapped knowing the wrath she would encounter if she ever disobeyed him. Sofia had no friends and her father had disowned her many years before, so she had no choice but to endure her fate with the man that she had once loved.

Since their first meeting all those years before, Marco had slowly and subtly groomed her to be his submissive slave. Mental, emotional and physical abuse chipped away at her self-confidence and self-esteem until she felt worthless. He had successfully dissolved her spirit, just as pouring bleach over a shit-stain in a toilet. She felt no better than that disgusting skid-mark created by the excretion of Marco's arse. She had no fight left in her and wished for the day that water would flush her around the u-bend. She was being controlled and became incapable of making decisions, having to ask permission just like a child. Seeking his approval was the best she could hope for.

Marco spent most evenings at his nightclub, returning home in the small hours; sometimes he never appeared. Sofia was expected to wait up for him and provide a meal as he walked through the door, whatever time that was. The smears of lipstick and the smell of cheap perfume would indicate to her whether he would force himself on her or if he had been satisfied by one of the sluts at the club. The sight of the man he had become turned her stomach in revulsion, she hated every fibre of his being and often wished he was dead; in his seedy world maybe he would confront the wrong person, someone that wasn't consumed by the fear she held.

Sat on a tall stool at the end of the bar, Marco surveyed his palace. It was filled with raucous teenagers and thumping music, but nothing could drown out the sound of the ring of the cash registers as they played the tune of money. He ensured that he got his cut from the profiting drug dealers, plying their trade in the darkened shadows and the prostitutes preying on vulnerable middle-aged businessmen that occasionally came to the club looking for a one night stand. Marco ruled with an iron fist, learning from his past that no one dare to do business without his permission.

This was a night when the stars aligned and fate stepped in to unite people in new beginnings. Marco noticed a group of high-spirited girls heading for the exit, dancing to the music as they weaved through the crowd. The one leading the pack was a tall redhead wearing a birthday sash over her shoulder; she stumbled to the floor in drunken laughter. A petit blond girl helped her to her feet and guided her through the exit door. The bevy of scantily clad girls that had ignited his lustful eye, had now disappeared into the night. Marco scanned the room looking for more leggy girls in high heels to ogle over.

As Marco emptied the contents of his glass of brandy in a large gulp, he heard a commotion in the corridor near the toilets. Two of his security guards were rushing to the incident, one almost bowled over by a tumbling victim of the affray. Marco could see an averagely built teenager with a shaven head; skilfully avoid a bottle attack and flooring the assailant with a swift kick. Clearly he wasn't average, he had dispatched four attackers with ease during the altercation. Marco was curious to find out more. He had to step over a groaning man curled in the foetal position, clutching his groin and another moaning with a bloodied face, as he approached the scene.

His security guards had pinned this shaven headed youth to the wall. Marco briefly held back in the shadows to study this intriguing character; he showed no emotion or signs of remorse. He appeared unscathed by the brutal fight and hadn't even broken a sweat through his exertion. The only evidence that he had been involved in the battle, was the split skin over his knuckles that were splattered with blood. Marco stepped out of the shadows and pushed his face between the two heavyweight security guards so he could look into the eyes of the man called Casey. He stared at his unflinching glare, delving deeply into the blackness of his soul. All Marco could see was a younger version of himself staring back. Leaning over so he could whisper into Casey's ear, he eerily demanded, *"I could do with someone like you, do you want to work for me?"* It wasn't a question, no one ever said no to him.

Part 10

Casey stumbled back into his room at the hostel in the early hours of Sunday morning. He had been living there for quite some time and had managed to change his bunkroom, for a private room so he didn't need to share anymore. Although it was small it contained a single bed, wardrobe and a chest of drawers. He still had to share a communal bathroom, but this room gave him privacy and a secure place to leave his belongings. He had bought himself a small television, which resided on top of the chest of drawers, along with a single photograph of his mum and a small cross.

Staring deep within the simple photo frame, he could see his own reflection superimposed on the glass, his focus flickering between himself and his mother; arguments ensued between the two images, bringing them to back to life. *"You slut, I saw you..... I bloody heard you!"* roared the reflection. ***"No stop ..... You're turning into your father!"*** screamed the photograph. Casey hung his head in shame. Pangs of guilt swept through his body as he recalled their argument, he blamed himself for her death. The few moments of unspoken love that they shared slipped into insignificance; his tough bravado was in turmoil with his vulnerable inner child. Through frustration he punched the wall, causing searing pain to explode from his knuckle, rippling up his forearm. The painful distraction gave him respite from the nightmare in his head.

Working at the supermarket didn't give him enough income to improve his situation, but the offer of work from the nightclub owner only a few hours before, may change that.

His mind was in spin from reliving the past and planning the future. They were complete contrasts that he struggled to reconcile. The thought of how his life could change seemed unreal. He had to see Tess again and also arrange a meeting with the nightclub boss, both prospects scared him and excited him at the same time. Sleep was sparse, he was so restless weighing up the pros and cons of both situations.

Casey was feeling hungry so headed off to the local café near the train station. An all-day breakfast, accompanied by a couple of cups of hot sweet tea usually cured his hangover and helped him to think. During the week they opened at seven o'clock for the commuter trade, but Saturday and Sunday it was ten o'clock. Casey had been watching the time, waiting for them to open and chuckled to himself as the ten chimes of the church clock coincided with the rumbling of his stomach. He was the first customer through the door and was greeted with a cheery, *"Hello,"* from the waitress.

*       *       *

A bleary-eyed Tess skulked into the kitchen and sat quietly at the table, Doris was busy baking and only noticed her as she turned to reach for some flour. With a giggle in her voice Doris teased, *"It looks like someone had a good night."* Feeling sorry for herself she pleaded, *"Please mum, could you make me a cup of tea?"* With an unsympathetic smile, Doris brushed the flour off her hands with a tea towel and filled the kettle with fresh water, *'Oh to be young again'* she thought, reminiscing on her own youth.

Tess took the hot brew into the lounge to find Bert engrossed in his newspaper. She curled into a ball on the

132

sofa and clung to the mug with both hands as if it was her prized possession. *"Hello sleepy-head, did you have a goodnight?"* Bert cheerfully chirped. *"Ummmm, yes thanks dad."* She remembered the screams of delight from the group of girls as they arrived outside The Roxy. Tracy looked stunning in her beautiful dress and long red hair, proudly donning her birthday sash. The loud music and sipping several drinks made her very giggly making the evening blend into one, with the exception of Kelvin. She felt a wide grin spread across her face as she thought about the boy in her class, who had become a confident young man. She remembered giving him her phone number and hoped he would call.

\* \* \*

Marco yawned as he woke from his bed, turning to sit on the edge so he could slide his feet into his slippers. He broke wind as he stretched for his silk dressing gown, followed by a quick belch. *'It was his house and he could behave as he wanted'* flashed through his mind as he loudly urinated in the bathroom. As he caught his own reflection in the bathroom mirror, he smirked recalling the grope he had had in his office with the new barmaid. His arrogance led him to believe he could have anything he wanted.

Sofia was already downstairs preparing his breakfast, just as he expected. Her sleep had been disturbed by his inconsiderate noise when he came to bed at five o'clock. She gripped the duvet tightly and feigned deep sleep, in an attempt to dissuade any sexual demands. Slipping quietly out of bed around seven o'clock, gave Sofia at least a couple of hours to shower, apply makeup and do her hair. Marco expected her to look pristine at all times or suffer his rage, especially first thing in the morning. No words or pleasantries where exchanged as she presented him with coffee and a large plate of smoked haddock and poached eggs. Sofia went into the conservatory, not wanting to look at him, waiting for him to demand more coffee and a newspaper.

When his breakfast had been consumed, Marco retired to the lounge to smoke a cigar. Sofia quickly cleared away the dirty crockery, because only then would she be given permission to go to church. They were both Roman Catholics; the church gave her sanctuary and peace from her dominated lifestyle. Marco never went to church, scoffing her attendance, but it gave her an opportunity to make friends and socialise. Occasionally she would be allowed to entertain coffee mornings at their house, but could only invite people that Marco considered suitable. She always referred to it as their house, never her home.

*   *   *

Realising that he'd overslept, Casey quickly dressed and headed for the supermarket. Mr Yates never seemed to be in a good mood on Monday mornings. Casey had been late last week, he didn't want to cause any more friction; he had also been reprimanded last month for his attitude and needed to keep his job, well for the moment. Yates had taken him under his wing and over the five years that they had worked together, had been very considerate to the young Kelvin. Although he appreciated his kindness, Casey felt he had outgrown the role. He wanted something bigger that would keep his wallet full, something that would give him the lifestyle he could only dream of.

With minutes to spare, Casey slipped into the staff room to collect his uniform, managing to miss the watchful eye of Mr Yates. *"Morning Boss,"* Casey chirped, *"Good morning Kelvin,"* he replied, deep in conversation with Joyce from accounts. Casey swaggered along the corridor towards the storeroom, relieved to overcome his close shave. During the day his mind wandered, daydreaming of what life could be like with money to burn and Tess on his arm. The vision made him smile, but also more dissatisfied with his Groundhog Day existence, he had to find a way into the big time. His skills had come from the school of hard knocks, his feral streetwise education, rather than from any classroom. Exploring his options, he knew that he only had one choice.

*"Oh crap!"* Casey cursed himself as he absentmindedly knocked his bruised knuckle on the wall, whilst moving a cardboard box. Doreen threw him a disgusted look, to which he replied, *"What are you looking at, you old bag?"* then continued with his task, although blood had started to run down his hand. Casey had never warmed to the prim and proper Doreen, as she always seemed to be looking down on him, yet she was a shop assistant just like him. With the carton securely stored, he trotted off to retrieve a plaster from the first aid box.

Casey managed to dodge the deep puddles on his way home from work. There had been a heavy downpour; a hole in the bottom of his shoe allowed rainwater to soak his sock. Every other step emitted a squelching noise as he walked. A flash of lightning was the cue for the heavens to open once more. Casey dashed for cover under a shop canopy. Knitting patterns and balls of wool adorned the window. He chuckled to himself, *'Just my luck to get stranded outside a do-it-yourself jumper shop.*' There was a picture of a man in an Arran cardigan smoking a pipe, with a woman in matching clothes. Casey struck the pose and mimicked the man with the pipe, *"What's for tea tonight Gloria,"* he scoffed.

Searching his pockets, he found Tess's phone number. It was almost six o'clock. The downpour created a curtain between him and the phone box on the other side of the street. He had to wait until it eased. *'Should I? Shouldn't I?'* wrestled in his mind. *'She's far too good for a bum like me'* seemed to be his conclusion. He yearned to see the only friend he had at school, his first love, even if she didn't know it. Regardless of the rain, he seized the moment and dashed to the phone box opposite.

Nervously he rummaged through his loose change to find a ten pence piece. His fingers pressed numbers on the phone. *"Beep, the number you have called has not been recognised,"* the automated recording informed. Casey cursed when he realised that he had misdialled. His second attempted was acknowledged with a ringing tone, after seven tries, Casey decided to end the call. He would try later.

Doris quickly brushed the flour off her hands and sped towards the ringing telephone. Just as she placed her hand on the receiver it stopped, *'Oh well, I'm sure they'll call again.'*

As the rain eased, Casey decided to take a detour via The Roxy. He wanted to check the opening times, so he could speak to the boss about his offer of work. The entrance was locked and to his frustration, he couldn't see a sign listing their opening hours. He kicked an empty coke can to vent his annoyance, causing a loud rumble along the pavement, drawing the attention of people passing by. A click, then a creak alerted him to the fire exit door opening in the alleyway next to The Roxy. A cleaner carrying two sacks of rubbish, headed towards the refuse bin. Casey seized the opportunity and shouted, *"Hey mate, is the boss in?"* The bewildered worker turned quickly to face him, then replied, *"If you mean Mr Rossi, he'll be here Thursday about seven o'clock."* With a nod of acknowledgement, Casey shouted, *"Cheers mate!"* He felt a splatter of rain on top of his head and decided to run back to the hostel before the next downpour could soak him.

The rain did drench Casey just yards from his hostel, *"Crap!"* he spat, dripping water on the floor in the entrance hall. He could feel the wet pocket of his trousers sticking to his thigh as he rummaged for his door key. Inside his room, he quickly removed his sodden trousers, *"Crap, crap, crap!"* he vented at the wet garment. He needed them dry for work tomorrow, so hung them over his radiator. *"Crapity, crap, crap."* The flyer with Tess's number on was also soggy; he carefully peeling the paper apart, relieved the numbers were still visible due to the waxy lipstick. Discarding the remainder of his wet clothes, in a heap on the floor, he headed for a hot shower in the communal bathroom. Singing at the top of his voice, *"Winding your way down on Baker Street … just one more year and you'll be happy!"* followed by his mimicking of a saxophone player soon lightened his mood, as he allowed the warm water to wash his shivering skin. Although he wasn't a great fan of Gerry Rafferty, he could see himself entwined in the simple lyrics that weaved through the song.

Afterwards, propped up on his bed Casey felt dry and refreshed; he enjoyed the luxury of a steaming hot shower, something he never had at home. His mind wandered back to that mildew covered room where he washed in lukewarm water, in a stained white bath, ingrained with a tidemark. A pedestal sink accompanied it with a chip out of the corner and also a toilet with a broken pine seat. The door had been crumpled with raging kicks from his father's frustration; the door shaken from its hinges would no longer close, there was no privacy. The bathroom's distorted open frame was in sharp contrast to his mother's adjoining bedroom door, which had withstood the barrage. Although that received a similar pounding, the door was tightly sealed, consuming the blood soaked body of Brenda, encased in her own crypt. Casey buried his face into his pillow and screamed muffled cries of furious guilt, before he pounded the wall with his injured fist.

Casey's moods could turn one hundred and eighty degrees in a matter of moments for no apparent reason. Flashbacks from his past pounded on his conscious tormenting his soul, yet left just as abruptly, leaving him confused.

His anger dissolved as he focused on the fire throbbing in his knuckle and the warm trickle of blood running down the back of his hand. He used a piece of toilet paper to blot the open wound and remove the blood splatter on the wall. Life had to change; doing nothing wasn't an option anymore. The thought of meeting up with Tess lifted his mood. Before he could chicken-out of the call, he quickly dressed and headed for a public phone just outside the hostel; he quickly dialled before he could change his mind.

*"I'll get it mum,"* called Tess from the lounge. *"Hello,"* she said picking up the receiver. There was a moment's pause, which felt like an eternity. Casey stuttered his words, *"H-hello its Casey, o-oh I mean Kelvin, is that you Tess?"*

After another pause, Tess quizzed, *"Yes, hello Kelvin it's great to hear from you, but who's Casey?"* He wasn't prepared to reply to any question and merely said, *"Oh it's a nickname I use. Do you fancy meeting up for a drink on Wednesday?"* changing the subject quickly before she could press him further. Without a second's hesitation she enthused, *"Yes that'll be great, shall we say seven o'clock in The Rose and Crown?"*

Casey's heart sunk as he recalled standing outside that pub, raging at the sight of his mother with those men; those dirty, disgusting bastards, pawing over her! Thinking on his feet, he suggested, *"Let's meet in The Bell, it's nicer in there."* Tess chirpily replied, *"Great see you there."* The call ended, leaving them both in high spirits.

Tess dressed casually to meet her old school friend. As she approached The Bell, she tried to recall her events over the past five years. To her surprise, she had butterflies in her stomach, which distracted her, clouding her memory. Casey was sat at a table just inside the door and promptly stood up as she walked in. She nestled into a chair, whilst he fetched her a drink from the bar. Conversation was easy between them; they had lots to catch up on.

*"Last orders please!"* shouted the barman, as he rang his bell. They couldn't believe how quickly they had chuckled their way through the evening and enjoyed each other's company. Casey walked Tess home along the quiet streets,

until they stopped outside her front door. *"Well this is where I live, goodnight Kelvin."* Without thinking he leant over and kissed her on the lips. Tess was a little taken aback, but smiled and returned for another. *"I'll call you,"* Casey reassured her, as Tess closed the door behind her.

Casey walked home as if he was stepping on a cloud. A beaming smile spread across his face as he thought about the evening, nothing could dampen his mood. Sleep came easy for him that night. His jovial mood continued through the next working day, mulling over his meeting with Rossi that evening, as he went about his duties. From four o'clock in the afternoon, Casey checked his watch every five minutes, counting down the time with excitement until he could leave work. The only task left to do, was to change out of his work clothes into something that would give him a meaner persona. In his bedroom he slipped on a black polo shirt and black trousers, then finished off with a black bomber jacket. Satisfied, he counted down time on his watch until just before seven o'clock, when he could leave. Casey felt a mixture of nerves and excitement as he walked to The Roxy, *"Life is on the up,"* he tried to convince himself.

The main entrance of The Roxy was closed, but he found the side door open and crept in. The place was silent apart from the clink of bottles being stacked behind the bar. *"I've come to see Mr Rossi,"* Casey confidently said to the barman who was crouched in front of a refrigerator. "*Go through the door marked 'Staff Only' then up the stairs. His office is on the right, you can't miss it,"* the barman said without turning his head, continuing with his chores. Casey didn't reply.

140

He could see a red door to his left with the *'Staff Only'* and for a moment questioned his intention to speak to the nightclub owner. A sharp intake of breath cleared his mind and drew him to the entrance. The bright red door needed some repair, the paint was starting to flake and there was an impact dent, about two feet from the floor. The frame was painted the same as the door and was in a similar state of disrepair. Casey noticed how dingy the place looked, something not obvious with the flashing lights and the darkened shadows of a raucous night of revellers. As he pushed open the stiff door, it felt as though he was prising apart the jaws of a devil. A voice in his head whispered, *"Hello Satan,"* as he stepped into the dark corridor.

The muffled sound of a single voice became clearer as each stair was trod. He could see at the summit of what seemed an endless staircase, an open door with its light illuminating the upper passageway. Casey realised the voice that he heard was that of Mr Rossi in a heated telephone conversation. Unsure what to do, he hid in the shadows outside the doorway waiting for the call to end. He heard an angry Rossi demanding payment of a debt. When the phone was slammed into its cradle, Casey stepped forward into the doorway nervously saying, *"Err, hello."*

Marco Rossi just raised his eyes to meet the eye-line of Casey, then grinned and slouched back into his leather bound chair. There seemed to be an eternal silence whilst the burly Italian man studied Casey from head to foot. His sausage-like fingers entwined, as he joined his hands across his protruding stomach. Casey's attention was drawn to the intimidating glisten of his chunky gold rings donning each finger; which was in deep contrast to the comical sight of his hairy belly, exposed through an unbuttoned gap of his over stretched shirt. *"Umm, so you've decided to work for me? I knew you would,"* Marco said with a chuckle. People only refused his wishes at their peril.

Casey became distracted by the scar running down Marco's cheek as he was given the rundown on the work he was expected to do. He was on trial for a month, working with Benny who would show him the ropes, and then he'd be off on his own collecting outstanding debts for his new boss. *"You may need to give them some gentle persuasion,"* smirked Marco, *"But if they don't pay, I'll take it out of your wages."* Once Casey had calculated how much money he could make his mood turned to excitement, realising that he could eventually give up his work at the supermarket, but not just yet. He was instructed to come the same time next week; he would shadow Benny for the next month.

He didn't need to persuade himself too hard, to celebrate his good fortune over a beer in The Bell on his way home. Standing alone at the bar, he reminisced about the evening with Tess and how his life could change for the better. Although his work for Marco scared him a little, it was a way out of the poverty pit that was going to be his future. He could collect Rossi's money during evenings and weekends, therefore still work at the supermarket until he earned regular money. The more debts he collected, the more commission he could earn. His mind wandered into a daydream, visualising which sports car he should buy first, yet he'd never taken any driving lessons, *'Just a minor detail'* he thought.

Part 11

Daydreaming of his future life, Casey worked on autopilot at the supermarket; he could only imagine a world that could be so different from his feral past. Fear froze his thoughts with self-doubt. His upbringing had not equipped him with the life-skills to deal with other people's idea of normal life. He desperately wanted to feel the warmth of a loving relationship and a loving home, but these were alien concepts to him. The thought of failure hung heavily on his shoulders dampening his mood.

*"Kelvin there's a call for you!"* shouted Teresa from Mr Yates's office.

*"Hello,"* he said answering the call. *"Hi Kelvin its Tess. I'm on the office phone so I've got to be quick, would you like to meet up later?"* Casey's mood barometer swung to sunshine as a huge smile spread across his face, *"Yes great!"* They arranged to meet at The Bell again at seven o'clock. Casey thought nothing could darken his state of mind, until he reached into his pocket and realised he was almost broke. It was another few days until he got his wages, but his second date with the lovely Tess was worth every last penny.

They chuckled like school children, making up time stolen from them. When they caught glimpses of their eyes meeting, they both knew they were no longer school children and they wanted to be more than friends. Casey nervously asked, *"I'm broke this week, so do you want to come back to my room and watch some telly instead?"* Tess sniggered as she grabbed her coat, *"Yes come on then."*

*"Kelvin, why do you always wear sunglasses, even inside?"* she asked. He said nothing, just removed them and hung his head in shame. Tess looked closely gently running her finger down the scar on his forehead, more obvious now. Her mind shocked at the damage to his eye, her heart in knots, *"What happened?"*

*"It was my dad. He punched me when I was younger."* After a pause he continued, *"My fringe always covered it, but now ......"* Tess pressed her forefinger to his lips, a gesture to say, *'You don't need to explain.'*

Not much television was watched in Casey's dingy room. They started to get to know each other intimately, an unexpected surprise for both of them. Sex hadn't been a thought in their minds up until that point, but the lustful connection was electric and couldn't be stopped; neither wanted the passion to stop.

Casey fumbled in vain to unbutton her blouse, failing to appear experienced in these matters. Tess nervously chuckled and pinged the buttons open for him, her face flushing in the process. From then on, they both tried to scramble out of their own clothes, without making eye contact with each other. When naked they locked their glares, almost too embarrassed to look any lower at each other in detail. Tess folded her left arm across her breasts and her right hand over her groin shyly hiding her modesty. *"Kelvin could you turn the light out please?"*

He was relieved to oblige. His erection was starting to grow and was feeling awkward. Looking at the bashful Tess made him excited, yet he didn't believe he deserved such a beauty; someone that he'd put on a pedestal in his

144

schooldays was stood naked before him. Casey didn't feel good enough for her, which made his penis wither. The darkness came as a welcome relief.

Their first sexual encounter was clumsy and brief, neither being experienced. Tess was cocooned in a warm bubble of emotion, her feelings growing for the new Kelvin. Casey couldn't believe how the wonderful Tess could be interested in a bum like him; he was elated but confused not knowing what he should feel. They hugged closely on his single bed deep in their own thoughts, until their playful lust that had to be quenched yet again.

*"You've got a glow on your face this morning,"* Cathy teased her with a wink, as Tess entered the office. Flushed with embarrassment she replied, *"It was just a date,"* then busied herself with the duties of the day. Colin overheard the banter and felt a pang of jealousy. He would look after her and make her happy if only he had a chance; he wanted her to notice him.

\* \* \*

Casey marched to work with an air of confident purpose. He had Tess on his mind. *"Oh the sexy Tess, damn she looked hot,"* he thought, feeling smug as he pictured her naked body. The rampant desires that rushed through his body the night before became vivid in his mind once again, encouraging a slow erection to grow in his pants; he became self-conscious of his daydreaming and his tightening trousers, as he stepped through the doorway of the supermarket. *"Shit, damn, bollocks…. Think about something else, football, or cleaning, or stacking shelves. God anything else!"* In an attempt to deflate his rising cock

145

he pinched himself really hard to cause pain; the distraction began to work. He had to make something of his life to win her over.

He was also excited about his impending induction with Benny, not really knowing what to expect. Marco Rossi thought he was up to it; must be a doddle of a job if the big man called it *'Easy money.'* Casey mumbled to himself, *"Life is sweet".*

The day of reckoning arrived later that week, Casey's first day at The Roxy. His duties at the supermarket melted into insignificance, as he counted down the hours, then minutes to the end of his shift. He was so preoccupied that he'd skipped his lunch, causing his stomach to rumble. Time dragged its weary legs around his watch face, refusing to accelerate under his scorn. *"I'm off now Mr Yates,"* he shouted pulling off his work coat at the end of his shift. *"Um, okay Kelvin see you tomorrow."* Casey grabbed a cheese sandwich and a bottle of coke from the kiosk; cursing himself that he'd forgotten his discount card, and had to pay full price.

*"Oh shit!"* Casey complained as he nicked himself, shaving his head. He wanted to engulf himself in his tough guy character. The trickle of blood running down his temple, merged into the shaving gel on his face. A momentary thought of raspberry-ripple ice cream made him chuckle in the mirror. Once showered, the razor mark only left a faint red line. Casey scowled at his reflection, pulling menacing faces, just as a singer would practice their scales before a performance. He was dressed, satisfied and heading out the door for a new chapter in his life.

Benny was stood at the bar as Casey walked into The Roxy. He was a short man, that appeared as round as he was tall. It was difficult to age him, with his closely cropped hair and greying goatee beard, he may have been in his early forties. His loose fitting blue bomber-jacket appeared bulky in places and hung heavily at the front, pulling apart the zip fastener. *"You must be Casey?"* squeaked a voice that seemed out of sync with his appearance. *"Yeah, that's me"*, Casey cockily replied. *"We're doing the evening collections, come on,"* Benny beckoned as he walked away, not waiting for Casey.

The pair almost looked like a modern-day remake of Laurel and Hardy without the comedy. Benny was a man of few words, only replying to Casey's constant questions with, *"You'll see."*

Their first appointment was with Fraser, a low-life drug user and dealer. His haunt was an alleyway next to a convenience store. The local youths congregated around the shop entrance, giving him a regular stream of customers and also provided a lookout for him. Benny had several dealings with him and found Fraser to be a slippery character, evading his payments. *"Casey, you walk past the front of the shop and down the alleyway. The kids don't know you. I'll sneak around behind him."* Casey became excited by what he saw as military game planning, pulling his shoulders back, he did as instructed.

Fraser was a slender guy of about six feet tall, with a black leather jacket and stubble chin. As Casey approached he said *"What do you want mate, pills or weed?"* Benny appeared from the shadows behind him and bellowed in a commanding voice, *"Neither prick, just our money,"* before he landed a punishing blow into his kidneys.

As Fraser hit the ground, Benny swiftly kicked him in the ribs. *"You're two weeks over due, I'll take a hundred now!"* Wincing as he spoke, Fraser spluttered, *"I've only got fifty,"* and then gurgled in pain, knowing he'd suffered broken ribs.

*"Not enough,"* Benny spat his words, reaching inside his blue bomber-jacket he pulled out a pistol, *"I'm gonna take all you've got."* Fraser's shaking hand pulled out a wad of notes, which Casey counted; seven ten-pound notes, three five-pound notes and a couple of single notes. Benny nodded his approval, *"And for our trouble, I'm taking your stash too, just because you've dirtied my shoes,"* smirking with satisfaction.

*"See you next week, prick,"* Benny eerily said as he left Fraser with a parting kick to his groin. Both Casey and Benny walked from the front of the alleyway past the silent stares of the crowd. *"Onto the next job, sonny!"* Benny joked. *"It could be a profitable night."*

Casey felt electrically charged from head to toe. *'Wow bloody wow!'* rang through his head, surprised how slick Benny had been to dominate Fraser. Riding shotgun to a thug excited him, making him feel almost untouchable. With mixed emotions Casey thought, *'I'm a thug too .... Shit!'* The prospect gave him an adrenaline rush.

That evening was Casey's baptism of fire, helping Benny extort money from people on his debt list, some easier jobs than others. They were back at The Roxy by eleven o'clock,

148

receiving a nod of acknowledgement from the door staff, as they slid past the waiting queue outside. Marco Rossi was perched on a bar stool; seeing them approach, he slipped through the red '*Staff Only*' door to return to his office, shortly followed by Benny and Casey.

*"How did you do boys?"* Marco said without expression. *"Three hundred boss,"* Benny replied, not declaring all the money from Fraser or the drugs he'd taken. Marco palmed off thirty quid for Benny, *"That's your ten percent,"* then looking at Casey, *"And a tenner for the trainee."* They both said, *"Thanks boss,"* as they retired to the bar for a couple of beers. Casey was pleased with his payment for four hours work and excited at the prospect of earning big bucks when he could go it alone. *"Cheers!"* as they chinked glasses, *"Here's a couple of quid for keeping your mouth shut,"* Benny said as he slipped the money into Casey's pocket.

With his days working at the supermarket and his evenings split between The Roxy and the lovely, sexy, damn hot Tess, Casey's diary was pretty full. With money in his pocket, he could treat the lovely Tess to cans of beer in his room and Chinese takeaways. That's all he knew from his feral upbringing, so he thought he was treating her like a princess. Sometimes she complained that he never took her out, so a few drinks in The Bell and a drunken fumble under the duvet was his idea of a perfect night.

*"Oh shit!"* exclaimed Tess, ***"Oh shit, shit, shit, shit!"*** from the confines of her bathroom. *"Are you ok Tess?"* called Doris. *"Yes mum, I've just knocked over my makeup".* That wasn't the real reason, *"Oh shit what am I going to do?"*

For the rest of the day Tess completed her office duties in silence, not wanting to idly chat. When the office emptied, she bravely picked up the phone to make a call. *"Kelvin we need to talk, can I come over to see you after work?"* Bemused he replied, *"Yeah sure, what's up?"* Tess's heart seemed to be pounding in her throat, stopping her from speaking clearly, *"I'll tell you later,"* then quickly hung up before he could reply.

Casey heard a faint tapping on his door; Tess was stood there with a tear rolling down her cheek. He was expecting a roasting from her, so he was taken by surprise. *"What's up?"* he blurted, *"Kelvin I'm pregnant, my Dad's going to kill me."* It felt like a gong had struck inside his head, freezing his thoughts to silence; then a tsunami of questions hit the inside of his forehead. *"Shit, shit, arseholes, are you stupid, didn't you take protection?"* he ranted, *"What are you going to do about it?"* Tess was upset by his response, hoping for more sympathy, *"I could never have an abortion, I'm going to keep it."* Casey could feel the blood drain from his face, how could he be a father, when he could barely look after himself? Screaming in his head was his mother's voice shouting, ***"You're turning into your father!"*** He turned to look at the solitary photo of his mother and bowed his head in shame.

They stood in his small dingy room without a word being spoken, without eye contact and without compassion; neither wanting to speak first. Tess stuttered, *"I'm scared to tell my dad, will you come with me?"* Casey nodded in silence. The enormity of the situation still not registered in his conscious brain. The short walk to Tess's home seemed as if someone had pressed the mute button on all ambient sound, apart from the uncontrollable sobbing that echoed

150

down the street. There were no more tears left to fall down her cheeks, just a pathetic cooing of sadness. She gripped his hand tightly as they shuffled along, as if they were heading towards the gallows.

Although Bert and Doris knew their daughter was dating a young lad, they had never met him, only knowing that they had gone to school together. She seemed happy so they were happy. Tess tugged a reluctant Casey into her house, leading him through the darkened hallway into the brightness of the lounge. Bert and Doris were sat watching television and were surprised they had company. *"Mum, Dad this is Kelvin."* Bert cast a disapproving look at the shaven youth, instantly thinking he wasn't good enough for his princess. *"Hello Mr Clifton, Mrs Clifton,"* Casey mumbled. Doris replied with a smile, whereas Bert remained stone-faced. Before her parents had an opportunity to speak, Tess burst out, ***"I'm pregnant."*** It was almost as if the world had stopped turning in a surreal vacuum of silence, until Bert stood up raging at Casey to get out of his house. As Casey closed the front door behind him he could hear shouting and arguing, crying and doors slamming. He walked home bewildered, wondering what fate would bring him.

The following day, Tess waited outside the supermarket for him to finish work. He felt nervous seeing her sat on the car park wall but needed to talk to her. Tess threw her arms around his neck and sobbed on his shoulder. *"We need to talk,"* she pleaded. Everything was moving too fast for Casey to process, his head began to spin recalling his feral existence as a child, yet determined to not make the mistakes of his parents. Only time would tell how he would cope. Casey reassured Tess that he would standby her, to provide as best as he could; earning money from Marco Rossi was now a necessity.

Bert's temper had waned as he came to terms with the situation. Although, the circumstances could have been better, he was secretly looking forward to becoming a granddad. Accepting that *'This Kelvin lad'* would be part of his daughter's future, he had to get to know him. Casey was invited for Sunday lunch, where the four of them could become acquainted over a meal. Sitting around Doris's infamous kitchen table, she took the role of a mothering matriarch; light-heartedly she quipped, *"Well, you've made your bed, and you've got to lay in it,"* trying to lift the tense mood. Although the atmosphere wasn't jovial, it was civil and they managed to talk about Tess's future baby without too much hostility. Before Doris had an opportunity to clear away the dirty dessert dishes, Bert said, *"I will always provide for my Tess and want the best for the baby. I'm going to buy you a house, where you can both raise the child."* Focusing his gaze, he jovially threatened, *"You're not going to let us down, are you Kelvin?"* All he could reply was, *"No sir."*

The overly protective Bert Clifton surprised him at his surreally civilised *'Baptism of fire.'* Doris appeared to be the nurturing mother that he never had, which made him reflect on missing chunks of his childhood. Bert took the reins from his matriarchal wife and laid down the law as to how life was going to be for his daughter. Although Casey was glad that *'An adult'* was taking control, he looked at Bert and thought, *"What an arse!"* The icicles of fear that were once stuck in his veins were now flowing as sniggering Emojis spitting contempt. *"That's what he thinks. Dickhead,"* scoffed the voice in Casey's head.

152

Part 12

The debt collectors, worked as a team three evenings a week for Casey's month long probation. Benny was an ex-soldier who missed the adrenaline of the army. He had a day job working for a security company and worked the evening shifts at The Roxy, in his words, *"For an extra few quid and lotsa fun."* Casey did feel out of his league at first, but was allowed to take the dominant role on occasions, with Benny as backup. After his trial period, Casey was given his own debt list to work on, skyrocketing his earnings, but also his vulnerabilities; he had to put himself on the line to earn the big bucks. A couple of times he had to make a quick escape, especially if he was outnumbered.

Casey and Benny always compared lists before venturing out, doubling up on the *'Troublesome ones'* and then sharing the commission. They built up a strong bond and trusted each other when the chips were down. It suited Casey to stash his earnings away and continue at the supermarket for the moment. There were no daytime debt lists available at The Roxy; they were the more lucrative business owners, so the boss's favourite people got first pickings. Casey would have to bide his time to go up in the pecking order.

As fast as Tess's pregnant stomach increased, her sex drive diminished, much to Casey's frustration. She never came to his hostel anymore; anytime they spent together was under the watchful eyes of The Clifton's. Although, Doris had taken a shine to him and furnished him with an endless supply of tea and cakes, he wasn't used to so much attention and felt like a caged animal. The sickly sweet homestead was the polar-opposite of his upbringing and the exciting life he had at The Roxy. *"Maybe, I can have the best of both worlds, if I play my cards right,"* he thought to himself. He needed his solitary independence, his own comfort zone, where he didn't have to wear a pleasant mask with a fake smile. Somewhere he could hold hands with his demons and offload his fury like an erupting volcano. The Clifton family were too nice, too sweet, and too friendly, to understand his dark side, it was never their world to comprehend.

The amount of nights that he claimed to be working increased, offering a perfect cover for him to satisfy his sexual appetite that Tess no longer was interested in. Girls at the club would engage with his flirtatious banter; excessive alcohol making them easy prey. Casey realised that Tess was no longer as *'Hot'* by comparison, to this bevy of buxom, leggy beauties that were far more adventurous than she ever was. His hostel room was a convenient place to take them; only having a single bed was the ideal excuse to ask them to leave directly after sex. *"Sorry babe, there's no room for you to sleep here, so I'll see you around,"* became his parting shot, as he bundled them out of his room in the early hours.

Casey told her that he had to work at The Roxy to save up for the baby. Tess tried to quiz what he did there but he clumsily evaded the question by saying, *"Just a few errands, filling in where I'm asked to, you know the sort of thing."* Although Tess wasn't satisfied with his guarded answers, she knew pursuing her questioning was futile and only fuel for an argument. In her quiet thoughts, she wondered if he was being unfaithful or involved in crime, both options scared her.

With a couple of months to spare, Bert managed to secure a property in the same street as their factory. He felt more comfortable being able to keep a watchful eye on them and had been holding out for the right house. Tess was really excited as Bert showed them around the house. Doris offered advice on décor and gave Kelvin decorating tips as he trailed behind. *"This place is so clean,"* he blurted, *"And look, the bathroom door closes*!" This made the group chuckle. He couldn't believe his luck.

Bert and Kelvin spent weekends together decorating the house, whilst Tess and Doris went shopping for furniture and kitchen equipment. There were only a few weeks left to get the place ship-shape for the baby, so they decided to get the place homely before they moved in. This gave Bert a chance to get to know Kelvin and to share his do-it-yourself skills with his daughter's boyfriend, the father of his grandchild. This thought made him ponder how his young princess had grown up so quickly; she was moving out of their family home to start a new family home of her own.

It was almost midnight when Tess let out a load scream from her bedroom, ***"Mum, the baby is coming!"*** Doris tied her dressing gown as she entered the room, reassuring her daughter to stay calm. Bert came to join the commotion to see how he could help. *"Should I phone an ambulance or bring the car around?"* Bert asked. *"She's okay for a bit, so bring the car around, we'll take her to the hospital,"* suggested Doris, *"And, oh by the way you had better let Kelvin know"*. Bert decided to call at the hostel on route as it was on the way to the hospital.

155

Bert pulled the car to a halt before jogging to the hostel entrance. *"Room fourteen dad. Argh!"* Tess called after him as a contraction pounded her body. He puffed his way up the staircase using the handrail for support. The corridor seemed bleak and dark only lit by the occasional ceiling light. *"What a dive,"* he thought to himself searching for the numbered doors. Outside fourteen he tapped on the door, no answer. Again he tapped to no avail. Scribbling a note, he pushed it under the door and headed back to the car. *"Where in the bloody hell is he?"* cursed Bert.

\* \* \*

Casey's heard a tapping on his door whilst he was mauling a naked brunette in his hostel room. He held a hand over her mouth to muffle any noise, *"Shhhh."* Footsteps faded away before they both relaxed and continued their drunken sexual romp. *"Who do you think that was Casey?"* she asked after they had both been satisfied. *"Dunno,"* he grunted, annoyed at the interruption. Casey spotted the note on the floor in the early hours of the morning, just as Sandy left.

Well, he thought she said her name was Sandy, or maybe Mandy. He chuckled to himself, *"Anyway, she was Randy alright, ha!"* He scooped up the paper to read an irate note from Bert saying that Tess had gone into labour, ***"Get to the hospital quick."*** Casey dressed quickly and ran towards the hospital, cursing himself as he went, *"Shit, shit, shit, how am I gonna explain this one. Shit!"*

Doris comforted Tess through her painful contractions, until she successfully gave birth to a baby boy just after five o'clock. Much to Bert's disgust, there was no sign of the absent father; Casey ran to the hospital, arriving half an hour after the birth of his son. *"Where in the hell have you been, didn't you get my message?"* fumed Bert. *"Dad don't start, he's here now"* Tess said, eyes transfixed on her new buddle of joy. Kelvin sheepishly squeezed through to greet his new son. *"Sorry I was fast asleep."* It was the most perfect thing that he'd ever held in his arms, his bravado had dissolved into a vulnerable child, just like his son.

The hospital room was illuminated with happiness from the new parents and new grandparents, Casey's misdemeanour was quickly forgotten; but he did regret missing the birth. Doris suggested that Tess and the baby stay with them for a week before settling in their new house; this way she could help her daughter and selfishly steal cuddles with her new grandson. Kelvin was invited to stop at their house too, but declined to share Tess's single bed, saying, *"Tess could do with her mum, so I'll pack up my stuff at the hostel and move into the house when she is ready."* This seemed to satisfy everyone and allowed Casey to have a little more freedom away from the scrutiny of The Clifton's.

Casey was relieved that Tess would leave hospital and spend time with her mum, giving him more time to exploit his alternative lifestyle. The thought of losing his *'love nest'* where he satisfied his sordid liaisons, troubled his mind for a couple of days, until he realised that he could keep paying the rent on the room without Tess knowing. It would also be a good place to store spare clothes and money that he didn't want her to see. *"It's a win-win!"* he thought to himself. He celebrated that night in his hostel room, with a bottle of vodka and busty barmaid.

Carefully dividing his clothes, Casey left his best garments in the hostel room wardrobe. His day-to-day wear easily filled a couple of black bin liners and his meagre possessions fitted into another. He slit the side of his mattress, forcing bundles of money through the opening, along with his prized designer watch; he'd taken it from someone on his debtor's list that refused to pay his instalments. He only wore the watch for Mr Rossi's work, as he was too embarrassed to explain to Tess, how he'd come by it and certainly didn't want her to know about the money he was stashing away. Casey smirked to himself as he closed the door of his bolthole, then jumped into a taxi, heading for a new life with Tess and Thomas.

Each day, Tess strolled along to the factory to see her parents and proudly show off to the employees, her buddle of joy, which they named Thomas Albert Clifton. Cathy was always the first to step forward to hug Thomas, even before Bert could escape from his office to greet her. *"Dad can I change Thomas in your office?"* Bert winced at the thought of a soiled nappy on his precious leather-bound desk, but replied, *"Yes Tess that's fine."*

Much to Tess's surprise, Colin showed a keen interest in her baby, blowing raspberries to make him laugh. When Thomas cried, Colin was the first to nurse him to sleep, rocking him on his shoulder. Tess's heart melted whenever she saw Colin weaving his soothing magic. She thought, *'He's a really nice guy.'* A steady stream of factory workers made excuses to coo over the baby, often teasing Colin over his nursing skills. *"He looks just like you Colin, is there anything you want to tell us?"* Jenny cheekily asked with a wink.

*"I'm working tonight, so I'll be home late,"* Casey informed Tess over breakfast. *"Not again Kelvin, you are never here.*

158

*You treat this place as a hotel,"* she ranted, making Thomas cry. *"Yes baby, you tell Daddy that he should spend more time at home!"*

Casey swigged the dregs of tea from his cup and left the house without saying a word. *"Nag, nag, nag, that's all she does!"* he cursed, as he kicked an empty coke can out of frustration. He stopped at his hostel room for a large slug of vodka to ease his bad mood, before heading to the supermarket to work.

It was a short walk to her home, *"Oh, her parents' home,"* mentally scolding herself. It had become a daily ritual for Tess and Kelvin to have their evening meals in the Clifton household. Doris stopped mid-task to scoop up little Thomas for a quick hug, before continuing to prepare their meal, *"Is Kelvin coming for dinner today?"* Sulkily she replied, *"Nope, he's going to work at The Roxy tonight, the third time this week."* They cast each other a quizzical look, they knew it would be another late night for him.

*"Well mum, he is trying to earn more money,"* Tess said, trying to defend him. *"He should be at home helping you with the baby, instead of coming in at all hours!"* ranted Doris. Tess knew there was tension between her parents and Kelvin, they didn't see him as suitable, but had to accept he was the father of their grandson. She tried to be the peacemaker, not telling them about Kelvin's late night antics. Her mother's words rang through her ears, *"You've made your bed, and you've got to lay in it."* Tess had to make the best of the situation.

* * *

Marco was pleased that Casey managed to cover Benny's shift at short notice; he had been ambushed the night before and ended up in hospital. Tonight Casey would do the rounds with two heavies called James and John. They were no-nonsense brothers who had a nasty reputation, Casey would be their backup. First call was payback for the beating Benny received, and then they heavy-handedly collected instalments from other reluctant payers. They had to send out a message to the community that they were in control and would inflict their fury on anyone resisting.

The bounty from their evening's exploits was laid on Marco's desk for him to count. The boss grinned like a Cheshire cat as he flicked through the notes. He'd used their skills to extract payments from the toughest debtors on his list, the ones where he had to stamp his authority. *"Fifteen percent commission each tonight boys as a bonus. I'm sure no more smart-arse pricks will try it on for a while,"* Marco boomed. *"A quiet word Casey before you go,"* was the hint for James and John to leave. His sausage like fingers knitted together, as he leaned forward on his mahogany desk, *"I like you Casey you're a good boy. I've got some regular day shifts I want you to do, as well as your evenings."* Casey knew that he wasn't given an option to say no, *"Yes boss, whatever you need."*

Casey joined James and John at the bar. Between them they quickly consumed the contents of a bottle of whiskey, before heading their separate ways. *'I've hit the big time'* Casey thought as he stumbled along the street to the house he shared with Tess. Navigating his key into the lock, that seemed to dodge his advances, was the biggest challenge of the night. It was only when he closed the front door behind him that he realised his oversight to change at the hostel on

160

the way home. *"Oh crap. Oh stuff her, who cares? Hic!"* he mumbled loudly as he knocked over a table in the hallway. *"Shhhhhhhhhhh,"* he scorned the offending item.

Tess was sat up in bed with her arms folded, throwing him a disapproving look. His last memory of that evening, was to throw her a handful of money to, *'Stop her nagging.'* *"Here you go Tess, have some money,"* he loudly spoke, as he stumbled across their bedroom just after one o'clock in the morning. Tess was annoyed to be woken from her sleep, *"Shhhh, be quiet, you'll wake the baby. What time do you call this?"* The room started to spin as he reached for the rubbish bin next to the bed to puke. The springs of the mattress complained as he fell on the bed fully clothed. Sleep swept over him, as if he was being buried in a concrete grave, leaving him incapable of moving.

Tess noticed that he started wearing trendy clothes and an expensive watch. His extra money seemed to be spent on himself, rather than the house or the family. Casey thought he could buy her happiness and her silence, with a few notes. Although they lived rent free, they still had bills to pay, groceries and clothes to buy. Tess was grateful for her parents help, and the small allowance Bert slipped her each week without Doris knowing. What he didn't know was, Doris gave the same secret allowance without Bert knowing. She still relied on Kelvin's wages from the supermarket to keep their head above water.

*"I think I'll leave the supermarket and work full time at The Roxy,"* Casey mulled over a breakfast cup of tea. ***"Are you shitting me?"*** yelled Tess, throwing a cup into the sink; *"What are we going to do for money Kelvin?"* Before he could answer, she continued, *"You're hardly here now,*

*we'll never see you!"* Casey calmly took another gulp of tea and dominantly replied, *"I'm the master of the house, and I'll do what I want."* Tess slammed the door behind her, as she headed up the stairs to attend to Thomas's cries.

Part 13

*"You're a good for nothing gobshite!"* screamed Brenda at a cowering Kelvin. *"You're turning into your father!"* she continued to rant. *"It's your fault I'm dead, you could have been a better son!"* Kelvin rocked his head from side to side to avoid the rain of slaps targeted around his face. *"No mum, no. I'll be good, I promise!"* pleaded the pathetic image of a repentant child. A slap to his face shocked Casey from his regular bad dream. As his eyes gained focus, he could see a smiling Thomas patting his father's cheeks and gurgling. *"Another one of your nightmares Kelvin?"* asked Tess, who was propped up in bed drinking a cup of tea. He could only muster a grunt in reply, before heading to the bathroom to empty his bladder.

*"Your tea is getting cold,"* Tess reminded him, pointing to his bedside cabinet. Casey took a swig of his lukewarm brew and grimaced as he climbed back into bed. *"Dad, dad, dad!"* chirped a playful Thomas as he climbed onto his father and then started to bounce, shrilling with laughter. Casey's mood lifted as he wrestled his son in horseplay, ignoring the complaints from Tess as he almost spilled her tea in the process. As much as Kelvin drove her up the wall, she loved to see the softer side of him that was dwindling from his character. The world only saw his tough exterior, playful moments like these were rare; they were only revealed when he dropped his guard, and she knew at times like these he felt vulnerable. She worried that the caterpillar Kelvin, who had become a butterfly that she loved, was turning into a monstrous moth. He was out of control; she didn't know him anymore. Demons deep within his soul

163

were driving his behaviour down a path that Tess couldn't even comprehend; his mood swings caused so many arguments.

* * *

*"Watch what you're doing, you clumsy idiot!"* screamed Doreen, as Casey knocked her chair in the supermarket canteen. Their working relationship had diminished into a feud, finding any opportunity to bicker. *"Shut your fucking trap, you ugly witch!"* he ranted kicking the chair from beneath her; a thud and screams of complaint followed as Doreen crashed to the floor. The altercation brought silent stares from the onlookers, including a shocked Yates. ***"Kelvin, in my office, now!!"*** he screamed, as the two men marched from the canteen. Co-workers comforted the distressed Doreen.

*"What in the hell do you think you are doing?"* Yates continued to scream, as he closed the door behind Kelvin. *"The bitch is always having a go at me,"* he growled in reply. Then the more confident Casey continued, *"I've had enough of this shit-hole anyway, I'm leaving,"* as he opened the office door and left. *"Kelvin get back here, Kelvin!"* shouted Yates. His words fell on deaf-ears, as Casey threw his uniform jacket on the corridor floor. He never looked back, just continued to march out of the store.

Casey psyched himself up for the inevitable roasting he got from Tess, the minute he told her the news. *"Yeah, whatever!"* was his only response to her yells.

He marched down the street to the telephone box and promptly tapped out the numbers on the keypad. *"Hello*

164

*boss, I'm free to work any days or nights that you want me."* After a moments pause, the gruff Italian said, *"You're a good boy. See you tomorrow."*

Casey soon earned the trust of Marco, thinking on his feet to out-smart some of the most elusive payers. The boss was impressed with his comic genius, luring his prey to part with their money using his mind rather than his brawn. Although Casey was very capable with his fists, his streetwise past had armed him with the skills to read body language and anticipate situations, before they had even happened. He wasn't academically clever, but he certainly knew how to manipulate people in the darker community and get what he wanted. Casey could have made a perfect poker player, with his pan-faced expression and his quick sleight of hand; others found him difficult to read and unpredictable, not knowing how he would react.

Casey had to wait by the telephone box for Marco's call around ten o'clock. Sometimes it was a challenge to stop people using the phone while he waited for the call. For anything up to an hour, he would have to ward off people's complaints until the device rang. Once the list was delivered, he had to collect the debts and be at the club before the end of the day. Casey was often the first one to complete his list. *"The early bird catches the worm,"* he would say sniggering to himself.

*"A quiet word. Shut the door,"* Marco ordered as Casey dropped off his daily takings. *"I have a special job for you. It's just exchanging bundles of money, with other bundles of money,"* he continued. Casey was less known to his associates and also the police. The boss wanted to replace his regular runner, who had been arrested doing Marco's

money laundering. *"Get a cab from outside the train station and come to the back entrance of my house for midday tomorrow,"* Marco instructed, *"And, cover your tracks."*

Casey starting to visualise '*The Pink Panther*' sneaking around, with Peter Sellers as the hapless Inspector Clouseau on his tail; raincoat and magnifying glass in hand. *"Da-da, Da-da, Da-da-da-da-da, da-daaaa!"* sung in his head as he struggled to keep the smirk off his face in front of Marco. The boss was being serious so couldn't understand Casey's nonchalant expression; little did he know the comedy sketch running through his mind.

The following day Casey did as he was told, but out of devilment wore some pink socks. Upon arrival, he asked the cab driver to wait for him in the lane behind Marco's house. The garden gate was unlocked, yet complained with a loud squeak as Casey pushed it open. As his eyes started to scan the length of the manicured lawn, his glaze gravitated to an ornate water fountain of a stone angel, showering water into a fishpond below. A click of the back door opening broke his moment of absentmindedness. Marco was stood there silently, staring at him as if to say *'Hurry up.'* Casey marched quickly towards the house.

Marco had seen the taxi approaching up the lane and had unlocked the back gate in readiness. Casey was in awe at the extravagance lavished on his boss's lounge. Expensive sculptures of china and gold were placed with precision on highly polished cabinets. The marble fireplace was almost obscured by a vast amount of delicate glass ornaments, reaching a crescendo on the mantelpiece with a prized glass domed carriage clock.

Casey was ushered to sit on a sumptuous tapestry sofa. On the coffee table before him sat a black holdall, which Marco prised open. *"In here is five grand of used notes. You go to this address and exchange it for ten grand of newly printed notes, then bring it straight back here. Capisce?"*

Casey nodded as he zipped up the holdall. Just then a timid woman shuffled into the room. She had long black hair and was dressed immaculately. She was slightly overweight, which exaggerated her round face; Casey thought she looked beautiful, yet he could see the pain in her eyes and lips that had forgotten how to smile. *"I won't be here when you get back, I like to have an alibi. Give the money to my wife Sofia and she'll give you fifty quid, not bad for a couple of hours work,"* Marco chuckled. Casey looked at the boss, then his downtrodden wife, then cast his stare back to Marco. With a nod Casey left to complete his task.

The taxi took him to a part of the town that he didn't know. The address Casey had been given, took him to a bakery situated in a parade of shops. *"Wait here for me,"* he told the driver. The instructions which he had on a scrap of paper, directed Casey down an alleyway next to the bakery, and into a small arcade of bow-fronted craft shops. He imagined them covered in Christmas decorations, enticing shoppers to buy their wares. *"Number five, where's number five?"* he questioned himself, as most of the units only had names. He found a clock-makers door with the number five painted over, obscuring its identity. A small bell rang above the door as Casey pushed it open. Behind the counter an elderly man was working on a dismantled clock. Briefly glancing up he said, *"Take the bag into the back room,"* then he continued with his task.

167

*"Hello dear,"* greeted Casey as he opened the connecting door. A small grey haired woman was sat a workbench, polishing the wooden case of a grandfather clock. *"Close the door dear, we don't want any prying eyes."* Casey did as instructed.

Casey had entered a surreal world of normality that he didn't expect; far removed from the tough world he battled in, he found a charming yet perfect cover that no one would question. The little old lady beckoned Casey to place his holdall on the bench for inspection. Once she was satisfied with the contents, she unlocked a drawer beneath her workstation, revealing wads of bank notes. *"Come on dear, let's get busy,"* as she started to empty the holdall, counting the contents as she went. With a nod of approval, she proceeded to refill the bag with wads of notes from her drawer. Casey was amazed at her slick movements, cramming the holdall to the brim. There was little time for pleasantries; she ushered him out of the door, saying, *"Thank Mr Rossi for doing business."* He was back in the arcade as if the last few minutes were an absentminded daydream. Moments later, the taxi was returning him back to his boss's house.

Casey pushed open the stiff gate allowing him access into the Rossi's back garden. He could see Sofia watching him approach the house from behind patio doors, her eyes appeared to be watching his every step. She opened the door and beckoned him inside. *"Err, hello Mrs Rossi,"* he said cautiously, handing her the holdall. Their eyes locked for what seemed to be an eternity; her dark brown eyes drew him in, as a moth to a candle flame. *"Call me Sofia,"* she muttered, shyly dropping her gaze.

Sofia placed the holdall on the coffee table, leaning over to check the contents. Casey noticed her blouse gape open, giving him a glimpse of her ample cleavage. *'No, no this is wrong,'* he thought to himself, only managing to avert his gaze before he got caught out. *"Here's your wages,"* Sofia said handing him a plain envelope, *"I'm sure I'll see you next time."* Casey's stare was transfixed on her shiny lipstick mouthing her words. With a smug smile he replied, *"Yeah, for sure,"* before heading out the patio door. As he reached the garden gate, he turned back to see her stood in the doorway. He thought to himself, *"Ummm, M.I.L.F."* as she waved him goodbye.

Part 14

"*Boo!*" joked Colin, screeching with laughter from a hiding place behind his desk. He loved to tease Thomas when Tess brought him into the office. The infant would giggle with laughter as Colin chased him around the room, much to the delight of Tess. "*Shhh! Keep it down, you two,*" teased a grinning Bert. "*Why can't Kelvin have more fun with Thomas?*" she sighed under her breath; the youngster was a bundle of energy that just wanted to play.

Colin had never had a girlfriend so far and considered himself as a happily single, although he had always hoped his friendship with Tess would be more than friendship. His affection for Thomas was clear to see, whereas his affection for Tess was a closely guarded secret. Sometimes when their eyes met, he felt a connection, or maybe he was just living in hope. '*That waste of space boyfriend of hers,*' didn't treat her right, not the way he would, if only he had half a chance; fate was a cruel master, he doubted Tess would ever love him the way he secretly loved her.

Still living at home with his parents William and Winifred, he felt comfortable in his man-cave of a bedroom; the walls adorned with Space and Sci-Fi posters, his favourite being Star Wars. Colin had stood in line at the cinema on the first day that the film was released, soaked to the skin but undeterred to see the film on the big screen. He'd picked up the poster in the foyer, thankfully the rain had stopped when he left, so his prized procession got home unscathed. Harrison Ford's eyes seemed to follow Colin around the room, enticing him to wave a pretend light sabre in mock battle, recalling scenes from the film.

*"Morning Colin,"* Cathy chirped, as he walked into the office carrying a packet of doughnuts. *"Umm, you know how to get on the right side of me,"* she chuckled at the sight of cakes, *"Hope they are all for me?"* Colin loved the banter and replied with a smile, *"No, but you can have the first pick."*

Just at that moment Bert appeared in the doorway of his office and joined into the horseplay, *"Is there one there for me too?"* Colin laughed at the verbal ambush and said, *"Okay you win, and you'll be wanting a brew with that. I'd best put the kettle on,"* he said scurrying off to the kitchen. Colin saw Bert as more of a father figure than his own dad; he had huge respect for his boss.

* * *

*"You've filled this bloody cup to the brim again!"* Will ranted, as he spilt his cup of tea over his lap. His shaky hands tried to dab the spillage with a tissue as Winnie fussed over him. *"Get out of the bloody way woman!"* he ranted, storming out of the room to change his trousers. *'Here we go again, another one of dad's moods,'* thought Colin; he decided to keep his head down to avoid being drawn into the argument. He'd noticed his dad occasionally jerked his movements and thought nothing of it, but the arguments were becoming more frequent; hence he spent more time in his bedroom. *"I'd best go and help your father,"* Winnie muttered to Colin as she headed out of the room.

172

Colin could hear snippets of the conversation coming from their bedroom. The tone had calmed and he heard his father say, *"Sorry Winnie, I didn't mean to shout."* His parents seemed to get along, although the only comparison he had was Bert and Doris, who were much more playful.

William and Winifred ran a small grocery store, situated in a row of Victorian terraced houses. They had been working there for well over two decades, taking the family business over from William's father, who had died suddenly of a heart attack in his mid-fifties. His mother couldn't cope and had to move in with her sister in Oswestry, leaving Will and Winnie to bring up the youngster in the flat above the shop. Colin had no back garden to play in and the frontage was directly onto a busy street, leaving him little chance to build friendships with other kids. Therefore, a solitary world was born in his bedroom.

Will was great with the customers and had a spiv-like charm about retail, but the tax man was always on his back and it was clear that times were changing, much quicker than he'd liked. The suppliers started to used automated systems and talk in a language that he didn't understand. The last few years had been a confusing time for Will, with the introduction of Value Added Tax, making his bookkeeping more of a chore. *"Colin, your mother and I think it'll be good for us if you went to college, to learn about these business studies things that people are talking about,"* Will instructed him in a matter-of-fact manner. Colin's heart sank at the thought, yet after much persuasion by his parents, he reluctantly agreed.

Almost a year into the course and he'd had enough of studying. His classmates all had aspirations to seek out top

173

jobs, whereas this seemed way out of his reach. They had wealthy parents who would give them generous allowances, his parents gave him a pittance. Colin was desperate to earn a wage, to stand on his own two feet and buy some trendy clothes that he just couldn't afford. He had his eye on a pair of baggy trousers with a fashionable three-belt waistband and a pair of platform shoes. Will scoffed and said that fashion was a waste of money.

The fickle finger of fate spun its magic, as he scanned the local newspaper for latest cinema times. The adjacent page was the job vacancy page, something that Colin never thought to explore; yet one advertisement caught his attention.

*Office junior required for local manufacturer, no experience required. Apply to Bert Clifton.*

On his way home from college, he summoned up the courage to detour to the factory. Taking a deep breath, he rang the bell next to a small plaque stating *'Reception.'* A plump lady in an apron opened the door and said, *"Yes dear?"*

Colin's cheeks flushed with embarrassment as he spoke, *"Excuse me madam, but I see you are advertising for an office junior."* Doris chuckled and said, *"Come on in dear, you can speak to my husband Bert."*

Another argument ensued when Colin told his father that he had found a job and was dropping out of college; this time Will directed his rant at Colin, who scampered to his room before his father really lost it. A few minutes later his mother tapped on his bedroom door, *"Don't worry son, here's a cup of tea. If that's what you want to do, I'm sure your father will come around."* Colin seemed to walk on eggshells for the next few days, waiting for the same argument to erupt again, but it never did and it was never spoken about again.

Colin noticed that his father was becoming more frustrated with his own clumsiness, chastising himself openly. *"Don't worry dear,"* became Winnie's answer to all his mishaps, although Colin could see the concern in her eyes with his mood swings. Since he had left college, there was a tension in the air making him feel uncomfortable. His father seemed to be constantly stressed and confrontational. Winnie fussed around to keep the peace wherever she could, often receiving more wrath for her trouble. Colin felt guilty, as if he'd abandoned the ship, but he did work around the shop most evenings to make amends.

* * *

*"Hello Colin,"* welcomed Cathy on his first day in the office. Colin was very nervous to start his new job, although he'd had a lot of work experience in his parents shop. *"I'll show you around,"* Cathy continued, prompting the young lad to follow her. Tapping on the boss's office, the door creaked open. *"Hello Bert, Colin's here."* He was greeted with a handshake from his new boss and a beaming smile from a petit, blonde girl in a school uniform. Bert went on to say, *"This is my daughter Tess, and she'll be working for us when her exams have finished."* Colin seemed frozen with nerves not knowing what to say, until he muttered, *"Um, Err, hello."*

Obviously blushing and stumbling over his words, was the first impression he left Tess. *"Hello Colin,"* she said, *"I don't bite,"* giggling to herself. Colin could have kicked himself, because of his embarrassment, but, *'Wow,'* he thought to himself. That was the first time he saw her and throughout the years he'd known her that feeling never changed. She saw him as a brother and confided in him, but he wanted more than just friendship, yet being friends was still a good thing, although he had eyes for no one else.

Colin took an instant dislike to the cocksure Kelvin when they first met; he felt that he'd taken advantage of an innocent princess, impregnating his vile seed inside her. He didn't like conflict, so Colin gave him a wide berth, although their chance meetings were few and far between.

*"Here you go Tess,"* said Colin, sliding a hot water bottle down the back of her chair, to ease her painful backache. *"Oh thanks, you are a darling,"* she replied with a grimacing grin. Their friendship had grown throughout her pregnancy; seeing her through bouts of morning sickness, puffy ankles and constantly cursing the thoughtless future father of her child became a daily routine. Colin didn't mind pandering to her needs, which she gratefully accepted. He looked forward to seeing her every morning, but was fearful that his world would fall apart when the baby was born. She would be leaving work to play happy-families with Kelvin: the thought made him feel jealous.

Tess allayed his fears by bringing the new baby into the office most days. Their friendship had been cemented and Colin felt privileged to be classed as family. It was clearly stressful for Tess to cope, but she had a good support network of Bert, Doris, Cathy and now the lucky Colin. She and Kelvin had moved in a house not far from the factory, close enough for the watchful eye of Bert Clifton.

* * *

*"Tommy, Tommy where are you?"* Tess called from her father's office. She had taken him to the factory to see Bert. Whilst she was engrossed in conversation, he had slipped out of the room. ***"Thomas! You little sod, where are you?"*** The two-year-old infant was curious and knew the place well. Colin noticed the side door open, which led to the main road. He peered through the door, only to see the toddler stood in the street playing with leaves blowing in the wind; oblivious to the danger of a speeding car heading towards him. As quick as a flash, Colin bolted across the road, managing to scoop up the toddler in his arms, as the car squealed to a halt. There seemed to be an everlasting moment of silence before Thomas started to cry and Tess started to scream.

Colin stood frozen to the spot, with Thomas tightly nestled in his arms. Tess rushed to her son and prised him from Colin's grip, so she could cradle him reassuringly. With her spare arm she tightly hugged Colin around the neck and kissed him on the cheek. *"Thank you, thank you, thank you,"* she repeated, before sobbing on his shoulder. Colin felt a little uncomfortable with the attention and was relieved when Bert arrived to console his distressed daughter.

Cathy made a pot of tea for them all as they returned to the office; soon they were all giggling with relief and cursing the unlocked door. Thomas soon forgot the incident and continued to play with the few toys left for him in the

177

office. *"Thank you Colin,"* Bert said shaking his hand, with sincere gratitude. Colin wanted to avoid any more attention or conversations about the incident, so he slid onto the floor to play with Thomas. Doris arrived with cakes, turning their play into a tea party under the desk.

Part 15

The shards of glass hitting the pavement, sounded like the gentle rustle of a wind chime. The searing pain from the breaking bottle on the back of Casey's head, distorted his vision. A punishing blow to his lower back forced him to the floor, where his assailants took advantage with fierce kicks to his body. Casey winced in agony unable to scream out the pain, which exploded inside him. His breath rasped as he struggled to inhale, for it only to be kicked from him with another punishing blow. Realising the more he reacted the more punishment he would receive, he accepted his fate until he was on the verge of passing out.

He could feel them rifling through his pockets and a muffled sound of them talking but nothing was audible above the ringing in his ears. A honk of a car horn sent the assailants fleeing. Casey could only see the two blurred figures running from the scene; there was nothing to identify them. He could only assume the getaway driver had signalled them as it sped off soon after.

Casey pulled himself up so he could check the damage. Blood trickled down the back of his head and he was sure he had a broken rib, but visibly he had survived quite well. On checking his pockets he screamed, *"Bastards!"* as he realised they had robbed him of two hundred pounds. *"The boss will go ape-shit,"* he thought. Staggering along the darkened alleyway, he headed for the hostel to clean himself up.

Marco was sat at the nightclub bar, writing in one of his ledgers when Casey arrived. *"Boss, I need a word in your office,"* Casey firmly said. As Marco entered his office, he lowered himself into the leather swivel chair behind his desk, listening suspiciously to Casey's version of events. The boss unemotionally ordered, *"You know the rules lad, unless I get the money back, you work for me for free until the debt is paid."* Casey nodded without saying a word; his pride was dented more than his pocket. The boss continued to say, *"You can do another money exchange for me tomorrow as a down-payment."*

\* \* \*

*"What in the hell happened to you?"* Tess snapped as Kelvin walked into the house. *"Two guys jumped me on the way home. Stop nagging woman!"* he retorted, heading off to the bathroom to shower. Standing naked in front of the mirror he could see a couple of bruises developing on his ribs, one was extremely sore to the touch; the knock to the back of his head was only a small cut once the blood was cleaned away. He considered himself lucky.

Cleaned and refreshed he retired to his bed, where the scowling Tess cast him an icy stare. *"I'm sorry Tess for snapping, it's just been a bad day,"* Kelvin mumbled, then kissed her on the cheek. Tess accepted his apology, turning to put her arm around him. Sleep came easy for both of them.

*"Are you going to report the attack to the police?"* Tess questioned Kelvin over breakfast. He raised his head in shock at the prospect, almost spitting his tea across the kitchen table, *"Err, no. It was all so quick and I wouldn't*

180

*recognise them again."* He quickly munched noisily on his toast, to avert any more conversation. The less contact he had with the police the better; he had been lucky to keep off their radar and that is how he wanted things to stay.

The taxi's brakes squeaked to a halt at the back of the Rossi household. *"Wait here,"* Casey instructed the cab driver. He found the back gate unlocked, giving him access to the rear garden. Tapping on the patio doors didn't draw any attention; the door lever smoothly turned, silently opening the lounge door. *"Hello, is anyone there?"* Casey called. In reply, he heard a torrent of muffled shouting from upstairs. Marco was screaming abuse, although the words weren't clear, Casey froze on the spot. He imagined dry ice cascading down the staircase, forming into an effigy of his father bellowing at a cowering silhouette of his mother. In that fleeting moment, he resorted to being the abused child of many years before.

The young Kelvin had a favourite toy, a green plastic soldier that stood two inches tall. It had a small shield and an upturned sword. The model was fixed to a base, rigid and firm, but unable to move. Today Casey was that toy soldier, glued to the floor, unable to free the shackles of his solidified stance. The memories of his childhood fear, streamed like lava through his veins.

*"Casey! Casey!"* broke his trance. *"Casey!"* screamed Sofia from the doorway, *"He's in a right mood, grab the bag and go."* His eyes flicked across the room to see a dishevelled Sofia, clearly frightened. *"Just go!"* she prompted him. Casey nodded, grabbed the bag from the coffee table and left. He could still hear the ranting as he approached the gate, although glancing back, Sofia was

stood at the patio doors; maybe the boss was venting at someone else rather than his wife, but Casey was worried for her safety.

The taxi ride became a blur, as Casey's mind was occupied with the affray at the Rossi household. Although he knew that Marco had a foul temper, he'd never experienced it first-hand. The roar of the beast from the room above, echoed through his head, his thoughts kept returning to the vulnerable Sofia. *"Hey mate, is this the place?"* asked the taxi driver as he pulled up outside the bakery. Casey's consciousness was shaken back into the moment, flicking his eyes between the driver's gaze and the row of shops outside, *"Yeah, wait for me, I won't be long."*

Clutching the holdall, he headed down the alleyway to find the clock-maker at number five. Soon after Casey rang the bell, a frail figure unbolted the door. The elderly man had been tinkering at the counter with the mechanics of an old timepiece; without saying a word, he beckoned Casey to go through to the back room to make the exchange with his wife.

* * *

Marco was sat on the edge of the bed tying his shoelaces when he received a call from Benny that firstly stunned him into shock, and then sent his anger into orbit. *"Boss, I've heard James and John are dead."* These were Marco's best lads, his most trusted and loyal men. The brothers had been found sacrificed in an alleyway. They had been tied side by side to some railings, arms outstretched as if bound to a crucifix. Their throats had been cut and their tongues pulled through the bloody slits to give the appearance of human

182

cravats. This was clearly a professional hit aimed at the heart of the Rossi Empire; a ritual killing with an unspoken message.

As the description was relayed to Marco, visions of the bloody mutilation spun around in his head making him feel vulnerable and exposed. Searing lava gauged across his throat, imaging how the fatal injury would feel if he had been tethered to the fence alongside his *'Boys.'* The thought that he was no longer invincible scared him like never before. He had fled from those feelings a long time ago, when he had to flee The Scorpion; then he was young and naïve. Even with his violent maturity, this incident unnerved him.

Flashing through his mind were the stories of Mafia hits when he was much younger, how they had brutally killed those who had crossed them and left their bodies mutilated for all to see. *"Was this their trademark? Was this a warning of worse things to come?"* The not knowing unnerved him. Maybe he was just being paranoid, as twenty years had passed since he had fled Italy. As much as Marco had a list of small-time enemies that would gladly see him suffer, this was different; he had no idea who was brave enough or stupid enough to take him on. His arrogance had always left him feeling untouchable, yet this was the first time in recent years that he felt vulnerable. He had gained so much exploited wealth, demanded so much false respect from the community, that now he had so much to lose. When he had nothing, he had nothing to lose; now he had weaknesses that could be exploited.

Whether he was becoming sloppy or self-absorbed, he hadn't seen this coming. There had been no word on the street about anyone trying to muscle-in on his patch or confrontation that could put him on guard. This faceless enemy screwed with his mind, twisting and distorting logic that could only be vented with rage. Benny could only stay silent and listen to Marco's roar of profanities during their telephone call; even the muffled conversations from downstairs that he assumed would be Casey, didn't dissuade the verbal attack on his anonymous assailants.

Marco ended the call abruptly by throwing his phone violently against the wall, smashing it on impact. He bellowed like an injured lion as he punched the bedroom door. In one swoop of his arm, he swept the contents of Sofia's dressing table crashing to the floor, her vanity mirror smashed to pieces. Marco launched the dressing stool with such force, that it broke a picture over their bed and dented the wall. Storming down the staircase, he saw a petrified Sofia stood in his way, transfixed at his approach. *"Get out of my way!"* he demanded, just before his hand swiped the side of her face with a violent blow. She lost her balance and fell to the floor. The front door was left wide open as Marco leapt into his car and sped off.

Sofia managed to pull herself up from the floor and closed the front door. She needed to block the world out before she could sob uncontrollably. Curling up on the sofa, she cried until her tear-ducts ran dry. She felt so empty, so alone and so ugly. Her inner-self chastised her weakness, but also endorsed her worthless existence; she had made her bed and had to lay in it, even if it was a loveless bed with an adulterous and abusive monster. Her thoughts were consumed, trying to make sense of a twisted dark mess, only to be interrupted by a noise in the garden. The unexpected rattle of the back gate made her jump out of her skin. Cowering, she peered from behind the cushion pressed firmly to her chest, to see Casey walking up the path.

She wasn't sure if she felt relieved to see him or fearful that she would have to explain the incident. Sofia used the back of her hand to wipe the smudged makeup from her face, before Casey reached the patio doors. Rummaging for a tissue, she blew her nose and dabbed a stray tear from her eye.

*"Oh my god, are you okay?"* asked Casey with genuine concern. She didn't say a word as Casey sat next to her, just bowing her head so her hair could hide her sorrowful face. He gently swept away her locks to reveal her bruised eye and split lip. She didn't move her head, but her eyes turned to catch his gaze; her tears started to flow once more as she buried her face into his shoulder. Casey uncomfortably put his arm around her as she sobbed once more. He had no words to console her.

Sofia's wailing softened to a whimper as she lifted her head to look at Casey. Their embrace felt warm and comforting to her, in way that she'd never experienced with Marco; not even in their early days, when she had fallen head over heels in love with the young waiter, had she felt anything near to affection from him. She stared into Casey's eyes as if time had stood still, and then kissed him on the lips. He was taken aback by her unexpected boldness before responding, locking their mouths in a passionate moment of madness. Sofia's body yearned to feel wanted, to feel desired as they pawed at each other's clothing.

Sofia unzipped his trousers and forced her hand inside his pants to grip his growing erection. He recoiled slightly in

185

unexpected embarrassment, but her hand held firm stopping him from resisting her; Casey slid down his trousers and pants much to her approval. There was a moment of stillness, maybe anticipation or disbelief. The only thing visible was their panting chests; the sound of their excited breath broke the silence.

Casey slid his hand up her skirt to an unusual sensation for him, of her unshaven thighs. Looking down he could see her legs smooth below the knee, yet above, fine black hairs tickling his palm. A little higher, his hand was greeted with the fabric of a functional pair of black knickers, which he quickly tugged down revealing a thick mop of black pubic hair. Lust blocked out all sanity as they writhed half naked on the sofa, not even considering the consequences of getting caught. Intercourse was frantic and brief before Casey's orgasm exploded inside her.

Both left panting and bewildered as to what just happened, Sofia said, *"You'd better go,"* as she pulled down her skirt. Casey nodded as he buttoned his trousers and shuffled towards the door. Looking back he saw an embarrassed woman wrapping herself tightly with her clothes, *"Will you be okay?"* Sofia was fidgeting with her buttons then snapped at him, *"Yes, just go!"*

The enormity of what had just happened, struck him when he realised the waiting taxi had gone. *"Shit, shit, shit,"* he rebuked himself; he had been in the house far too long. The fare would be paid by The Roxy's account, but he was worried about the gossip. *'Heyho'* he thought, it was a new driver so maybe he would think that was normal. As he walked down the lane towards the main road, he became aroused once again at the memory of their passionate encounter. *"Man, she was fricking hot,"* he voiced to himself with a huge grin.

Casey bumped into Jenny, one of the barmaids at The Roxy as he got off the bus in the town centre. *"The boss is looking for you. He's raging so you'd better get your arse down to the club, pronto!"* His mood changed to pure fear at what could be waiting for him.

Part 16

*"Oh crap!"* he rebuked himself heading towards the club, *"I'm in deep shit now."* He really wanted to go home rather than face the angry Marco, but knew his fate would follow him wherever he went. Veering off course through the doors of the first bar he found, two shots of whiskey quickly slid down his dry throat. *"I've got to front this out,"* he muttered to himself as he consumed the third double whiskey. Leaving the bar, he nervously headed for The Roxy, imagining the punishment due.

After a deep intake of breath, he swung open the doors to the nightclub. In the middle of the dance floor stood Marco, surrounded by six muscle-bound doormen; as he approached they all stopped talking at the same moment, turning to stare at him. Trying to seem brave, he pulled his shoulders back and swaggered towards them. Benny appeared from the shadows behind him, and followed Casey to the circle of men.

He was now surrounded with no means of escape. Turning his head slowly, he locked glares with each man in turn; Benny shuffled uneasily behind him. Casey could feel his heart pounding as sweat trickled down his forehead. "*Shit, Shit, Shit!*" shouted in his head. Marco was pacing from side to side just like a pacing lion stalking it's prey; staring directly into Casey's eyes, he burned a channel to his core. He was more frightened than he'd ever been outnumbered and extremely vulnerable. *"Shit, shit, fucking shit!"*

*"W-what's up boss?"* Casey's voice echoed around the room.

*"What's up? What's up? I'll fucking tell you what's up!"* Marco ranted. *"James and John were sacrificed last night, and I don't know who in the hell did it!"* the boss continued. Casey expelled a sigh of relief at the most inappropriate moment, which raised some confused looks from some of the doormen. Trying to defuse his reaction, Casey said, *"That's awful boss, what are we going to do about it?"*

After a stony silence, Marco addressed his troops, *"We can't show any weakness on the street so business as usual, but I've gotta find out who's trying to muscle-in on my operation. I've got to squash them quick! So everyone get out there and lean on people."*

As the group dispersed, Marco called after Casey, ***"A quiet word in my office!"***

His feelings of relief skyrocketed to nervous fear in the space of those six words. Bowing his head in a submissive pose, he followed the boss up the back staircase. As Marco sat behind his leather bound desk, Casey's stomach cramps made him involuntarily break wind. Marco stared deeply in the young man's eyes for what seemed an eternity, before saying, *"Your recent mugging must be linked to the executions last night, so your debt to me has been wiped. Hit the debtors hard this week and you'll be able to do another money exchange next week."*

Casey swaggered out of The Roxy with a cocky arrogance. *"The dickhead hasn't gotta clue I banged his missus,"* Casey chuckled nervously to himself. The next bar he

190

reached was called The Stag. It seemed an appropriate place to down a few more whiskeys and reminisce about his sexual encounter with the horny Sofia. It was just after seven o'clock when Casey decided to stagger home.

*"Where in the hell have you been? Look at the state of you,"* scorned Tess as he noisily stumbled into their house. *"Thomas has just fallen asleep and you're going to wake him up. You selfish bastard,"* she continued. Without saying a word in reply, Casey sat on the sofa, kicked off his shoes and promptly slipped into a deep sleep. *"You drunken tosser!"* Tess spat in disgust, as she headed off to her bedroom, leaving him there to sleep it off.

Casey abruptly woke from his comatose sleep, as Tess noisily banged saucepans in the kitchen. She promptly switched on the radio, and then sang loudly along to the track playing, which was Donna Summers', *'I will survive'*. *"Daddy, daddy!"* screeched little Tommy, just before he launched himself onto his delicate father.

Tess slopped the contents of a cup of tea, which she set down on the coffee table in front of him. *"I only seem to see you when you're pissed, it's the third time this week!"* thundered Tess. All he could see stood over him was the image of his raging mother, as if blasting his father, ***"You drunken gob-shite, you treat this place like a doss-house!"*** Brenda had to pick her battles, whilst the hung over Terry was unable to retaliate. Now her scorn was directed at the young Kelvin, cowering under her wrath, ***"You fecking eejit, you're turning into your father!"***

Bowing his head in shame, the timid Kelvin apologised to Tess and headed for a shower; a cold shower, or maybe a

191

cold light of day shower. Kelvin only had negative role models to follow as he grew up, maybe dragged up would be more appropriate. His life with Tess was filled with the comfort and security of a clean family home, but also, he was enticed by the glamour of working for a mobster, the money and the bevy of easy girls. He was too immature to reconcile the two; he was naïve to think he could have both.

Rossi was frustrated at being unable to contact his employees, that he bought them all the latest Motorola Pager on the market, so he could get hold of them anywhere. The device bleeped. The message simply said, *"Call me."* Marco was the only one with the number, so Casey found the nearest pay phone and called him. *"Casey! I'm going out of town for a couple of days, but I need you to do a money exchange tomorrow, Capisce?"* Without a second thought Casey replied, *"Yes boss."* A large grin spread across his face.

\* \* \*

Tess was engrossed washing up the breakfast things as Casey entered the kitchen. Tommy was running around the table, arms outstretched pretending to be an aeroplane. *"Err Tess, I'm not working today so shall we take Tommy to the park?"* Tess was shocked at his interest in them and nervously replied, *"Oh, ok. That would be nice,"* then softened her stern expression. *"Maybe we could take a picnic,"* she continued. Casey nodded, already preoccupied with the thoughts of tomorrow.

For Tess, this was the best day they had spent together as a family in ages; watching Kelvin play with little Tommy, picnic in the park, then dinner at her parent's house. Bert and Doris seemed pleased to have Kelvin to visit, a rare treat for all of them. She was glad that Kelvin had made the effort for a change. They spent the evening making passionate love; it had been quite a while. She thought that he'd lost interest in her, but cocooned in her warm bubble she enjoyed the moment. Casey enjoyed the same moment, yet he was fantasising about what he wanted to do to the sexy Sofia.

The taxi journey to the Rossi's household seemed to take ages, with traffic delays and road works. Casey felt frustrated but also excited. Thoughts returned to his fantasies whilst wrapped in the arms of Tess, his erection starting to grow. *"Wait here,"* he instructed the driver as they reached the rear entrance of his boss's home. The click of the gate latch seemed louder than normal, maybe he was just heavy-handed with excitement. Sofia was stood at the patio doors, watching his every step across the lawn.

Casey paused for a moment as he reached the doorway, staring into Sofia's eyes. His gaze soon dropped to her ample cleavage; as he reached to paw her, she stepped back into the room. *"Easy tiger, you have a job to do,"* she teased. *"You, are the job I want to do,"* he flirted. She could see the obvious bulge in his trousers and encouraged it further by rubbing her hand over the taut fabric of his trousers. Her eyes became transfixed as her palm toyed with his penis, as if she was using a rolling pin to flatten pastry. Dropping to her knees she unzipped his trousers to free his frustrated erection, then she quickly gave Casey the best blowjob he'd ever had. *"That's just for starters,"* she chuckled, *"Now get going before the taxi driver suspects anything."* Grabbing the holdall from the coffee table, he trotted across the garden towards the gate.

A quizzical look from the driver made Casey feel a little uneasy, but nothing could hide the huge grin he had across his face. He floated in a daydream as the taxi bounced over the potholes, his trance only broken the when driver repeated, *"We're here now."* Casey cast him an embarrassed look and replied, *"Ok, I won't be long."*

*"My, we are in a good mood today,"* chirped the grey haired lady from behind a bench in the back room of the clock maker's shop. Casey tried to play it down by adopting a more serious demeanour. Contents checked and holdalls exchanged, Casey parted with, *"See ya next time."* His thoughts already on session number two with the sexy Sofia.

*"I'll make my own way back."* Casey said dismissively to the taxi driver as they reached the gate to the Rossi's garden. The gate opened swiftly with a loud squeak, clattering behind him as he closed it. Casey swaggered across the lawn with the holdall draped over his shoulder. At the patio doors his mood went from excitement to pure fear within the blink of an eye.

Marco was pacing the lounge, engrossed in a telephone conversation. Sofia walked into the room holding a cup of coffee; at the sight of Casey, her bland expression turning to shear panic as she handed the brew to her husband. Marco was too preoccupied with his call to notice anything. He glanced up at Casey and gestured him to leave the holdall on the coffee table as he continued to pace the room. Sofia and Casey froze to the spot like two naughty children waiting to be scolded.

*"I know its business, but they've made it personal,"* Marco chanted into the receiver, *"Yeah, yeah, we have to show strength,"* he continued. His pacing led him into the hallway, giving the two lovers a moment to themselves. Casey hesitantly instructed, *"Sofia, I've got to see you again. Come to the Hostel in Kings Street tomorrow at midday."* Their eyes locked for a brief moment before Marco came back into the room. Casey nodded as Marco handed him an envelope in payment for his services. He left not knowing Sofia's response.

Tess noticed that Kelvin was preoccupied when he came home, but he seemed in a good mood so she was satisfied. They both played with little Tommy, and then later walked over to her parents for dinner; it felt like a normal evening for her. That night Kelvin was a passionate animal in the bedroom, exciting Tess more than ever before. She felt wanted and desired; she felt a spark that had been missing for so long. *'Why?'* she didn't question; whereas Casey had Sofia firmly on his mind.

Casey was up and out of the house early before Tess could question his movements for the day. He treated himself to a cooked breakfast at the café near the train station. He'd always flirted with the lovely Sarah, who worked there on the morning shift, but today Sofia was firmly on his mind. Stomach full, he took the short walk to his love nest; the grotty, rundown hostel that didn't look so special in the cold light of day.

He found a half empty bottle of whiskey stashed in his wardrobe and took two large mouthfuls of the harsh liquid. Casey thought, *"Dutch courage or drown my sorrow,"* depending whether she shows up or not. Looking around his

195

shabby room, he straightened it as best as he could. It was eleven o'clock and he was pacing the room in anticipation, checking his watch every few minutes. At eleven thirty, he could wait no longer, so decided to wait outside the hostel on the steps; after all, she didn't know which room he was in. Scouring up and down the street, he was on lookout, but through the busy bustle of pedestrians, he saw no Sofia. It was now twelve twenty-five, *"I'll give her another five minutes,"* he voiced to himself.

*"Casey?"* a familiar voice spoke from behind him. He turned to see an unrecognisable Sofia stood in sports clothing and a baseball cap; dark sunglasses covered her eyes. *"I didn't want to be noticed,"* she reassured him as they stepped into the lobby. Maybe, it was more to reassure her as Marco had a lot of friends in the town.

Sofia's eyes surveyed the tiny bedroom, sterile of personality, lacking of any warmth. It was a seedy venue for their sordid liaison, but the setting seemed to excite her even more. Glued to the spot, Casey started to peel off her clothes, leaving her naked to his gaze. Goosebumps formed all over her body as he ran his rough hands over her flesh. Sofia could feel the hard skin on his callus ridden right palm as it scratched the skin of her buttock, sending a shiver to her core. Excitement built in her body, yet cement seemed to flow through her veins, rendering her immobile; unable to move herself to respond to him. *"Oh just fuck me Casey,"* she muttered squirming with pleasure to his touch. Casey just grinned and continued to tease her.

She was longing to undress him, but it was only her eyes that could move. She had to watch Casey undress himself, exposing the obvious excitement that he had. He walked naked towards her, proudly displaying his ridged cock, pressing it flat against her stomach as their bodies met. His hands grabbed her buttocks and collided their hips together. Sofia let out a gasp before he started to kiss her. After a moment, Sofia flung her arms around his neck as she responded passionately to his probing tongue.

He pulled her onto the tiny bed. Their bodies became lost in exciting and passionate intercourse. Sofia had never felt so aroused and exhilarated. She felt a freedom that had escaped her life up until now. Their sticky bodies writhed on the confines of the mattress, until they fell on the floor to continue their antics. They didn't care if anyone could hear their cries of ecstasy; they were lost in space and time.

Exhausted, they wrapped themselves in the duvet. Casey grabbed the remains of the whiskey bottle and poured the fiery spirit in a single tumbler that they could share. *"Have you lived on your own for long?"* Sofia asked before sipping from the glass. Not wanting to confess his relationship with Tess, he massaged the truth by stating, *"I've had this room for about three years."* Sofia tipped the dregs of whiskey from the tumbler on Casey's chest, and then started to lick the spillage. Their excited bodies returned to a place divorced from reality as she straddled his body once more.

Sofia looked at her watch and exclaimed, *"Oh crap! Its four o'clock I'd better go home."* Casey glumly nodded, wrapped himself in a towel and headed for the communal toilet. Sofia dressed whilst he was out of the room, but playfully pushed her soiled knickers in his discarded jeans pockets. *"A memento for him later,"* she chuckled to herself.

197

*"Okay lover-boy, I've got to go,"* Sofia quipped as Casey came back into the room. She pecked him on the cheek and said, *"I'll see you soon, very soon."* Leaving before Casey could talk her into staying any longer.

Casey lay naked on the bed staring at the ceiling. *"Wow, fucking wow!"* he screamed, and then let out a '*Whoop!*' sound.

After quickly showering at the hostel, Casey dressed and headed for the nearest bar for a couple of celebration drinks. He hadn't eaten since breakfast, so the alcohol was starting to go to his head. He was feeling very mellow, even an insult about his shaven head from one of the locals didn't provoke a reaction. Nothing could upset his mood.

A supermarket near his house provided a pit stop for cans of beer to take home. Tess was at her parents when he went in, allowing him to consume a couple more beers before she came in. He was very chilled when he heard the front door open. *"Daddy, daddy!"* squealed Tommy.

Tess could clearly see how drunk he was, and then scowled, *"You've been drinking again. Get yourself to bed whilst you can still walk!"* Remorseful he nodded in agreement and stumbled up the staircase. As mad as Tess was with him, she also remembered the last couple of wonderful days. Thinking to herself, *"I'd better not be too hard on him."*

Tommy chuckled as he splashed in the bath. It was soon his bedtime. Tess curled up on his bed and read his favourite story; soon his eyes were dropping so she bid him good night. Last chore of the day was to put the washing in the machine so it would clean overnight. She gathered the

198

laundry basket from the bedroom and also the discarded clothes, which Kelvin had scattered on the floor.

Casey woke at five o'clock the next morning. It was clear that Tess hadn't been to bed; her side had not been slept in.

Part 17

Casey could see Tess slumped over the kitchen sink as he stepped into the room. His footsteps broke her trance; a glare of pure hatred flashed from her eyes as she hurled a cup at him, breaking against the wall next to his head.

*"You dirty rotten cheating bastard!"* Tess hissed, holding up the offending underwear. *"What slapper have you been with?"* Spittle sprayed from her lips like a venomous snake. She suspected his betrayal for some time, but the harsh reality was a sucker-punch that took her unawares. *"Get out! Get out you bastard!"* were the only words she could summon up; her mind was in turmoil, but the very sight of him turned her stomach.

Casey hung his head in shame and mumbled, *"Sorry."* Quickly dressing, he stepped out onto the street, clicking the front door quietly behind him.

*"You stupid little gob-shite, you fecked up a good thing,"* ranted Brenda in his head. *"Yeah, just like your good for nothing father. He was a bastard too,"* she echoed around his empty skull.

Casey shuffled along the empty street; it was just as empty as he felt. A milk cart rattled passed, making its early morning deliveries. His mind flashed back to his childhood and the tatty grocer's van, that appeared weekly outside his house. *'Fat bastard Fred'* abusing his mother for a bag full of food. Casey never appreciated how low she had to sink just to survive, the sacrifices she had to make. Now he was becoming *'A Fat Bastard Fred'* taking what he wanted. He wanted to be different from his role models, but didn't possess the skills or knowledge to change. His shame turned to contempt, his insecurities turned to bravado and his innocence to arrogance.

He had money in his pocket and women on tap, *"Who gives a fuck!"* he shouted at the top of his voice, echoing his contempt along the hollow street.

The café near the station was just opening as he approached. *"Time for a good breakfast,"* he said to himself. The regular waitress Sarah took his order and supplied him with a brimming cup of tea, *"Don't spill it,"* she joked, and *"I'll bring your breakfast over in a minute."* Casey's mind was preoccupied, so much so, that his breakfast had gone cold before he even realised it was there. *"She will take me back,"* he mused, *"When she calms down, she'll take me back."*

The Crown Inn was nearby and opened early to cater for its regular heavy drinkers. Stomach now full, Casey needed some *'Dutch Courage'* to talk to Tess or maybe a *'Hare of the Dog'* to settle his hangover; either way he was just making excuses for his increasing dependency for alcohol. After a couple of hours, the bar became filled with men slurring and talking incoherently. Casey was happy to join in with the revelry. Midday arrived, as Casey stumbled outside into the sunlight. The golden orb in the sky burnt his sensitive eyes. *"Time to face the music,"* he thought.

Nervously, he negotiated his key into the front door lock, and then pushed the door open. Stood in the hallway was a stern-faced Bert towering over three stuffed black bin liners.

*"She doesn't want to see you,"* Bert barked with authority, *"Its best if you move out."* Casey was taken aback, as he had not seen the dominant side of Bert before; his arrogance turned to guilt and didn't want any confrontation, so picked up his meagre belongs without uttering a word. *"Oh, and I'll have your door key as well,"* Bert continued, outstretching his hand.

Three bags of belongings were the sum total of his life so far; but not forgetting his wardrobe of designer clothes and bundles of cash at the hostel, *"I'll be okay,"* he mumbled to himself. Returning to live in the hostel filled him with dread. Although it was okay as a love shack, he had become used to a better way of life. He felt his tiny room had out served its purpose.

Over the next few days Casey scoured the local letting agents, until he found an exclusive city centre apartment, fully furnished with a security entrance. It would provide a sanctuary from the seedy world that now entwined him. Six month's rent in advance was easy to find from his stash.

Tess eventually responded to his messages, begging to see Tommy. She agreed to meet him every Sunday morning in the park, in exchange for maintenance money to support his son. Those couple of hours each week become precious and the highlight of Tommy's week. Casey's constant apologies fell on deaf ears as he disappointed his son week after week by not showing up; Tess could no longer trust or rely on him. Although she could see that Tommy enjoyed spending time with his father, it was an unacceptable situation.

Casey continued to work for Marco, piling in the cash whilst doing his dirty work. His new apartment impressed the sexy Sofia, christening every room with their lovemaking. His life was now a toxic mix of promiscuous sex, violent clashes and heavy drinking; his days blurred into one and his nights were filled with one-night stands from The Roxy.

* * *

Tommy had just nodded off to sleep when Tess heard a rap on the front door. Anxiously she opens the door a few inches, restricted by the security chain that Bert had fitted. Her fearful expression turned to a beaming smile, when she saw Colin stood on the step with a bunch of flowers. *"Come in, come in, it's lovely to see you,"* enthused Tess. *"Are those for me?"* pointing to the flowers. *"Err, yeah. I thought you may need cheering up,"* Colin spluttered.

Tess had already opened a bottle of wine and was happy to share it with Colin as they scornfully chastised Kelvin's despicable behaviour. Colin comforted her by putting his arm around Tess's shoulders as she started to sob. *"He's just a wrong 'un, you deserve much better than him,"* Colin tried to reassure her. *"You're a good man. Why can't he be more like you?"* Tess replied, as she looked deep into his eyes, and then kissed him on the lips. There was an awkward pause, where they both moved away to reach for their wine glasses. *"Um, sorry Colin, I don't know what I was thinking,"* Tess embarrassingly blurted.

*"I'm not sorry,"* replied Colin, *"I've always had a crush on you."* They both took a large swig of wine and continued their passionate embrace. Pawing at each other's clothes they were soon making love; unashamedly and genuinely making love. The intense feelings they both felt in that

204

moment of madness, surprised them and changed them, there was no going back. Retiring to the bedroom, they feel asleep in each other's arms.

*"Colin, Colin!"* screamed Tommy as he jumped on their bed at first light, *"Will you be my new daddy?"* Awkwardly, Colin pulled the duvet up to his chin to hide his bare chest, and then replied, *"Hello Tommy, is it breakfast time?"* Tess grinned and chirped, *"Come on Thomas, let's go down stairs."* Her son trotted behind her requesting cornflakes and milk.

Once Tommy was fed and engrossed in his favourite cartoon on the television, Colin sheepishly walked into the kitchen. Tess smiled at him and kissed him on the cheek. This reassured him somewhat. *"Err, are you okay? I m-mean, a-r-e we okay?"* stuttered Colin.

Tess's mind and emotions were in a whirl. Looking back at the quizzical Colin she replied, *"I wasn't expecting to feel like this, but yes and yes I'm very okay."* She leaned forward and gave him a hug, *"Do you want a coffee?"* At that moment little Tommy came running into the kitchen, *"Mummy can I have some juice?"* Then he continued, *"Colin, come and play with me."* Colin cast Tess a glance; she responded with a nod as Tommy grabbed his hand and dragged him into the lounge.

The next few weeks became a roller coaster for Tess and Colin, where they grew very close, very quickly. They weren't strangers and knew each other very well, but they hadn't seen or expected the intimate side of their friendship, which was now developing into a relationship. Bert and

Doris were delighted to accept Colin into the fold; he was far more suitable in their eyes than the tearaway Kelvin.

Casey felt a little putout when little Tommy announced in the park that mummy had a new boyfriend. Tess quickly changed the subject with a bribe of sweets, but the information was registered in Casey's mind. *"Guess she's moved on,"* he said to himself. *"She's better off without me,"* lingered in his thoughts for quite some time. There seemed an awkward atmosphere between the adults for the rest of the visit. Casey handed Tess a wad of notes and said, *"See you next Sunday,"* waving to Tommy who was still playing in the sand pit.

* * *

Sofia arranged to meet up the following day for an afternoon of excitement in his new apartment; although, he was drunk by the time she arrived. He seemed angry whilst making love to her, reminding her of her husband, something that made her feel a little uncomfortable. Casey wasn't in the mood for conversation, just to get down to business. Sofia could tell he was troubled and preoccupied, so left just after Casey rolled off her and fell asleep. She was worried about him, yet she knew nothing about him; he never talked about his past or anything going on in his life. Maybe they were both using each other to fill a gap in their existence.

The *'Brrr ... Brrr ... Brrr'* sound from the trim-phone next to his bed woke Casey from his sleep. Looking around he could see no trace of Sofia. The phone continued to ring. *"Yeah!"* barked Casey as he answered the call. His boss Marco was just as abrupt back at him, *"Get down the club,*

206

*we've got work to do!"* A cold shower brought Casey back down to earth, *"Yeah, we've got work to do,"* repeating the instruction to himself.

The New Inn enticed Casey on the way to his employer. *"Stuff Marco, he can wait a bit longer,"* he mused, as he swung the pub door open. It was a family pub filled with chatter and clinking of glasses. Sitting on a bar stool, he ordered a beer.

A young lad caught his attention, running around the room arms outstretched like an aeroplane. *"Neeee-oooooow!!"* screamed from his lips, much to his excitement. Casey smiled and thought of his son and their play times. It was a bittersweet moment, yet Casey took warm satisfaction that he was Tommy's dad. The child's mother called him over, so she could quiet his noisy excitement; although continuing her conversation with her friends as he escaped her grasp.

Casey's attention panned around the room a little further, to overhear the heated exchange of two drunken men. One appeared as the image of his father, spilling beer from his glass, as his arms made grand gestures to emphasise his point of view. Casey was lost in time with morbid curiosity, studying the two men's animated conversation; the words were muffled, but it seemed like regular banter from a pair of friendly adversaries.

As his gaze scanned further around the room, he found a table of four people sat around a table in the corner of the room. Three dishevelled men and a small timid woman, the vision of his mother. She looked a pitiful sight, slumped over the table, clutching a glass in both hands; her knuckles white from the tight grip on her alcoholic support. The three men laughed and appeared to taunt the woman into embarrassed submission.

The young lad was still screaming around the room. When he came face to face with Casey, he looked up and blew a raspberry, chuckling to himself at his bravery. The lad ran off once again, arms outstretched, *"Neeee-ooooow!!"* screaming from his lips. *"You little bugger,"* Casey laughed to himself, lightening his mood.

Lifting his gaze, the image of his father had gone, leaving two men chuckling at the bar. His vision panned to the corner table, where his mother had transformed into a young woman, who was laughing with the three men. These flashbacks haunted him on a regular basis, stirring up confusing, disturbing memories of his past.

After swallowing the dregs of his beer, he stepped out onto the street. *"Yeah, we've got work to do,"* repeating the instruction again to himself.

Marco was having a meeting with the Cartwright brothers, when Casey walked into The Roxy. Clearly they didn't want to be disturbed. To occupy his time, he loitered by the bar flirting with Anna, one of the cleaners. She was busy mopping up the spilt beer behind the counter; each of her footsteps sounded like a plaster being ripped from a wound, as her trainers became stuck to the congealed liquid. They both quietly chuckled trying not to draw the attention of the boss.

It was clear to see over the past few weeks, that Marco was worried about the anonymous calling cards from his faceless foe. If only he knew the perpetrator of these acts of

208

aggression, he could take action, but the not knowing screwed his head; hence the meeting with the Cartwright brothers. He wanted the assistance from these notorious mobsters from Nottingham, but was guarded with his concerns about 'The Mob.' He didn't want to spook them, as he needed them; obviously there would be a heavy price to pay for their help. A prolonged suspicious stare, followed by a cautious handshake, signalled the end of their meeting.

Casey waited until they were out of sight before approaching Marco. *"Hey boss, how's it hanging?"* Casey joked to lighten the mood. It failed miserably as Marco barked back, *"Go and see the drug dealer on Grafton Street, he owes me two hundred!"* Without saying another word, Casey did as instructed, not wishing to create any friction.

Marco Rossi was clearly living on the edge and unable to reconcile the breaches to his business. Were they random attacks from people chancing their luck or the pure genius of a calculated assault? He couldn't fight an enemy that didn't show its face. The not knowing drove him crazy; the uncertainty of what happens next made him sloppy. He was becoming vulnerable.

Part 18


Tess invited Colin over for an evening meal. She was filled
with nervous anticipation as she tucked Tommy up in bed.

After spending a few minutes changing into her prettiest
dress and adding the final touches to her makeup, she
headed to the kitchen to finish preparing the meal. She
wanted to make this a special evening, just the two of them.
She was looking forward to seeing Colin, yet the butterflies
knotted her stomach. Tess felt a little confused; she had
mixed emotions; dread – anxiousness – happiness –
uncertainty. No feeling took precedence over another.

The tap-tap on her front door made her jump, distracting her
thoughts as she eagerly rushed to answer it. Colin was stood
on the step with a beaming smile, waving a bottle of wine.
They kissed as Tess invited him in. *"You look lovely,"*
complemented Colin. *"And dinner smells good too."*

*"Thank you Colin,"* she replied as she ushered him to sit at
the kitchen table. They made small talk as Tess served up
her feast, both enjoying each other's company. Tess spilled
gravy on the table as she placed Colin's plate before him,
and then cursed at her clumsiness. Colin chuckled as he
dabbed up the spillage with his napkin.

Colin pulled the cork from the wine bottle and leant over
the table to fill Tess's glass. She covered the rim with her
hand and said, *"No best not."* Colin looked confused and
replied, *"Why not?"*

Tess looked nervously into his eyes and mumbled, *"Because, I'm pregnant."*

Part 19

*"I need a money exchange done tomorrow at the clockmakers,"* Marco instructed. Casey nodded accepting his orders.

It had been a couple of weeks since the sexy Sofia had been at his apartment; he'd not heard from her since. Casey developed a smug grin across his face, imaging them naked, shagging on his boss's sofa. *"A drink to celebrate,"* he thought to himself; any excuse he could find to consume alcohol. He was reaching the stage where he didn't need an excuse, drinking was becoming a big part of his life. He saw it as a comforting friend offering escapism, whereas the unseen demons were starting to control him.

The hinges complained with a loud creak as he opened the garden gate of the Rossi's household. The taxi waited patiently to continue its journey to the rendezvous point for the exchange. Casey was his usual cocksure self as he opened the patio doors and swaggered into the lounge. Sofia stood nervously by the black holdall. Her eyes followed his every movement.

*"Hello sexy,"* Casey chuckled with a confident grin. When he got within reach, he leant over to kiss her. Sofia recoiled, raising her hand to create a barrier for his advances. *"N-no we can't do this,"* she stuttered, *"I can't see you anymore. Well not in that way."*

Casey's confidence dissolved into the floor, his grin turned to confusion. *"But, why?"* he asked.

213

Sofia looked nervously into his eyes and mumbled, *"Because, I'm pregnant."*

Part 20


Colin placed the wine bottle on the table and stared at Tess with a stunted expression. *"Pregnant! Wow!"* trying to contain his excitement. He had no idea how she was going to react, although inside his heart was pounding with hope that she would be pleased. They had only been in a relationship for a very short time, yet they seemed to have known each other forever. For her to have fallen pregnant so soon was a shock; they hadn't used contraception but he thought it would take ages, not first couple of times they'd made love.

Tess's nervous expression turned to a slight grin as she asked him, *"Are you pleased?"* Colin's huge smile put her mind at rest, so she flung her arms around his neck. *"It'll be great Colin,"* trying to reassure them both, *"I do love you,"* she continued. A warm relief radiated through her body as they held each other close. She was certain that he would make a good dependable father for their child and a solid stepfather for Thomas. Tess had dreamt for a stable family life, now she had the opportunity to make it happen. *'Did she love him?'* She believed so. Maybe she was in love with the dream of playing happy families.

She had never said those words to him before. Colin blushed a little as he replied, *"I've always loved you Tess."* Their meal was forgotten, neither were very hungry at this point; their excited conversations were much more important than the rumble of their empty stomachs. Retiring to the sofa, they hugged, talking about their future life together.

* * *

Doris was covered in flour as she rolled out some pastry; Bert busied himself making tea, as he hummed the tune '*Moon River*' to himself. Spending time together in the kitchen was their usual Sunday morning routine. Little Tommy ran into the kitchen ahead of his mother shouting, *"Nee Naa, Nee Naa!"* trying to copy the sound of a police car. *"Mum, Dad, we've got something to tell you,"* enthused Tess as she tugged Colin into the room behind her. He looked a little sheepish at this daunting moment. She continued, *"I'm pregnant, we're going to have another baby."*

Time seemed to pause as her parents slowly turned their heads in their direction. Tess and Colin held their breath for what seemed forever as they tried to study the expression on the Clifton's faces. Shock turned to happiness as a huge smile spread across Doris's face. She rushed to hug her daughter. Tess ended up with a dusting of flour in the process and a smudge of butter on her cheek. *"Oh Tess that's wonderful,"* exclaimed Doris. Bert proudly stepped forward to shake Colin by the hand, and then pecked Tess on her unsoiled cheek. *"Congratulations to you both, I'm sure Colin will make a great dad."*

Colin's tension subsided with a deep sigh. The joy in the room was contagious and Colin soon joined in with the smiling faces. *"I think that calls for a Sherry to celebrate!"* Bert gestured to the drinks cupboard; Doris nodded in agreement. *"Not for me dad. I'll have a cup of tea and a piece of mum's cake, as I'm eating for two now,"* Tess chuckled.

*"That went okay,"* thought Colin. *"I wonder how my mum and dad will take it."* His parents weren't the maternal type, only just tolerating children whenever they were around. They had met Tommy once before and never really showed him any affection, which disappointed Colin. He thought they would be happy for him, so dropping them with this new bombshell filled him with apprehension.

Little Tommy was left in the capable hands of his grandparents, as Tess and Colin headed off to tell their news to his parents. *"What do you think they'll say?"* asked Tess, then continued, *"Do you think they'll be happy?"* Colin wanted to reassure her and also reassure himself but the seeds of doubt were firmly embedded. *"I'm sure they'll be fine about it,"* was all he could muster.

Tess had only been to their home a couple of times. It was a dark flat above their grocery shop. The sombre atmosphere made her feel a little uncomfortable, by comparison to her own family home. The shop remained closed on a Sunday, so Colin took Tess through the back yard and up the metal staircase. The letterbox rattled as Colin slammed the door behind them, leading Tess into the lounge.

William had just finished eating his lunch off a tray on his lap. A soiled napkin was tucked in the open neck of his shirt, protecting his clothes from food spillages. He was struggling to navigate his cup of tea to his lips with his two shaky hands. Colin noticed recently that his condition was getting worse, but his mother's mollycoddling cast a smoke screen over any concerns he had.

Winifred was busy clearing away the plates as they entered the room, *"Oh hello dear. You didn't warn me that we were*

217

*having company,"* she said dashing past them to the kitchen. Colin didn't have a chance to reply, so just gestured Tess to sit with him on the sofa. His father noisily slurped his tea, paying no attention to the couple.

A few moments later Winnie reappeared. *"Mum, dad, we've got something to tell you,"* Colin crackled through a dry throat. *"We're going to have a baby."*

*"Oh that'll be nice dear,"* Winnie offhandedly answered, before saying, *"William, you're spilling your tea."* She left the room to fetch a cloth to mop up the mess. Colin and Tess felt totally deflated from her bland reaction; his father was focused on the television blinking in the corner, having made no acknowledgement of their news. Colin and Tess awkwardly looked at each other both wanting to make an excuse to leave but neither having the courage to say. They felt awkward, squirming uncomfortably on the sofa as though they were an imposition.

As she came back into the room, Colin tugged Tess to her feet and said, *"We'll be off mum. We've got to pick up Tommy."* Winnie preoccupied with mopping up William's mess, replied, *"Ok dear, see you later."*

Outside, Colin gave Tess a hug and apologised for his parents. *"It's okay Colin,"* she reassured him. *"It must be a shock for them."* Linking her arm through his, they tottered along the uneven pavement, back to the Clifton household. *"As we're going to be a family, guess you'd better move in,"* Tess joked, but her message was sincere. Colin beamed and kissed her on the cheek. *"That'll be great,"* he laughed, and said *"We'll be like a proper couple."*

Winnie had a more severe reaction to the news that he was moving out, than that of becoming a grandmother. *"What am I going to do with the shop? You know your father can't cope with the lifting and I can't run it on my own!"* Colin eventually agreed to call in for an hour each night to stock the shelves and tidy the stock room. This seemed to appease her complaints; he just hoped Tess would understand.

*"Daddy! Mummy has got a baby in her tummy,"* little Tommy proudly announced in the playground. Kelvin was a little taken aback. He knew that Tess had been seeing Colin, but didn't expect her to think about extending her brood so quickly. Feeling rejected, he looked at Tess and said, *"Hope you'll be happy."* He was far from happy about the situation. He knew she deserved better than him; he'd made his bed and had to lay in it.

Colin managed to cram his Sci-Fi collection into three cardboard boxes. *"Hum,"* he said to himself, *"Guess I got to grow up now."* He kept a few books separate, with his favourite Star Wars memorabilia; he doubted Tess would mind his little weakness. His room now stripped from clothes and personal items, he was ready to go. The only thing left hanging on his bedroom wall was a large poster of Wonder Woman; he was looking forward to having a real life wonder woman to fall asleep with.

Bert tooted his horn. He'd parked his car in the street outside the shop, so he could help Colin move. *"Pleased to meet you,"* Bert said shaking William's hand, then turning to Winnie to repeat the introduction. Between them, Bert and Colin managed to negotiate the heavy boxes down the precarious staircase. The 'goodbyes' were as brief as the 'hellos' as a new chapter began for Colin. He had never lived anywhere else and felt a little overwhelmed with the speed that change was happening. He reassured himself that it was a good move. Tess and her family were good people and he was starting a new family of his own. "*Exciting times ahead*," he convinced himself.

Colin and Tess fitted together as a couple very well. After all, they had known each other for a few years and had become best friends; now they were lovers and making a life together. Little Tommy had accepted him without hesitation; their bond was already strong. Tess understood the need for his nightly errands at his parent's shop. He was usually home by seven o'clock, just in time to tuck Tommy up in bed, then they would have the rest of the evening to themselves. Life felt good.

* * *

Just after midday on Tuesday 15th May, Colin answered the ringing telephone at work. *"Colin, you've got to come home."* The call from his mother ended abruptly.

Colin grabbed his coat, before briefly explaining to Bert that he had to go. The heavy pounding of his feet rattled his head, as he ran the half-mile to the shop. His mind was spinning as quickly as his racing stride, wondering what the urgency was. As he turned the corner into the street, his fears were amplified by the sight of an ambulance with flashing lights outside the shop.

Dashing into the shop entrance, he was greeted by two ambulance men and his distraught mother, sobbing into a handkerchief. He hugged her to console her, but could get no sense from her. One of the medics called Dave, placed his hand on Colin's shoulder and beckoned him to join him in the back room. *"I'm sorry to say that your father lost his balance and fell. He tumbled down the metal staircase at the back of the shop and hit his head on the ground."* Colin struggled to compute what he was being told; only following the dialogue as a series of pictures. Dave continued, *"We did everything that we could, but I'm sorry to say that he's gone."*

Tuesday the 15th May would be a day that Colin wouldn't forget, couldn't forget; it was his birthday.

The shop remained shut for the next seven days. A simple sign on the door stated *"CLOSED UNTIL FURTHER NOTICE."* The regular customers would understand the tragedy that the family were going through. Colin had to take on the responsibility of organising the funeral; his mother was in no fit condition to cope with practical issues.

Tess was a tower of strength, supporting him however she could. Bert likewise gave him the freedom to deal with the sombre necessities of the situation, and also a cash advance to cover the expenses. Colin was humbled by everyone's generosity. He was glad that he had moved out of the flat, into his home with Tess, it gave him some respite to grieve.

*   *   *

The hearse pulled up outside the shop at nine forty-five on the morning of Monday 21st May; it was followed by a simple saloon to transport Colin, Tess and his mother. They were the only family to attend this meagre ceremony. A few of the neighbours lined the street to show their mark of respect, but William had few friends to speak of and even less that would mourn his demise.

The ten o'clock service at the local chapel was attended by a handful of people. Colin felt the heavy rain showers were fitting for the mood of the occasion. The trickle of water running through the broken gutter near the entrance door distracted his attention as the vicar performed his duty. His mother remained silent, almost in a trance; Tess sat close to Colin squeezing his hand throughout the service. *"Can we all rise?"* instructed the vicar, as the pallbearers carried the coffin outside to the pre-dug grave.

The rain had stopped, yet the ground was sodden; it was soft under foot. The silent convoy followed the coffin to its place of rest. Winifred let out a muffled sob as the coffin was lowered into the ground; Colin put his arm around his mother's shoulder, Tess gave him a tight embrace. The three of them locked together, trying to comfort each other. A shocked wave of happiness flooded over the soon-to-be parents, as they felt the baby kick for the first time. Their touching bodies experienced this precious moment together. They felt guilty for smiling at such a sad time, but it created a happy memory from an otherwise bleak day.

Colin knew that his mother wouldn't be able to cope with the shop on her own. It was almost like a repeat of his tragic grandparents in this ill-fated shop. His grandmother moved out when his grandfather had a heart attack, he now questioned the destiny of his mother. Colin felt a responsibility. He knew he had to take over the reins or the shop would falter and possibly never recover; his family pride would not allow that to happen, he had to protect his mother.

After long discussions between Colin, Tess and Winnie, it was agreed that Colin would leave his job at the factory, so he could work full time in the shop. His mother could stay in the flat above and work in the shop whenever she wanted to; Colin and Tess would continue to live together. Colin would be able to keep the Trott name above the door and become a managing partner of the business. Potentially he could earn more money to provide for his new family and also support his mother in the process.

*   *   *

Little Tommy's curiosity grew along with the size of his mummy's tummy. Tess encouraged him to get involved and held his small hand on her stomach as the baby kicked. *"Would you like a baby brother or a baby sister?"* she asked him. With a cheeky grin he replied, *"I want a puppy."* He then kissed Tess's stomach before running off squealing with laughter. *"Little bugger,"* Tess chuckled to herself.

Kelvin had cancelled the last few visits with Tommy, which upset Tess. She could understand that he may feel pushed out with Colin on the scene and a baby due, but it annoyed her that Tommy was being punished for the situation. The times she did bump into Kelvin in the street, he was either drunk or nursing a hangover. Their chance meetings were brief, but he would always give her a bundle of cash to support his son. Tess felt sorry that he had lost his way in life that he had become a troubled soul; in hindsight it wasn't surprising with the upbringing that he'd had.

*"Oh Tommy,"* she tried to explain to her son, *"Mummy's tummy is too big to pick you up."* Tess was now over eight

223

months pregnant and was suffering a sore back. Tommy accepted the reasons and kissed his mummy's tummy, then asked, *"Can I have a brother and a sister and a puppy?"* Tess chuckled to herself and replied, *"No Tommy just a brother or a sister."* He shrugged his shoulders and went running off, arms outstretched, shouting, *"Neeee-oooow!"* as he mimicked the noise of an aeroplane.

Colin had been working hard to maintain the shop. His mother spent much of her time watching daytime television, locked away upstairs on her own; although he did encourage her to serve at the counter whenever she could do it, keeping contact with the regular customers. She always looked preoccupied and sad. Today was delivery day from their supplier. Colin had his hands full shifting the new stock, therefore Winnie had to man the counter and serve the customers. He kept a watchful eye on her, stepping in whenever she had a problem. It was a tough day and Colin was exhausted.

Tess chuckled to herself as she peered through the door of Tommy's bedroom. Colin had read him a bedtime story and they had both fallen asleep on his tiny bed. She felt happy with her life and blessed that Colin was such a kind man. He had taken Tommy on as his own and she knew that he would make a brilliant dad to their new baby. *"Colin,"* she whispered as she gently shook him. *"Colin, I think it's our bedtime too,"* she chuckled.

*"Ummmm, okay,"* he replied in a sleepy voice. Colin and Tess headed for their bed and sleep came easy for both of them. It was just after three o'clock in the morning when Tess shook him again and said, *"Colin! Colin wake up!"* He

murmured a reply, but woke up with a start when she continued, "*The baby's coming!*"

Part 21


Casey picked up the black holdall in stunned silence. He stared into Sofia's frightened eyes once more before leaving to complete his task. He had no recollection of his walk to the taxi or giving the driver instructions; he was brought back to consciousness by the blast of the taxi horn, as they avoided a near collision.

*"Shit, shit, shit!"* screamed through his head. Had he been literally caught with his trousers down? Scenarios rushed through his mind visualising Marco's raging reaction, all with dire consequences and bloody exchanges.

The old grey haired man wasn't sat at the counter in his usual place today, his wife occupied the seat. She opened the shop door then locked it behind Casey as she ushered him into the back room. *"My husband isn't feeling very well today,"* she informed Casey without being prompted. After a swift exchange of notes, Casey climbed back into the taxi for his return journey. Questions were bombarding his thoughts, but no answers were forthcoming. The stream of words cascaded down a funnel in his mind, until the individual letters distilled into one simple question.

Casey dismissed the taxi driver at the rear of the Rossi residence. He felt like a prisoner on death row; like a dead man walking across the lush green lawn. Sofia was stood at the open patio doors. As he approached, she stepped back into the room to let him come in. His simple, but most difficult question blurted from his lips, *"Shit, what do we do now?"*

Sofia paused for a moment before responding. *"He'd kill us if he knew,"* then continued, *"So I made sure I had sex with him last night, I'll tell him the baby is his."* She looked so lost in her thoughts; staring at Casey, he could see she was looking far beyond him, passed the glass doors and well into the distance. Her body jerked back into the moment, her focus resumed and said with authority, *"He can never know, right?"* Casey nodded in reply and their pact of secrecy was sealed.

Casey left feeling anxious, but also a little relieved. His life was a roller coaster at the best of times, yet up until now he had managed to hold onto the safety harness in the cart. He needed a drink to calm his nerves. No, that was just another excuse; he just needed a drink.

The loud ringing of trim-phone jolted him awake from his drunken stupor. He knocked over his bedside lamp trying to silence the offending racket. *"What?"* barked Casey as he answered the call. *"I need you at the club by four o'clock. Capisce?"* replied Marco just as sternly. *"Ok boss,"* Casey said apologetically.

Casey sat on the edge of his bed and took a large swig from a half empty bottle of whiskey. He coughed as the burning liquid hit the back of his throat. The second swig gave him a reassuring warm glow. A moaning from behind him made him turn his head, to see a naked blonde stirring from her sleep. *"**What the ....**"* he mumbled inside his head, not recalling what had happened the night before. Just another one of his one night stands.

*"You'd better get dressed and go,"* he coldly ordered her, *"I've got a job to do."* She looked through a gap in her

228

dishevelled hair and simply replied, *"Okay."* Casey walked nakedly to the veranda window and took another large slug from the bottle. He could see people beneath him scurrying along the pavement like an army of ants. *"Will you call me?"* enquired the blonde as she left. Without turning to face her he said, *"Yeah, sure,"* but as the door closed, he continued with a chuckle, *"When I remember your name."*

Casey had distanced himself from everyone. He kept Marco at arm's length and avoided Sofia wherever possible. All the people he knew in the club and also on the street became nothing more than useful commodities. His only loyal and trusted friend was found at the bottom of a bottle. His mother's voice resonated through his brain, ***"You're turning into your father,"*** but he was beyond caring anymore.

Alcohol gave him the bravery to intimidate his victims, without it he was no more than a scared child, frightened of the shadows. Kelvin was his sober ego; an ego that couldn't survive in the dark places Casey had to dwell. He had created a lifestyle that was now taking over him and controlling his actions, there was no going back.

With a cocky swagger Casey he headed for an empty table at the far side of the cafe. He always placed himself with his back to the wall, away from any doorways; a position where he could be on guard against any surprise attacks. Even in the most innocuous places, he was still on heightened alert. Sarah soon followed with a feast for him. *"Here's your breakfast Casey, and I hope you like it?"* Casey replied, *"Yeah thanks,"* he was a man of few words with a hangover, which happened most mornings.

Tea rained on the table, as his shaky hands failed to control his brimming cup of tea. *"Oh crap,"* he cursed as a drop soiled his Ben Sherman shirt. *"Oh crap,"* he cursed again as he rummaged in his trouser pocket to locate his ringing pager, *"Call me pronto."*

Casey called Marco from a payphone to receive his instructions for the day. *"I want you to pay Fraser a visit. That drug dealing prick is taking the piss!"* After a pause, his boss continued, *"Make sure you lean on him good and proper. He can't disrespect me anymore."* Casey knew exactly what was expected from him, to give him a public beating, so he was put back in his place.

The last time Casey had encountered Fraser was with Benny in an alleyway next to the estate shop. As before, ambushing him from behind sounded a good option. Casey was more confident with his deadly skills and wasn't fazed by taking the assignment by himself; in fact it would look less obvious if he worked alone.

Casey watched Fraser from the shadows, waiting for his opportunity, waiting for him to be alone before he pounced. As stealthily as a cat stalking its prey, Casey crept up on his victim, landing a punishing blow to his back. As Fraser fell to the ground groaning in agony, Casey grabbed him by his collar and dragged him into view of a gang loitering in front of the shop. *"This is a message from the boss!"* Casey screamed before pounding Fraser's bloody face with vicious blows.

Casey felt two burly men drag him from his attack and pin him to the ground. His face buried in the pavement and his hands behind his back; Casey heard an undercover cop say,

*"You're nicked,"* as the click of handcuffs restrained his wrists. *"Fraser's been under surveillance for months and you've blown our operation. Who in the fuck are you?"* vented one of the officers.

At the police station Casey was thrown into a cell. He had always been careful in the past and never been involved with the police. This was a stupid mistake; he'd taken his eye off the ball and hadn't checked around beforehand. Usually police would stand out to him like a neon sign, but this time he was sloppy. The hangovers he experienced each day had dulled his senses.

After several hours waiting in a cold cell, he was taken to an interview room to be questioned by the two undercover policemen who had arrested him at the scene. Once establishing that his name was Kelvin Carter AKA Casey, they continued to bombard him with questions, which he refused to answer. They sent him back to his cell once more so he could be appointed a solicitor.

An elderly man called Mr Baker was the duty solicitor assigned to the case. His baggy clothes and stubble chin didn't instil Casey with any confidence in the system, yet his manner was very concise. He explained the seriousness of the charge and suggested it was in Casey's best interest to comply.

Back in the interview room, the policemen continued their questioning. Casey was determined to remain steadfast and claimed it was a disagreement between him and Fraser over drugs. He didn't want to implicate Marco in anyway; he already had enough worries with his boss.

Casey was released on bail to appear the following Tuesday, 27ᵗʰ September at the Magistrates Court. His duty solicitor would be present, but he wasn't optimistic, as Casey had been caught red-handed by two police officers. Casey wasn't optimistic either.

On leaving the Police Station, Casey weaved a trail through the back streets to ensure he wasn't followed, concluding his journey at The Roxy. *"Is the boss in his office?"* Casey asked one of the cleaners. They nodded, so he went through the red *'Staff Only'* door and headed up the stairs. Marco was sat with his feet on his desk, deep in a telephone conversation. On seeing Casey, he quickly spoke into the receiver, *"I'll call you back,"* and promptly ended the call.

Marco had heard rumours through the grapevine, but wanted to hear it directly. Casey spoke with a nervous stutter, *"I-I've been p-pulled by the police. I'm getting done for beating up Fraser."*

There was a prolonged silence where they both glared into each other's eyes. Marco broke the impasse by saying, *"Keep me out of it and I'll see you are alright."* Casey nodded and replied, *"Of course boss."* Both of the men appeared suspicious of each other's intent, but had to trust one another in this delicate situation.

The next week was tense for Casey. His days were spent clinging to a bar stool, whereas his nights he caressed a bottle of whiskey. He was genuinely worried and felt extremely alone. Alcohol seemed his only respite, so he indulged in a lot of liquid respite; the downside of his trance state, was to unlock the demons in his head. It was like a seesaw of destruction between his rational and irrational thoughts. News broke on a television special. The News Reader introduced the show, *"Its Sunday 25th September,"* then continued, *"IRA prisoners armed with guns, hijack a lorry and escape from The Maze Prison."* News reports were normally of no interest to Casey, yet this seemed a sucker punch of reality, highlighting how he could so easily be caged like those men without an escape plan; with no one trying to break him out of his concrete cell, he would remain friendless and alone. Prison felt like a real possibility.

His court appearance was very brief, with compelling evidence to refer the matter to The Crown Court. A judge and jury would consider his case on the 11th October 1983. Casey's solicitor remained pessimistic and suggested he put his affairs in order; just in case he received a custodial sentence for his crime.

For the next few days Casey resumed his alcoholic binge, looking no further than the bottom of the next bottle. Day and night blended into one, as he lost all concept of time. His distorted reality was trying to reconcile his irreconcilable past. The guilt of his mother's suicide hung heavy on his shoulders, and the pain he had caused to others; emotional pain to Tess and physical pain to all those on the receiving end of his fists. He despised the bullies at school that took away his dignity, yet he was now one of those bullies; he was ashamed of his actions. *'Live by the sword, die by the sword'* became his self-destructing mantra.

The court date was fast approaching and Casey knew he had to prepare for the worst outcome. He purchased two large holdalls to hatch his plan. Casey divided equally all his designer clothes, personal items and wads of illicit cash, into the two holdalls. The picture of his mother and his pager were stowed into a side pocket. He had built up quite a financial stash and he wasn't giving that up easily. He thought if one bag was discovered, then he would still have a nest egg to fall back on. Leaving only the bare minimum in his apartment, he took the holdalls to the local railway station and secured them in two left luggage lockers.

His rent on the apartment was due and the worst-case scenario, he would lose his deposit and a few meagre possessions, if he ended up in prison. It was the best he could hope for under the circumstances; a consolation drink or two or maybe a few were now in order.

The morning of the 10th October came and Casey felt very uneasy. He had no one to talk to, no one to confide in. Casey walked aimlessly through the streets, until he was drawn to the entrance of The Roxy. He wanted reassurance, so he pushed the door open and walked inside. The red 'Staff Only' door looked ominous, like the mouth of a fire-breathing monster. Yet, he had to dance with the devil and enter the hellhole; the door creaked as he pushed it open.

Marco was sat behind his desk with a waitress on his lap. Casey tapped the door and entered without invitation. Marco dismissed the girl and stared at Casey with concern. *"What do you want lad?"* Marco asked. *"Nothing boss, it's just that my court day tomorrow and I'm worried,"* replied Casey. This seemed to put Marco at ease; he opened his desk drawer and pulled out a wad of money, *"Here's a grand to keep your mouth shut. There'll be more for you when the dust settles."* Casey scooped up the cash and said, *"Okay boss, thanks."*

Before Casey could continue the conversation, Marco was on his feet ushering him out of the door. *"I've got to go now lad, my wife has just had her baby."* Casey was stunned by the news. Marco followed him down the staircase and through the club. The sunshine dazed his eyes as they went in separate directions, on the street outside.

First port of call was to divide the cash between the two holdalls in the left luggage lockers, then secondly the nearest pub to compute the information that he'd just been told. *"I'm a dad again,"* he told himself, wondering if it was a boy or a girl. He lifted a large tumbler of whiskey and said loudly, *"**Cheers!**"* Apart from receiving a few strange looks from other customers, no one else was there to celebrate his news.

He spent the afternoon mulling over the bombshell that had been dropped on him. He'd guessed Sofia's baby was due soon, but with the recent events resulting from his arrest, it had slipped his mind. Twenty-four hours until his fate was sealed and he had a new conundrum to resolve. Casey's mind was being driven by reckless thoughts, but the yearning was too strong. He had to see his child before going to court; it may be his only chance.

* * *

Casey sat in the shadows of the hospital car park, staring at the entrance to the maternity ward. He had noticed Marco's car in the car park, so he had to bide his time. He couldn't afford to get caught, there was too much at stake. Just after seven-thirty Marco left the building, jumped into his car and sped off out of sight. Casey's stomach churned at the prospect of going in, but his mind left him no choice.

235

Scurrying through the darkness, he took one final look across the car park before entering the brightly lit entrance; the electric doors slid open and sucked him inside.

As patients, doctors and nurses went about their business, Casey blended in unnoticed. He approached the reception desk and enquired, "*Where can I find Sofia Rossi?*" The receptionist without saying a word buried her head into her journal. Moments later she replied, "*Ward seven. Are you family?*" Casey just nodded and headed for the staircase.

The place was spotless with a strong smell of disinfectant; he hated hospitals and felt uneasy, but needs must under the circumstances. Not wanting to join the queue of people waiting for the lift, Casey pushed open the adjacent green door and climbed the staircase to the first floor. As he opened the next door, he could hear a dull rumble of activity from the wards.

The wards were clearly marked along the corridor, ward seven was easy to locate. He hesitated in the doorway, his heart pounding, doubting his resolve; yet he could see Sofia sat in her bed reading a magazine. Her hair was tied back in a ponytail and she was wearing her pink nightie, not as flattering as he remembered her.

A deep breath propelled him into the room, heading towards her. She looked up and smiled. Then a voice echoed from the other corner of the room, "*Kelvin? What are you doing here?*" Casey spun around to see Tess lying in a nearby bed. His eyes flicked back to Sofia, she shook her head and buried her vision back into her magazine.

Casey changed his direction and walked over to the bemused Tess. Trying to cover his tracks, he muttered, *"Errr. I heard that you had had your baby."*

Part 22

Casey tried to hide his disappointment as she stared into his empty eyes. Tess was pleased to see him, but she also felt a little suspicious; she hadn't seen him for a few weeks and he had never shown her any compassion before. *"What's up Kelvin?"* she asked. He glimpsed back at Sofia once more, she was still immersed in her magazine, and then said, *"I'm in court tomorrow, and I may go to prison."* Tess seemed a little shocked at the news. She placed her hand on his to reassure him, although he was lost in his thoughts.

Sofia was steadfast in her reading pose, yet her eyes had swivelled in their sockets towards him. She was digesting the news, but couldn't react. Amazement swept through her body that Casey should know her and from their conversation knew her quite well. He had never mentioned an ex before, yet he'd never mentioned much about his personal life either. *"And why call him Kelvin?"*

*"Did you have a boy or a girl?"* Casey asked Tess. He wasn't really interested but had to make small talk to justify his visit. Plans to see his child had been scuppered; this may be the only opportunity he'd ever get to see his offspring. He didn't even know if his child was a boy or a girl either. *"I had a little boy. Colin and I are thrilled,"* Tess informed him, then blushed at her insensitivity. Conversation was awkward between the two of them, neither knowing what to say. After a pause Tess said, *"Tommy misses you."* From his recent news, she knew it may be some time before he could see him.

"*Oh my God,*" echoed in Sofia's head, realising that he was a father already from a previous relationship, then continuing her thoughts, "*Well I never.*" She was also seeing a more vulnerable side to him other than his open bravado, this she found quite endearing. She wanted to speak to him, especially with hearing the news of his court appearance and was now frustrated that she couldn't.

Casey stood up and muttered, "*I'd better go.*" There was no point prolonging his pain or his disappointment any longer. "*Goodbye Kelvin, good luck,*" Tess spoke with genuine concern.

His exit route took him almost past Sofia's bed. Casey could see her eyes following him and when he got close she gave him a contorted smile. He could see congratulations cards on her bedside cabinet saying '***It's a boy.***' That gave him a small amount of comfort, yet drove his urgency to see his son even more. Once the child was taken to the Rossi household, he may never see him; he would have no excuse to visit.

Outside the ward, Casey thumped his hand against the wall. An echoing boom resonated along the empty corridor. "*Shit, shit, shit,*" he said to himself as he spun around to look at the closed doors of ward seven. Above the door there was a direction sign, '*The Exit*' to the right and, '*The Nursery*' to the left. He had to see his son, as this may be his only chance.

Casey headed to the far end of the silent corridor; only his footsteps could be heard. The last door on the right had a simple sign pinned to it '*QUIET PLEASE*' and above it '*The Nursery*'. His heart was pounding and his mind was

240

spinning. Quickly turning to look back down the long corridor, he could see no one. From behind the green door he could hear a choir of gurgling babies.

The door was the colour of a football pitch, the white edges of the peephole windows reminded him of goalposts. *"Maybe he'll be a soccer player,"* Casey mused as he peered through the glass. He could see six babies lying in cots, some sleeping, some kicking their legs; there were two cots empty. No one else was in the room; the babies had been left unattended. He had to take his chance, yet he was anxious to push open the door.

The door became an emerald green with his mother's face transposed into the paintwork. *"You're a little gob-shite, just like your father,"* spat from Brenda's lips. *"You can't look after yourself let alone a little nipper."* He recoiled from the verbal attack in his mind, closing his eyes and shaking his head to make the vision disappear.

The door was just a green door, no more than that; time was running out. Casey pushed the door ajar and slid through the gap. All the cots had medical notes hanging on clipboards at the foot of the cribs. The third one along said *'Sofia Rossi.'* Casey stood glued to the spot, staring at the sleeping baby, his son. Without thinking, Casey reached into the cot and picked up the new born child, he murmured, but continued to sleep.

He was dressed in a plain white baby-grow, wrapped in a blue blanket. Casey pulled out one of his tiny hands the baby gripped his finger. A plastic nametag secured around his wrist also labelled him *'Sofia Rossi.'* *"I wonder what she will call him?"* he asked himself.

241

The memories of baby Thomas came flooding back into Casey's thoughts. Those perfect times shared with his innocent son. Sofia's baby, no their baby, would receive no such affection from the violent Marco, even if the monster accepted him as the fruits of his loin. Fear flooded through Casey's mind at the horrors his son could face, and he wouldn't be there to protect him.

He paced the ward, rocking his son in his arms, staring at the various babies. Casey chuckled to himself, "*All babies look the same*" Then he stopped in his tracks and confirmed to himself once again, "*All babies look the same.*" Casey looked closely at his son and compared him to the other babies, one by one. Some had blue eyes and some had brown, but to him, they all looked the same. When he reached the cot labelled '*Tess Clifton*' a baby boy looked back at him with the same brown eyes. He laid them both side by side in the same cot they could have been twins.

Reckless thoughts cascaded through his head. The thought of his son growing up in a mobster's world froze him with fear. Tess was a warm and caring mother to Thomas and she would also be to her next child; she had a secure home life and great parents. "*I wonder if I could get away with it?*" he asked himself.

If only he could swap the babies, Tess would become the surrogate mother of his child, without even knowing. He could watch him grow up when he visited Tommy and his child would be safe. The babies were only a few hours old, she would never know; Sofia would never know either, he hoped anyway. In Casey's blinkered mind, logic wasn't a luxury he possessed. His emotions were highly charged and panic drove his thinking, time wasn't on his side to hesitate or reconsider. A split-second decision was all he had.

Casey rushed to the door and opened it a fraction so he could see down the corridor. No one was in sight. He took a deep breath and seized the moment to hatch his plan.

Tess's baby was dressed in a blue baby-grow with a small teddy bear embroidered on the front. He was then wrapped in a white blanket. Casey quickly went about undressing them both and swapping their clothes. He used some liquid soap from the sink to ease their nametags, so he could slide them over their wrists. It was a little trickier to replace the nametags on the opposite child, smudging the ink slightly in the process.

Wrapping Tess's son in the blue blanket to cover his white baby-grow, he closely checked his work, before placing him in Sofia's cot. His son now in the white blanket and blue baby-grow was being checked for detail; Casey was satisfied with his work. Kelvin junior would now have a different future. At that moment he heard the door click open.

*"What are you doing?"* ordered a surprised nurse. Casey turned casting her a look of fear. *"Umm. I'm just having a quick look at Tess's baby, before I go to work abroad,"* he said in panic. The nurse wasn't happy with his excuse, saying in a stern voice, *"It's most irregular, I'll have to report it."* Casey gently placed the baby into Tess's cot and pleaded with her not to say anything. She grunted in reply and asked Casey to leave.

Casey quickly marched down the corridor purposely not glancing into ward seven, and then flew down the back staircase. He needed to make a hasty escape. Casey would be in serious trouble if he was caught and didn't want to face an interrogation. In the entrance, he could see a security guard talking to the receptionist. Casey lowered his head and continued to walk with purpose until he was in the safety of the car park shadows.

*"Shit, what have I done?"*

Part 23

*"Kelvin Carter, you have been found guilty of grievous bodily harm,"* concluded the Crown Court judge. *"You will receive a custodial sentence of two years."* Although expected, Casey found the decision hard to accept, cursing the court officials as he was led to the cells.

Casey had time to reflect during his two hours wait to be transported to his assigned prison. The holding cell echoed noise from the corridor outside, the stomping of heavy footsteps from the guards, the clanking of the doors closing and indiscriminate loud chatter. Each invasion of the silence interrupted his thoughts.

Guilt racked through him, as he thought about the dastardly deed that he had executed the night before. In his twisted rationale, he found justification in protecting his new born son from a future life of misery. Casey didn't want him to grow up as he had, he didn't want him to stir his monster within. *"You're turning into you father!"* bellowed through his head. He didn't want his son to turn into him.

Little Tommy danced in his mind, playing happily with his mother. This reassured Casey a little, justifying his actions even more. Yet, the deceitful plan he had imposed on the oblivious Tess darkened his mood. She was a good person and would never forgive him if the truth ever came out. He had robbed her of her own child. He was a thief from the shadows no better than a Magpie stealing an egg from the nest, and then allowing a cuckoo to replace it. *"Do birds have a conscience?"* he pondered.

*"Would Sofia understand?"* Casey doubted it. What if Marco found out about his affair; fathering a child with his wife, would he be a dead man?

The only solace he could find from the turmoil of hurt and pain was the knowledge that the profits from his villainy were safely stashed in left lounge lockers at the railway station. He could make a new start when his prison term was completed. Marco had said that he would pay him for his silence; that was something Casey had to follow through to avert any suspicion.

His cell door swung open, *"It's time to go,"* instructed one of the guards. Casey complied and followed him along the corridor. As each door was unlocked, then relocked behind them; he started to realise what prison would mean and his loss of liberty. He could only surmise what to expect.

\* \* \*

Marco arrived at the hospital to collect his wife and child. The sentence that Casey had received was playing on his mind, although the lad had kept his mouth shut as instructed. Sofia was nervously sat on the edge of her bed, dressed and waiting, as Marco entered the ward. *"Are you ready?"* he asked. Sofia nodded. He turned on the spot and started to leave; Sofia grabbed the baby and her belongings, and then tottered along behind him, trying to keep up.

They had never used contraception during the years of their marriage, and she hadn't fallen pregnant, *"So why now?"* Marco questioned to himself. He'd had many affairs with the waitresses at the club; none of those had fallen pregnant. *"Why now?"* he was suspicious. Their car journey home

246

was in silence; Sofia was content to fuss her baby. Her son was the first thing she had ever loved.

*"Vincenzo,"* Sofia announced. *"I want to call our baby Vincenzo. Little Vinnie,"* she chuckled. After hearing Casey's real name at the hospital, she thought it was the nearest name she could suggest without being questioned. *"Kelvin = Vinnie,"* she thought to herself, blushing a little in the process. Marco shrugged his shoulders, showing his lack of interest. *"Yeah, sure,"* he replied.

A beaming Colin walked into the ward with a very excited Tommy holding his hand. *"Tommy,"* said Tess, *"This is your new baby brother."* The youngster leant over and kissed him on the forehead. *"Is he a puppy?"* he cheekily asked, with a snigger. Tess chuckled out loud, replying, *"No Tommy he's a baby boy,"* then continued, *"And, he's named Samuel, but we'll call him Sammy."*

Colin gathered up all her belongings, carrying them in one arm, whilst carrying little Sammy in the other; he insisted that Tess didn't exert herself. She agreed and allowed Tommy to lead her by the hand out of the hospital. Bert was eagerly waiting outside in his car to take them home. Doris would have loved to come along, but there wasn't enough room in the car for all of them; she had prepared tea and sandwiches for their return.

Night fell, and an excited Tommy was tucked up in bed; baby Sammy was dozing in his crib, whilst Tess and Colin were curled up on the sofa counting their blessings. Life felt good. They believed nothing could spoil their happiness.

\* \* \*

247

Casey handed over his clothes and few possessions when he eventually arrived at the prison. His belongings were placed into a simple cardboard box and sent to a storage room. He was issued with prison issue items, such as a grey tracksuit, tee shirts, underwear and slip on canvas shoes. A towel and basic toiletries were given to him in a bundle, before he was escorted to his cell.

The metallic clicks of the locks and the banging of the doors, created an eerie atmosphere as he was guided through a series of doors along a sparse corridor. The floor shone reflecting their images, a sterile comparison to the dirty grey wall. As they passed through each chamber of this endless passageway, the mood darkened. Eventually they reached a metal caged door; beyond it, a bright room filled with the murmurings of dozens of people.

The eyes in the room followed his every movement. The chatter ebbed and flowed as he passed the individual groups of men huddled in conversation. Casey noticed a group that stood out more than the others; a large shaven-headed man surrounded by four heavies. They were silent, just tracking his steps like a sniper following its target. Casey locked on to their vision, assessing the situation before turning away.

The door to his cell was already open as the prison warden led him into the room. It was a small room containing a bunk bed, a toilet and a sink. Another inmate was lounging on the upper bunk. "*Jenson, this is your new cell mate Kelvin,*" informed the warden. Jenson was engrossed in a magazine, but peered over the top of the pages and said, "*Alright? Yours is the bottom bunk,*" he said before resuming to read. Casey crouched down and sat on his bunk; no more conversation was said.

A few minutes later, a huge shadow cast over the doorway as the four heavies squeezed into his cell. The large shaven-headed man remained in the doorway, then instructed, *"Jenson, take a walk."* Clearly this wasn't a request, so Jenson scuttled from the cell, leaving Casey to confront the mob. Two of the men dragged him from his bunk, pinned him to the wall, and then proceeded to bludgeon him with punishing blows. Casey could do nothing to defend himself in this confined space, just had to accept his beating.

Casey curled up on the floor bloody and bruised, the five men towered over him. The only one to speak was the shaven-headed man, *"I'm Frank by name and Frank by nature,"* he barked. *"This is my wing and you abide by my rules!"* Frank landed a kick into Casey's ribs to emphasise his point. He continued, *"You think you are tough? I hear you are a pussy Kelvin, a pussy with a shaved head."* Casey turned his head from his foetal position to look at his abuser. Frank continued to bark his orders, *"I'm the only one in here with a shaved head. If you shave yours again, you'll get another beating!"* Frank kicked him again as a parting shot, and then the five men left the room.

Jenson came back into the cell as Casey was climbing back onto his bunk nothing was said. The door slammed shut and a key locked it securely. *"Lights out!"* boomed from a warden outside, and then darkness engulfed the room. He thought to himself, *"Seven hundred and thirty days to go,"* then fell asleep.

Bang, Bang, Bang on the door, woke Casey at six o'clock; Jenson slid off his bunk and urinated loudly into the toilet. There was going to be no dignity here. *"I'll take you to the shower block,"* suggested Jenson, *"There's less people about early. Less trouble.*" Casey nodded, grabbed his towel and followed Jenson outside. Purple bruises had developed on his sore ribs and his grazes stung as the water ran over Casey's body. He didn't want to dawdle, he felt vulnerable; Jenson was hurrying him along, before others arrived.

After depositing his wet towel in his cell, Casey followed Jenson to the food hall to get breakfast. There was a constant stream of chatter from the inmates between mouthfuls of food. Casey had always been a loner, keeping himself to himself; here it would not be possible. The thought of being surrounded by so many men all the time made him feel anxious. Following Jenson's lead, Casey grabbed a tray and mimicked his foraging movements to gather food.

Sat at the corner table, Frank and his heavies sniggered to themselves. "*Morning Kelvin,*" Frank shouted across the room in a patronising tone, then proceeded to blow him a kiss. Others sat nearby turned to look at Casey; he lowered his head and followed Jenson to the other side of the room. "*Kelvin, don't let him get to you,*" reassured Jenson. "*Just stay out of his way.*"

\* \* \*

Sofia adored little Vinnie. He was her world, far removed from the seedy and abusive side of Marco. Her baby also created a good excuse not to pander to Marco so much. "*Shut that screaming baby up!*" became Marco's signature phrase; Sofia didn't mind little Vinnie crying, it gave her a reason to cuddle him. Her and her son dissolved into one.

Marco felt a bit awkward when little Vinnie started to walk around the age of one year old. He couldn't escape the sticky hands of his tiny tearaway as he freely lunged at his father; oblivious to his father's reluctance to entertain him. Vincenzo's curly brown hair was always a topic of argument between Sofia and Marco. *"Italian children don't have curly brown hair,"* Marco ranted, suspiciously. *"My Papa had curly brown hair,"* Sofia said, defending the accusation. Her husband had not met him so he couldn't argue the point; yet it was untrue.

The club became almost a second home for Marco. He spent most days there and also many nights. He blamed the crying baby on his lack of sleep, yet it was just a ploy to have sexual encounters with his favourite waitresses. Sofia didn't mind his absence; in fact she enjoyed her newfound freedom. She and Vinnie were becoming very close he meant everything to her.

*"Mummy, mummy look!"* shouted Tommy as he walked into the room holding Sammy's hand. *"Oh my goodness,"* squealed Tess in delight. It was Samuel's first steps. "Come to mummy," Tess said holding her arms outstretched. Letting go of his brother's hand, Sammy tottered precariously across the room. Tess scooped him up and planted a big kiss on his cheek. *"We'll have to surprise daddy when he comes home from work."*

Colin had been working hard at his grocery store. The business had been signed over to him and his mother had taken a back seat. She worked very little in the shop, becoming almost a recluse. Colin had to hire an assistant to keep things ticking over. He had streamlined some of the processes and purchased different stock; he was starting to make a healthy profit. His mother living above the shop was an ideal situation, he could check in on her several times a day.

An excited Sammy shouted, *"Da, da, dad, dad!"* as a beaming Colin walked through their front door. Tess was crouched in the lounge holding Sammy poised to toddle to his father. A stunned Colin watched in awe as his son made four steps then landed on his bottom. *"Wow, look at you!"* chuckled Colin as he sat on the floor next to him. Tommy sidled sheepishly up against Colin and sat on his lap, and then said, *"Colin. Can I call you daddy too?"* A tear rolled down Tess's cheek. *"Yes of course you can,"* Colin replied, choked with emotion. He looked at Tess and then at the boys and thought to himself, *"This is the best day of my life."*

\* \* \*

Casey found his second Christmas in prison particularly tough. He felt so alone; alienated from the outside world. There was no one there for him, no friends or family to care about him, no one would give him a second thought. He felt extremely sorry for himself and spent much of the day moping on his bed. *"Three hundred and fourteen days to go,"* he spoke to himself in the mirror. He'd had a couple of skirmishes during his sentence, so doubted he would be released early.

*"Happy Christmas Kelvin,"* said Jenson handing him a piece of cake. Casey smiled.

Jenson was due to be released in a few weeks. They had built up a friendship under these adverse circumstances and

Casey would miss his company. The two of them looked out for each other, something that he'd never had before; someone that would genuinely cover his back. The thought of sharing his cell with someone new wasn't something that Casey wanted to think about.

*"Kelvin,"* Frank said with a nod in acknowledgement, as they passed on the landing. He had relaxed his intimidating attacks on Casey, refocusing on newer targets. They had both reached an understanding how to coexist. Casey had conformed to his orders and hadn't shaven his head. He now had a mop of curly brown hair, just like his school days. The softer image had helped him to blend into the crowds and have a quieter life. Maybe Frank had done him a favour.

Two hundred and fifty eight days left for Casey and Jenson was ready for release. *"Keep your nose clean, or don't get caught,"* chuckled Casey as they shook hands. Jenson handed him the tobacco he had left and two bars of chocolate. Casey wasn't keen on either, but it was currency. *"See ya,"* Jenson said as he left with the warden. Later that day a replacement cellmate arrived. He was a small guy called Steve; he'd been charged with shoplifting for the umpteenth time. Casey had already commandeered the top bunk to show his seniority. They never developed a friendship, but just rubbed along together.

*"Kelvin Carter, the governor wants to see you,"* ordered a prison officer. They both marched along the landing, navigating the series of locked doors, until they reached the office door. A plaque positioned at eyelevel stated, Mr Smallbone, Governor. His name had always amused Casey, *"I bet he's got a small boner,"* was the joke.

Inside the office, Mr Smallbone informed Casey that his application for parole had been accepted and he was eligible for early release. *"Thank you Mr Boner, err I mean Mr Smallbone,"* Casey responded. He was due to leave prison on Easter Monday, in just a few days. The prospect excited him, but also scared him at the same time. He was unsure what his future would bring.

The day that he stepped through the prison gates went without recognition. He was stood outside alone staring at the empty space that surrounded him. He had put on weight during his sentence and his trousers wouldn't fasten up, they were only secured in place by a loose fitting belt. It was starting to rain, so Casey pulled up the collar on his jacket and headed for the bus stop. His only port of call would be the railway station left lounge lockers, then find a pub for a beer.

Casey sighed with relief when he discovered both of his holdalls were safe in their respective lockers. He palmed fifty quid from one of the bags, and then headed for his old haunt, The Hostel, as a temporary stopgap. He paid for a single room, stashed his bags, and then headed for the nearest pub. It didn't take him long to get drunk and stagger back to his room to sleep.

The next morning came soon enough, waking him at his usual six o'clock without being prompted. Showered and dressed, he headed to the café for breakfast. The short walk felt like de ja vu, but to his disappointment Sarah no longer worked there. The cafe had been taken over by a trendy chain of restaurants; Cappuccino and a Panini had to suffice.

Plucking up the courage to make the call, Casey phoned Marco. *"Hello boss, I got out early!"* There was an uncomfortable pause, and then Casey continued, *"You said you'd look after me if I kept you out of it."* Another uncomfortable pause ensued before Marco replied, *"Ok. Don't come to the club, I'll meet you by The Boathouse at midday."* The call ended abruptly.

Casey wanted some more comfortable clothes so headed to the sports store to buy a new outfit. A blue tracksuit with a hooded top and matching trainers put a smile on his face. He wore them out of the shop, with his own clothes stuffed into a plastic carrier bag. The hood pulled up, gave him some anonymity from prying eyes, he didn't want to get recognised until he was back on his feet.

It was only ten thirty and Casey knew he had to keep a low profile, so headed back to the hostel to deposit his clothes. He plugged the charger into his pager and the device flashed to life. *"At least Marco can contact me,"* he thought. The clock turned very slowly as he sat on the bed, anticipating his meeting with Marco. Maybe he'd give him his job back? Maybe he'd find him some work? Or maybe he'd just pay him off to disappear? Meeting Marco by the river worried him, an ideal place for an ambush, so Casey had to go early to check the place out.

With thirty minutes to spare, Casey arrived at the river and quickly checked around for anyone loitering. There were a few couples walking, the occasional jogger and dog walker, but nothing that gave him concern. He found an empty bench positioned evenly between two footbridges, both some distance away. He had a good view and also a means of escape if needed. Casey pulled his hood further forward over his face and sat on the bench in preparation. Every few moments, he surveyed the one hundred and eighty degree viewpoint, looking for hazards.

Midday came and went, nothing happened; was Marco messing him around? He was never known for his promptness. Casey sighed with relief, when fifteen minutes later Marco appeared from the bridge and started walking along the footpath. He was wearing his usual long black coat, which was unbuttoned; his large stomach bulging over his tight waistline. His black hair slicked back and glistening rings on his fingers. Quickly surveying each direction, Casey was reassured everything was okay. As Marco came close, Casey stood up, pulled down his hood and said, *"Hello boss."*

Marco already had a sizable brown envelope stuffed with cash in his hand, but froze to the spot in total disbelief. He couldn't speak, he couldn't move, time frozen. *"No, no, it can't be!"* screamed in his head, as he saw the adult image of Vincenzo stood before him. He had never seen Casey with hair before, his curly brown hair; the same as Vinnie. Marco scrutinised his features, his nose, his chin, his eyes; they all matched. ***"No, no, it can't be!"***

Realisation turned to rage as fire-breathing dragons exploded in Marco's head. *"He's your son, isn't he?"* Marco spat, before the volcano of anger erupted. *"I'm gonna fucking kill you and that bastard boy!"* he raged, lunging to grab Casey. He managed to side step the attack and retreat a few steps as Marco stumbled to the ground. Casey stood in shock as Marco got to his feet and pulled a pistol from his coat. Casey turned and fled as fast as he could. *"I'm gonna fucking kill you!"* ranted Marco as the first shot was fired.

Casey glanced over his shoulder as the bullet spat dirt from the pathway. Marco had the pistol aimed directly at him; he had no choice other than to dive into the water. As he plunged into the murky refuge of debris and silt, two further bullets hit the water just missing him. Casey had to swim for his life, through this putrid sludge; he had to swim as far as he could underwater, as he didn't know what was waiting for him above the surface.

Part 24

Casey could no longer fight the urge to take a breath. He would drown if he stayed under the water, alternatively he could be shot above; he had to take the risk and surface. Just as a crocodile stalks its prey, Casey raised his head just enough to expose his eyes and nose. He was in the sanctuary of the overhanging shelf on the far side of the riverbank. He could see Marco running away along the towpath, still waving his pistol. Casey pulled himself up a little more so he could open his mouth and take a gasp of air. His heart was pounding rhythmically to the stomping of Marco's feet as he disappeared into the distance.

Once the coast was clear, Casey pulled himself from the dirty water, and then ran as fast as he could to his hostel. He peeled off his dripping clothes, throwing them into a soggy heap in the corner of his bedroom floor. Naked, he streaked across the passageway into the communal shower room, to wash the stench from his body. A wisp of dirty water swirled around his feet, as the shower did its work to cleanse his body, yet his mind was in turmoil reliving the moments from the river.

Realising he had forgotten to pick up his towel, he had to dash naked and dripping back to his room. A couple met him in the passageway; the girl squealed in surprise, whereas her boyfriend cheered. The last view they had was to see his bare bottom disappear from sight as he closed the door behind him.

He sat on his bed for quite some time, allowing the droplets of water to run down his body, soaking the mattress. *"**Shit, shit, shit!**"* he screamed out loud. *"He'll fucking kill me! Oh shit!"* He knew without question, he had to leave the town and never come back; to run as fast and as far as he possibly could. It was too dangerous to leave in daylight; he could easily be spotted. He had to wait for nightfall and hope he wasn't found beforehand.

Sofia was surprised to hear the squeal of Marco's car on the driveway. He very rarely came home during the day. It was just after four o'clock and Vinnie had just gone down for his afternoon nap. *"Shhh!"* she said with her finger to her lips, as Marco came storming through the door. *"Vinnie's asleep,"* she continued. Without warning Marco punched her in the face, knocking her backward through the doorway into the kitchen.

*"I fucking know, I've always known, that bastard child isn't mine!"* Marco ranted before landing a punishing kick into her ribs. *"That f-fucking Casey ........... And you!"* he spat. *"I'll kill him, I'll kill you and I'll kill that bastard child!"* he continued to rant.

Pulling Sofia to her feet by her hair, he landed another punishing slap to the side of her face, spraying blood from her mouth over the work surface. She struggled to remain on her feet, holding onto the counter for support. Marco roared as he approached her again; Sofia pulled a large knife from the rack, and then turned to plunge it deep into his chest.

His look of pure hatred turned to complete shock in a split second. Marco clutched his chest, the blood trickled over his fingertips; the blade was deeply embedded; only the handle was visible. Marco fell backwards with lifeless eyes, hitting the floor heavily; his facial expression not changing as his head split open on the tiled floor. Sofia was unable to move for what seemed eternity, just left panting heavily through her mouth; then she burst into tears, sobbing for what she had done, sobbing for the end of his abuse and sobbing for the consequences ahead.

Sofia was thankful that young Vinnie hadn't seen the carnage, and that he'd slept through the ordeal. She ran the cold tap, scooping a handful of water to rinse her bloody mouth, spitting the contents into the sink. The tap continued to swirl water down the plughole, mesmerising her; was this symbolic of her future?

Casey was already dressed and ready to flee. The daylight was turning to dusk. He had been waiting for darkness so he could leave the hostel. His worldly possessions stuffed in two holdalls; he had put five hundred in his jacket pocket to pay for his escape. A strange buzzing sound came from the side pocket of one of his holdalls. The unexpected sound made him jump out of his skin, making his fearful state worse. *"What the fuck!"*

He struggled to free the knotted zip and reached inside the pocket to discover his pager ringing. The message said, *"HELP ME - S."* Sofia needed him, he owed her that much.

He feared for his own life, yet needed to know what she wanted. He ran to the phone box and dialled the Rossi house phone. Within two rings Sofia answered, *"Casey is that you?"* He remained silent not knowing what to say; eventually he cleared his throat and said, *"Yeah."*

261

Sofia burst into tears, sobbing uncontrollably, *"I need your help …… Marco is dead."* With a mixture of dread and also relief, he replied, *"Oh shit! Ok, I'll come over."*

Arriving at the back of the Rossi house he found the gate locked. Casey scaled the fence and jogged across the lawn. He pulled open the patio doors to an eerie silence. He crept as quietly as he could through the lounge, not knowing what to expect. The kitchen door was open and he could see Marco lying in a pool of blood, the handle of a knife still erect from a gashing wound to his chest; Casey reluctantly stepped inside.

In the corner he could see Sofia sat on the floor curled in a ball, knees pulled tightly to her chin, propped up against a wall, her clothes covered with blood. Her eyes flashed in his direction, but she never moved, she never murmured. Casey walked over to her, his eyes still glued to the image of the dead man. Crouching down next to her he said, *"Are you ok?"* Clearly she wasn't okay, what a stupid thing to ask. Sofia didn't reply, just extended her hand to stroke his hair, the same as her son's. She then burst into tears and hugged him, sobbing onto his shoulder.

*"Fuck what a mess, we've got to sort this*," Casey instructed as he pulled Sofia up. His heart was pounding and he had to think on his feet. He had to help her he owed her that. He had to make amends for stealing her child, to ease his conscience. He hoped that she hadn't realised and hated him for it. Casey guessed not as she had called him, maybe as a last resort, but at least as a friend.

Casey pulled the knife from Marco's chest, wrapping it in a kitchen towel and placing it inside his jacket. *"This is what* *you **must** do,"* ordered Casey. *"Take off your clothes and put them in the washing machine, we must destroy the evidence."* He continued, *"Take a shower to wash off his blood,"* Sofia could do no more than silently conform to his instructions; she wasn't thinking clearly enough to question him.

Sofia stepped out of the upstairs bathroom, wrapped in a dressing gown, her hair dripping water onto the floor. Casey was stood on the landing to meet her. *"Now phone the police. Tell them you were taking a shower and heard a scuffle downstairs, you found Marco dead in the kitchen."* Sofia nodded her head, still not really comprehending what Casey was telling her to do; she felt like a zombie in a surreal world following inane commands. A sleepy cry from an adjoining bedroom brought her back to reality, *"Its Vinnie, he's awake."* She disappeared into his bedroom before Casey could interrupt her thoughts.

Casey waited, distracted in a weird respite of normality, in a toxic situation. Sofia reappeared holding the child. ***"It's impossible!"*** screamed inside Casey's head. Before him was a young child with curly brown hair. *"What happened?"* continued to bombard his thoughts, *"Did someone switch them back?"* Tess had blond hair and Colin was ginger, how could they produce a baby that looked like Tommy, just like him? *"No, no, no, it can't be. Shit, shit, shit!"* continued to attack his mind.

He looked back at Sofia in disbelief and spluttered with a choking voice, *"C-call the P-police. Now!"* Then he ran down the stairs and out the patio doors.

263

His mind was cascading into a deep abyss. The shock that his plans had been uncovered, that his plans had been destroyed, consumed him. Up until this moment, his son had been still at risk from the vile Marco, he had still been living in a mobster's world. God-knows what future lay ahead for him; Casey's mind was on overdrive with the endless possibilities of anarchy and violence.

The street lamps appeared to illuminate pyramids of light onto the pavement; car headlights flashed past as if streaks of light from a laser display. The din of their engines rhythmically whooshed by, in a hypnotic tone. Everything was raining down on him like a raging cyclone as he stepped off the kerb.

A squeal of tyres broke his trance. The first impact of the car tore his legs away from under him. The second impact bounced his body on the bonnet of the car; the third impact cracked the car's windscreen as his head pounded the glass. As the car ground to a halt, his limp body slid off the vehicle onto the tarmac. He lay there still, and lifeless; darkness consumed him as he blacked out.

Beep ….. Beep ….. Beep, rang through his ears from the heart monitor. He could see a bright light creeping through the slit of his ruptured eye, then heard a squeak from a passing trolley. Pain racked through his body; opening his eyes he could see that he was lying in a hospital bed. Casey tried to move to get more comfortable, then realised that he was handcuffed to the bed. A policeman was stood guard outside the closed door.

Part 25

Once Casey was well enough to be discharged from hospital, he was officially arrested for the murder of Marco Rossi.

*"You're not going to wriggle yourself out of this one,"* said the detective in a condescending tone. Two police detectives interrogated Casey in an interview room for a couple of hours. His solicitor advised him to say, *"No comment,"* to all the questions that were being bombarded at him by these two police officers. *"How can you sit there and say nothing?"* ranted the detective, *"We have a stack of evidence against you."*

*"You had his blood on your clothes."*

*"You had the murder weapon in your jacket."*

*"Your fingerprints were on the knife."*

*"You had a large sum of money on you."*

*"What was your motive for killing him?"* quizzed the detective towering over him. *"Did you argue over money? What happened Kelvin, tell me what happened?"* Clearly Casey's silence was frustrating the officers, who were hoping for a confession.

Casey's mind wandered back to Sofia holding her child on the landing; their child on the landing, he should have been living in safety with Tess. His plan had backfired. He

265

couldn't implicate Sofia, she had to look after their son; he couldn't deprive him of his mother. Casey had no choice other than to take the rap. He was implicated anyway and he had to do the right thing for his son.

He lifted his head to look at his interrogators and said, *"Yeah I did it, I killed him."*

The interview was terminated and they returned Casey to his cell. He was detained at the police station a little longer, until he was transferred to a prison, pending trial. With such a serious charge, they couldn't risk the chance of him absconding. He had only left the same prison gates a few days before, yet he was back already. He didn't feel daunted by the prospect, he knew how the system worked, keep his head down and do his time. His impending court appearance left him no hope, clearly the evidence was stacked against him; he'd be seeing the inside of prisons for many years to come.

*"Hello Kelvin, did you miss me?"* Frank chuckled at the sight of Casey, returning so soon after his release. *"Yes Frank, I couldn't live without you,"* Casey returned the banter. He wasn't feeling very jovial, but had to remain composed; any weakness could be exploited, any hostile reaction would land him another beating. Casey had to play the game.

The prison warden led him to his allocated cell, where a stern inmate called Jack, one of Frank's henchmen, greeted him. *"Back again, did you steal some sweeties?"* Casey was in no mood to pamper to his jibes, *"No, I killed someone,"* he snapped. A look of shock swept over Jack's face as Casey slumped on to the bottom bunk.

Casey became the talk of the prison wing; many prisoners gave him a wide berth. Frank and his henchmen gave him healthy respect by not riding shotgun over him. Casey wanted to keep his head down, until the trial. He still had lots of issues to deal with in his head. He tried to make sense of what happened in the maternity ward a couple of years before and what had happened in the meantime. He had to reconcile his involvement with the killing of Marco; if only he hadn't made that phone call, his life would have been so different. He would have been miles away spending his money and free as a bird; now he was trapped in a cage.

*"Why get involved? …… Fucking idiot!"* screamed through Casey's head.

It felt unreal that Casey had left prison for such a short time, yet been involved in a violent confrontation with Marco that nearly cost his life, and then turning the tables to become an accomplice in his murder. If only he could rewrite those few days, his life would have been so different.

Casey was appointed a solicitor called Margaret Graham. She was a stern older lady, with short grey hair and a large hairy mole protruding from her chin. The buttons of her jacket struggled to withstand the girth of her bulging stomach, as she sat across the table from him. *"It's not helping your case, refusing to give a statement,"* she lectured him, and then continued, *"The judge may be more lenient if you showed remorse."* Casey leaned across the table, as if having a direct conversation with her mole, *"I did it, and I'll do the time. That's all you need to know."*

The police took several weeks to compile the case against Casey, leaving him to remain incarcerated pending trial. For him, the time behind bars was no different to that of the last two years, no visitors, no contact with the outside world, just a forgotten life. He had no one to care for him or about him. He hoped Tess would visit one day, but she had no reason to. He hoped Sofia would visit one day, but she couldn't implicate herself. His family had become the varied and colourful characters detained with him.

*'Margaret the Mole'* as Casey referred to her, had one last meeting with him before his trial. She wanted to prepare her paperwork and her defence for him, but she had very little to offer to vindicate his actions. Casey continued to take sole responsibility for Marco's death and refused to reveal a motive. She could do no more than to explain to him, the consequences of his actions and the possible outcome of the trial. As she left the interview room, Casey was left feeling cheated of his future and regrets for his past. With his feral upbringing and subsequent lifestyle, he didn't stand a chance. The cards were stacked against him at every turn. He didn't have the role models to guide him along the straight and narrow; his fate had been sealed the day he was born, it was just a matter of time.

The prison warden woke him early on the day of his trial. Casey went to the shower block to freshen up, and then he was taken to the reception block, where he was given a black suit and white shirt from the clothing lockers. He had no formal clothes of his own and felt uncomfortable being dressed in a cheap, ill-fitting suit, like a penguin. Casey guessed that was the least of his problems right now.

Handcuffed to a guard, he was led into the courtyard, where he boarded a secure vehicle to take him to court. Casey felt quite blasé about the journey, not appreciating the enormity of what lay ahead; for him, it was just another day at the office. Being incarcerated had numbed his expectations of life, he had formed a strange attachment to prison life and the camaraderie of the inmates; possibly the family unit that he'd never had before.

*"All rise,"* instructed the court official as the judge entered the room. As he sat into his superior chair, everyone else in the courtroom sat in unison.

Casey scanned the faces in the room, and spotted Sofia in the front row of the pews. Their eyes locked. For a brief moment she smiled discreetly, before dropping her gaze. The charge was read out to him, before the proceedings commenced. He watched a procession of people take the stand to give evidence, but he was stunned to see Sofia take the stand; his heart pounded fiercely in anticipation. He felt a little betrayed, yet she was only following his instruction.

Sofia looked uneasy as she gave her account, *"I was upstairs having a shower, when I heard raised voices and a commotion downstairs. I dressed as quickly as I could and rushed down the stairs, to find my husband dead on the kitchen floor."* She sniffed and dabbed her eye, as if to blot a tear; Casey knew she was acting. Her cross-examination took a few minutes more, and then she was allowed to resume her seat in the pew.

The jury, which was sat to Casey's right-hand side, listened to every word spoken.

Casey was led to the stand to give his own account of the event. *"Marco owed me money. We argued and I stabbed him."* His brief defence brought on a bombardment of questions from the prosecution solicitor and also his defence solicitor, '*Margaret the Mole*'. Casey remained steadfast in his resolve to take the blame. He was determined not to implicate Sofia and leave his son without a mother. He couldn't allow his son to go into foster care as he had done.

During a lengthy recess, Casey was placed in a holding cell, where he was given a tray of lukewarm food. "*The last supper,*" he thought.

Returning to the courtroom Casey was instructed to stand as the jury read their verdict, "*Guilty!*"

The judge turned to him and said, "*Kelvin Carter, you have been found guilty of the murder of Marco Rossi.*" He then continued his summery by saying, "*As punishment for this heinous crime, you will receive a prison sentence of no less than twenty-five years.*"

Sofia shed a genuine tear, as Casey was led to the cells. He briefly glanced at her and thought to himself, "*Life's a bitch ... then you get fucked over by one.*"

Part 26

Sofia was overwhelmed with guilt when Casey was sent to jail, but she had to focus on her own liberty and do the best she could for Vinnie. He was the centre of her world, the reason she existed; she had never known true love before her son, the beat of a mother's heart. Nothing or no one would ever be allowed to tarnish that.

She wanted to visit Casey, to write to him, to contact him in some way to say how sorry she was; to say how grateful she was for his sacrifice, but she couldn't. She couldn't implicate herself in the deception, the web of lies that had brought her to this point. Sofia prayed for him every night and also prayed for herself; she would never forgive herself for the evil deed she had committed, yet at the same time felt huge relief from the end of her abuse. In her whirlwind of emotions, Vinnie remained her guiding light.

Sofia wanted no part of Marco's empire or what it represented. The Cartwright brothers gave her a handsome sum to buy The Roxy; they knew the purchase also included the territory to continue practicing the illegal street antics. They were just as, if not meaner than Marco, so it would be a profitable patch for them to own. Sofia was just pleased to cut her ties from that sort of lifestyle.

She also sold her house. The place was never a home to her and she had to escape all the memories oozing from every shadowy corner. It was a tomb that imprisoned her and consumed her thoughts. She had brought to an end her abusive marriage, yet Marco was still controlling her

271

routines and her habits. It was just like he was still there barking his orders into her head. Sofia needed a completely new start, for her and for Vinnie.

*"Here's the keys to your new home Mrs Rossi,"* beamed the estate agent on completion of their transaction. Sofia had found a spacious cottage a few yards away from the church where she had infrequently attended before. Since the demise of Marco, she had found solace with the congregation. Now Sofia had the freedom to attend the services each week and become involved in the social activities they held. They had been very supportive and friendships had grown; she felt safe for the first time since she could remember.

Everyone he met adored Vinnie. His cheeky antics and boundless energy won the hearts of all he came into contact with. The church was a place where Sofia was comfortable to let the toddler explore and interact with other children; something that her previous life wouldn't permit. As difficult and traumatic as her marriage was, and her heinous actions, which killed her husband, she felt a huge weight had been lifted from her shoulders. Sofia felt extremely guilty that Casey or should she call him Kelvin, had taken the blame for her crime, yet understood his selfless act to protect his own son. She thought about him every day; their affair was brief, but the events had changed her life.

\* \* \*

Sofia dropped a tear at the sight of Vincenzo Rossi dressed for his first day at school. With his maroon blazer, grey shorts, white shirt and school tie, he looked so grown up. His long mop of curly brown hair created a halo-like aura around his head. Sofia was so proud of him, as she led him into his first classroom; then embarrassed him by kissing him goodbye. Outside she dabbed away a tear as she met other mother's in a similar state. *"It's tough to see them grow up,"* said a Chinese lady, holding a tissue in her hand. *"Yes,"* replied Sofia, *"I know how you feel."*

Later that same day, all the parents were lined up outside the school entrance to collect their children. Several seemed anxious whether their child had settled during their first day at school. Vinnie came wandering out the entrance, trailing way behind everyone else. *"Come on mister slowcoach,"* joked Sofia. He was holding a painting and promptly handed it to her, *"This is for you mama,"* he said. *"Oh that's lovely Vinnie,"* she replied with a proud smile on her face. It was a crude mixture of bright colours, with two stick figures in the middle, one large and one small. She asked, *"Is this you and me?"* He nodded then quizzed, *"Do I have a papa?"* This was the first time he'd mentioned Marco since his death and it floored Sofia for a moment. *"No darling, he is in heaven. Why do you ask?"* He looked up at her with sad eyes and replied, *"Other children painted a mama and a papa."*

*"Let's get an ice cream as you've been such a good boy,"* Sofia piped up. She had to distract the youngster from any more awkward questions. They both skipped along the street to the shop.

Sofia had been on a roller coaster for the last two decades. Falling in love with the bad-boy Marco when she was a teenager, being disowned by her father, and then being dragged into a loveless, abusive false marriage fifteen hundred miles away from her home. The one decision she

273

made all those years ago to defy her father's advice, took her down a path of no further choices. She felt lonely and controlled by a tyrant. He had institutionalised her and even since his death she felt powerless to make her own decisions.

The parishioners of her church were empathetic and supportive, but they never knew the full story of Sofia's past, so couldn't comprehend her plight. Vinnie was her world, the reason she had to fight through the quicksand of toxic emotions that engulfed her mind. She was still that innocent little girl inside, yet her eyes had seen things that no one should see; her body had endured violent punishment and her mind stripped of rational thought. She realised that her son had become her obsession, so she needed to get help.

*"Hello Sofia. Please come in and sit down."* Esther Goldberg was a counsellor whom Sofia had plucked up the courage to contact. It had taken several attempts for her to just pick up the telephone to make the appointment; Sofia's anxiety about the meeting caused her to reschedule three times. Vinnie was safely at school and Sofia had to summon up the courage to face her fears. *"Can you tell me how you are feeling?"* Esther softly asked. Sofia just broke down in tears, sobbing uncontrollably.

It was the first step, a major step that Sofia had taken to come to terms with her life so far. She had to unravel almost four decades of her life, to reconcile the irreconcilable; she didn't know where to start, yet she felt safe to be guided by the non-judgemental Esther. Sofia had never revealed her inner thoughts before and although she was willing to discuss her issues, she remained guarded over the details of

274

Marcos death. She could never trust anyone else with that knowledge.

The first few weekly sessions with the counsellor, were emotionally charged with tears, anger and frustration. Esther's skilful approach, reassured Sofia that she had to go through this painful process to create any sort of future life for herself. She could no longer live her life as a frightened recluse, being controlled by a ghost from her past.

The church group could see a difference in her as Sofia's confidence grew. These were the closest people that she associated with, these were her friends; more so, they were the closest people that she considered to be family. One of the elders at the church reminded her of her father. She longed to see her father, to talk to him, to beg his forgiveness.

*"Dear Papa and Mama,"* she wrote, *"I know it has been many years, and I don't know where to start."* Sofia screwed up the piece of paper and tossed it into the rubbish bin, along with dozens of other discarded sheets. Words didn't flow well, words didn't seem to be enough, to explain how she was feeling, but she knew she had to write something. It was just after midnight when she finally finished her brief note; sealing it into an envelope, she hoped her parents still lived in their family home.

A few weeks later, the letter was returned unopened, saying, *"Return to sender."*

Sofia was devastated to receive the returned item and thoughts bombarded her mind. Did her father see her address on the flipside of the envelope and refuse to open

275

it? Had they moved? Were they still alive? The not knowing stirred her emotions much more than she ever realised it would. The thought of leaving so much unsaid punished her mind. She wanted to explain, to say that she had made a huge mistake, to say they were grandparents. Sofia sobbed until her tears ran dry.

*"Is this the Private Investigations Agency?"* Sofia nervously asked down the telephone. *"I've got a job for you."*

Dave Banks, an ex-policeman turned sleuth, met Sofia in the reception of The ABC Bureau. His back-street office had an unassuming black door, which led from a quiet street, up a staircase to his office. His advert in the local newspaper was quite elaborate compared to his meagre business premises and Sofia realised his operation consisted of him and his receptionist / administration assistant. On reflection, this was a good choice and very low-key. *"Mr Banks, I would like you to find my parents,"* Sofia instructed, and then continued, *"But they live in Italy, is that a problem?"*

Dave Banks quizzically smiled and replied, *"Yes that's fine Mrs Rossi, but you'll need to cover my fees and expenses."* Money wasn't an issue for Sofia, having banked Marco's illicit wealth. After a brief discussion, they agreed a cost and Mr Banks jotted down the minimum information that she had. Sofia left the office with a mixture of excitement and apprehension; many years had passed with no contact and she didn't know how she would be received, if and when they were tracked down.

*"Hey Mama, can we bake some cakes?"* Vinnie excitedly asked. He had been cooking in his school class and loved to

stir the ingredients together. Sofia called him her little chef as he spent hours in the kitchen with her preparing food, but Vinnie enjoyed getting messy with flour and eggs. Just like any other eight year old, his treat was to lick the spoon of the raw cake mix; Sofia would pass him the spoon and dab the contents on his nose, much to their amusement. She wanted to pass on to him her knowledge and replicate the warm memories of her own childhood; her Mama was a great cook and taught her so much.

Sofia let Vinnie enjoy a warm cupcake from the oven with a glass of milk before his bedtime. Staring at him munching on his supper, she got lost in a fantasy world of innocence and security. She could see herself dressed in her pyjamas, sat at the dining table nibbling away at her mother's latest batch of fruitcake. Raisins and crumbs would litter her lap; she quickly brushed them off onto the floor when her mother had turned away. It just strengthened her resolve to track down her parents even more.

*"Vinnie, please put your shoes on, it's time for school,"* Sofia cursed out of frustration. Scooping down to pick up the post, she quickly scoured the letters; one stood out from her usual bills, a letter from The ABC Bureau. Sofia ripped open the envelope. *"Dear Mrs Rossi, please contact the office. We have information regards your search."* The letter was brief and official, giving away very little. She wanted more details. Their office wasn't far from Vinnie's school; she would call there directly after dropping him off.

*"Ah, Mrs Rossi,"* Dave Banks acknowledged as she entered his office, *"Please sit down."* It had taken three weeks for him to gather information; little time for him, yet an eternity for Sofia. *"I have to sadly tell you that your mother passed*

*away five years ago, but your father is still alive and is residing in a nursing home,"* he informed her before passing Sofia an address printed on a piece of paper. She recognised the area, but the address was unknown to her. *"Thank you, Mr Banks,"* she replied. She left with bittersweet feelings; sadness that she had missed her mother's funeral, but happiness that she may get to see her father.

*"Would you like to go on a plane?"* Sofia asked Vinnie. He was a little bemused until she explained they were going on holiday and it would be fun. Vinnie had never left the country before, nor had Sofia for many years; she had to plan her trip in advance to organise a passport for them both. She had found a website of the nursing home where her father was staying and had called them to ensure it was okay to visit. It seemed strange for her to speak in her native tongue; she had been speaking English for many years, yet conversing in Italian stirred up warm memories. Sofia was becoming excited about the trip, yet sceptical about her father's reaction. The nursing home warned her that some days he wasn't very receptive.

The days, hours and minutes felt like an eternity until they boarded the plane for Naples. Throughout the flight Sofia's stomach was churning, but she kept a brave smile on her face, so as to reassure her nervous son. It was the first time on a plane for both of them; Sofia had fled with Marco almost three decade before, escaping by train and boat. Reality struck her when it was time to alight the plane, suffering a mild panic attack. The airline steward quickly recognised her plight and discreetly told them both to sit until all the other passengers had left, *"To avoid the rush,"* she said with a wink. Sofia was grateful for the short respite to compose herself, Vinnie hadn't noticed anything was wrong.

A taxi took them to a hotel on the outskirts of Naples, to a suburb she was familiar with. Memories flooded over her as they travelled along streets that she recognised. The hotel was tucked away in a quiet side road; although many years had passed and she had changed in appearance, she didn't want to get recognised or draw attention to herself. When the grey haired lady in reception engaged in chitchat, she asked her the nature of her visit. Sofia paused for a moment and replied, *"Oh, just passing through."*

*"Mama, these people talk funny,"* little Vinnie said out of innocence. Sofia chuckled and replied, *"They speak Italian, just like me."* He shrugged his shoulders as he pulled a game from his suitcase and started to preoccupy himself. Sofia stared out of the bedroom window, rehearsing conversations in her head for the following day. She hoped her father would be forgiving.

The nursing home was very bland and unassuming from the outside, almost unidentifiable as a dwelling. It reminded her of an office block with curtains. The entrance was a simple double glass door leading to a reception area; an unattended desk stood before her, with a sign saying, *'Ring bell for Attention.'* Sofia gripped Vinnie's hand tightly as they waited for a member of staff to come. *"I've come to see Luigi Costa, I'm his daughter,"* Sofia informed the receptionist. They were instructed to take a seat whilst a porter was called to take them to him.

A short overweight man seemed to waddle through an adjacent doorway to greet them. He was a man of few words, just asked them to follow him to the communal lounge. Sofia grabbed Vinnie's hand and they trailed behind this man along what seemed to be an endless corridor. Noises of chatter came from rooms they passed. Occasionally Sofia would catch a glimpse of residents staring silently at her through open doors, this made her feel quite uneasy.

They entered a spacious room with several residents sitting around the outskirts in upright lounge chairs. A television blared from the corner and a couple of people were loudly chatting to be heard. Sofia scoured the room, unable to recognise her father, but continued to follow the porter. They reached an alcove by the window, where a frail figure was staring outside. She didn't believe it was him and almost questioned the porter's introduction. *"Luigi your daughter is here to see you."* As Sofia and Vinnie stood before him, his blank eyes looked at her. She could now see that it was him, or rather a shell of his former self. *"Hello Papa,"* she said, but there was no acknowledgement of her words. The porter interrupted by saying, *"He's suffering with dementia and struggles to remember anyone. Don't expect too much."*

Sofia crouched down to hold his hand and said, *"This is your grandson Vincenzo."* His eyes flickered towards the youngster but there was no reaction, he just mumbled something inaudible. The porter brought over a couple of plastic dining chairs for them to sit on and left them alone. Sofia felt heartbroken inside seeing the husk of what used to be a strong man. She tried to make conversation with him, translating her words in English to Vinnie, who sat awkwardly watching; he was too young to understand.

An hour or so passed with Sofia trying to communicate to her father, occasionally she would get an incoherent mumble; she was unsure whether it was a reply to what she had said, or random chatter. She was struggling with her own emotions and Vinnie was becoming restless. Sofia leant over to kiss him on the forehead and whispered, *"Forgive me Papa."* There was no reaction from him, no movement; he just stared blankly through the window. Sofia left without the resolution she wanted, still not knowing if he had understood her words; she never looked back. Outside she dropped a silent tear, so as not to alert Vinnie that she was upset.

The taxi ride back to their hotel was a time for Sofia to quietly reflect on her visit. Her thoughts were interrupted with Vinnie's chatter, a welcome distraction for her. Sofia realised that this may be the last time that she would ever come back to this region; her father didn't recognise her and may not have much time left, therefore she would have no reason to return. Her childhood memories flashed through her mind, some she had the urge to share with Vinnie.

Back at the hotel, they packed their suitcases and headed for Gaiola Beach a few miles down the coast. It was a special place for her with happy childhood memories. The trip had been tough on her and also Vinnie, so she wanted to treat him to some fun. Checking into another hotel overlooking the sea, they spent a few days laughing and playing on the beach. This was a rare treat for Vinnie. Living in the centre of England, he didn't often get the opportunity to swim in the sea or build sandcastles. Sofia had time to put things into perspective and focus on what really mattered to her, the welfare of her son.

Part 27

*"Slow down Sammy,"* shouted Tess as the three year old rushed around the house. Ever since he could stand on two feet, he ran everywhere. Sam was a stocky young lad with jet-black hair. He had similar features to Tommy, but his hair colour was always a mystery; Colin had red hair and Tess was blonde. She could remember her father having dark hair when she was a child, but now his locks had turned grey. The youngster seemed to follow the genes of Bert with his portly stature and olive skin.

Samuel and Thomas played and also fought like brothers do, but they were close and spent all their time together. Doris always said, *"They are as thick as thieves,"* when they were up to mischief. Sammy seemed the sly one, leaving his older brother to take the blame for any misdemeanours. Tommy was now attending school, leaving the days free for Sammy and his mum to bond.

Colin looked weary when he came home from work. *"Has it been a tough day?"* Tess asked, handing him a steaming cup of tea. Colin flopped into his armchair before replying, *"Yeah, we had a stock delivery, and mum was playing up."* He sipped from his cup before continuing, *"She was calling me upstairs every few minutes, so I got nothing done."*

Winnie was almost a recluse in her flat above the shop, Colin was the only contact she had with the outside world. Her days were spent glued to her television and seeking attention from her son. Her mental health had been suffering since William had died; she had spent all her life with him and now she felt lost. As a consequence of her reluctance to leave the flat, her physical health started to deteriorate. Her mobility became laboured and she began to neglect herself.

Tess brought Colin his dinner on a tray, and then herded the boys up the stairs to bath them before bed. Once fed he poked his head around the bathroom door to join in the raucous of laughter as the boys splashed in the tub. In the small bathroom, there was no escape for Tess and Colin to avoid the spray of water as the boys excitedly played. They didn't mind, they loved to spend family time and eagerly joined in the revelry.

Colin and Tess took a child each, wrapping them in a towel and briskly rubbing them dry, much to the youngsters' amusement. The boys both ran naked to their bedroom squealing with laughter, followed in hot pursuit by their playful parents; Colin stomped along the corridor, arms above his head imitating a monster, whereas Tess chanted, *"We're the cuddle monsters!"*

Once the brothers were dressed in their pyjamas, Colin snuggled up with them on Tommy's bed for some quiet-time, reading them their favourite bedtime story about monsters. Tess went downstairs to wash up the dinner things, leaving the three men of her house to their nightly ritual. She was surprised that Colin hadn't come down before she had tidied the kitchen. Tess crept upstairs to find him fast asleep on a single bed with both of the boys. She chuckled to herself and felt a warm glow of love, seeing them cramped precariously on Tommy's bed. She scooped Sammy up and returned him to his bed; he didn't stir from his slumber. *"Come on sleepy-head,"* Tess whispered, giving Colin a nudge. He opened his eyes and grinned. As he slid off the bed, he wrapped Tommy in his duvet, before they both crept from the room. A click of the light switch plunged the room into darkness.

* * *

Tess had a lump in her throat the day Sammy started school. Watching Thomas and Samuel walking hand in hand through the school gates with their lunch packs over their shoulders, she thought how grown up they looked. Sammy was as big as Tommy; they were different in shape and hair colour, but similar features. From the back they looked like classmates, yet from the front clearly brothers.

She had never had the house to herself for the last seven years, one or the other child under her feet, yet the house felt so empty; she felt lost so went to her mother's for a cuppa and chat. Doris was elbows-deep in flour as normal, baking cakes for the factory workers, Tess joined in the task. *"Mum, how did you fill your time when I was at school?"* already knowing the answer. *'What a stupid question'* Tess thought. Doris just smiled and replied, *"Keeping house for you, your Dad and the extended factory family,"* pointing to her cake mixture. Her mum was the hub that kept the wheels spinning.

*"Mummy, Sammy got told off by the teacher for running along the corridor,"* barked Tommy in a telltale tone. Sam took no notice when questioned by Tess, he just ran into the garden to kick his ball. *"He can never sit still,"* she muttered to herself, then smiled when he celebrated, scoring between the painted goal posts on their back fence. *"He is a little monkey,"* she thought.

285

Tess and Colin settled down to watch a film after the boys had gone to bed; Tess recalled her events of the day. *"Don't worry Tess,"* Colin said and then continued, *"The boys have to grow up sometime."* With a chuckle Tess replied, *"Maybe we should try for a girl."* Colin gulped, and then burst into laughter, *"You had me going for a minute."* They both continued to laugh, but deep down Tess was feeling broody.

*"Mummy, I've wet the bed,"* Sammy said bleary-eyed, as he walked into the lounge. *"Don't worry, mummy will sort it."* It was an unusual event, but she guessed he was feeling unsettled starting at school. Colin picked him up and went about changing his pyjamas, whilst Tess went to change his sheets. *"Colin, come here!"* she called. He abruptly stopped as he walked into the bedroom with the sleepy Sam in his arms. Tess was holding back the duvet to expose the urine soaked bottom sheet; within the contents of the liquid were traces of blood.

Colin and Tess had a sleepless night, fretting over Sammy, wondering what had caused him to pass blood. He didn't seem to be poorly, but they had to get it checked out. Colin had to begrudgingly go to work the next morning, he had no one else to open the store, but Tess promised to call into the shop on the way back from the doctors to give him an update. Colin's mind wasn't on the job, overcharging and undercharging the customers, much to their annoyance.

*"Well Miss Clifton, Samuel seems fine, but drop in a urine sample and I'll get it checked,"* said Doctor Phillips. Sammy was full of life and full of cheek, asking the doctor what each of the instruments were for. The doctor gave Tess

286

a prescription for antibiotics, just in case he had an infection, but he didn't seem concerned.

Colin felt reassured when Sammy came stampeding into the shop, quickly followed by Tess. They briefly chatted about the conversation with the doctor, before Tess returned the youngster to school. On the way back home Tess felt extremely alone and anxious; she didn't want to spend the rest of the day on her own, so she returned to the shop. *"Colin, I thought you might need a hand."* He was pleased to have her there and gave her a peck on the cheek.

Tess realised that working with Colin may fill the void she had experienced with the boys being at school, so this became a regular arrangement. They never heard back from the doctor regards the urine sample, which they had left; they assumed no news was good news.

*"Mummy, I saw Tommy kiss a girl,"* Sam said with a giggle. Tess didn't know how to reply, so just chuckled and continued preparing their evening meal.

Sammy seemed to be slowing down, not racing around at a hundred miles an hour anymore. Tess assumed school was wearing him out; often he would doze watching television and have to be woken up for his dinner. She could never remember Tommy looking so tired.

*"Mummy I've wet the bed,"* Sam said as he waddled into the lounge, trying to keep his wet pyjamas off his legs. Colin picked him up, whilst Tess raced up the stairs to check the sheets. Colin carried the sobbing youngster back to his bedroom to fetch clean clothes, only to find a tearful Tess

transfixed at the sight of his bloody urine sheets. The three of them hugged, oblivious to the transfer of his wet clothes.

It had been several months since the last episode. The parents thought it had been a one off incident, but now they were worried. Colin managed to contact Barry his part time work assistant, who agreed to open the store for him. The following day Colin and Tess insisted on seeing the doctor although his schedule was fully booked. He agreed to see them at the end of the morning session.

*"There is no record that you previously brought in a urine sample,"* the doctor retorted to Colin's sharp questioning. Clearly the sample had gone astray, leaving everyone assuming there was no cause for concern. Tess took Sammy into the toilet and after several minutes of encouragement, he managed to fill the urine file. Doctor Phillips assured them that the sample would go to the laboratory and he would have the results by the end of the week. Although Tess and Colin weren't satisfied with his response, they knew that they would have to wait for their answers.

Samuel wasn't his usual boisterous self and lacked his boundless energy. Tess picked up on his clingy nature and felt the need to reassure him with endless cuddles. She was worried, she was anxious, yet couldn't show her concern to her vulnerable son. Sammy was allowed to stay off school that week and snuggle under a blanket on the sofa with his mother, watching daytime cartoons, whilst he dozed. Although Tess had the support of Colin, he still had to work; she felt so alone, isolated with her negative thoughts.

The ringing of their telephone on Friday morning jolted Tess back to reality from her wondering thoughts. *"Hello*

*Miss Clifton, this is Doctor Phillips."* Tess's heart sunk with worried anticipation. *"I'm a little concerned with the results,"* he said, and then continued, *"I'd like to refer you to the hospital for further tests."* Tess was speechless and racked with worry. She managed to mumble, *"Okay,"* as a tear rolled down her cheek.

*"It's only me!"* called Doris as she opened Tess's front door. Stepping into the lounge, she was greeted with the image of Tess and Sam nestled under a blanket, television randomly blaring but not being watched. Tess's blank face turned into a stream of silent tears running down her face; her chest rhythmically bouncing in time to her faint sobs. Doris sat down beside Tess and cradled her head to her chest, nothing was said; the tears soaked Doris's blouse, she stroked Tess's hair to comfort her. *"Mummy,"* muttered Sam. His words brought Tess back into the moment, with a sniff she replied, *"Yes Sammy,"* but he continued to doze.

*"What is it dear?"* asked Doris. Tess instantly began relaying the conversation with the doctor, then proceeded to share all her worries and anxieties; not just about this incident, but about what she had endured over the last few years. This was the catalyst that lifted the lid on many issues that had overwhelmed her for so long. Clearly Tess had been living on an emotional knife-edge for a while. Although she had functioned adequately under the circumstances, she had never reconciled the turbulent life she had with Kelvin and the consequences of his actions. Tess had deep-seated insecurities anticipating that Colin would let her down also; the reality was he never would. Doris listened intently then reassured her that everything would be okay. *"We'll get you some help,"* Doris gently said before giving her another hug.

Colin had a stressful day working at the shop and tending to his mother. When he arrived home, the news from Tess bounced off his numb, hollow core just as another problem to be solved. Although he appeared to say the right words of reassurance, Tess felt the context was lacking sincerity, compounding her feelings of insecurity. He wasn't being uncompassionate or unsympathetic; he also was living on an emotional parapet; stressing about his mother and grieving for his father. Something had to change before he also snapped.

Tess's conversation about Sam bombarded him, allowing him no time to tell her about his news. He was naturally worried about his son, but his thoughts were being hijacked by the moment, being swept along out of control. He now had two pressing issues to deal with, both as important as each other, but now neither having the gravitas they deserved. He was stressed beyond words, yet he couldn't burden Tess with his worries. That day he had snapped with his mother. She could no longer cope at home, nor could he look after her anymore; he had called the Social Services Department to inquire about her going into a care home.

A letter was posted through their letterbox early on Monday morning, hitting the hall floor with an ominous thud. Colin, Tess and the boys were sat around the kitchen table having breakfast. Colin and Tess linked eyes both too scared to move; eventually Colin slid his chair back to retrieve the envelope. Opening it gingerly he read the contents out loud. *"It's from the Nephrologist at the hospital. Sammy has an appointment tomorrow at ten o'clock."* Thomas looked puzzled and said, *"Daddy, what's a Neffoliest?"* Colin stuttered a little as he replied, *"Its s-someone who will help*

*Sammy to get better."* Samuel was preoccupied aimlessly stirring his cereal bowl, so he didn't hear what was said.

Neither Tess nor Colin could sleep that night. They both lay speechless staring at the darkened ceiling of their bedroom, consumed by their worrying thoughts. Negative scenarios played out in their minds, fearing the worst, nothing could reassure them. Shortly after four o'clock, Colin said to Tess, *"Would you like a cup of tea?"* She looked at him and nodded.

Colin returned a few minutes later with two half-filled cups; clearly some of the contents had been spilt on the carpet, yet he was oblivious to the drips still running down the side of the cups. He placed them on the bedside cabinet, and then climbed back into bed to hug Tess. No further words were said and their tea went cold; they forgot the drinks were there.

*"Mummy is it breakfast time?"* asked Tommy, with his usual cheerful tone. Tess jolted back to consciousness, unaware that she had dozed. *"Ummm, yes Tommy. Go and wake Sammy up."* Colin was lying in a contorted position clearly uncomfortable, but he was asleep. Tess left him to slumber and headed to the kitchen to make breakfast.

Doris tapped on the front door about eight o'clock. *"It's only me,"* she chattered in a reassuring tone, although she was as nervous as hell inside. *"Is Tommy ready for school?"* Doris was to look after Thomas for the day so Tess and Colin could attend the appointment with Samuel.

*"Do I have to see the Neffy-man at the hospital today?"* asked Sammy. *"Yes,"* replied Tess, *"He'll make you feel*

291

*better."* That seemed to pacify the youngster, who continued to munch on a slice of toast. He seemed a little brighter today, but Tess and Colin were still anxious and studied his every movement.

The three of them felt as though they'd walked miles along the seemingly endless hospital corridors to reach the clinic. Sammy walked between them holding their hands, taking every opportunity to lift his feet and swing. The feeling of dread swept over them as they approached the reception desk. Colin spoke up, *"We have an appointment at ten o'clock for our son Samuel Clifton."* The receptionist nodded in acknowledgement and gestured them to take a seat. Two minutes after ten o'clock they were ushered into a side room.

*"My name is Mr Prithpal Singh, I'm a Nephrology Consultant. Please take a seat."* The next few minutes were taken up with formalities and a summary of Sammy's symptoms. The consultant gave the youngster a quick physical examination before informing them of other tests he wanted to carry out, which included blood and urine samples and a scan; all of these to be completed before they left. *"These are just precautionary,"* he explained, *"So we can assess what is happening to Samuel."*

Sammy was very brave navigating himself through all the tests required of him; he seemed far less stressed than his parents, although he was oblivious to the potential severity of his condition. Once the tests were concluded, they were advised to get some lunch and return to the consulting room for a three o'clock appointment, to speak with Mr Singh.

The seconds seemed to bang like a gong inside Tess's head, marking a long arduous wait for the results. Colin sipped on a cup of tea, whilst Sammy munched on a sandwich; Tess just chewed on her fingernails, transfixed on the wall clock on the opposite side of the room. At two-thirty they could wait no longer, so headed back to the waiting room in the clinic. Tess had taken some medical books from the library and had convinced herself every worst-case scenarios for her son. She was almost a hypochondriac by proxy just waiting for confirmation of a tragedy.

At three-twenty Mr Singh called them into his consulting room. *"Please sit down,"* he instructed. *"The results haven't come back conclusive. Samuel's kidneys seem to be slightly enlarged, possibly an inflammation. This could be for several reasons, including an infection."* Mr Singh spoke in a bland tone, very matter of fact. *"I'll give you some strong antibiotics and I'll see you in three months."*

*"But, but that's a long time to wait,"* Tess snapped back, feeling very agitated. A moment's pause seemed to make time stand still, before Mr Singh replied, *"There is nothing to show there is any immediate concern, so we have to eliminate one thing at a time. Let's see how he responds to the medication first."* Colin picked up the prescription and thanked Mr Singh for his time. They left with many unanswered questions. The burning question was, *"Is Sammy going to be okay?"*

The telephone was ringing as they walked through the front door of their home. *"Hello,"* said Colin as he picked up the receiver. *"Hello Mr Trott, this is Claire from Social Services. Can we come and see you tomorrow?"* He agreed and ended the call. Colin hadn't had a chance to talk to Tess

293

and now wasn't an option, she had enough to deal with; how could he tell her now? He felt like the world was hanging on his shoulders, he was ready to break.

Part 28


"*Carter, wait outside your cell!*" barked the prison guard, as they barged into his room for regular search. Kelvin hadn't made many friends during his term in jail and was often ridden roughshod by the wardens. They were a corrupt bunch that insisted on contraband, to as they say, "*Grease the wheels of harmony.*" His exploits before his incarceration hadn't won him any loyal friendships, so he had no visitors whatsoever or any means to placate the greedy guards; therefore, he had to endure these regular disturbances.

"*Bloody hell Kelvin,*" complained his cellmate returning to the dingy room. "*We've been busted again.*" Their room had been ransacked; mattresses and bedding from their meagre bunk beds were scattered on the small tile floor. The contents of their lockers and drawers also joined the pile of debris. Jonah who was Kelvin's long-serving '*roomy*' wasn't happy about these regular invasions by the prison guards; he had paid his contraband dues, yet was still subjected to the same treatment. "*For God-sake Kelvin, just give them something to keep them off our backs.*"

When the legendary Casey strutted his stuff in civvy-street he demanded respect. His altercations were planned with precision, with a means of escape; a place in the shadows where he could ambush his prey and slide back into anonymity. Jail offered him no such luxury and any of his outbursts resulted in painful reprisals that he couldn't hide from. The prison community had a hierarchy that he hadn't become privy to. Although his reputation as a murderer gave him some form of kudos, only a few were intimidated by him. The persona of Casey had to fade and die in exchange for a quieter existence as curly-haired Kelvin.

He had great contempt for the penal system and the corrupt officers that enforced the regime. Kelvin did the bare minimum to conform and took every opportunity to get one over on them. He felt a degree of honour amongst thieves and villains, but despised the two-faced bullies in uniform that were as crooked as any of the crooks that he associated with.

His cellmate Jonah had a run-in with the guards when he first arrived on the wing. When he was getting booked in to the prison, one of the guards took a pair of expensive trainers from his possession box; he tried them on and said to Jonah, *"I'm having these!"* Jonah flipped and he had to be restrained by other guards, *"You thieving screw!"* he spat. The prison guard flexed the trainers on his feet before squaring up to Jonah, nose to nose. *"Ummm, you'll learn who is boss around here."* The guard turned to his colleagues; they were pinning Jonah's arms behind his back and said, *"Take him to solitary, twenty-four hours should cool him down."*

Most long serving prisoners were given jobs of responsibility, Kelvin was no exception; rather, Kelvin was singled out as a special case for work so the guards could have a cut of his meagre wages. He had no other way to pay their racketeering. Yet, he did barter with other prisoners without their knowledge and con the vulnerable amongst them, but he didn't want to rock the boat too much; just to serve his time and one day, get out.

296

*"Happy birthday mop-head!"* scoffed one of the prisoners. *"Thanks you ugly twat,"* Kelvin replied. Banter helped them all get through the day; usually there was no malice. *"Just another day,"* mused Kelvin. It was his thirty-ninth birthday and he still had over a decade left in prison. The thought hung heavy in his mind, every day the same, no excitement. He decided on that day to make his fortieth birthday a day to remember.

After several years doing cleaning duties and clearing garbage, he was promoted to washing the dishes in the kitchen. It was sweltering on summer days, yet he was grateful during the winter to work indoors. He enjoyed the chatter in the confines of the kitchen, with regular horseplay breaking the routine. *"Oh you twat!"* Kelvin screamed with laughter as a rotten apple bounced off his head and splattered into pieces against the wall. He retaliated by launching a mug of soapy water at the offender, barely missing some freshly cooked pies. *"Oi, cut it out you two!"* barked the chef, *"And clean that mess up!"*

Kelvin went about scraping the remnants of the apple off the wall, whilst Billy grabbed a mop. *"My dad used to make wine out of old apples,"* whispered Billy, *"Maybe we could give it a try?"*

Billy's job was to prepare the fruit and vegetables for the chef. He had to wash, peel and chop everything from potatoes to pears, then dispose of the waste. It was a laborious task considering the numbers they catered for so any excuse for joviality was most welcome; carving faces into the potato skins and fashioning carrots into penis shapes broke the monotony.

In their recreation time after their lunchtime shift, Billy and Kelvin discussed how they could stealthily concoct a homemade brew, under the watchful eyes of the authorities.

At the back of the kitchen was a large walk-in storage cupboard. One side housed all the crockery, pots and pans, whereas the other side held all the non-perishable foods, such as pasta, rice, sugar etc. along with all the tinned goods. The shelves were deep to accommodate the large quantities that were required and gave good hiding places, especially at the back of the lower shelves; a great place to hide their new venture. Kelvin purposely hid a couple of three litre glass containers behind some large casserole pots on the bottom shelf; he knew from his cleaning chores these pots were rarely used and his glass containers wouldn't be missed.

*"Hey Billy, what-cha got for me?"* whispered Kelvin as Billy was preparing the food.

*"You can have some potato skins,"* Billy replied without distracting his concentration from the sharp knife whizzing through his hand. Kelvin dropped his gaze and became transfixed watching his partner in crime slice the vegetable with precision, removing the unwanted skins. His mind started to wander as the image of Billy morphed into the silhouette of his mother. She spat, *"You little gob-shite, you're turning into your father!"* Kelvin felt like a small child being chastised by a ghost from his past. He muttered under his breath, *"Sorry mum, I'm already like my father."*

*"What did you say Kelvin?"* asked Billy. *"Err, nothing,"* replied Kelvin, *"Yeah, just leave a couple of handfuls in the storage cupboard. You know where the jars are hidden."*

Lunchtime was the best time for phase two of their operation. The kitchen was almost deserted whilst the kitchen staff served the food at the counter, a valuable few minutes for Kelvin not to be supervised. He crept into the store cupboard and retrieved the glass jars. Billy had followed his instruction and placed the potato skins in the jars. Kelvin pilfered some sugar and yeast from the food storage and added these to the vegetables. He peered through the doorway to ensure the coast was clear, then dashed across the kitchen with the jars to fill them with water. Safely back in the store cupboard, he completed his task by tying a cloth over the neck of the jar, before stowing his bounty back in their hiding place.

Later that shift Kelvin and Billy met up and smacked their hands together in a high-five, saying in unison, *"Team work."*

For the next few days, Kelvin eagerly checked his liquid experiment. Bubbles started to rise after five days, much to his excitement, but to his dismay a couple of days later it stopped. He pulled the jars out from their hiding place to discover the contents in the jars had turned to a thick sludge, almost like a wallpaper paste. *"Oh crap!"* he cursed before emptying the contents down the sink. Speaking to Billy, they agreed that it must have been the starch in the potatoes that was the problem. Plan B, Billy was preparing apples the following day.

Just as before, Billy placed the apple skins in the jars and Kelvin added the sugar, yeast and water. After four days of regular checks the liquid started to bubble, much to their excitement.

*"Kelvin get me some saucepans from the cupboard,"* instructed the chef. *"Yes Boss!"* Kelvin replied. As he opened the door he was hit with the smell of brewing yeast. It had been seven days now and it was obvious to him what it was. He knelt down to view the jars and was greeted with a frothy contents spewing out of the cloth covers. The liquid had crept down the side of the jars and covered the shelf. *"Oh crap, crap, crap,"* he said out load. Returning to the kitchen with the saucepans as instructed, he was on hyper-alert at being discovered. Kelvin intercepted anyone heading into the cupboard, offering to fetch and carry for them; he had to bide some time until lunchtime to clear up the mess.

*"Come on guys, let's get lively!"* barked the chef, signalling for his staff to take the prepared trays of food to the serving counter. It reminded Kelvin of a line of soldier ants going about their business, carrying food in procession. As the last of them disappeared out of sight, the door behind them swung closed. He had ten to fifteen minutes to clear up the mess in the store cupboard; leaving his washing up duties he headed swiftly to complete his impeding chore.

The stench of yeast overwhelmed him as he swung open the door. There was no time to dither the clock was ticking. He pulled out the heavy casserole pots from the bottom shelf; they had splashes of the frothy residual dripping down their sides and their bases were deeply encrusted with the now solidified gel. Kelvin removed the sodden cloth covers from the glass jars and strained the contents through a sieve into a large bowl. The soggy apple mush and the soiled clothes were wrapped and secured in a black plastic sack, before being discarded into the rubbish bin.

Kelvin quickly mopped the spilled contents off the shelf, before wiping down the casserole pots and swilling out his glass jars. *"Yes boss, just coming!"* echoed through the closed storage door. Kelvin's heart missed a beat as he gently opened the door a fraction. He could see through the crack, Danny retrieving a tray of food from a work surface, and then disappearing back to the serving counter. *"Phew, that was close,"* whispered Kelvin to himself. He quickly tipped the now fizzing liquid back into the glass jars and recovered them with a fresh cloth. As he stowed them back in their hiding place, he could hear the chef's voice calling him, *"Kelvin, where in the bloody hell are you?"*

*"Shit, shit, shit,"* Kelvin muttered. As quick as a flash, he grabbed a container of curry powder and tipped it over the floor; grabbing a brush, which was propped up against the wall, he started to sweep. The store cupboard door flew open. The chef stood in the doorway dumbfounded; his expression turned to anger as he barked, *"What in the hell happened here?"* Kelvin shrugged his shoulders and replied, *"Sorry boss, I knocked over the curry powder."* After a few more profanities from the chef, he left Kelvin to clean up the mess. Kelvin was thankful that the pungent spice hid the smell of his secret stash.

*"Hey Billy, the bubbles have stopped rising."* Billy looked at Kelvin in a confused manner. *"The bubbles in the wine jars, you twat,"* Kelvin continued. A huge grin spread across Billy's face and he seemed to rock on his toes with excitement. *"Hey Bro, that's great. We gotta taste it."*

The following day Kelvin made an excuse to go to the store cupboard, where he scooped a cupful of the concoction from the jar. He took a large swig and almost choked, as the acidic liquid hit the back of his throat. He took the remainder of the contents for Billy to try. After sampling a mouthful, he smirked, *"It's as rough as a badger's arse. But, it's booze."* They agreed to leave the brew in the jars for a couple more weeks, before filtering it through cloths into empty apple juice bottles, which the prisoners had at breakfast. The two litre plastic bottles filled with wine were placed out of sight on a high shelf.

*"Billy I've got an idea,"* chirped Kelvin. *"We can drink two of the bottles, but I want to save one."* Billy looked confused, but said nothing. Kelvin continued, *"I want to keep making batches of wine and always keep a bottle back. Then, have a knees up for my birthday."* Billy grinned and nodded in agreement.

* * *

*"Happy birthday Kelvin you wrinkly old bastard,"* joked Alfie, one of the prisoners, as he slapped him on the back, *"It's your big Four-O."* Kelvin smirked and replied, *"Thanks knob-head, just another day at the office." "Or was it?"* he chuckled to himself. He had plans to celebrate, plans to break the monotony, to get one over on the system.

Billy and Kelvin had been hatching their plan for several days, preparing to execute their mayhem at breakfast time. They had for months before, been brewing their apple wine and storing it in innocuous empty apple juice containers. They had managed to accumulate many litres of their alcoholic contraband, enough to fill a regulation cardboard box of fruit juice; it was then easy to hide amongst other supplies.

Billy was a designation server at mealtimes, whereas Kelvin was assigned to the washing up duties. The previous day they had tipped away a whole box of orange juice, so as to tip the balance of choice to apple. Billy struggled to hide his sniggers as he and the serving crew prepared the breakfast feast for the wing; Billy made sure that he was assigned '*Juice Duties*' for that day.

Frank had been released many years before, so Dixy was now the lead gangster on the wing and always first in the queue for every meal. His henchmen reserved his place, no one ever complained. "*Try our apple juice Mr Dixon.*" Billy offered him a small sample to try. His eyes bulged as the nectar hit the back of his throat, then he started to cough. Billy recoiled as the red-faced man stared at him. "*That's bloody good lad, a large glass for me,*" Dixy said with a smile and a wink. "*Phew,*" thought Billy.

"*Dixy recommends the apple juice,*" Billy instructed every inmate with a wink, as they passed through the counter. Some looked quizzical but no one refused. Jeff, one of Dixy's henchmen, came back for another glass for his boss just before the supplies ran out. Billy was relieved that the contraband had been consumed and no evidence was left.

Kelvin had been watching the proceedings through a crack in the door, swiftly returning to his duties whenever anyone came. He was chuckling like a small child over a schoolyard prank.

The usual muttering in the room started to increase in volume with heckling and laughter. The prison guards seemed uneasy with the increasing hilarity and nervously scanned the room for the cause. Alfie the prison joker, jumped up on to the table and started to sing and dance, much to the raucous applause of other prisoners. The guards rushed to intervene, being showered with food for their trouble. A food fight ensued much to the amusement of the inmates. Billy laughed uncontrollably, along with Kelvin who was stood in the kitchen doorway. Billy turned to his friend and said, "*Happy Birthday Bro.*" Kelvin nodded in thanks.

It was like a slapstick scene from a black and white comedy film; maybe Laurel and Hardy or the Keystone Cops, where food was being smeared into the faces of others and people were slipping on food debris, sending furniture flying. Fights and skirmishes broke out; the guards had clearly lost control. The alarm bells rang as a mob of heavy-handed officers entered the large room, in an attempt to break up the mayhem. Picking off the prisoners one by one, they managed to return them to their cells. Dixy and his posse had been sat at their usual corner table observing the chaos without being drawn into the affray. Dixy had been studying Billy and Kelvin, watching their reactions and said to himself, "*Umm, interesting.*"

"*Mr Dixon, please return to your cell,*" politely instructed one of the prison guards. He stood up, unscathed from the food fight, nodded and led his entourage calmly away. The room was a total mess, furniture upturned and food trampled into the floor. The prison governor arrived to survey the damage, "*What in the hell happened here?*"

Kelvin, Billy and the rest of the kitchen crew had scurried into the kitchen to keep a low profile. Billy quickly rinsed and disposed of the empty containers into the refuse bins, whilst the others busied themselves with domestic duties. It was a hive of activity when the governor stormed into the kitchen; everyone ignored his arrival and continued to beaver away. Even the chef tried to keep his head down, before being summoned for an explanation with the governor.

No answers were forthcoming; no one revealed the cause of the outbreak. Dixy had put pressure on the inmates to keep quiet, having his own agenda in mind. Everyone complied with his wishes; they had no choice. The governor could only concede that it was high jinks started by Alfie's jovial performance. The whole wing lost privileges and Alfie was put on the punishment block.

Exactly seven days later, Kelvin and Billy were summoned to Dixy's cell. Muscle-bound Jeff escorted them along what seemed to be an endless corridor. They had purposely avoided such confrontation, as it never seemed to bode well for those who had been sent for before. Jeff stopped them outside the furthest door along the darkened passage, and then tapped gently on the door. He waited patiently for an invitation to enter, before herding Kelvin and Billy inside.

Dixy was sat in a comfortable upright chair, nothing like the prison issue; clearly he had powerful connections to acquire such luxury. *"Come in boys,"* he gestured with a hand movement. The two stood nervously before him. Kelvin piped up and said, *"You wanted to see us Mr Dixon."* A long stony silence ensued. The guys squirmed at the eternity of time.

*"Umm, it looks like you've got a racket going on without my permission,"* Dixy eventually spouted. Kelvin and Billy looked at each other, not knowing how to reply. Billy

305

eventually said, *"Sorry Mr Dixon, but it was only for us, we weren't trading it."*

*"I can be a generous friend or a pain in the arse, if you know what I mean,"* stated Dixy, then an impasse of silence shrouded the room. Billy and Kelvin didn't know how to reply, they just remained statue-like. *"I'll tell you what,"* continued Dixy, *"I'll take two-thirds of your production and I'll make sure you're not bothered. Deal?"* Dixy extended his shovel-like hand to confirm their cooperation. There was no choice in the matter, no one dare to refuse him unless they wanted to experience his dire displeasure. Kelvin was the first to nervously shake his crushing grip, quickly followed by Billy. They said in unison, *"Deal."*

Part 29

*"Hey Mama, that looks cool,"* enthused Vinnie looking at the front of their new restaurant. He was a bright lad but never applied himself at school, leaving at the age of sixteen with minimal qualifications.

Sofia wanted to provide a future for him and also give her a business interest where she could invest some of her late husband's wealth. Hence, she decided to open a new Italian restaurant called *'Vinnie's'* something she hoped her son would be proud of and take control of when he was old enough. He had just left school, so he couldn't have a trading licence and he had no experience of business; neither did she to be fair, but she was a quick and determined learner.

Between them, they had spent the last few months finding a suitable venue and refurbishing it to their taste. Fortunately, it wasn't far from their home, a short walk in fact, which made their decision more palatable. Using Sofia's contacts through the church, they found a promising chef that they could employ. Things were starting to come together at last.

Standing quietly inside the empty restaurant space, Sofia's mind wandered back to when she was a young and innocent teenager staring at the handsome Marco, the waiter she fell in love with, many years ago. The atmosphere of that café gave her a sense of naïve excitement, far removed from the illicit deeds that her young eyes overlooked. Her eyes were only for Marco everything else was a blur.

"*Heyho,*" she thought, "*A new millennium a new start.*" It felt like the year two thousand would be a clean slate, fresh beginnings on her terms. Letting go of her rose-tinted youth was always an issue. Although she knew how toxic and abusive her relationship was with Marco, she still clung to her early memories hoping he would change. He was never going to. Sofia had been swept along by circumstance rather than choice; now it was time for her to put behind her the sordid past and her own murderous actions; although the bloody pool on her kitchen floor still haunted her.

A loud '*Tap-Tap*' on the glass door jolted her consciousness back to the present. "*Delivery for Mrs Rossi,*" announced a burly man in overalls. Her tables and chairs had arrived for the restaurant; she was excited that her venture was starting to feel real at last. As the tables and chairs were positioned, she started to visualise the plethora of customers brimming from every corner. She smiled and gently nodded to herself, life was good.

Vincenzo arrived shortly afterwards. He had been sent on an errand to fetch coffee for the pair of them from a neighbouring shop, "*Its looking great Mama,*" he said passing her the cardboard cup of hot liquid. He took a sip from his own cup before saying with a grin, "*Only seven days to go before we open.*"

The next few days turned into a blur. Vinnie spent his time in the kitchen with Marlon the chef. Vinnie cleaned and stacked all the crockery and cutlery, whilst Marlon attended to the cooking equipment and food store. The entire dried foodstuff could be stowed away; the freezer could be filled, whereas he had to place orders for the fresh meat and vegetables for their opening day.

Sofia occupied her time with front of house, making the restaurant feel homely and welcoming. Tablecloths, pictures and accessories were her forte, creating an Italian ambiance. She polished the glasses and stocked the small bar with bottles of wine and spirits. The finishing touch was to hang a personal picture behind the counter, a black and white photo of her Mama and Papa on their wedding day; she wanted them to be proud of her. Vinnie appeared from the kitchen to admire her work. *"Do you remember visiting Grand-Papa?"* she asked. Vinnie stared at the photo, transfixed at the image, with a smile he just nodded in acknowledgement.

Her father had died a few months after their visit. She was thankful that they had seen him, but didn't attend his funeral. Vincenzo had been poorly at the time and wasn't well enough to travel. Sofia couldn't leave him, so she spent the day in quiet retreat whilst Vinnie slept. She sent money to the nursing home for his burial, a joint plot with her Mama, with a promise to herself that she would visit the grave; as yet, she had not kept her promise.

It was eight o'clock on Friday evening and the three of them were exhausted. Sofia and Marlon sat at a table in the deserted restaurant, sharing a bottle of wine, while Vinnie had to console himself with a glass of coke. *"A great job boys, thank you so much,"* said Sofia with a heartfelt smile. Tomorrow was their big day. They had hired a kitchen assistant to help with the chores and a waitress to help Vinnie serve the customers. Sofia would remain the matriarch, greeting the customers and overseeing proceedings. They each had their roles to play, although the reality would be a testing time.

*"Five – Four – Three – Two – One. Let's open the doors!"*
Sofia shouted in a cheery voice. Vinnie unlocked the door at exactly three o'clock on that Saturday afternoon, much to the excitement of Sofia's churchgoing friends waiting outside. They had loyally turned out to support the opening ceremony, or more so to gorge on the free buffet that was laid on; she didn't mind, and was grateful to receive the compliments from her friends. Vinnie and the new waitress Monica handed out glasses of champagne, before directing them to the self-service buffet table. There was a real buzz in the air from the restaurant, although Marlon and his assistant Josh missed the frivolity. They were busy preparing for the evening bookings. At eight o'clock they had five tables booked and a couple at nine o'clock, leaving three tables spare for anyone walking in. There was much work to do.

Sofia ushered the last of the afternoon revellers out of the restaurant by five-thirty, so they could clear away and have the place spick and span by seven o'clock at the latest. *"Well son, we've done it, we're open for business,"* Sofia said with a huge grin on her face. She was proud of their achievements and proud of the maturity of her son, *"He will make an excellent manager one day,"* she thought to herself. *"Now let's get cracking!"* she said in a firm but jolly manner.

Mr Johnson on table three sent his soup back because it was cold and Mrs Freeman on table seven complained her Lamb was undercooked, but apart from that everything seemed to go smoothly for their first evening of trading. Marlon was a little stressed and bellowed at Josh a couple of times. By the end of the evening, he had apologised and they worked more in unison. Vinnie seemed to charm the clients,

310

whereas Monica endeared herself by appearing a little scatty, apologising to everyone for it being her first day.

The last customers left just after eleven o'clock. Vinnie bolted the doors and let out a sigh. Sofia called them all together and said, *"We all worked as a team and did a fantastic job, thank you so much."* By eleven-thirty, the place was clean and tidy so they all went home for a well-earned rest. *"See you tomorrow,"* they all chirped in unison as they headed off in different directions.

Vincenzo revelled in his new job, charming the customer's and flirting with the young girls. *"Hey my name's Vinnie, welcome to my restaurant,"* became his icebreaker. Sofia was proud of her son, how handsome he was and oh so confident. Naturally, as his mother she was biased, yet he did become a popular lad and his cheeky demeanour earned him a lot of money in tips.

*"Not another pair of shoes Vinnie?"* Sofia remarked. He was a normal teenager with money in his pocket, spending rather than saving. She didn't complain too much, as he was proud of his appearance, buying clothes and attending the hairdresser on a regular basis. *"Hey Mama, I gotta look good,"* he replied with a cheeky smirk. Sofia chuckled and ruffled his curly hair. He'd allowed his hair to grow into long curly locks, styled and gelled to a dishevelled perfection. *"Hey Mama, don't mess up the hair,"* he joked. Sofia laughed out loud, *"Not that you would notice."*

\* \* \*

*"Amen,"* the congregation said in unity. Sofia had built a close friendship with her churchgoing friends. She found

311

comfort and solace from their company, always looking forward to the Sunday morning service; the church was important to her. Her faith had seen her through some very dark times and she had never taken that for granted. Reverend Peter continued with his service, offering thanks at this Christmas time service. The pews were unusually full, but not surprising at this time of year; Sofia was grateful that people made the effort to attend, keeping the church a focal point of the community. There was always a warm compassionate atmosphere, which she loved, much in contrast to the cold, dank day outside.

It was just a couple of days before Christmas and it had rained constantly for three days. Sofia was looking forward to closing the restaurant for a few days, but they still had a full diary for Monday evening and Tuesday, which was Christmas Eve. After that, the bookings resumed for the Saturday. With the suppliers closed, there was a lot of preparation to do.

Jackie handed Sofia a cup of tea and a mince pie, *"Hope you have a lovely Christmas."* Before Sofia could say her thanks, Reverend Peter interrupted asking her what her plans were for the festive season. With a cup and saucer balanced in one hand and a mince pie in the other, it was difficult to consume her refreshments without stopping the conversation; the tea soon went cold, but she managed to tactfully nibble on the pie. Noticing the clock on the wall, Sofia interjected by saying, *"Oh my goodness, is that the time!"* It was almost midday and she needed to prepare Sunday lunch.

Vincenzo was having a lazy morning in bed; she doubted he would make any preparations. She hastily put on her coat

312

and bid farewell to her friends, before heading out into the downpour outside. A gust of wind blew rain into her face as she stepped out of the church, blurring her vision for a moment. She lost her grip on the slippery top step and cascaded down the next six steps, landing in a wet puddle. The intense pain spiralling up her body from her swelling ankle, quickly superseded by the indignity of her landing on the ground with her skirt riding up to expose her underwear. Her screams were heard from inside the church. She soon had her friends running to her assistance.

Jackie and Gillian were first on the scene. Gillian discreetly pulled Sofia's skirt down over her knees, whilst Jackie tried to comfort her. Sofia winced in pain as she pointed to her ankle; her foot was resting at a precarious and unnatural angle. Reverend Peter and Matthew Jones from the congregation, helped lift Sofia up so she could stand on her undamaged leg; between them they supported Sofia as she hopped back into the sanctuary of the church. Placing her on a comfortable chair, they phoned for an ambulance. *"Please, phone Vinnie for me,"* Sofia pleaded.

Vinnie was too preoccupied with the naked girl in his bed to answer his phone. He heard it ring but only when he reached over to silence it, did he realise what the time was. *"Shit, Shit, Shit!"* he yelled as the clock showed twelve-ten. He had little privacy to entertain girls under the watchful eye of his mother, so her visits to the church on a Sunday morning gave him a couple hours freedom to satisfy his urges. Mandy was usually obliging. He saw her as a casual fling, whereas she was smitten and wanted a relationship. He kept her on the hook to keep her interested.

*"Shit Mandy, you've gotta go. Mama will be home soon."* They both dressed rapidly and Vinnie bundled her out the back door. He sighed with relief, then answered the phone as it started to ring again. *"Vinnie, this is Jackie from the church. Your mother has had a fall."*

Vinnie grabbed his coat and ran to the church. It was only a few minutes away, but the rain was still pounding down, making it almost impossible to dodge the deep puddles. He was only wearing material trainers and his feet were soaked by the time he reached the church. There was an ambulance outside with its back doors wide open. Sofia was being wheeled out on a stretcher; Vinnie was stunned with worry.

*"Mama what's happened?"*

The ambulance crew continued to guide the stretcher into their vehicle to avoid the rain. The paramedic ushered Vinnie to join his mother so they could close the doors. *"Don't worry son, I slipped on the steps,"* Sofia tried to reassure him. *"They think I've dislocated my ankle, and I need an x-ray at the hospital."* Vinnie sat holding his mother's hand as they travelled to the Accident & Emergency Department of the Shrewsbury hospital. He was soaked to the skin, his feet sodden and his curly hair hung lankly against his face.

A couple of hours passed before Sofia was attended to at the hospital. The nurses had given her pain-relief, yet it was still an anxious wait to get x-rayed. The doctor confirmed that her ankle was dislocated; he could manipulate it back into place without surgery, but even with a local anaesthetic it was still a painful procedure. Finally the joint was bound with a plaster cast. *"Rest up for six weeks. We'll look at it*

314

*again then,"* instructed the doctor before she was discharged with a prescription for painkillers.

In the taxi on the way home, Sofia started to fret about the busy schedule at the restaurant. Vinnie tried to reassure her, although she knew that she had no other choice than leave him in charge. The restaurant had been open eighteen months now and everyone knew their roles. The stock had been ordered already, so it just needed managing. Vinnie was secretly excited about being the boss, so encouraged Sofia that she had to rest. There were only two days left before Christmas, and then the restaurant would be closed for a few days. She had to concede that she was no use to them; a few days with her foot up would help her recovery.

Sofia spent a frustrating Christmas period lounging on the sofa with her foot elevated on a stool. Gillian from the church offered to call around once a day to help her bathe and prepare for bed; this was certainly not a sight for her son to see, so she was grateful for the help.

Vincenzo was in his element being '*The Boss.*' He organised the last couple of days before Christmas with military precision, sometimes ruffling the feathers of his co-workers, but all in all it was a successful effort. He so wanted to prove himself to his mother.

"*More sprouts?*" Gillian asked as she passed around a bowl of vegetables. Sofia and Vinnie were invited to join Gillian's family for Christmas lunch. It was a challenge to all fit around their small kitchen table, especially with Sofia's leg in plaster, but they managed and had a few giggles in the process. "*Don't drink too much wine Sofia, or you'll be legless,*" joked Gillian's husband Ray. "*Oh*

315

*don't,"* replied Sofia with a chuckle, *"It hurts when I laugh."*

Sofia insisted on returning to work at the restaurant for the New Year rush, although she was still on crutches. The pain had only eased a little, yet she was determined to do what she could to help. Vinnie placed two chairs behind the bar, one for her to sit, the other to elevate her leg. She would be able to chat to the customers and serve drinks from their limited bar. Sofia stood when she needed to with the support of her crutches and sat down when she could. Although she often winced in pain, the attention she received from sympathetic customers lightened her mood.

A couple of months of light duties and rest passed before she could finally have the plaster cast removed from her leg. It had become increasingly itchy; not even her longest knitting needles could reach far enough inside the cast to give her relief. The pleasure was indescribable when she could soak her scaly leg in a warm bath.

Sofia still felt a little uneasy on her feet so continued to use her crutches. She had suffered a degree of muscle waste so needed physiotherapy and an exercise regime to build herself up again. Just being independent again was all the tonic she needed. The next few weeks were business as normal, albeit at a slower pace.

Sofia picked up the receiver to quell the noisy telephone.

*"Hello Vinnie's Restaurant, how can I help you?"*

*"Yes we do have a table free on Saturday evening, what time would you like?"*

*"Ah-ha - Ummm - Okay - that sounds lovely. So it's a birthday celebration?"*

*"Your son's eighteenth! What a coincidence, it's my son's birthday on the same day."*

*"And your name is? Tess Clifton. Okay Tess, it's booked for you."*

Sofia ended the call and returned to her cleaning duties.

Part 30

Colin was racked with guilt having to place his mother in a nursing home. He could no longer cope with the pressures of running a business and caring for his mother; also, on top of his constant stress, he was deeply worried about Sammy. He shielded a lot of his overwhelming feelings from Tess as she was consumed with Sam, ensuring he was healthy. Therefore, Colin suffered in silence, ultimately affecting his own health.

Winifred passed away a few short months after moving to the nursing home. She didn't really comprehend where she was or engage with other residents, remaining in her room most of the time. Colin visited most days, but she didn't even recognise him, an upsetting experience for him, adding to his shame.

Her funeral was a quiet affair, as most of her friends had either died or she had lost contact with them. She lived as a recluse for many years. Just a handful of people attended including Colin and Tess. It was one of the rare occasions she allowed Doris to look after their sons; this was a time she had to let go, albeit the minimal time they had to be away. She left Colin to reflect over the grave as she left directly after the service.

Sammy attended several hospital appointments over the next year, having various tests and trying different treatments to eliminate options, but they never really got to the bottom of his symptoms. His condition seemed to ease and disappear as strangely as it arrived, leaving them with no answers, just a seemingly healthy child. Mr Singh informed them, *"There are no more symptoms to investigate, and so I'm happy to discharge him from my care."* Tess and Colin looked anxious but couldn't argue with his comments. He continued by saying, *"If you are ever worried in the future, please phone me straight away."*

Tess became overprotective of Samuel, but knew she was stifling him. She had to let him be a normal child, running, shouting and playing with his brother. She had to let him enjoy his school time with other children without being paranoid, although she did struggle to let him have his independence.

Life never seemed to be the same again for the two of them. Tess had invested all her time worrying over Sammy whereas, Colin's mind was spinning, between his guilt for moving his mother into a nursing home and the welfare of his son. When Winifred died, Colin felt entirely alone. Running the shop was the only constant thing in his life, a perpetual wheel that kept turning, although it came with some challenging memories? Tess and Colin's relationship had developed a huge void, both feeling let down by the other.

Colin suffered in silence with his thoughts and his feelings, teetering on the edge of depression with a black abyss looming in front of him. He tried to talk to Tess, but she didn't seem to understand; she just kept switching the conversation to her own *'Tales of woe',* which considered to be more important than his issues. Colin felt very alone. Even the love from Thomas and Samuel rarely lightened his mood. Tess no longer showed him affection.

Tess had expected Colin to literally down-tools and to be by her side with Sammy's illness. She never understood the pressure he was under to keep the corner shop open and contend with his mother's issues. Tess had never really gelled with Winifred, whereas Colin saw her everyday so her perspective of the situation was a pole apart from his version of events. They both suffered in their own way, but Tess had the support of Doris and Bert. Without the support of Tess, Colin had no one.

The next twelve months was a stressful time, not in the way of the dramatic events that they had endured, but more so dealing with the aftermath of tragedy. Tess was in a constant state of hyper-alert, feeding her anxiety, worrying about what may happen in the future with Sammy. Colin dwelled in the past, trying to cope with grief and guilt. The only thing they had in common, the only thing that kept them functioning as a couple, were their boys.

*"You're always working in that bloody shop!"* Tess ranted, *"And you missed Thomas's sports day at school!"*

*"Sorry I couldn't get anyone to cover,"* he replied in a snappy, sarcastic manner. The shop was all he had for himself, almost his sanctuary. He had lived there all his childhood and then adopted a career managing it, when his mother could no longer cope. The memory of an ambulance outside, when his father died often flashed through his mind, as brightly as the flashing blue lights of the vehicle. There were so many memories within the four walls of the building; good and bad, but it represented his past. *"I'll try and make it next week for Samuel's sports day,"* he said in a less aggressive way.

Colin sidled up next to Tess at Sammy's sports day without saying a word. Tess felt someone had stood close, when she looked and saw it was Colin. She squeezed his hand and with a strained grin, she said *"Thank you for coming."* Sam was standing on the start line of the hundred-metre race; when he saw both of his parents he waved vigorously with a beaming smile. He wasn't an athletic child, but this support spurred him on to win third place.

*"I've got to get back to the shop, we're due a delivery,"* mumbled Colin. Tess nodded and replied, *"Okay, see you later."*

The strain on their loveless relationship either manifested in arguments or solitude. They never mentioned separating, or trying to improve the situation. There was an air of inevitable failure which neither wanted to admit. They stayed together for the children, accepting their fate as how most relationships end up. Marriage was never discussed.

Tess had her parents to talk to and a few close friends to meet with, but Colin had no one. He lived in a lonely bubble without any family, without any friends, only Tess and the boys. He couldn't understand or rationalise the depressed feelings that had become the norm. An invisible black cloud hung over him even on the brightest of days. He found life difficult to cope with. He wanted to feel happy, he wanted to be with Tess and the boys, but he couldn't deal with his feelings of despair. Tess had noticed his mood swings and tried to talk to him about them. He just shrugged it off with whatever excuse came to hand.

\* \* \*

*"Oh, come on Tom, let me come to the pub with you,"* Sam pleaded. Thomas had turned eighteen and could legally drink, whereas Sam was barely sixteen. He wanted his elder brother to buy him alcohol that he couldn't get for himself without any ID. Tom had a group of friends that he socialised with in The Cherry Tree pub most Friday and Saturday evenings; he was working in Bert's factory so he hand money to burn. Although Sam was in his last year at school, he looked much older.

*"Oh, come on bro, p-l-ease,"* he continued to beg.

*"Okay, okay, okay,"* Tom replied, *"But don't let mum find out."*

*"See ya later mum!"* Tom shouted as he headed out for the evening. Sam left with him, not saying a word. The front door slammed behind them before Tess could answer. She was busy in the kitchen washing up the dinner things and tidying the mess she had made. Colin had left the table abruptly after eating she hadn't seen him since.

Once the clatter of her chores had subsided, Tess could hear a strange sound coming from upstairs. It sounded like a muffled panting, no more like an injured animal. She headed to the foot of the stairs and called, *"Colin are you okay?"* There was no reply. She went up the staircase to investigate. The sounds became louder as she opened the bedroom door.

Colin was curled up in a ball in the corner of the room sobbing into his lap. He was sat on the floor with his knees pulled to his chest and his head bowed. *"Colin, what on earth is the matter?"* He didn't reply. Tess sat on the floor

323

next to him and put her arm around him. He responded by nestling his head on her shoulder and wailed uncontrollably.

"*Okay Sam, you sit at the table by the window and I'll go to the bar,*" instructed Tom. Although Sam looked eighteen, he didn't want the barman to question his age. Tom soon returned with two brimmed pints of frothy beer. "*Cheers,*" they both said chinking their glasses together.

"*It's a beautiful day .... Don't let it get away*," played over the din in the pub. Sam tapped his fingers on the table in sync to the drummer and said with enthusiasm, "*Bono is great.*" Tommy nodded in agreement then joined in singing the lyrics, albeit his version mixing up words. They both spat in unison, "*Oh crap, she's done it again,*" as Britney Spears erupted through the speakers, and then they both laughed.

Sam passed a pound note to Tom to buy the next round, Tommy paid for the third. The boys chuckled and joked, making fun of even the least funny topic. The alcohol was clearly making the evening an enjoyable time. This was Sam's first experience of beer; his head was swimming and his bladder was full. "*I need a piss,*" Sam said standing up abruptly. "*Easy bro,*" Tom joked as Sam wobbled into a chair. Sam chuckled; he was in a happy mood.

Swinging the toilet door open brought him back to reality, like being struck by a snowball. Stood at the urinals was his English teacher Mr. Franklin. "*Shit, shit, shit!*" screamed through his head, "*I'm busted!*" Just as Mr. Franklin turned heading toward the washbasin, Sam bolted into one of the cubicles and locked the door. Within a split second Sam had gone from a foggy elation to stone cold sober. His heart was pounding as he stood with his back resting on the inside of the cubicle door, then he realised that he had to empty his bladder before he wet himself. As the stream of warm urine splashed into the toilet, he started to laugh, *"S-h-i-t, I got away with it."* Yet, he still had to find a way of getting out of the pub without being seen.

Sam gingerly peered around the toilet doorway, scanning the bar for Mr. Franklin. He spotted him standing with a group of men near the bar, but clearly in eyeshot of his brother. Sam ducked his head and walked purposefully towards the exit door, out into the cold night air. He snuck around the side of the pub and found the window where Tom was sat. Sam tapped on the window until he got Tom's attention, and then beckoned him to come outside. *"My English teacher is inside, I'll get busted,"* Sam explained.

*"I've just bought two more pints for us,"* Tom complained. He continued a little more light-hearted, *"You go home and I'll see you there. I've got beer to drink."*

*"All in all it was still a good night,"* Sammy reflected as he walked along the street to his home. He quietly swung the front door open just after ten o'clock. The house seemed empty as he stepped into the hallway. The television was playing to itself in the lounge and no one was in the kitchen. Sam took his opportunity to avoid confronting his parents smelling of alcohol and headed upstairs to his bedroom. He could hear muffled chatter coming from behind the closed door of his parents' bedroom. Sneaking into his own bedroom, he closed the door quietly. *"Phew,"* he thought, *"I got away with it."* Sleep came quickly to him.

* * *

325

It took some time for Tess to comfort the sobbing Colin. She had no idea what had brought this on, as she had never seen him in such a state before. Eventually she managed to coax him to sit on the bed, where she continued to hug him. Although their relationship had been strained at times, Tess felt a genuine concern for him; a closeness that she hadn't experienced for quite a while. She asked him a couple of times to tell her what had happened, but he remained silent.

Eventually Colin whimpered, "*I can't cope anymore,*" then continued to talk non-stop for an hour or more. He spoke about the loss of his parents and the loneliness he was experiencing; mourning their passing and the grief he hadn't dealt with. The shop was a constant reminder of the bittersweet memories of his past. He discussed the guilt he felt for letting his mother down and putting her in a home, then continued to talk about her funeral and worrying about Sammy's illness. More so recently, he was feeling unwell but couldn't explain why. He had developed a twitch and sometimes struggled to remember how to do simple tasks or make decisions. This irritated him and he vented his frustration on the people he loved.

"*Don't worry Colin,*" she reassured him, "*Everything will be alright.*" Tess helped him to undress and tucked him up in bed. She went downstairs to make them both a cup of tea. She returned with the steaming brews and joined him in bed, holding him tightly; their cups of tea went cold. "*We'll call the doctor and make an appointment.*"

Colin slept through the following morning; he had had a restless night and was clearly exhausted. Tess called Barry, Colin's shop assistant, informing him that Colin was unwell and he would need to cope with the shop as best as he could.

*"Would you like me to come in with you?"* Tess asked Colin when the doctor asked him to step into his consulting room. Colin nodded and replied, *"Yes please."*

Colin was reluctant to explain how he was feeling, maybe he didn't know himself, but after a couple of probing questions, Colin couldn't be quietened. He talked constantly for twenty minutes without taking breath, his words spewing out of his mouth at a hundred miles an hour. Eventually Colin ran out of steam and abruptly stopped. He felt emotionally and physically drained and could have easily dozed on the spot. It felt like a dark cloak was cocooning him, weighting heavy on his shoulders. He was being drawn in to pull the hood over his head and close his eyes; he wanted to shut the world out, shut his thoughts out.

*"It sounds like you may have depression,"* concluded the doctor. *"I'll give you antidepressant tablets to help with the symptoms and I suggest that you see a counsellor."* Colin took the prescription, but was reluctant to talk about it anymore. He needed to escape from that room before being interrogated, having to explain his words. Colin couldn't rationalise what he didn't understand and that frightened him; maybe he had said too much. He pacified the doctor by saying he would call the counselling service, but wasn't sure he would.

After a few days of vegetating on the sofa, Colin's frustrations got the better of him and he insisted on returning to work. *"The shop needs me,"* he tried to justify to Tess. She could see how agitated he was becoming, so agreed, on the proviso that she worked with him. Tess needed to make sure Colin could cope; spending time with him would help her understand what he was going through. She wasn't sure that the shop environment was the right place for Colin under the circumstances, but that was all he had.

Tess carefully monitored Colin's behaviour during his hours of work, comparing what she saw to his time at home. She had been consumed with her own life, assuming Colin was just being moody at times; what she observed concerned her. He wasn't just being frustrated with her or the boys, or even life in general; he was becoming frustrated with himself. His confidence had waned and he seemed to be struggling to make decisions. Colin's handwriting had become almost illegible due to his twitch, so he had delegated several administrative chores to Barry.

*"I'll put the kettle on,"* chirped Tess whenever Colin's mood dipped. The distraction seemed to help him. The antidepressant tablets took several weeks to start reducing some of the symptoms, easing further as the dosage was increased. Yet, Colin never seemed to improve any great deal.

Between Barry and Tess, they almost managed the shop without Colin's input, although he never really noticed. They left him to the tasks that he was comfortable with, reassuring him how well he was doing. Tess had given Barry the heads-up that Colin was struggling with depression and he needed a little more support than usual. The three of them seem to find a natural rhythm of working and shielded Colin from anything that would cause him stress.

The doctor contacted them to request that Colin should make an appointment for a review.

*"How are you doing Colin?"* asked the doctor. *"Oh I'm fine thank you,"* he replied, knowing full well that he wasn't. He wanted to bury his head rather than face his problems and fears. Talking about it just encouraged his negative feelings and frustrations, so if he could ignore it, maybe it'd go away.

Tess interrupted by saying, *"Actually, Colin still struggles to concentrate at times and still has his twitch."* Then continued to say how worried she was that he, *"Wasn't his usual self."*

Colin started to become irritable at her comments and insisted that he was doing okay. The doctor paused to observe their minor bickering, and then said that he would like to conduct some further tests, which he described as, *"Purely routine."* Blood samples were taken and Colin was instructed to go to the lavatory to produce a urine sample. Whilst he was out of the room Tess asked, *"Is he okay?"* The doctor looked directly at her and replied, *"It may be nothing, but I'm a little concerned."* At that point Colin returned, so the conversation couldn't continue.

It was an agonising wait for Tess to hear the test results. Colin was oblivious to her concerns and was unaware that anything was wrong. Tess tried to continue as normal, yet in the dark hours of the night when Colin was snoring, she lay awake racked with worry.

Tess answered her phone on the first ring, seeing that it was from the surgery. *"This is Vicky from the surgery,"* said the receptionist. *"The doctor has asked to see Mr Trott and suggested that you should come along too."* Tess's mind was bombarded with thoughts, exploding in her subconscience; none of them were positive. *"Oh, o-h, y-e-s,"* she stuttered, *"Okay, we'll see you on Thursday."*

*"Who was that?"* inquired Colin. Tess cleared her throat, and then replied; *"Only the doctor, we've got to see him again on Thursday."* Colin just nodded and continued stacking the shelves with tins of baked beans.

Every minute that exceeded the midday appointment pounded in Tess's head like the chimes of a church bell. Fifteen chimes erupted in her head before they were eventually asked to step into the consulting room. As they sat down, the doctor wasted no time with pleasantries. *"I'm sorry to say that the results have confirmed what I suspected."* Then the doctor continued before any questions could be asked, *"It appears that Mr Trott has Huntington disease, so I'm going to refer you for specialist help."*

Tess and Colin were bemused, not really knowing what the condition was or how it would affect Colin. The doctor broke the silence by saying, *"This is a genetic condition, and so we need to also screen your children."* Tess reacted badly to this comment, barking, *"What in the hell do you mean?"*

The doctor remained monotone and explained that it's a hereditary condition that has no cure. *"Early diagnosis can help to manage the symptoms better, but there is an inevitable deterioration in the quality of life for those effected."*

Tess was stunned. Colin stooped his head and shed a tear, not for him but for the fact that he may have infected Samuel. How could he possibly tell him that he may have given him a life-sentence of a cruel disease that would eventually eat him away? Colin could remember some of the traits that his father had, which had now become his own way of life. Maybe his father had the disease, but died before it had been diagnosed?

They both walked home in silence, almost as strangers walking in the same direction; both consumed with their thoughts. The house was cold and empty on their return.

Since leaving school Sam had joined his brother working at Bert's factory as a warehouse porter. Tom had been promoted to supervisor and enjoyed light-heartedly bossing Sam around. It was hard physical work, but both brothers loved the banter from their fellow workers. Bert occasional brought them back in line if their horseplay became out of hand, but he also gave them a lot of leeway to do the job. There was a mutual respect between everyone in the factory.

Tess and Colin sat in silence, listening to the tick of the clock. It was just after one o'clock when they got home, they had four hours before the boys came home from work. They had to talk, they had to discuss what had been said, but neither wanted to. Tess went to the kitchen to make a cup of tea. Colin could hear her sobbing, her cries muffled by a towel held tightly to her face.

After quite some time Tess reappeared carrying two steaming cups of tea. She said, *"It's only two weeks until Samuel's eighteen birthday. Can we not say anything until after that?"* Colin lifted his bowed head and nodded, just saying, *"Okay."* They sipped their brews in silence, trying to compose themselves for the return of Tom and Sam.

Laughter broke the chilled atmosphere as the two brothers burst through the front door. *"Take off those dirty boots,"* Tess shouted from the lounge in her usual manner, trying to avoid any suspicion. Colin seemed to click back into life from his comatose state and said, *"Hello lads, had a good day?"* Tom was the first to reply joking, *"Yeah except Sam is being a knob as usual."* Both brothers laughed as Sam punched Tom's arm to deaden it.

Tess busied herself in preparing dinner. She placed three plates of food on the table, making her excuses for not feeling hungry. *"I'm just going to pop over to see Granny Doris,"* she said closing the front door behind her.

Although Bert and Doris had semi-retired they still managed the business, just giving more responsibility to their line-managers. Doris still baked cakes for the workers, who visited them daily. Life hadn't really changed for them except Bert was now at home more, often under Doris's feet. She jokingly complained, but liked having him there. He was now approaching seventy years old and needed to slow down.

*"Tess what on earth is the matter,"* Bert asked as she stumbled through the door crying. He knew that she and Colin had been having problems for some time, but he'd not seen her so upset before. Doris scurried to the kitchen to boil the kettle, and then joined Bert to hear the explanation.

*"Oh my word,"* was all Doris could muster. Bert said nothing just cradled Tess in his arms. They all agreed to keep things under wraps for now.

The following day Tess had to start making birthday preparations. Once she had dialled, the phone only rang a couple of times before it was answered.

*"Oh hello Vinnie's, can I book a table for four on Saturday?"*

*"We are going for a birthday drink first, so can we say about eight o'clock?"*

*"Yes it's my son's eighteenth, he can have his first legal drink. But, you know what lads are like, best I don't ask questions."*

*"Yes book it under my name, Tess Clifton."*

Tess ended the call and started to think about what present they should buy.

Part 31

*"Make room for the old-uns!"* Sam cheekily joked as he ushered Colin and Tess into the pub on his eighteenth birthday. Tom was already at the bar ordering their drinks.

Tess steadied Colin through the doorway as he was struggling to negotiate the step. Despite the fact that he needed her help, Colin insisted that he could manage; Tess ignored his complaints and held his arm until he was seated at a table. She was determined that nothing was going to spoil this special day.

*"Cheers Sam, happy birthday,"* they all said raising their glasses in unison. The bartender wasn't impressed to see the '*I'm 18*' badge pinned to Sam's tee shirt, as he had been illegally serving him for the past year or more, without realising. After consuming two drinks each, it was time to head to Vinnie's Restaurant for a feast. A short taxi ride was all that was needed for them to be standing on the pavement outside, queuing to go into the busy restaurant. They could see through the window that there were only a couple of empty tables left. The group in front of them would take one theirs would be the second.

Tess led the four of them through the doorway to be greeted by a well-groomed lady stood by the bar holding a register. *"Hello, we've got a table booked under the name of Clifton."* At that moment the waiter arrived also to greet them.

As if taking a screen-shot from a movie, the whole place froze to a complete standstill. Time had no concept and every character stood statue-like. A deep sinking horror chilled Tess to the core. Tess couldn't move, she was as much a mannequin figure as everyone else in the room. The only thing that could move were her eyes, scanning the room for clues.

Tess first saw a few birthday cards on the counter, not just any cards, but eighteenth birthday cards. *"To Vinnie, love Mama",* was scribed inside one of them. A bottle of champagne with a bow around it stood proudly between the cards.

Her eyes panned across to the waiter who had introduced himself as Vinnie. He was a good-looking lad of average build, with a very distinctive mop of long curly, brown hair. Her eyes caught a glimpse of Tommy standing nearby, with the same physique and flowing curly locks. She quickly compared; they could have been brothers. Her mind started to scream, *"Kelvin!"*

Scanning back to the bar, Tess could see an old black and white photo behind the bar. A couple that had just got married. Was her mind playing tricks? The man in the photograph looked just like Sammy. No it couldn't possibly be, she must be dreaming. What sick twisted game was being played in her mind?

Tess brought her eyes back to the lady stood behind the counter. She squinted to focus, the woman looked familiar. Although nearly two decades had past, she hadn't changed; it was Sofia from the maternity ward, she had given birth the same day. "*Oh my god!*" roared from her silent mouth. No one could hear her screams.

Sofia experienced the same moment of silent terror. Likewise she had joined the same mannequin state, where the world had stopped spinning. She was frozen to the spot, as if surrounded by a concrete suit, only her eyes were free to move.

She could see the look of sheer horror spread across the face of the woman stood before her. Up until that point nothing had alerted her, yet that stare had driven her soul into a spiralling abyss. Sofia traced the movement of Tess's eyes, flashing between her, the photograph, the cards, and her son.

Sofia too, couldn't comprehend the young man standing before her looked the image of her father on their wedding day. The same smile, the same nose and very much a Mediterranean look about him. His straight dark hair was longer than her father ever wore, but still hung in the same lank way. Her eyes stopped at the *'I'm 18'* badge pinned to his tee shirt; he was born on the same day as Vinnie.

Stood next to him was another young man with a similar build, but displaying a long mop of curly brown hair. She quickly compared him to Vinnie and was shocked at the likeness. The words spewed out of her mouth, words that she didn't want to say, "*They could be brothers!*" Without giving her thoughts time to recover she continued, "*He looks just like Casey!*"

Sofia's eye returned to the horrified Tess standing in front of her; then she remembered where she knew her. The maternity ward on the day she gave birth to Vinnie. The day Casey came to visit her, to see his son, but was distracted to see someone else; his ex-partner Tess! *"Oh my God!"* screamed through every fibre of her body, *"What is going on?"*

Vinnie broke the impasse by chirping obliviously, *"Can I show you to your table?"* Colin, Sam and Tom followed him, whereas Tess headed for the toilet and immediately threw up. She sat in the toilet stunned and totally lost for words. Nothing made sense. She tried to process what was going through her mind and when reality struck, she was violently sick again. Tess shuffled to the table and explained that she was unwell and was going home. She left before they could complain.

Tess headed for the door to leave, but had to run the gauntlet past the bar and Sofia.

Sofia saw her headed for the exit and blocked her path. *"We've got to talk,"* pleaded Sofia. Tess gave her eye contact but couldn't respond; she burst into tears and navigated her way through the obstructed doorway. Sofia was left dumbfounded, forced to complete her shift as best as she could. They could read each other's thoughts; they could remember the tiring first night in hospital, when the babies were taken to the nursery. *"NO, NO, NO, it can't be! It must be a sick, evil joke?"*

Part 32

A psychic link joined Tess and Sofia that night, neither comprehended nor wanted to face an alternative truth.

Tess walked the distance between the restaurant and her home, not even thinking about hailing a taxi. Her mind was overloaded with negative thoughts and unbelievable scenarios, questioning any form of reality that existed. She tried to reassure herself that she had imagined the evidence that had unfolded before her very eyes; maybe if she could blank out this evening, then it couldn't possibly be real. *"That was it,"* she thought, *"My mind is playing tricks and it'll be okay in the morning."* She hoped that her mind was recalling a plot from a novel she had once read, a twisted tale of fiction.

She reached her home without remembering how she got there. Out of frustration, she kicked the front door, as the key couldn't find the slot to unlock the entrance to her home. Eventually a satisfying click allowed the door to swing open. The house was dark and eerily quiet not giving her the comfort that she had hoped. Fear swept through her as she reached for the light switch; she dreaded to see the simple normality that could mock her feelings. Tess chose not to illuminate the hallway; instead she headed up the staircase to her bedroom in darkness.

Tess scrambled out of her clothes, and then buried herself under her bed covers, just leaving her eyes free to stare out of the window. The streetlight outside their house uncomfortably lit the room, but she had no inclination to close the curtains.

After a couple of hours, the hall light was switched on and the peace was shattered with the raucous chatter of the men returning from their celebrations. Colin crept into the bedroom and asked, *"How are you feeling?"* Tess ignored him. She had her back to him and pretended to be asleep, although her eyes were wide open transfixed on the dancing images that the streetlight was superimposing on the window. Colin assumed she was deep in slumber as he slid into bed and wished her good night.

A heavy nightmare eventually consumed her shortly before Colin's alarm clock rang at seven o'clock. He chose not to disturb her, albeit she would have been unable to respond to his rousing. Tess jolted to consciousness as she heard the front door slam behind Colin just after eight o'clock. Her sons' chatter in the kitchen soon subsided as they also left for work. *"My sons, my sons?"* screamed in her head. It was a question, which she was unable to answer. She had to find the truth.

Tess had to eventually release herself from her linen shackles as she felt the vomit rise in her throat. Dashing to her bathroom, she didn't quite reach the toilet bowl, so threw up in the sink. Her stomach was empty, therefore only watery bile splattered in the bowl. Tess ran the tap to allow the swirling water to clear the mess. Scooping up a cupped handful of water she rinsed her putrid mouth.

She couldn't recognise the withered woman staring back at her from the mirror. She seemed to be a hollow ghost with an ashen face and hair of white straw. Piercing red eyes burnt uncomfortable wounds deep inside her. As much as she wanted to avoid confronting this frightening image, Tess was unable to move.

The ringing of her phone broke the silent impasse. She chose not to answer it, just allowing it to cease of its own accord. It was ten-fifteen and she needed to face her fears, find some answers. Tess quickly dressed and left the house in a daze. She didn't take her handbag, purse or mobile phone, just aimlessly walked in the direction of the restaurant. Her keys rattled loosely in her hand as they swung in time to her stride.

When Tess arrived at the restaurant it was closed. She hadn't thought of that as a possibility and felt frustrated and deflated. Sitting herself down on a bench outside, tears rolled down her face. With her head stooped, Tess hadn't noticed the figure of a dark-haired woman approaching. *"Tess?"* Sofia asked hesitantly. Tess lifted her head in response. Sofia then continued, *"You'd better come in."*

Tess followed the footsteps of Sofia as they walked to the locked door. Sofia opened it and they both stepped inside to a cold dim room. It had none of the energy of the previous night; the tables were neatly laid in preparation of the next intake of customers. Sofia chose not to switch on the lights, just directing Tess to sit at a window table.

Both women had spent the last twenty-four hours agonising over the same thought, *"Had there been a mix-up at the hospital?"* Yet, the possibility scared them beyond belief.

Sofia didn't give Tess a chance to speak, she just launched into a non-stop barrage of words.

341

*"I know what it looks like, but it can't be true."*

*"Vinnie is my son, I know he is. I don't care what you think."*

*"I don't care about biology, Vinnie is mine. Oh God he's mine!"*

*"Kelvin is the father, that's why they look alike."*

*"They can't know, they can never find out."*

*"You must promise me to keep this a secret."*

*"For the love of God promise me,"* she pleaded.

Tess couldn't find a way of interrupting her, so had remained quiet. When Sofia had run out of breath Tess managed to speak. *"I totally agree with you, in my heart Samuel is my son, but we have no choice but to find out the truth."* Sofia looked on in horror. Tess continued, *"My partner Colin has a genetic illness called Huntington Disease. We have to warn his son, whoever that is, that he may also contract the disease."*

Sofia wailed, *"Oh God no!"*

Neither had any idea how to have that conversation with their sons. It was a conversation that no mother should ever have to have and no amount of life experience could ever prepare her for it. They both sat dumbfounded in silence. Tess broke the hush by saying, *"I can't deal with this, I have to go."* She stood up and left. Sofia never moved, she just continued to stare into an endless space.

The sound of screaming tyres and a loud thud jolted Sofia's attention. She turned in time to see Tess being thrown into the air by a speeding car. Her legs had been swept from under her, before her head shattered the windscreen. As the car skidded to a halt, her limp body slid to the ground. Tess's numb body and numb mind wasn't aware of the impact of the speeding vehicle. She hadn't noticed traffic racing past as she stepped off the pavement. The breaking of her leg bones didn't cause any pain, nor did her hips crunching on the bonnet or the loud crack of her skull as it hit the tarmac. She was aware of her pulsing head wound and a sticky warm liquid covering her face, but not pain; just nothing. Muffled voices surrounded her. Tess's only conscious thought was the slowing heart beat pulsing through the gash in her head.

Her heartbeat became weaker, and then it stopped.

Part 33

Two police cars and an ambulance arrived within minutes as the crowd began to grow. Sofia couldn't bring herself to venture further than the entrance to her restaurant, so she was unaware that Tess had died. It was only when the ambulance lifted her body on a covered stretcher that the enormity of the situation struck home.

Police officers had closed the road and were starting to obtain statements from passers-by. Sofia had poured herself a second glass of brandy before a female police office walked into the restaurant. She said, *"Excuse me madam, did you see anything?"* Sofia started to sob uncontrollably.

After several minutes, Sofia managed to utter, *"Yes she was in here moments before. We were talking."* The officer sat next to her to offer comfort. Sofia grabbed a napkin to dry her eyes, and then explained the content of their conversation. *"Oh goodness,"* said the officer, *"Are you up to giving a statement?"* Sofia shook her head and replied, *"Not yet."*

PC Joan Harris arranged for a police car to collect Sofia and take her to the station later that day. Vinnie was distraught to see his mother so upset and offered to go with her. Sofia refused and instructed him to cancel the bookings for that night. The restaurant would be closed. She was in no frame of mind to share information with him; Sofia didn't even know where to begin.

The officers showed her patience and understanding as she relayed her statement to Police Constable Harris and Senior Investigating Officer Boyle. The essence of her tale confounded the officers as they gave her heartfelt sympathy. They took a break at the end of the interview to digest what was said.

SIO Boyle returned with a cup of tea and said, *"I'm really sorry Mrs Rossi but we have to explore all avenues of inquiry as the case is so complex."* Sofia struggled to comprehend what he was suggesting, so pressed him for clarity. SIO Boyle responded by saying, *"Miss Clifton was clearly distressed by the events of the past twenty-four hours."* Sofia nodded whilst he carried on speaking, *"And, we need to understand her state of mind at the time of the accident."*

He continued to say, *"The driver may be charged with serious criminal offences, so we need to understand if Miss Clifton intentionally walked into the path of the vehicle or not."* This had crossed Sofia's mind but she didn't want to think about it. SIO Boyle summarised by saying, *"The content of your statement and the statements of others will be disclosed in a court of law, so it may be kinder for everyone involved if they knew the truth beforehand."*

*"B-u-t I can't. I can't tell Vinnie,"* Sofia stuttered. She knew that he had to learn the truth as he may be infected with a hereditary disease. She would be heartbroken to be told that he wasn't her flesh and blood and even more devastated if he had a terminal illness also.

*"We have specially trained officers that can help. They can support you and everyone else through the process. We may*

346

*need to conduct DNA tests, but they will be with everyone's consent.*" SIO Boyle had asked PC Joan Harris to join them. She continued their conversation by trying to reassure Sofia that they would have all the difficult conversations with the individuals involved. Sofia was mentally and physically exhausted and asked if she could have some quiet time alone. She curled up in a ball and fell asleep.

As Tess had no identification on her, it took the police a few hours to track down her address.

Doris was stood at the kitchen window and saw a police car go past. It was unusual to see the police in such a quiet street; her curiosity got the better of her and she peered out of her front door. To her horror, she could see them banging on Tess's front door at the other end of the street. She quickly called Bert to walk down and investigate. Doris stayed on her doorstep, fussing with a tea towel in her hands as she watched proceedings.

Bert managed to catch their attention, so they waited for him to meet them. From their conversation and the way Bert reacted, Doris could see that something was wrong, so she bolted down the street. The couple howled and held each other as the news that their beautiful daughter had been so tragically killed, was being relayed. The officers walked the couple back to their home so they could record more details. Tom and Sam were called from the factory floor to receive the devastating news, whilst another police car headed to the shop to tell Colin.

Forty-eight hours passed before the police started to speak to Colin, Thomas, Samuel and Vinnie about the circumstances leading up to the accident. There was never going to be an easy way to broach the subject, let alone encourage them to help with their investigation.

Tom and Sam were unaware of Colin's illness or the severity of his condition. It was a conversation he and Tess were going to have after the birthday party, but they never had that opportunity. All three of them couldn't comprehend the concept that Sam may not be Colin's son or Tom's brother. It was totally absurd to think such a thing. Colin was there at the birth; surely he would know his own son. Samuel was always at his mother's side in hospital or so he thought; not realising that Samuel was nestling in the nursery on the first night to allow Tess time to recover.

*"I don't believe you,"* Colin screamed at the officers. Yet, turning to Samuel, Colin said, *"We had better do the DNA test and any other tests to make sure you are safe."* Sam was apprehensive and reassured by Tom that he would also agree to a DNA test to prove them all wrong.

Vinnie didn't take the news well, storming out of their home to process the information. He text Sofia later in the day, to say that he would stay with a friend for a couple of nights, to get his head straight. Sofia needed to explain things to him, the way she felt and what he meant to her. She had to bottle it all up inside her, until he was ready to listen.

He reappeared the following day looking quite dishevelled. Vinnie had been sleeping on Jeff's sofa, a friend from school. Sofia didn't know what to say, so she just flung herself at Vinnie to give him the biggest hug. They both shed a tear. *"Mama, I don't care what they say, you are my mother."* Sofia hugged him once more as he whispered in

348

her ear, *"And, I'll take the stupid test to prove them wrong."*

Part 34

Seven long gruelling days passed before they were invited to the police station to receive the results. SIO Boyle thought it best if they all attended at the same time.

Sofia couldn't face working at the restaurant until she knew the outcome of the tests. Nor could Vinnie face his duties with his usual joyous charm; they both decided to have a break, leaving Marlon in charge. It was a quiet time of year and it would be easy to close on the weekdays and run on skeleton bookings over the weekend.

Vincenzo and Sofia spent time together chatting and also time apart in solitude. They both had their own issues to deal with, but hoped that their bond was still as strong as ever. Sofia had to make one more confession to Vinnie before the test results were revealed, that Marco wasn't his father. With everything going on at such a fast pace, it wasn't the first thing on her mind. It was another load that Vinnie would have to carry, knowing that she had an affair with an employee of Marco's.

Sofia worried how much more news he could take, so decided not to tell him that his father Kelvin, was the man in prison for the murder of her husband Marco; she felt that news would tip him over the edge. She worried that if he knew, he'd never forgive her. She prayed that he would never find out. He could never find out, that she in fact had killed him; that his mother was a murderer. Sofia was sure he would never forgive her for that.

Vinnie shrugged off the confession, but Sofia could see that it had hurt him badly. Regardless of what a total bastard his father had been, he expected his mother to behave better than that. He only had a few memories as a child; most had been locked away in his subconscious to protect him from emotional pain. Yet, he did remember his father playing with him once in the garden, a game of football as he recalled. Although he'd heard a lot of arguments, he had not witnessed many, so he had to rely on his mama's account of the hostility.

Sofia started to panic as memories came flooding back. Just a few days earlier, her life was filled with sweet smelling flowers and now it was filled with black thorns. The skeletons from her past were coming back to haunt her. The lies that she had buried could be unearthed at any time destroying everything that she had strived for. She would lose her son, if in fact Vinnie was her son. She would lose her friends, her house, her business and her liberty. Her life had been a fabrication of lies, a smoke screen of deceit. Sofia had created an angelic persona that she could no longer live up to. She envied Tess, wishing that the car had taken her instead.

Colin was a broken man, without the energy or health to fight back. It was bad enough that he could have passed on the festering genes within his body to his offspring, but now he didn't know for sure who that was. He hoped that Samuel was his son, but also hoped that he would be spared the anguish that the disease would cause him. Yet, how could he possibly wish that evilness onto a total stranger? There was no happy solution to his plight and he now had to contend with the enormous sense of grief through losing the true love of his life. Tess was his rock and he had no one to help him through this horrendous ordeal. Without her he had no life to live for. Not knowing the truth about his son was a cruel bitterness that he couldn't face alone.

Samuel had always questioned his dark hair, knowing his father had ginger hair and his mother was blonde. She had shown him old black and white photographs of Granddad Bert when he was younger saying, "*You're the spitting image of him.*" Maybe the non-coloured images didn't reveal the true colour, just a way to reassure him, to give him a plausible explanation. In the school photographs displayed on the mantelpiece, it was clear to see that he was different from his brother Thomas. In hindsight he hadn't questioned it before, now he questioned everything.

Thomas couldn't believe the strange waiter he met in the restaurant looked so much like him. It was like staring into a mirror. He hadn't realised it at the time, he was celebrating his brother's eighteenth birthday; he had no reason to, but now! What in the hell was happening to the family? His step-dad was terminally ill, his mother had just been killed and maybe his brother wasn't his brother after all. How could he possibly process all of that information at once? Up until a few days before, his life was normal.

Doris hadn't stopped crying since receiving the news of her daughter's death. Bert tried his best to comfort her, but didn't know how to react himself. He felt obliged to make funeral arrangements, but was prevented by the police inquires. There had to be a post mortem to establish the cause of death, then an inquest. Not to mention, to unravel the mess of fatherhood. He couldn't imagine a fictional plot so bizarre, yet still had to endure the reality of this fragmented situation and deal with the emotions that went with it.

* * *

Colin, Thomas and Samuel were directed into a conference room at the police station for their two o'clock appointment. Sofia and Vincenzo were already there and were sat at the opposite side of the large table. SIO Boyle asked the three of them to sit; their position was on the other side, so everyone faced each other. The atmosphere was tense and silent. PC Harris entered the room and joined her boss at the head of the table. Everyone seemed on tender-hooks, even the officers.

PC Harris broke what seemed to be an endless silence, by saying, *"Thank you all for coming."* There were no thanks or gratitude from the families, they were there under painful duress, but also knew there was no choice the stakes were too high.

SIO Boyle took a back seat, allowing his female officer to take the meeting. PC Harris continued, *"We do have some information for you which will be submitted to the inquest, but we are unable to give you a conclusion to the accident until they have made a decision."*

Colin and the Clifton boys shuffled in their seats, they seemed a little frustrated from her comments, but allowed her to continue.

*"With regard to the DNA tests that we have conducted, we do have conclusive evidence that we can share with you."*

354

The rustle of white paper cut the atmosphere with a knife. Five pairs of eyes watched her every movement. The officer was clearly nervous and dropped the detailed report on the floor. The room seemed to take a sharp intake of breath simultaneously as the piece of paper floated downwards; the officer tried to grab it in vain, over-reaching and losing her balance. Eventually retrieving it she said, *"Err, sorry about that."*

*"We have compared DNA samples taken from Sofia and Tess. We are sorry to confirm there is a DNA match between Sofia and Samuel and also Tess and Vincenzo."*

A tear rolled down Sofia's face as she stared across the table at the young man called Samuel, who looked a youthful version of her father. She knew the moment that she saw him enter her restaurant that there was a connection. Their eyes locked for what seemed a long time, yet in the corner of her eye she could feel the jealous glare of Vincenzo looking straight at her. Sofia turned to face the man she believed to be her son from birth, but could offer no words of comfort.

Tom's eyes flicked between Sam and Sofia, trying to make sense of what was happening. He could only break the silence by saying in disbelief, *"Yeah, but .. but .. but?"* Tom noticed Colin hunched over his crossed arms on the desk, he was clearly a broken man.

Colin raised his head and asked PC Harris, *"So, does Vincenzo have my illness?"*

Five heads turned towards the officer, waiting for her response. SIO Boyle squirmed in his seat and spoke for his colleague who clearly didn't want to answer.

He said, "*To answer your question we had to do further DNA tests as things weren't as straightforward as we first thought.*"
"*As you can now understand, you do not have a DNA match with Samuel and you knew that you weren't the father of Thomas.*"

"*But, you don't have a DNA match with Vincenzo either.*"

Colin's face was racked with confusion, not comprehending what had been said.

"*We did find the same DNA trace through all the three samples, Thomas, Samuel and Vincenzo.*"

"*Because we knew that Tess and a man called Kelvin Carter were the parents of Thomas, we checked his DNA on the criminal database.*"

"*Kelvin Carter is a parental match for all three men. They are in fact all brothers.*"

Colin tried to stand, then collapsed to the floor struggling to breathe. A panic attack swept through his body as he realised that he hadn't been a father to anyone. Everyone just sat and stared at the crumpled man on the floor, no one rushing to his rescue until PC Harris broke the impasse; just like the 'Bionic Women' running in slow motion, she took three strides to reach him.

Part 35

Kelvin lay in his bunk completing a crossword, before his cell door was locked for the night. It was just another boring day for him. His highlight of the day was to pilfer a cereal bar from the store cupboard for his nighttime snack.

He was unaware that Tess was already pregnant when she kicked him out; nor was she.

He was unaware that the truth was being unravelled; the way lives had been changed.

He was unaware of the pure hatred being sent through time and space towards him.

# Sofia

Part 1

She looked down at her bare feet and gazed at her chipped nail varnish. The cherry red lacquer appeared crazed on the big toe nail of her right foot; the varnish was chipped in the corner, exposing a white filed edge that was manicured to perfection. The varnish on the other smaller toenails seemed to have grown with the nails, leaving a pink band around the cuticles, like four small halos on her toes.

Her left foot also adorned dishevelled nail varnish, but the chipped lacquer was less obvious as splatters of blood had seeped into some of the crevasses. *"Damn,"* Sofia thought. *"I should have painted my nails,"* flashed through her mind as she stepped onto the ledge of a multi-storey car park. She hadn't felt the broken glass that she had kicked whilst taking off her shoes. Her green coat had been folded neatly on the concrete next to her shoes and her spectacles placed inside the open pocket.

The trivial details of Sofia's plight held her attention. She had lost everything, so trivia was all she had left. The balls of her feet rested on the edge of the concrete shelf, allowing her toes to dangle freely; the breeze seemed to soothe away the tense reality of what she had to do. Looking back at her toes she could see the traffic shuffling through the congestion five floors below. There were people walking on the pavement below, she had to wait until there was a clearance, Sofia didn't want to hurt anyone else; she didn't want to traumatise anyone being witness to her impact on the ground.

Sofia raised her head to survey the busy city. It was eight o'clock in the evening, the light was starting to fade, but the streets below never slept. She could see a cleaner vacuuming in an office opposite, panning further around someone else engrossed in a telephone conversation at a brightly lit desk. On the floor above, she noticed a young woman, maybe in her twenties staring directly at her. She was excitedly talking on a telephone, her hands vigorously gesturing to whoever she was in conversation with. Needless to say they could only hear her words, not see her actions.

The young woman was wearing a business suit. In any other situation Sofia would assume she was calm and calculated, but now she looked extremely worried. Ending her call, she placed both hands on the glass window in front of her and stared directly at Sofia. There seemed to be a brief connection between them, which warmed Sofia's mood a little, but Sofia had to look away and return to the task in hand.

The breeze gusted a little stronger, bringing goose bumps to her arms; her attention became heightened recalling the events of the last few days. Her son was not her son and he hated her for the deceit. She had loved a stranger, as her own for eighteen years without knowing that he wasn't her child. Nothing could ever make this situation right, to remedy the feeling that her heart had been ripped from her body in such a cruel way. Today was a good day to die.

*"Ca-can you step down from the ledge?"* stuttered a worried security guard. At first Sofia didn't realise he was talking to her. *"M-my name is Dan. Ca-can you step down from the ledge?"* Sofia turned her head towards him and saw a young man no older than Vinnie with an outstretched hand. *"He is just a boy in a uniform,"* Sofia said to herself. *"Someone else's son."* She couldn't face him or speak to him; she didn't want to reason with him or tell him how she felt. How could he possibly know the excruciating pain she felt inside? She had to ignore him, to blank him out. She had to end the pain; she had to end her life.

Looking back at the ground below, she could see the flashing blue lights of a police car screaming to a halt beneath her. The officers frantically cleared the street and occasionally peered up towards her. Another police car arrived also with its blue lights flashing, but this one didn't stop, it raced into the entrance of the car park. Moments later she could hear the squealing of tires approaching. Dan continued with his efforts to coax her off the ledge, Sofia just blocked out his pleas, *"He's just a boy!"* howled inside her head. Sofia clamped her cupped hands over her ears and let out a bellowing scream.

As she dropped her hands from the side of her head a women spoke behind her. *"My name is PC Samantha White, you can call me Sam. What is your name?"*

361

Sofia started to shake and felt cold. She wrapped her arms around her body to find some comfort. She wanted to quietly end her life, not to be exposed to this fiasco. Her mind started to race.

*"Sam! Sam! That's my son's name. He's not a girl, he's a boy!"*

*"I don't even know him, yet he's my son. But, Vinnie's my son isn't he?"*

*"How can I be a mother, when I don't even know my own child?"*

*"What sick fucking joke is being played on me?"*

PC White calming asked again, *"What is your name?"*

Sofia turned her head to see two police officers standing behind her. One was a middle-aged blonde women, the other stood a little further away by the Police car, a tall man of Asian appearance. PC White continued, *"Would you like to step down so we can talk?"*

Sofia continued to scrutinise PC White by peering over her shoulder. She didn't want to talk, she had made up her mind to end her life; Sofia wanted them to all go away so she could jump without having to justify it to strangers, to be judged.

She turned slightly to face the officer, who was stood nearby with her hand outstretched. *"Why don't you all fuck off and leave me alone!"* bellowed Sofia, just before her foot slipped and she started to tumble ........................